A Penny for the

To Anne

Best wishes,
Francisco

Music

28 NOV 2015

Françoise Adams

Published in Great Britain by Argenté Publishing 2015
Copyright © Françoise Adams 2015

ISBN 978-0-9932340-0-2

'A True Love' Lyrics by Françoise Adams

www.apennyforthemusic.com

Printed and bound by CPI Group (UK) Ltd, Croydon, CR0 4YY

Acknowledgements

To Barbara O'Driscoll. Thank you for sharing your time,

experience and unstinting encouragement so generously

Dedication

To my wonderful husband, Alex, for his support,

invaluable contribution and unending patience while I

wrote this book. And to my mother, May, whose

enjoyment of it finally made up my mind to publish it.

Prologue

She stood by the window and watched as he walked down the path to the waiting taxi. The two bags he carried held the last of his belongings. He handed them to the driver and at the sound of the car's boot shutting with that dull 'clunk', she took a sudden and sharp intake of breath. The moment sounded so final. The driver disappeared inside and waited. But before climbing in, Laurent stopped, turned around and looked back at the window; it was as if he sensed her watching. He stood for a few moments staring at the window. Then, without ceremony, he slid into the back seat. And as the car pulled away and faded out of sight, a single tear escaped. She felt it roll, warm and gentle, down her cheek.

Part One

Chapter One

Home

"Happy Birthday, Mum!" Natascha called, as she entered the kitchen via the back door. The cold December afternoon had been heralded by a brisk, winter breeze and the warmth and smells of the kitchen were wonderfully comforting.

Natascha was speaking to the chic coiffure of russet brown hair peeking from behind the breakfast bar. And as she watched her mother surface, holding a tray of freshly baked pastry cases, Natascha adjusted her mind-set, changing it from 'aware and alert' having driven for nearly two hours from her home in London, to 'comfortable and relaxed' now that she had arrived at her parents' home in the most idyllic village in a far corner of Oxfordshire. She was good at that. She could shift her state of mind to accommodate any given circumstance in moments; to adapt to any occasion at will as easily as changing gear in her Audi. That's how Natascha operated, that's who she was; very rarely ruled by emotion, always guided by her head.

"I've got a little something for you," she continued, waving a small silver coloured gift bag in the air.

"Oh Natascha, it's lovely to see you darling. Be a dear and hand round those little cheesy biscuits, would you?" her mother said almost seamlessly, putting down the golden baked canapés and pointing an oven glove-clad hand towards the worktop, "I need to..." She stopped mid-sentence and smiled apologetically. "Oh, I'm sorry sweetheart, it is lovely to see you, really it is, and thanks for the gift but I really want to get these to the table before I put in the quiches. Everyone seems to have come with such voracious appetites! Long drive?"

Natascha hid a smile. Although her mother always showed signs of mild panic, in truth, she loved the whole entertaining thing, especially her annual birthday drinks party. Making the conscious effort of modifying her mental state hadn't really been necessary. Simply hearing her mother's ramblings was enough for Natascha's mind to settle back into her 'safe' zone all on its own.

Her high heels clicked sharply on the kitchen floor tiles as she went to kiss her mother's cheek, before crossing the room to scan the scene across the hallway. She peeped into the lounge and listened to the buzz of animated voices, the chinking of plates and glasses and Frank Sinatra crooning in the background. Guests stood eating, drinking and chatting; the sound of raucous laughter every so often escaping into the effervescent ambience.

"Party in full swing, I see," Natascha said, as she turned back to see her mother, again distracted by the oven and more pastries. "Hey, Mum, you don't need to do that. I'll get the rest of my bags from the car. When I get back I'll put those in the oven. In the meantime you can go and mingle with your guests." From the lack of any reaction to a single word, it was evident her mother was not listening. Natascha gave an affectionate sigh, being all too familiar with her mother's easily diverted attention and lifted an eyebrow. "Mum," she said, a little louder, "your guests! Go on, go! You can leave those to me. You can't be the birthday girl and spend all your time socialising from the kitchen! I'll be back in a minute to take care of everything here. Don't worry, I'll have it all under control." Natascha gave her another peck on the cheek and waited while her mother put the tray back onto the worktop and reluctantly untied her apron, grumbling something about a bossy daughter under her breath as she left the kitchen. Natascha shook her head in gentle exasperation and made her way to her car along the path that ran alongside the little house.

As she approached the end of the garden, any unimportant thoughts in her head flittered away when in front of her she saw the wide-shouldered back of a man leaning into the open door of a car and impatiently rooting around in the glove compartment. It hijacked her attention. She came to an involuntary halt in the middle of the path and continued to watch as he began to ease himself out. After locking the car he turned around and stopped dead when he caught sight of her. Something stole Natascha's breath leaving her to stand staring. For her to take notice of, let alone be interested in the attributes of the opposite sex, was an extremely rare reaction. But this was different. This was a *very* attractive man. His tight jaw line, high cheekbones and the faint shadow of a dimple in his chin were just too perfect. His dark hair was a little long for the current trend, granted; the back of which spilt way over the top of his collar but it was neat and glossy even in the failing afternoon light. Any breathing woman would have been taken by this man's good looks and Natascha felt dangerously close to being one of them.

Thankfully, shattering the moment, she heard her mother calling from the kitchen, jerking her out of her trance-like state and forcing her to take control of her wits. Inwardly, Natascha was very disappointed to have lost some of her self-control, reacting like a star-struck teenager.

"Natascha? Oh, Natascha, there you are. I was about to tell you that... Oops, no need. I can see that you've already spotted him!" she said as she came hurrying over. "Isn't it lovely to see him again? Oh, this is wonderful!" she gushed in a tone that supposed they already knew each other. "But you look as though you don't recognise him, dear," she said, looking slightly perplexed. "You do remember, don't you?"

Natascha realised she was still riveted to the ground. And, so as to regain her poise, she took a deep breath, straightened up and delicately shook her head to help her re-focus, allowing the soft waves of her dark hair to sway about her shoulders, its auroral shine reflecting the last rays of the winter sun.

"Come on, it's about time you two met up again, wouldn't you say? It's been far too long!"

Why did her mother keep saying 'again'? Natascha had never met this person. He had the type of face you couldn't possibly forget in a hurry. But before she had time to rack her brains some more, her mother grabbed the back of her arm and ushered her down the path towards the mysterious man until they were standing opposite one another. Natascha lifted her head slightly so she could see his face. Close up, Natascha could not help but fully appreciate him. Eyes, the colour of rich translucent caramel, so deep she knew that if she was not careful she could easily get lost in them. His almost feminine long and thick black lashes framed a dangerous stare, creating a dusky and smouldering gaze that only added to his mystery. It took her just moments to scan his flawless physique and note the well-cut jeans which suggested long athletic legs. He had that air of a Hollywood star that would stand him head and shoulders above a line-up of equally attractive men and a haunting aura that Natascha found far too beguiling for her own good. But it was too late. She couldn't explain why but she was already deeply drawn to him. Although she still didn't know him however, she had a strong suspicion that she should. His eyes were fixed on her as if he was studying her.

"You must remember. Goodness, Natascha, it's Richard! You must have been around twelve or thirteen years old the last time you saw each other. No, I tell a lie. Richard, you were a bit older. You were sixteen and Natascha, you were fourteen. But still, I would have thought..." Her mother looked over to Richard and was disconcerted. "Don't tell me you've forgotten too, Richard?" she asked, when she realised that he, too, had said nothing.

A dim light flickered in Natascha's head which gradually grew brighter. Of course she remembered Richard. But surely not? It couldn't be? She looked hard at him, her midnight blue eyes, usually as abyssal as the sea, suddenly sparkling like sunlight on water.

"Richard? Is that really you? I can't believe it, I didn't recognise you!" She looked into his face again. It was familiar but she would never have been able to recognise him had she not been told. Richard had been her best friend years ago when they were young. They'd known each other since junior school and had been very close. They promised they'd always keep in touch when his family moved away but after just a few phone calls and a couple of letters, he stopped writing and never returned her calls. There had been no further contact. And although she used to wonder what had happened to him from time to, it had been a while since he had last crossed her mind. But who would have guessed that Richard, whom she remembered to be quite nice but not altogether remarkable, could grow up to become such a good-looking man - so different that she hardly knew him at all?

However, in direct contradiction to her growing elation, he stood before her statuesque-like and expressionless; the only evidence of any kind of recognition at all was the very slight tinge of colour spreading over his prominent cheekbones and the darkening intensity of his beautiful eyes. His mouth, as sensual as it was, grew into an unnecessary smirk.

"Yes, I remember. How are you, Natascha?" he asked, drily. His voice was deep and as smooth as butter but lacked any warmth or humour.

The happiness began to ebb away from Natascha's face. What was wrong with him? Why the cool attitude?

"Well, I bet you two will have a lot of catching up to do," her mother said, blissfully unaware of the straining atmosphere. And feeling pleased with herself for initiating the grand reunion, she trotted away back to the house.

They both stood just looking at one another. His face showed no discernible emotion at all, except at one point she thought she saw something in those deep and mesmerising eyes but the look was unreadable to her. He turned them away. Natascha was a calm and optimistic woman by nature. She hadn't always been that way. Life had taught her the invaluable lesson that difficult situations or problems were never solved by impatience or loss of temper. She tried again with the upbeat approach.

"It's actually been twenty years! Can you believe that?" But it was to no avail. Her words were met by more silence. Very slowly, he turned back to look at her, continuing to stare as if he hadn't registered a single word she had spoken. Natascha wasn't usually one to show outward excitement - pleasant and polite, always; bubbly and animated - never. However, this was different. This was Richard. Taking her cue from his lack of any enthusiasm, she moderated her tone. "How have you been?" she asked more soberly. "What are you doing now? Did you ever become a scientist?" she asked with a restrained little laugh. Finally, he spoke.

"I work in IT." His reply was short, sharp and abrupt.

"Oh, I see. In software or..."

"Something like that."

Richard didn't elaborate or disclose any further information. Nor did he seem to be in the least bit interested in Natascha since he made no enquiries of her, even if it was only to be polite. It was clear that it didn't make the slightest difference to him whether it had been twenty years or twenty minutes since they had last spoken. And to think, all those years ago they were almost inseparable. But who was this Richard? Not the one she knew, not by the way he was acting. As far as she could remember they had spent nothing but good times together. Perhaps she was only remembering the good parts - 'the good old days' as most people did when reminiscing about the past. Maybe he had always been like this; cold and indifferent, bordering on the aloof, although at the time, she was so young she'd never really noticed? Natascha's mind quickly constructed her invisible wall, the one she always built in situations such as these, to act as a shield against the hostile vibes she was getting, allowing her to keep her cool and hold her composure, for what Richard did seem to have was the rare talent of causing Natascha's usually unruffled character to begin to wobble.

"I gave my parents a lift" he said, grimly. "My mother left this in the car and I was about to take it back to her. Perhaps you wouldn't mind handing it to her yourself." He outstretched his hand to reveal a small gift-wrapped box. Natascha glanced at it, deciding that it was unnecessary for her to be interested in what she was looking at.

"Of course," Natascha said, as she took the present from him. Any joy of seeing him again had now faded. She was also somewhat taken aback by what struck her as being more like an order rather than a request.

He couldn't even manage a thank you or goodbye before he got back into his car, fleeing like a villain from the scene of a crime.

Natascha watched him drive off. He had made it very clear that he was not the socialising type, regardless of the company. But was it necessary for him to make known his apparent condescension of such a gathering so blatantly? And in addition, had she just been insulted or not? Was his lack of concern deliberate or was it just the way he was now?

Had anyone else behaved in such a way as Richard had just done, she would simply have categorised and labelled him as rude and not given it another moment's thought. However, in this case, somehow his actions were a little shocking to her, she, who was not so easily affected. How could he be so impervious to meeting again after all this time? How could a reunion between two once very close friends leave such little or indeed, no impression on him at all?

"Bloody hell, gorgeous, you're a sight for sore eyes!" a young man suddenly announced as he walked past, his hands pushed firmly into the pockets of his jacket and face buried into its fleecy upturned collar against the cold. Natascha was shaken out of her thoughts, forcing her to abandon any search for answers to her questions. "You've certainly made my Christmas!" he added with an appreciative grin and a cheeky wink as he went on his way.

Although the use of a little more discretion was usually the norm, this was, by no means, an unusual reaction. Natascha had the beauty of every woman's ideal and the look of every man's fantasy. Flattery of her loveliness though, meant nothing to her. However, she was quite grateful for the young man's bold audacity; glad of the interruption to her useless speculations on Richard.

Natascha wrapped her arms around herself, briskly rubbing the tops of her arms to stave off the chill that had permeated her cashmere jumper. The smart matching linen skirt and stiletto heels were perhaps a little too formal for the occasion but she always dressed this way. The sharp yet classic style worked hand in hand with the self-assuredness and strong self-confidence she oozed, together with her steady character and tranquil personality. These were what were important to her, not a pretty face. They were attributes she had worked hard to achieve. Nothing and no-one was going to change that, not even an old friend, a 'once-upon-a-time' old friend.

Natascha turned back once more and looked into the distance where Richard's car had disappeared. Any disappointment had now changed to minor irritation. He had tarnished what should have been a wonderful moment.

She went to retrieve the rest of her bags from the car. She had luggage to take into the house, friends of her parents with whom she should share some polite chit-chat and a kitchen full of finger-foods with which she should be busying herself. Richard and his antics could evaporate into another galaxy. However, by the time she arrived back in the kitchen, despite her reasoned objectives, she knew that somehow, deep, deep inside, she would not be able to dismiss him quite so easily. This realisation did not make her happy but she would put that out of her mind, at least for now.

Chapter Two

"Nice to see Richard again, wasn't it?" Her mother was back in the kitchen arranging unfashionable cheese and tomato Vol-au-vents on a plate.

'Nice' was perhaps not the word Natascha would use to describe the meeting. He had been impolite and unfriendly but she didn't want to spoil her mother's day. "Yes, it was very nice."

"You don't sound very convinced, dear. You surely must have had quite a bit to chat about."

"He didn't actually say very much. He seemed to be in a bit of a hurry. There wasn't much time to catch up."

"Well, I suppose he was always a boy of few words. It sounds as though he hasn't changed much over the years," her mother said, scattering finely chopped parsley over the canapés.

The edges of the little box pressed against the palm of Natascha's hand. "He gave me this." She held up the dainty little box wrapped in light blue tissue paper and silver ribbon. "He said his parents were here and asked if I would give this to his mother. I'm sure I wouldn't recognise her now, though. I don't even remember her name."

Brushing the remaining bits of parsley from her fingers, her mother came over to Natascha. "Monica and Michael," she reminded her, taking the little box out of her hand and examining it. "His parents are Monica and Michael,"

Then, as it did with Richard, it all started to come back to her. Details she'd once known so well had completely eluded her. "Oh yes, I remember now. They moved to Scotland, didn't they? I didn't realise you kept in touch."

"Oh, we spoke quite regularly on the phone. Your Dad and I went to visit a few times. But they've moved back from Inverness and are living near St Mark's Church," she added absently, still studying the box. Her mother looked up and a slight frown hovered below the fine wrinkles on her forehead. "You don't remember, do you? Well, I suppose it was some time ago."

As Natascha thought back, she knew her parents had been to Scotland to visit friends. Perhaps her mother did mention names at the time but Natascha had never really made the connection. "It's the details that I've forgotten."

Natascha's mother, not having been able to work out what was in the box, handed it back. "Michael was offered a senior position in his company but it meant the whole family having to relocate to Scotland." Natascha vaguely recalled a goodbye scene. "Well, now that Michael has retired, they decided they wanted to come back to Oxfordshire. And moving back, of course, means they might be able to see more of Richard."

"Why, has he moved back here?" In spite of herself, Natascha was still curious to know more about him.

"I don't know where he lives exactly, but I do know that he was with them in Inverness until he was eighteen when he moved away to go to university. I can't remember which university it was but I'm positive it wasn't in Scotland and from what Monica says he never went back. I'm so pleased they've decided to come back. Monica tells me that she's taken up card making and has been doing it for quite some time, apparently. She wants to find out whether she can set up some card making classes down in the church hall and I promised I'd go with her sometime next week to have a word with the vicar to see if it would be possible..." For as long as Natascha could remember, sticking to the subject hadn't ever really been her mother's strongest point and very soon she'd lost interest in Richard and his whereabouts.

"I see." Natascha hadn't managed to glean much information, only that he didn't live in Scotland. And seeing as he hadn't even been bothered to talk to her, she wasn't going to concern herself with him. Anyway, he was gone now and she was unlikely to ever meet him again. "Anyway," Natascha added, in order to change the subject, "I thought I was going to take over in the kitchen?"

Natascha had barely placed the tray of clean glasses on the drinks table when she heard her mother behind her.

"Natascha, remember I told you about Monica and Michael? Well, let me introduce you..."

"Oh my goodness, little Natascha! Well, not so little now, of course!" Monica cut in, her words bubbling excitedly as Natascha turned around. "My, how you've grown and into quite a beauty! Mind you, I would have known you anywhere, what with all that beautiful jet black hair and those lovely blue eyes. Why, you must be the envy of all the girls in class!" She gave a hysterical little laugh at her own joke and furrowing her brows, she turned to Natascha's mother. "Vivienne, you never told me how stunning little Natascha has grown up to be!"

Monica and Michael were slightly older versions of the images that had begun to form in Natascha's mind. At that moment, her father appeared beside her.

"I didn't know you were here already, Tascha?" her father said, as he gave her a hug.

Natascha had an extra special soft spot for her father. "Hello Dad," she said, as she squeezed him back. "I haven't been here long." Then turning her attention to Monica and Michael, she added, "And we've just been introduced after twenty years."

Monica unexpectedly pulled Natascha in for her share of a hug. "Twenty years, gosh! It seems like only yesterday you and Richard were riding your bicycles into town to buy milk or sweets!" she said, all aflutter.

"It's very nice to meet you again... Michael," Natascha said, when she was at last disengaged from Monica's arms. He was still as tall as she remembered and stood as straight as a lieutenant-general leaving Natascha feeling compelled to address him by his surname, but it wouldn't come to her. Instead, she stepped forward and held out her hand for a polite handshake. Although she was a grown woman of thirty-four, it never failed to fascinate her how even when one is well into adulthood, the older generation will always be determined to speak to you as if you were still at school. For a split second Natascha felt like she was twelve again!

"Well, I'm sure we'll be meeting quite often now," Monica continued, still very excited.

"I hope we do," Natascha said, kindly, "but right now, I have to get some quiches from the kitchen. Maybe we can have a chat later."

Chapter Three

The long journey and the lively ambience of the party, which saw the last of the guests trickle out at around half past one in the morning, should have been enough to send Natascha to sleep without any trouble. But here she was, wide awake, staring into the near darkness at the outdated flowery pink Laura Ashley wallpaper that still decorated her old room. All sorts of pictures raced through her mind; work, her close circle of friends, the new coffee table she'd been contemplating. But in the end, all thoughts settled like tiny soft white feathers on Richard. The image of him, tall and more handsome than she could ever have imagined had taken its place at the forefront of her mind. Physically, he had kept himself in good shape and his features had become so refined and yet so strong. However, regardless of his good looks, they could never disguise the unwarranted behaviour, so frosty and distant.

Her mind travelled back to when they were young. Being neighbours, they had spent nearly all their time together. They had both attended St Mark's but naturally, since he was a couple of years older, he stayed with his classmates and she with hers. But always, it was 'see you at the gates after school' he'd say every day, so they could walk home together. They played childish games when they were very young and did their homework together when they were both at secondary school. 'What's up?' he'd ask, when it looked like she was struggling. He'd then leave his own work to help her with some maths problem or other. They ran errands together and went for country walks together. They spent so much time in each other's company.

Natascha remembered how Richard read incessantly. He had books on anything and everything. She went with him to the library just about every day. When they watched TV, she almost always lost the toss and would have to sit through numerous documentaries and science programs while Richard lay on his belly in front of the TV, chin resting in the palms of his hands and feet swaying idly behind him, oblivious to everything around him. She'd seen everything from slugs of the British Isles to the hunting abilities of grey seals; from the indigenous tribes of the Amazon rainforest to the Tuareg people of the Sahara desert. And although some may have been fairly interesting to watch some of the time, she could have done quite well without having to watch most of the others most of the time. Richard, on the other hand, soaked up every last bit of information, logging it somewhere in his head in case it was ever needed. 'You never know, it might be handy one day' he used to say. Lord knows what he would have been like had the World Wide Web been as prolific back then as it was today.

Natascha had always been in awe of him and his apparent bottomless pit of knowledge. Whatever questions she might have had, she asked Richard - Richard would always have the answer.

They were as close as any brother and sister could be. The bond they had formed was so strong that Natascha couldn't imagine how all communication could ever have ceased so suddenly, dying a rather unnatural death all that time ago. Maybe being fourteen and sixteen, it was easy to promise to stay in touch. However, contrary to what she had believed back then, maybe they were not as attached as she once thought. When they said goodbye, it really was the end. New chapters in their lives and the distance between them had taken them down very different roads that perhaps were never meant to cross. Things had definitely changed.

In any other circumstance, a situation such as this would have been like water off a duck's back to Natascha. She did not care for and therefore did not waste her time dwelling upon what didn't please her. This time, extremely unwillingly, she had to admit she was a little hurt and upset by Richard's cold off-handedness. She closed her eyes to stem the thoughts. Enough. I've wasted enough of my time thinking about him, she concluded. He could please himself; it would make no difference to her.

Sitting at the kitchen table for breakfast the next morning, the radio was playing to no-one in particular in the corner of the room. Natascha found Richard had infiltrated her mind again. His openly insolent behaviour still irked her. By now, she should have fenced off all thoughts of him and it annoyed her that she had not. Her strict mental process to assign Richard and all thoughts of him to the area in her mind marked as 'Unimportant/Irrelevant' was not working as it should. She would not allow this. This slight glitch in her methods would have to be addressed. Going back to London to leave the episode behind her was the first step. She stood up suddenly, startling her mother.

"Ooh, are you all right, dear?"

"I want to make an early start home today. Do you mind if I leave straight after breakfast? I'll see you and Dad in a couple of weeks for Christmas."

Chapter Four

Natascha was in her office at Colonia Events at seven thirty that morning, trawling the internet and searching through all the information she held, trying to find a conference room large enough to accommodate the three hundred or so attendees to Salter Investments' imminent annual meeting. The hall she'd originally hired had been double-booked by the business centre but they were unable to offer an alternative, which left her with the enormous task of finding somewhere else to put on the event at such short notice. To make matters worse, aside from June weddings, Christmas and the New Year were the busiest periods of the events calendar.

She loved her work as an events manager, being totally in charge of planning and organising conferences and galas from inception to execution. It was challenging, exciting and very rewarding but the job could entail long hours. But with her cool business acumen and unflurried character it was the perfect career for her and no other could suit her more. In equal measure to keeping on top of her work, coming into the office early allowed Natascha the satisfaction of being in command of and in absolute control of her working day; this simply being an extension of the way she lived her organised, personal life.

She had also agreed to spend some of her time assisting one of the company directors, Gavin Stewart, with his work until he hired a new personal secretary. Natascha was happy enough to help, however Emma, his previous secretary, had married and moved back to Wales six weeks ago and although Gavin and Natascha always had an excellent working relationship, it seemed he had become far too accustomed to the new working arrangement and was dragging his feet when it came to employing a permanent replacement. He found Natascha more than efficient and knew he could always rely on her, trusting her judgement implicitly. But he knew he was pushing her goodwill.

Natascha had a lot of work on at the moment but that agreed with her very well. Work, she found, always kept her fully and contentedly distracted. Any unpleasantness from the weekend would be relegated to nothing more than a mere and fleeting incident.

Her telephone rang.

"*Morning, Natascha. Can I see you for a minute?*" It was Gavin, wasting no time with niceties, as usual.

"Of course, I'll be there in a moment." Something was up - she could tell it in his voice.

Natascha pulled up a chair. "What can I do for you, Gavin?"

"We have a small crisis unravelling in the office this morning. Clayton has been called home on a family emergency so I'll be covering his meetings and Marissa phoned in to say that her doctor has advised her to have complete bed rest and there's no knowing when she'll be fit enough to come back to work. Hopefully, it should be before the start of her maternity leave but right now there's no guarantee that it will. The tiniest problem is...," he said, drawing out his words, "she's arranged a meeting with a prospective client this morning. Jules is on site and Steve's gone to visit a castle in the Highlands or something. So that leaves you, I'm afraid," he added, in a not so very convincing apologetic tone. "I know you've already got a plateful but we can't turn down potential new business, can we? Not just because of the small obstacle of having no staff available. Don't you agree?" Gavin looked at her rather sheepishly and batted his eyelids. "I was hoping that you might be able to take on another project, a Client Appreciation Party, so I've been told," he went on, "you know, pretty standard stuff, really. Nothing you can't handle." Gavin smiled sweetly. "Go on, you know how good you are at pulling successful dos out of the bag even when you're under pressure." The look of expectancy in his eyes developed into a plea which he could conjure up whenever he thought sweet-talking and praise were the best ways to get Natascha on side. He was wrong. But she let him go on believing it. "Don't worry about my diary. I can sort myself out," he said, with a confident grin.

Although taking on a new client so close to Christmas was not ideal - and no project ever turned out to be 'pretty standard', she knew she could cope with the extra work if she had to.

"Why not? You know I love a challenge," she said, ironically. "At least I can be sure that my Christmas bonus will more than cover the deposit on that rather nice Audi A4 I've had my eye on! Won't it?"

A look of relief crossed Gavin's face. "Thank you, Natascha. I knew I could depend on you. And you never know, I may be able to see to it that you can put a deposit on an Audi A4 *and* a nice red Ferrari for helping me out at such short notice," Gavin said with a wink. "A Mr Bradley Sampson from 'Sampson & French' is expecting to see Marissa. Can I leave it to you to sort out?"

"I'll go and see to it now. Don't worry, it'll be fine. Oh, and that's okay, the Ferrari can wait until next year. And one other thing; that's a brand new Audi A4 *Cabriolet*, to be precise," she corrected. Natascha stood up. "What time's the meeting?"

Gavin laughed, and then looked at her guiltily. "He's, er, due any minute now."

Natascha raised an eyebrow, "Wow! That is short notice."

"Shall I phone down to reception and ask them to call you when Bradley Sampson arrives?" he asked, carefully.

By the time Natascha got to her office door, her phone was already ringing.

"*Ms Hamilton, I have a gentleman here in reception from 'Sampson & French' to see you.*"

Chapter Five

As the lift bell sounded and the doors slid open, Natascha stepped out and turned to make her way towards reception. The breath that caught in her throat rendered her momentarily motionless. Her mouth felt dry and the accelerated beating of her heart pounded in her chest. 'This cannot be possible!' a voice bellowed in her head. At the other end of the foyer, Richard was standing beside the desk, tall and suave in a crisp white shirt and expensive suit. Natascha needed a few seconds to compose herself.

"Richard?" she asked as she approached him. "Richard, what are you doing here...?" It didn't take long before it began to fall into place... Sampson & French. She thought harder, Richard...Richard... Richard French! Yes, of course. He was Richard French. How could she have forgotten that? His parents were Monica and Michael French. Her parents always used to refer to them as 'our French friends'. Her mother hadn't mentioned their surname at the weekend and Natascha hadn't asked. The name had escaped her when she met them but it all started to come together now. Did coincidences on such a magnitude really exist? "I came expecting to meet Bradley Sampson but obviously you are not him."

"You work here," he said, drily.

"Yes, I do." Natascha expected him to say something more but he did not and she carried on. "So, you are the 'French' of 'Sampson & French'. What an incredible coincidence!" she said, as she welcomed him with a warm smile. Surely a small amount of her friendliness would be returned? But there was no response. Instead he gave her a cool stare, running his gaze from her face to her high heels and back up again. Presuming the phrase 'how nice to see you again' or words to that effect did not form part of his rather limited vocabulary, this meeting would soon disintegrate into a repeat of the weekend's distasteful incident if Natascha did not change tack. Therefore, replacing the relaxed manner which she reserved for friends to one created exclusively for business, Natascha presented herself as the professional she was and keeping her smile in place, she held out her hand for a brisk handshake, enabling her to conceal her miscalculations. She had made enough of a fool of herself already at the weekend and that, she reminded herself, would never happen again. If Richard was only interested in a business relationship, she would respect that. His reason for it was nonetheless puzzling but ultimately was none of her concern; she was here for her client and she would treat him as such. She continued, expertly. "Mr French, it seems there has been a change of personnel all round. I believe you were expecting to meet my colleague Marissa Clarke but unfortunately, because of unforeseen circumstances, she won't be able to meet you. But I have been given all the details and will be happy to work with you." Natascha had to keep control of the undesired effect he was having on her and retain her cool. She was also determined not to let their previous encounter colour her judgement.

"Yes, I am the 'French' of Sampson & French," he finally answered, entirely ignoring any other comments she had made. He paused, "I remember you as Miss Hamilton, unless you're now Mrs...?" he said formally, as though he was meeting a virtual stranger.

Natascha took a short moment before answering, feeling somewhat aggrieved at having to divulge this rather personal piece of information to him. "No, no, I was and still am Miss Hamilton, but of course, you must call me Natascha." She didn't feel a fraction of the geniality she was displaying. On the contrary, she was beginning to feel well and truly put out by his open surliness. "Well anyway, welcome to Colonia Events. If you would like to follow me we can speak more comfortably in my office."

"Thank you.".

She turned around and walked back towards the lift, a little in front of him, annoyed at her feelings. Negative thoughts and ridiculous emotions served no logical purpose.

The silence that fell between them as they took the lift to her office was particularly awkward. There was so much that should be talked about, so many questions to ask, so many answers to give but not a single word was spoken. A transparent wall had erected itself between them, keeping each to their half of the lift space. Natascha ventured an unsolicited glance in Richard's direction. She watched his impassive face as he studied the carpeting but all that was visible were his long, dark lashes keeping him hidden from her view. Then, as though he could feel her staring at him, she couldn't seem to tear her eyes away from his face as he lifted his own eyes to meet her gaze. Neither of them looked away as their eyes locked in what seemed like a battle of character. A slow hesitant smile began to creep uneasily to his lips and Natascha felt her own mouth begin to segue into a smile she could not wipe away. However, the spell was quickly broken when the lift came to a halt and the doors opened. She led the way to her office and ignored the moment.

"Please take a seat over by the window." Natascha motioned Richard to the small corner of her office where she had installed armchairs and a low bistro sized table to create a more relaxed setting. By avoiding the formal use of a desk and office chairs, her clients tended to be more trusting of her and her capabilities and the majority of the choices or suggestions she made were accepted without any unnecessary conflicts or disagreements. Whether it would have the same effect on Richard was an entirely different question. As she spoke she could see a picture of his cautious smile in the lift. But before it had a chance to fix itself in her brain she quickly erased the scene from her head.

"Please call me Richard."

Natascha shot him a look, surprised at the unexpected, albeit lukewarm attempt to appear more genial. "I'm sorry?"

"Downstairs you called me Mr French. Please, call me Richard," he said, matter-of-factly.

"Yes, of course." Natascha held her pleasant manner. "Can I offer you some coffee or tea or perhaps a cold drink, Richard?"

"No, I'm fine, thank you."

Natascha came over and sat in the chair opposite him. "I only need to get some basic details to start with then I'll go ahead and see what I can do to accommodate what you're looking for and we can take it from there."

Richard imperceptibly nodded.

"What sort of event are you hoping to stage?" She spoke to him as she would any other client.

"The company wants to host a 'thank you' party for all our clients. We'd prefer to get Christmas out of the way and hold it sometime nearer the spring."

"Something like a Client Appreciation Party?"

Richard nodded again.

"And did you have any particular idea in mind, perhaps a themed night?"

"Nothing specific but I definitely don't want a disco-type affair with flashing lights and a has-been DJ spouting out-dated jokes to eighties so-called hits," he said, completely straight-faced; without even a trace of wit.

 Having this cool and empty tone of conversation with Richard, quite simply, felt wrong. It was the sort of chat you had with a recently made acquaintance. Natascha was obliged to keep up the charade, however. "So, something of a classier style of food and drink, perhaps some live music, blues or jazz, maybe?" Natascha watched Richard's face for signs of his agreement or otherwise but saw nothing so she jotted down her suggestions as being acceptable. "Were you thinking of a black tie affair or would it be casual evening dress? That'll make a difference when I look for a venue."

"As long as it's not fancy dress, I'll leave it up to you. I'm sure you'll think of something appropriate."

"Of course, I'll make a note of it," she said, a little rankled. She picked up her pen again. "No... fancy... dress," she said aloud as she scribbled. "And would you like it to be held in the buzz of the city or in a quieter location."

"Quiet. I would prefer to avoid the centre of London if that is at all possible."

"That can be easily arranged." Natascha jotted down some more notes.

"There'll be around 150 people, including their partners," he said suddenly, without the need for Natascha to prise the information from him.

She looked up and laid her pen down. "Right then, I think I have enough here to make some initial enquiries and..." Richard got up before she could finish her sentence but she followed his lead and stood up from her seat holding out her hand. "Thank you, Richard. I'll be in touch as soon as I've put something together although that may well be after Christmas."

"I'll look forward to it," he said without emotion, as he shook her hand. And before Natascha could end the meeting a little more amicably, he was gone from her office.

Putting aside his testy manner, that must have been the easiest meeting Natascha had ever conducted. Gavin may have been right about it being a simple project, simpler than even he must have anticipated. All communication could probably be made via telephone or email and she might never need to meet with Richard again - not until the night of the event itself. In any case, he had given the impression that he couldn't be bothered to get involved, anyway; he would just want her to get on with it. Suddenly, his disinterest was of great comfort to her.

The advantage of the early start in the office that day made little impact on Natascha's unending morning. Emails were being delivered into her inbox thick and fast, each displaying a billowing red 'priority' flag and for every phone call she ended, another was waiting to be answered. This morning's unexpected events had rattled her more than she cared to admit and she had found herself making a conscious effort to move to one side unwanted thoughts of Richard every time images of him flashed up in her mind. He was just another client and she would deal with his project just as she would any other, she had to remind herself.

By the time she had her lunch she was one of only a handful of people left in the office restaurant. Usually, the place was noisy and energetic during the peak lunch period, vibrant with the sound of colleagues meeting up to relax after the morning over a hot cappuccino and lasagne in the winter months or a cold Pepsi and a salad when the pub across the road's beer garden had become too crowded in the summer. However, the busy lunch time had long passed and Natascha found herself sitting alone in one of the much sought after comfy armchairs at the far end of an almost deserted restaurant. After her busy morning, she found her appetite had dwindled away and didn't really want more than half a salad sandwich and a cup of strong black coffee. Gradually, the niggling taut sensation in her forehead began to relax. Her exhaustion after the morning was unusual but she couldn't be sure whether it was her work load that had demanded so much of her or the constant struggle to keep certain thoughts at bay. These thoughts were now impossible to ignore. The more she unwound, the more she could see how preposterous it all was. For twenty years he had all but disappeared from her life after having been one of the most important people in it and in one outlandish flash he was back, now one of her clients and more of a stranger to her than any man she would pass in the street. However, poring over her opinions of Richard was having an adverse effect on her. She let her head fall back gently against the cushioning of the chair, experiencing the satisfying mental massage she gave her whole body as she continued to unwind. Her eyes slipped closed. The remote sound of the mumble of voices drifting from the other end of the restaurant was very therapeutic.

Then, through her closed lids she felt a looming presence standing beside her, causing a shadow to fall across her face. She opened her eyes and saw Richard in front of her. The sight of him almost shocked her into springing bolt upright but she managed to straighten up gracefully and remain leisurely seated, avoiding the potential of spilling hot coffee into her lap.

"Oh, I thought you'd gone. I saw you leave the office hours ago," she said, as she calmly ran a tidying hand through her hair.

"Yes, I did but I left my umbrella in reception. I came back to get it," he said, as his blank face stared back at her. "It's started to rain again." Though obviously practical, his reason for returning all the way back to the office had an absurdity about it as Natascha visualised this fearless alpha male carrying an umbrella over his head, cowering from what she could see from the window, as only a fine drizzle. "I saw signs for the restaurant and decided to have a cup of coffee before I left. I didn't expect to see you here." An odd sort of expression played with his lips which he was trying to suppress. Was he mocking her?

The few moments of relaxation helped Natascha to stay cool-headed but with herself still seated and Richard towering over her, she needed to redress this intimidating arrangement. She stood up and said evenly, "Seeing as I work here, I suppose the possibility of seeing me was always quite considerable." She gestured towards the empty chair beside her. "Please, have a seat. Let me get you that coffee." For the sake of their working relationship, perhaps she should have bitten back the sarcasm. It was a slight lapse in judgement but one which she had no intention of worrying about. She would continue to be affable but be alert ready to deal with any possible disparaging remarks he may feel necessary to impart. He was no longer the same person she used to know, that was clear, but exactly what he was like now, she had not yet had the chance to learn - though it wouldn't be long before she found out, he would make sure of that. Returning to the table, she placed his cup beside hers and seated herself

"Thank you." He focused hard on the cup in front of him. Natascha watched his face as lo and behold, it seemed he was trying to find an opening for a conversation! He looked up.

"I should have asked this morning. Will I be responsible for sending out the invitations?"

Natascha was privately amused. If part of him was anything like he used to be, Richard would have researched thoroughly what Colonia Events Ltd could do for him. Her reply was, therefore, purely academic.

"Not if you don't want to. Let me have a copy of your guest list and their email addresses and I will deal with it if you prefer. I could arrange for a simple website to be created and send a single email to all your guests inviting them to visit the website. There, they can reply by ticking a box to state whether or not they will be attending and the site can be kept updated with any news. I'll keep an eye on it and update my records with any comments that may be left by your guests. It's a useful and time-saving way of staying in touch with your clients. No need for sending and receiving multiple emails." He must have known what she was going to say. She waited to see if he had any questions. "It's an idea."

In the past, this sort of information regarding new ideas and the use of technology would have been as fascinating to him as the makeshift science lab he had created when he was ten years old and then she wondered where this detailed recollection came from.

"That sounds good," he said. The bland reply was meaningless.

Blotting out the uninvited memories of the past, she reminded herself that this was business only. "This might be a good time to give you an estimate of the cost..."

"Would you like to go out for a drink sometime?" Richard blurted out.

His words came out of the blue and threw Natascha completely off balance. Had she heard him correctly? It sounded as though he was inviting her for a drink. The question was totally out of context and not one she was likely to accept but from somewhere far away, and through her bewilderment she heard herself reply, "That would be nice."

Richard instantly stood up. "I'll phone you to arrange where and when." And once again, before she was able to speak, he was gone.

His words had confounded her. It was strange that he had asked her to go out with him at all when it was plain that he had to propose it before having the chance to think about it. And if there was one thing that she could always count on Richard for was his inability to act on impulse. She stared at his untouched coffee cup and wondered why on earth she had accepted his invitation.

Chapter Six

Friday evening and Natascha sat at one of the tables outside the wine bar on the far side of the small green, wrapped in hat and gloves against the cold, waiting for Sue. Natascha organised all her Friday evenings so as to make sure she had time for a glass of wine and some down-time with her closest friend. But blocked drains at a charity event the week before and the non-appearance of the musical entertainment at a gala evening the week before that, meant that this was to be their first Friday night drink in a while. This week had been a difficult one, one which she would prefer to forget. But at least she could talk to Sue about it and get it out of her system.

The two had met at Colonia Events when Sue was hired as a temporary HR manager and Natascha was an assistant to one of the event managers. It began by some polite remarks as they stood together in the sandwich queue of the staff restaurant one lunch time but from that moment on, a close friendship had clicked straight away. That was seven years ago now but somehow it felt as though they had known each other forever. The only common factor between them lay in the fact that they had both grown up as only children. However, from that point onwards, their lives were worlds apart. Unlike Natascha's safe and innocent childhood, Sue's was full of tragedy. She was only a mere child when her father was fatally injured on his way home from work when a drunk driver lost control of his car and careered onto the pavement. Then, after her mother remarried three years later, Sue was forced to relive the same pain when both her mother and doting stepfather were lost to the horrific Zeebrugge ferry disaster in 1987.

At seventeen, she left her rather cold foster home to make her own way. Her unsettled childhood gave her little choice but to grow up at an unnatural rate but even at such a young age, she had found an unknown strength within herself and as a result had emerged a strong and fully-equipped adult. Life couldn't really throw much at Sue which she couldn't cope with.

Natascha was first attracted to Sue's quick wit and 'ballsy' attitude; so very different to how she, herself, used to be. Haggling for a bargain in a department store, simply for the challenge of it was one of Sue's fortes and demanding to see the chef if she found the restaurant food was not up to scratch was a must. It was not that she went out to deliberately cause a fuss but she disagreed with the reserved British way and liked to prove it.

As self-reliant as Natascha had become though, she could never envisage her life without Sue. Sue had been with her through the good times and had been a solid gold rock when times were bad. She was the only person who really knew Natascha and the only person Natascha felt she could open up to -

as much as Natascha ever did. She could not have wished for a more trustworthy and genuine friend.

Across the way, on the other side of a small green, the milky white rays from the street lights quietly lit-up quaint little shops, spot-lighting on the florist packing away racks of plants and flowers that decorated the pavement as she got ready to close for the evening. The cosy little café had a couple of customers sitting inside, huddled together at a table and a woman and her little boy were about to enter the grocery store. The small estate agents, however, appeared to have had its 'closed' sign displayed a long time ago. Colourful Christmas lights blinked merrily from every shop window.

The little patch of land was a treasured haven hidden moments away from the main shops that lined the noisy and hectic high road.

This welcome routine of Natascha's Friday evenings and the solace of the scene in front of her went a little way towards bringing back a sense of order to her recently cluttered mind.

In the distance Sue was walking across the green in her direction.

"It's good to see you. It's been so long," Natascha said, as Sue reached her, and gave her friend a more affectionate hug than usual.

"Come on, let's go in," Sue said, through chattering teeth. "It's absolutely freezing out tonight!"

Inside, the bar was warm and inviting; the walls bedecked with shimmering tinsel and the easy voice of Bing Crosby singing *White Christmas* mellowed the mood. They found a table near the open fire and sat down with their drinks.

"You look like you've had a hard week," Sue said, shaking her hair loose from under her woolly hat.

Natascha watched as her friend put away her gloves in her bag and considered her answer and suddenly realised that she didn't want to talk about Richard after all - not yet. "Well, it has been unusually manic in the office but there was nothing in particular that I haven't seen before. Maybe it had something to do with all the problems having exploded at the same time, I suppose."

Sue wasn't satisfied with Natascha's response and so asked outright. "And...?"

"What do you mean '*and*'?"

"And... what else?"

"There's nothing else," Natascha said nonchalantly, but she could see from Sue's face that she was not going to be so easily appeased by her answer.

"What are you not telling me? I can tell when I'm not getting the whole deal from you."

"Well, not much else happened."

"And what's your idea of 'not much'?"

Sue wasn't going to let it go. She had a keen eye when it came to Natascha being less than honest with her so she may as well come clean - to a degree. "Well, I did meet someone..." Natascha said, casually.

"Ooh... a male someone?" Sue's eyes were open wide in anticipation. Her friend finally meeting a man with whom she could have more than a platonic relationship was something Sue had spent a long time praying for.

"It wasn't quite like that," Natascha replied calmly, trying to play it down.

"What do you mean? Wasn't he single? Wasn't he attractive?"

"Well, I didn't have an opportunity to ask whether he was married or not and yet something tells me that he isn't..." Natascha trailed away when she found herself wondering about Richard's marital status. "And on the contrary, he is very attractive... He's actually an old friend, a very old friend or at least we used to be friends. The last time I saw him I was fourteen years old. We were very close, like brother and sister."

"You've never mentioned him before."

"We lost touch. But we met again at Mum's birthday drinks last weekend. I hadn't seen him in twenty years. He asked me, with as little interest as he possibly could, how I was although I don't actually remember him giving me the chance to answer. He handed me a present, asked if I would give it to his mother and was gone. We must have spoken for less than three minutes. He couldn't wait to get away."

"Oh, I see," Sue mumbled, disappointed.

"It was a really odd meeting. I was so pleased to see him but I'm sorry to say it but he seems to have become a bit snobbish and pompous over the years. He treated me as if he didn't know me from the next person." Natascha felt a slight tug inside as she recalled the afternoon. "But then, when I met him again..."

"You saw him again?"

"Yes, I did and it was under the most bizarre of circumstances. Gavin allocated a last minute project to me but didn't get the chance to give me much information about the client, only the name of the person I was to meet. When I got to reception, the person I was expecting couldn't make it and sent his business partner instead. I suppose you can guess who that turned out to be."

Sue sat shaking her head slowly from side to side. "Nooooo... You're never going to tell me..."

"Yes, this friend of mine - and I use the term loosely, was standing there as cool as ice. My client is his company. I had no idea. There isn't a single word in The Oxford Dictionary to fully describe the surprise I had." Merely speaking about that second meeting made Natascha shudder.

"And then what happened?"

"I can't say that he was any friendlier than he was the first time. He was very business-like and had no interest in mentioning anything about our previous friendship. In fact, he totally ignored it."

"Sounds like a crabby old git to me!" Then, noticing that Natascha didn't say anymore, Sue interrogated her further. "There's more to it, isn't there?"

"Well… maybe," Natascha sighed, now wishing she hadn't given in to Sue's probing. "I met him again, by chance, in the staff restaurant that same afternoon and after making some small talk, he asked me whether I'd like to meet for a drink."

"What did you say?" Sue asked impatiently, her interest again fired up.

"I don't know why but I said yes. I should have said 'no thanks'. I must be becoming a soft touch in my old age."

"Natascha Hamilton, I love you dearly but a soft touch, you are definitely not!" Sue said, adamantly. "When are you meeting him?"

"He said he'd phone to let me know where and when and then he rushed off and I haven't heard from him since. To be honest, though" Natascha continued, equably, "I can't see that he'll bother and I can't say I'd be disappointed. In fact, I'm quite relieved that he hasn't got back to me."

"Listen, he asked you for a drink and you agreed. You must think it's worth giving him a second chance. I'm sure he'll ring."

She was right. Despite her determination to accept Richard as he was now and any association with him would only be on a professional basis, Natascha admitted to herself that she wasn't quite ready to dismiss this person who had once been part of the happiest times in her life. She was curious about him. It may be that an invitation for a drink was his interpretation of good business etiquette. But in reality, perhaps part of her wanted to be absolutely sure that the Richard of today was definitely not the same Richard she once thought she knew. More worryingly, she found herself wondering whether his invitation was, in any way, a vague attempt to rekindle their old friendship.

"And what was your week like?" Natascha asked, trying to move away from the subject.

"It was much the same as usual although I did go to see Aunt Jessie a couple of evenings ago, you know, my step-father's sister. I don't see her very often and I suppose a visit was long overdue. Anyway, during a conversation, she let slip some very interesting information. It seems that before my step-father married my mum, he had a child from a previous relationship who was apparently given up for adoption. He and the mother were very young at the time and split up soon after, or so I'm told. If mum knew about it, she certainly never told me."

"But that means..."

"Yes, I know. Somewhere out there I have a step-something." Sue looked at Natascha for a long moment with a gleam in her eye. "And I think I'm going to investigate this further."

"Are you sure?" Natascha asked, a little concerned. "Some people are very disappointed when they meet long lost relatives, if, indeed, the one party wants anything to do with the other. The rejection can be quite traumatic."

"I'm sure I'm going to be able to cope with rejection from an absolute stranger. Well, that's what this person is at the moment, aren't they?" Sue gazed out into the distance. "Can you imagine? My family increased to an Aunt Jessie, her husband Martin and a step-someone overnight. Wow!"

"Hey, slow down. I think you may be getting a little ahead of yourself." But Natascha knew that once Sue had made up her mind, there was no convincing her otherwise. "Well, good luck with that but be careful - and prepared."

***

Richard pulled the key from the lock and banged the door shut behind him. He dropped his briefcase to the floor, wrenched himself out of his coat and threw it impatiently onto the chair in the hall before heading straight for the kitchen. He opened the cupboard, poured himself a large whisky and sat himself down heavily on a stool, pulling down the knot of his tie to half-mast and grappling with the top button of his shirt. He took a gulp of the clear golden liquid and closed his eyes. It slid down his throat, smooth and fiery. It was a satisfying feeling as it burned its way down, easing the tightness in his stomach.

He had worked late again. It was Friday and he had promised himself that today he would take it easy and get home at a reasonable hour. But then again, he said that every Friday and it never happened. It was a weekly Friday promise which, saving an unexpected life or death situation, never materialised. In fact, he would probably end up going into the office again tomorrow and may even work for a couple of hours on Sunday - the same as he did practically every weekend. At least Christmas was coming up and he would be forced to take a few days off. He needed the break.

Last Saturday was one of those unusual weekends. He hardly ever went to see his parents but on a rare impulse, he had climbed into his car and made the very rare and long journey to exercise his responsibility as the dutiful son. But God, what timing! He could so have done without meeting Natascha. After so long, he never thought he would ever see her again. It was stupidly very short-sighted of him. How had it never crossed his mind that of course, the likelihood of seeing her again was obviously not going to be totally off the radar? It was always possible that they could meet now that his parents had moved back to Oxfordshire. He should have thought of that. But in his defence, how the hell was he to know that the Hamilton's still lived there!

It was his first visit since they'd moved back from Inverness and he only intended to stay for a couple of hours. Of all the days he could have gone, he had decided to go last Saturday, on Vivienne's birthday! Of course, his parents would be at her time honoured afternoon drinks party. Natascha had been all smiles and surprise at their first meeting after so long but if it had really been so wonderful to see him again, why had she not tried to contact him in all that time? But maybe that was his fault.

Anyway, he didn't believe the show of friendliness to be sincere, though she had been very good at the pretence. She didn't even know who he was! And to top it all, he had chosen Colonia Events to handle the clients' evening. Out of all the Events Management companies he could have approached as an alternative to the disappointing company he had hired last year, he had to choose the one she worked for!

He had to admit though, she looked good - very good; better than he remembered. She was always beautiful as a girl but wow, what a woman!

At that surreal meeting at her office she looked sharp and business-like, giving him an enthusiastic handshake. Luckily, she seemed to be a good business woman, firm yet polite, revealing a capable and strong personality. He couldn't stand to have any old wishy-washy person handling his affairs. She had become so confident. Where the hell did that come from? She was such a sweet thing when they were young that he couldn't help but feel protective of her back then. Boy, it was obvious she didn't need protecting anymore! She had called him Mr French. Mr French! That had spoken volumes. He meant no more to her than any other of her clients. He was pleased that he had kept his cool though, dumbing down his initial excitement at the shock of seeing her again when he realised that she didn't even remember his name. He would have made such a fool of himself. Well, at least he could finally close that chapter of his childhood and forget about it.

Richard raised his hand to his temple and rubbed it roughly. Did he really ask her out for a drink?

***

Chapter Seven

By midday Natascha had straightened out her pristine flat. Her home was always immaculate but it never hurt to make sure that all was still in order. She had endured and survived her weekly trip to the supermarket, weaving in and out of the other shoppers to the jaunty sounds of Christmas songs having their yearly radio-play and was hindered only once by the crowd who had gathered around the cut priced Christmas puddings. Her regular visit to the hairdressers for a monthly trim was, thankfully, less of an unholy shindig and more of a dignified affair. The post had been delivered, depositing half a dozen Christmas cards on the door mat which she clipped onto the string of Christmas cards hanging over the mantelpiece. They joined fellow images of chubby Father Christmases and solitary robin redbreasts perched beside holly leaves. Soft glowing Christmas lights decorated a miniature Christmas tree that stood demurely on a small table, lighting up the cosy alcove, fading delicately into the rest of the sedately decorated room.

She had kept herself occupied all morning and now it was time to sit back and take a few minutes for herself.

Her guitar stood in the corner beside her, calling to be picked up. This might be a good time to try and do some more work on the song she had decided to rewrite.

Natascha's first love was music and she considered herself a bit of an amateur songwriter. A few years ago she used to sing in front of audiences with a friend and it was a great time in her life. Nothing had meant more to her than the two of them singing together. Music used to be an incredibly important part of her life. But she'd given all that up. Nowadays, she was content enough to play and write for her own amusement.

It was funny how emotions insisted on being put into words and played out through the melody of a song. Recently, Natascha had begun to rearrange the words of an old ballad she had penned when she was a teenager and which was the first song she had embarked upon with the theme of love. It had originated as a cheerful, positive song but she wanted to alter the lyrics and the chords to become more moody; to darken the song's colour. She looked at what she had scribbled so far:

'*You ~~are~~ were my rock whenever I stumbled,*
You ~~are~~ were my pillow whenever I ~~cry~~ cried,
I ~~give~~ gave you my heart and I ~~give~~ gave you my soul.
~~A warm love like ours can never grow cold~~
But a warm love like ours has somehow grown cold'

She then felt an urge to cross the whole thing through and start another song from scratch. Being around thirteen or fourteen years old when she wrote it, the concept of love was new to her and the words reflected that. But they touched her with a strong, sentimental feeling that came from somewhere inside where only her music lived.

She positioned her fingers, strummed the accompanying chords and immersed herself into the beautiful rich tones that rang out from her guitar; the sonorous harmonies sending her to a private place in her core where nothing could disturb her. The music filled a need she was longing for. It had a healing quality that nothing else could provide, soothing her unusually tired mind and weary spirit.

Singing again from the beginning she wanted to feel the new lyrics come to her but she had hit a creative wall, any new ideas did not fit comfortably. Picking up her pen, she did a little more juggling and made a few more amendments.

'Days ~~are~~ were covered in sunshine
And in the night sky the moon ~~turns~~ turned to gold
I ~~give~~ gave you my heart and I ~~give~~ gave you my soul
~~A pure love like mine will never grow old~~
But that pure love like ours has left me alone'

Natascha struggled with the rest and then wondered why she was tinkering with this old song. It was young and flowery and wasn't amazingly profound. But then perhaps that's how it should be. Maybe if she strengthened the verses, gave the song a decent new riff...? She leant back and let the instrument rest casually against her, inhaling deeply then let out the breath slowly. Although the song was proving to be more complicated to arrange than she had originally thought, she felt settled - far more settled than she had felt during the whole, long week.

The phone rang.

"Natascha? It's Sue. What are you up to? Not interrupting anything 'interesting', am I? You know, with a certain Mr 'I-haven't-seen-you-in-a-long-time'? Just say the word and call me back when you're free." Sue's hushed and hurried tone had that 'nudge, nudge, wink, wink,' expectancy about it.

"No, Sue, I'm at home - On My Own!" The bubble of amusement in Natascha's voice betrayed the good-humour in the scolding.

"Oh. Shame," said Sue, making sure that Natascha was fully aware of her disappointment. "Well in that case, let me tell you about our little dinner party tonight."

"Dinner party? I didn't know you were planning a dinner party?"

"Well, we fancied having a little spontaneous soirée. You can make it, can't you? Unless, of course, you have made plans to meet Mr 'I-haven't-seen-you-in-a-long-time'!"

"No, Sue. I don't have any other plans, thank you." Natascha shook her head gently. "What's the occasion?"

"Nothing very special. Call it me and Matteo's pre-Christmas do."

"And is poor fiancé Matteo aware of your little do?"

"How sceptical you are, Natascha. Of course he knows about it! I'll have you know, it was his idea, actually!"

"Mmm..."

"Don't 'mmm' me and come round! Come at any time but I hope to have dinner ready by about eight."

"Well, dinner sounds good. I'll bring the wine."

"Great! I'll call the other guys. Should be a good laugh! See you later!"

Natascha arrived at Sue and Matteo's house just as her friends, Simon, Dominic and Rachel, were going in. Simon, the lovable rogue amongst the close knit group, turned around at the sound of her heels on the path.

"Oh Natascha, there you are. What took you so long? I was beginning to miss you already!" he drawled woefully, as they hurried in out of the cold.

"Oh Simon, really! Don't be so dramatic!" Rachel squeaked, in her rather high-pitched, young-girl voice. "You've only just got here yourself!" She rolled her big baby blue eyes and ran a hand through her bob of sunny blonde hair after unravelling her thick woollen scarf from around her neck.

Simon didn't take any notice of her and continued with the long-standing lyrical recitation. "Oh, Natascha! May I be so bold as to tell you how beautiful you are looking again tonight? You've caught the sun, haven't you? Yes you have, I can tell! You're looking exceptionally radiant! Are you sure you're not ready to let me sweep you off your feet, yet?"

Dominic groaned. "God, Simon, give it a rest!". Even though he spoke with an amiable tone of voice to the familiar ravings of his friend, it still boomed across the room, matching his tall, brick-built frame which belied his gentle giant nature. Dominic and Rachel's own engagement was pretty much on the cards.

"Oh, be quiet, you big Philistine! Natascha is most deserving of every flattery. Unlike you, I know how to treat a woman!"

"Yes, so you keep telling us! But when are you going to get it into that stubborn head of yours? She's told you a thousand times, she doesn't want a boyfriend! She doesn't even fancy you!"

Natascha ignored the accustomed, rather childish repartee between Simon and Dominic and cut in before it could go any further. "Simon! How can I have caught the sun, it's December - in England!" she said, with a vague act of annoyance.

"And the candlelight," Simon went on, regardless, "is magically captivating the subtle tones in your hair and..."

"Simon. Read any good books lately?" Natascha interrupted, sweetness wrapped around her purposefully timed question to finally bring to a close the endless poetry.

Simon closed his mouth and took the hint. "I shan't say another word," he whispered and placed a finger over his lips.

Natascha looked thoughtfully at Simon. He was attractive in a rugged sort of way, he made her laugh and was always gentlemanly and chivalrous and at one time, she had seriously thought about starting a relationship with him; they got on so well. But no matter how hard she tried she could never see him as any more than a friend; he wasn't her type. In fact, she was still not interested in finding any man who might be her type. The cool stillness that ran under her light-heartedness and easy friendliness was not yet ready to be rippled. She enjoyed the company of others but was contented within herself, happiest when she closed her front door, leaving the world outside, allowing her to muse alone inside.

"So, what's everyone up to for Christmas?" Dominic asked, as they settled around the table. "We've got both sets of parents over on Christmas Day, so that should be fun!" he continued, feigning his excitement.

"Matteo and I are spending both Christmas and New Year with his parents in Italy this year," Sue said, "and that's really why we've invited you all here." She looked at Matteo who was sitting beside her and raised her eyebrows at him.

"Yes, Sue is right," Matteo started, his Italian accent warm and sweet. "We wanted to tell you all that we have at last set a date for our wedding."

"I'm soon to be 'Signora' Sant' Angelo!" Sue added with enthusiasm.

"You're kidding, right?" Simon asked, his mouth open with surprise.

"No, it's true," Matteo explained. "The wedding will be at the beginning of March and will be held in my home town of Siena. Each one of you must be there. And don't worry, I am arranging it so that you all have a place to stay."

"Congratulations! That sounds great and I'm really happy for you both," said Rachel, "but can I just say, there's not an awful lot of time to get the whole thing organised, is there?"

"Yes, I know," Matteo continued, "but it seems that my father's health is not so good and my parents wish to retire from their winemaking business altogether. And so they have asked me whether I would like to take over the business." He looked at Sue. "We have thought about it very carefully and think that it would be a great start for us. I know the business very well since I grew up on the estate and worked there before coming to London. It won't be easy to begin with but it is a wonderful opportunity for us."

"So, you'll be living in Italy permanently, then," Natascha said, a little quietly.

"Yes, we will be. In fact, we will be returning to England for only a short time after New Year. Of course, there may be occasions when we may have to come back before the wedding but the plan is to make the move with as little fuss as possible."

There was a hush around the table for a moment while everyone took in this little bit of important information. Then Dominic stood up and held up his glass "I think a toast is due to the happy couple. Here's to Sue and Matteo."

Everyone followed Dominic's lead and stood up, glass in hand. "Sue and Matteo!" And six glasses met in the middle of the table and clinked together.

The news was heart-warming, exciting even and Natascha showed her pleasure in a brilliant smile. But without warning, something feeling like a small rock fell to the bottom of her stomach with a heavy bump. Sue was leaving to live in Italy for good. Natascha left the happy look in place while she tried to will away the sudden wave of abandonment that washed over her. And before her mind could dwell on those thoughts any more, she went over to congratulate Sue and Matteo with kisses.

"This is just wonderful. I'm so happy for you both."

Natascha was by the front door buttoning up her coat. She was the last to leave.

"I gather you think it's all a bit sudden, don't you?" Sue said, from behind her.

Natascha turned around. "It is a bit of a shock that it's so soon but it's great news. I'm really happy for you."

The brief melancholic expression that had clouded Natascha's delight earlier had not escaped Sue's notice. "I wanted to tell you before we told the others but I didn't have the heart to. I knew how you would feel. I know how I felt the first time Matteo told me about the possibility of leaving everything behind and taking over the wine business."

"You've made the right decision. You and Matteo belong together and this seems to be the perfect time to set yourselves up for a great life. Moving to Italy is going to be such a fantastic experience, living 'La dolce vita' and all that. You're going to take to it like a duck to water!" Natascha managed a little giggle.

"But what about us? What about our Friday evenings?" Sue asked, with a seriousness that dismissed Natascha's attempt to lighten the mood.

"That, my dear, is just a logistical blip." Natascha answered, mimicking Clark Gable in *Gone With The Wind*. "Don't worry, I'll be turning up on your doorstep so often, you'll soon be fed up of me!" she teased. Then the tone of her words shifted and matched a sudden surge of honesty. Sentimental emotions that lay buried deep inside Natascha could only be roused by Sue. "You have done so much for me Sue, setting me straight, helping me to change my life around. I could never repay you for what you've given me. I'm just so glad that now it's your turn to have a settled life. God knows you deserve it. No-one can be happier for you than me."

"You will be my bridesmaid, won't you? My Maid of Honour?"

The two women held each other in a tight embrace, a hug laden full of friendship and a sisterly love, both holding each other with tears glistening privately in their eyes.

Chapter Eight

It was cold and drizzling as Natascha paced up and down Oxford Street. Normally she would avoid at all cost visiting the shops on a Sunday but she still had some so-called specialised baking equipment left on her mother's list of necessary requirements for Christmas.

She squeezed passed the hordes of bored looking children and harassed parents trying to finish their Christmas shopping on desperation driven autopilot.

Sue and Matteo's wedding announcement last night had elated Natascha. If there was one person who was long overdue every happiness, it was Sue. She had waited more than patiently for her share and now it was her turn to enjoy true stability. But the future had now developed a distinctly hazy outlook for Natascha. Sue was going to live so far away. Sue was such a constant in her life that, for the first time, Natascha realised how much she had been subconsciously depending on her friend. The self-confidence and self-assurance Natascha had built could only have been achieved by the generosity of Sue's loyalty and moral support. Natascha had been fortunate to find that one special person in whom she could confide everything, no matter how trivial or how mountainous the problem. They had grown so close that Natascha could almost feel Sue's happiness but she was also deeply ashamed of her own selfish thoughts.

Separation from a loved one was always a difficult and sometimes an agonising experience. Not only can the loss, be it by death or circumstance, result in loneliness, but a small part of yourself is torn away in the process, leaving ragged edges that had to be repaired. And in a lifetime, it could happen again and again. Natascha, to some extent, was becoming familiar with it. She had lost a favourite uncle from pneumonia a year ago and a few years before then, had to sit back and watch the love of her life desert her to be with another woman. Then, just at that point and with a bolt of sudden clarity, the feelings she had had to deal with when Richard had left twenty years ago ambushed her. She was amazed at how clearly she now remembered her panic when her mother had told her that Richard and his family were moving away. She recalled how she had begged Richard to tell her it was not true and how she had tried not to let him see her cry when he could not. She wondered whether Richard ever fully realised how much she had been affected when their friendship had come to an end. Natascha tried to halt her line of thought, feeling somewhat defeated as soon as she realised that Richard French was again skirting around the outer fringes of her mind and bringing with him some unwanted memories of a past love.

Having been dragged into Selfridges as part of the body of a crowd, she fought her way to the cookware department and found a calm and friendly-faced shop assistant, which in itself, was remarkable given the bedlam going on around her. She guided Natascha to exactly what she had been looking for. The long queue she was forced to stand in shuffled forward at a snail's pace and it took what seemed like an age before it was her turn to pay for the baking trays. It was a safe bet to assume that she would be spending time helping her mother to decorate mini square muffins and Christmas tree shaped biscuits over the holidays.

Something caught the corner of Natascha's eye as she made her way towards the exit. She looked across and without thinking, wandered over to the snowstorm paperweights. She stared at the rows and rows of clear, liquid-filled glass globes and the tiny figures of snowmen and churches with glowing stained-glass windows inside. Picking one up, she shook it gently and watched as the pretend snowflakes floated softly around, creating the magical fairy tale image that had enchanted her so many years ago.

Lost in the make-believe world within the glass, she was taken back to a time she hadn't been back to in years. Richard had given one to her as a Christmas present when they were children and it was almost identical to the one she now held in her hand. It was so hauntingly beautiful. She remembered it as being the most beautiful thing she had ever owned; her very own little piece of

Christmas magic she could keep perched on her grandmother's old dressing table all year round. It was as bewitching to her now as it was to her then.

Richard French's reappearance had impacted her life in a way that greatly unsettled her. He had a way of looking at her that conveyed his indifference and disinterest of their past and once close friendship. But why did it continue to bother her? Each of the little flashbacks she had been experiencing of late were becoming more and more vivid; every time stirring deeper and deeper inside. Her feelings frustrated her.

"Natascha!" The squeaky sound of her name at once erased her confused thoughts and behind her stood tiny Rachel and her tall Dominic. They were both laden with so many bags, it was apparent they must have been out shopping for some time. Rachel still looked chirpy. Dominic did not.

"You're not usually out shopping on a Sunday morning," Rachel said, looking quite happy to be part of the madness.

"Well, I try to make a point of not subjecting myself to this pandemonium but it doesn't always go to plan," Natascha said, lightly.

"For someone who doesn't want to be out here, you look incredibly calm and collected. Then again, I've yet to see you pulling your hair out!"

Whatever her outward appearance however, Natascha hadn't quite reached calm and collected yet but she managed to raise a smile, anyway. "Dominic, you don't seem to be quite as enthusiastic as Rachel, if you don't mind me saying so."

"No go ahead, feel free to say so! I can think of a hundred things I'd rather be doing instead of this." Dominic lifted up the half a dozen bags he was holding.

Rachel nudged him in the ribs. "You wouldn't let me go through all this on my own, would you?" she asked, craning her neck to look up at him and fluttering her eyelashes over big blue, sad puppy dog eyes.

Dominic shook his head in resignation. "No, of course I wouldn't, sweetheart."

"How about coffee? Are you both up for a breather?" Natascha asked, hoping it might lift her own mood. "I'm sure I could do with one."

"I'd love to say yes," Rachel replied, "but as well as old misery guts here, who's doing a bad job at pretending he's enjoying the shopping, there's a turkey in one of these bags that doesn't want to be out of the fridge for too long!"

Natascha laughed. "Maybe next time then."

Dominic shrugged his shoulders as if to say he could have done with a few minutes respite but conceded that Rachel was right. "Perhaps we could all meet up in the week."

"That would be nice."

"We'll see you soon, then," Rachel finished, as she turned to hurry away.

"I'll see you," Natascha managed to fit in, as she watched them both disappear into the throng.

Natascha looked down to see the glass ball still in her hand and she shook it again, wanting to see the snow scatter around the tiny figures one last time. With a sigh, she placed the ornament back on the shelf. As she walked away, something urged her to take a peek over her shoulder. The snow was still whirling about and without thinking twice, she turned back, picked it up and took it over to the cashier. And as she was handed her change and the carrier bag, she opened it up and peeped inside, feeling strangely content with her purchase.

Chapter Nine

Having poured herself her fourth cup of coffee of the morning, Natascha took it back to her desk stifling yet another yawn. She had hoped that the heavy intake of caffeine would help her move into a more productive gear but it was not having the desired effect. The weekend was usually her time to recharge and re-energise but today she felt tired and lethargic. To be fair, it hadn't been a usual weekend. Yesterday, she had been shopping in the rain on a Sunday morning and the day before that, had swallowed great spoonfuls of both joy and shameful sadness at Sue and Matteo's wedding news. And mixed in with all of that, she was trying to cope with the ceaseless invasion of random old memories of Richard. She scrolled through her emails. Brooke Park Hall, one of the venues she had approached for Richard's event, had replied to her enquiry. She was not at all keen to read it:

'Dear Ms Hamilton,

Thank you for you for your recent enquiry. I would be pleased to give you a tour of Brooke Park Hall's banqueting suite but unfortunately, the office will be closed until after the New Year. However, I will be in during the Christmas week, and would be pleased to speak to you then if it is convenient, since there is a

*particular issue I'd like to talk to you about. If not, I shall
hopefully hear from you in the New Year. Have a good
Christmas.*

Regards,

Jonathan Byers

Manager

Brooke Park Hall'

Great! Natascha sighed dejectedly. She should really give
Sampson and French the opportunity to visit any potential venue.
Natascha had no option but to call Richard's office to say that
she'll be speaking to the manager of the hall to arrange a visit
sometime in the intervening days before the New Year. Should
she also mention that her client will be accompanying her to the
meeting? The only saving grace was that she probably only
needed to speak to Richard's personal secretary or some other
assistant. Richard himself was certainly not going to be
concerned with such trivialities. Natascha picked up the phone
and dialled the number. In any case, maybe his office would be
closed for the duration of the holidays.

"*Good, morning, Sampson and French.*"

"Good morning. Would you put me through to Mr French's
personal secretary, please?"

"*I'm sorry, but Mr French's assistant is out of the office until
after the Christmas holidays. Mr French has asked that all calls
be put straight through to him. Who may I ask is calling?*"

This was unexpected. She hadn't anticipated the possibility of this situation arising and Natascha was momentarily lost for words. "Er..., my name is Natascha Hamilton and I'm calling from Colonia Events Ltd."

"Thank you. Just one moment."

Before she could say anymore, she heard the dialling tone indicating her call was being transferred.

"Natascha, good morning!"

"Good morning, Richard." Natascha paused, trying to decide how she would conduct the conversation since Richard, sounding so uncharacteristically cheerful, had thrown her. He's a client, he's a just another client, she reminded herself. "I didn't expect to speak to you. I was told your PA was away on holiday."

"Yes, her family lives in a small town in Pennsylvania and I usually like to give her a few extra days before the Christmas and New Year break to visit."

Over the telephone, Richard sounded pleasant; the smooth timbre of his voice was still cool and deep but had an engaging friendliness about it. And considerate to his staff? This was not what she had expected from the Richard she had encountered up until now.

"That's very good of you," Natascha said, trying to keep the astonishment from her voice. She shifted in her seat to help her focus on the issue at hand. "I'm phoning to let you know that I contacted two venues I thought might be suitable for your client's evening and I've received a reply from one of them. They want me to visit to discuss one or two issues and I'm planning to meet the manager on one of the days between Christmas and New Year and I was wondering whether I should mention that someone else will also be joining us at a visit to the hall? I thought I'd call you although I suspect your office is probably closed over the holidays." Then she added, with a little too much enthusiasm, "Obviously, there's no need for you to attend. I'm very happy to go alone and make a decision on your company's behalf." Natascha waited, sure of Richard's reply. It could not have been worse.

"Yes, I'd like to take a look myself, if you don't mind me being in the way."

Who was she speaking to? Natascha was nearly tempted to ask the person on the other end of the line to confirm his name. "Oh, okay, that's fine. I'll send you an email once I've confirmed some details. Get in touch if you have any other queries."

"I'll wait for your email." Richard gave a little cough and cleared his throat. *"Natascha, about the drink we spoke about last week. Are you free this evening after work?"*

The sudden change of subject tipped Natascha over the edge and left her speechless. She had previously come to the conclusion that his initial invitation in the office staff restaurant had been hasty and wrongly made and the longer he left it without mentioning it the easier it would be for it to be forgotten. But again she found herself thinking one thing and doing another.

"Yes, I should be free," she managed after a few moments.

"There's a small place not far from your office, 'The Lemon Tree', I think it's called. We could meet there at say, half past five?"

"Er.., yes, I know it. Half past five sounds fine."

"Good. I'll see you later, then." The line went dead.

Firstly, she was surprised that Richard had agreed to meet her to visit the venue for his company's party. Secondly, she was even more surprised that he mentioned having that drink again. And thirdly, his invitation did not sound very business-like at all. It was unheard of for her to meet a client on a social footing outside of office hours. She preferred to arrange all meetings within work's domain. And yet, she had made an insane exception in this case. Natascha toyed with the idea of telephoning him again to graciously bow out of the rendezvous, citing a prior engagement she had overlooked. However, thinking about it, she would only look foolish and disorganised. And anyway, she would only have to suggest another time as a matter of courtesy. Perhaps she could use this as her chance to ensure he understood that this was to be a business relationship only.

***

His office door shut with a loud thud as he closed it with more force than was necessary. Was he losing his mind? Strike that. He had already gone mad! What, in the Queen's name, did he think he was doing? Why did he say he'd meet her to visit a stupid venue and why the hell did he suggest having that drink after work tonight? He should have said no thanks to going to some boring banqueting suite or whatever she had arranged and definitely left the drink thing alone. He'd been dense enough the first time; opening his mouth before clearing it with his head. If he hadn't said anything about that ridiculous idea again, he was sure it wouldn't have bothered her in the slightest. In fact, he would probably have been doing her a favour, saving her the obligation of saying yes to drinks she'd rather not have. Damn it! What was he talking about? Natascha, obliged to say yes? No way! She was so cock-sure of herself nowadays, she would have had no qualms in saying 'no thanks' without feeling she had to offer any sort of excuse. He couldn't get out of it now, though. That would be just plain rude. He'd hoped that she'd call him back to say that she had an unexpected engagement she couldn't put off and would have to cancel, if indeed, she felt the need to explain at all but the phone hadn't rung again all afternoon.

***

What happened to the rest of the afternoon? It seemed to have bypassed her without her noticing. Thankfully, Natascha had used that time to settle down and compose herself once she was back in her office after lunch. Richard had invited her for a drink as a simple act of good manners and nothing more (although Richard linked with the words 'good manners' did not exactly fit the mould). Why she had agreed to meet him was the conundrum that was slightly more worrying. Perhaps they could use this time effectively, as an opportunity to clear up any unintentional misunderstandings and end the afternoon on better terms with each other. Trying to maintain this farce of civility was becoming rather tiresome.

Natascha made herself comfortable at a table near the window and could see Richard as he approached.

"I'm sorry I'm late. What can I get you?" he said, as he arrived at the table.

"No, you're not late. I've only just got here myself. A red wine would be nice, thank you."

"Right, I'll be back in a minute," he said, as he left to get the drinks.

Natascha watched in amazement as every woman's eyes in the room were drawn to the sight of Richard's dominating, tall figure as he passed them, striding purposefully yet gracefully towards the bar. His masculinity and air of mystery bolstered their compulsion to stare at him for longer than was decently discreet. It must be a reaction he produced wherever he went, for he incited the interest of every single woman and not just a handful as would seem more reasonable. Yet, he seemed oblivious to all the female attention he was arousing; blind to the lustful glances he was provoking. He remained ignorant of the stir he was causing amongst the fairer sex much to the annoyance of his male counterparts. His effect on the room was quite something! And it wasn't until he was making his way back did Natascha realise that her own eyes were still fixed on him and she hastily turned her head to look the other way.

Setting two glasses down on the table he took his seat. "I've been really busy this afternoon. The Christmas period is always so busy," Richard said, trying to sound causal.

"It must be last minute queries; everyone trying to finalise outstanding issues before the break."

They both stared hard into their drinks, both wrestling to find common ground without mentioning the glaringly obvious topic - 'The Past'. The atmosphere was forced and uncomfortable and ironically it was all because they had once known each other so well.

"You may know the venues that I'm interested in going to see, Brooke Park Hall, which I mentioned earlier, and Larkswood Manor. They're both on the outskirts of North London but far away enough to be in a rural setting, or so I'm led to believe. I'm not familiar with either of them so it'll be a first for me," Natascha said, realising that she was reaching for conversation but it was better than sitting in silence.

"I have heard of both but don't know much about them."

From the look in his eyes Natascha wasn't convinced that he was being truthful. It wasn't like Richard to know very little about anything. "It'll be a first for us both, then," she said, pleasantly.

Richard looked around him. "I really like this place, it has a good atmosphere."

Natascha nearly choked on her wine. Atmosphere? What did he know about atmosphere? What about the atmosphere here at this table? Was he just as enamoured with it? "Yes, I've been here before. It's always this relaxed," she had to say.

There was another pause in this semblance of a conversation and the meeting was fast deteriorating into a very bad mistake.

"So, what have you been doing these last twenty years?"

There, it was asked. Richard had asked the question to which explanations should have been exchanged the moment they met. But having been deferred for so long, it sounded clumsy and out of place. It should have been asked almost without thought but with interest and sincerity and not out of obligation or duty. The axiomatic question should have been an easy one to answer but Richard's disinterest up until now made it difficult for Natascha to do just that. And with the question hanging in the air awaiting an answer she was hesitant in providing one. Fine detail was no longer necessary and so she decided to keep it honest but vague.

"Well, I finished school and went to university to study Events Management," she said, in an informal tone. "Yes, I know what you're thinking, I was hopeless at school, and I'll be the first to admit it. I couldn't even organise my own homework without your help..." Natascha slowed her sentence to a stop. She could have bitten off her tongue for having fallen into the trap of being the first to make any reference to their shared past.

The moment the words left Natascha's lips, Richard seemed to inhale sharply and lowered his head just enough for her not to see his face, hiding an expression she could only guess at. She looked at his bowed head and wondered how she could have been so careless. It had been made quite clear that their history together was the last subject he wanted to touch upon. Although vibes were rather stiff and unnatural, so far, the underlying suggestion of hostility that usually formed part of Richard's manner had not shown itself. But with one negligent sentence Natascha had possibly changed all of that. However, when he lifted his head to look at her, she was surprised to see a look of acknowledgement on his face. There were no signs of animosity or embarrassment. He smiled very briefly and lowered his eyes to watch his finger tap the base of his glass repeatedly and in that split second Natascha wondered whether despite his outwardly cold demeanour and fundamental deficiency in charm, old Richard was still inside there - somewhere.

Natascha checked her galloping thoughts. She was reading into an undefined facial expression as if it might give her a clue as to what he was thinking. She shouldn't even be wondering what he was thinking. However, encouraged by the lack of a negative reaction she decided to continue. Smoothly, she sipped her drink and went on. "After university, I came to London and had a couple of rather insignificant jobs before working at Colonia Events. It's a good job. I enjoy what I do and it suits me." There was nothing more she wanted to add and so ended the shortened résumé of her life and she passed the role of storyteller back. "And how about you?"

"Much the same, really." It seemed Richard was to be just as unspecific. "I went to university too, doing Computer Science and Programming and went on to do a post-graduate degree. I was there for quite a few years. I then took a year out to travel before finally deciding that I really should start to work for a living. I had several short-term jobs until eventually I made up my mind to set up my own business in software engineering. It was by chance that I met with an old roommate and we decided to go into partnership. I'm surprised at how well it's done. Even in the very first year, we were a lot busier than either of us thought we'd be. We were lucky to have created the company when we did, in the boom of the late nineties when both large and small companies, whether they needed it or not, were desperate to update their software systems ready for the new millennium's much anticipated computer meltdown, that never happened."

"Congratulations are in order then," Natascha said. "And your parents have moved back to Oxfordshire. Do you see much of them?" she asked, innocently.

"No. No I don't," Richard replied, a shade abrasively. He shifted his eyes and looked down. The action was more animated than it had been so far and he seemed reluctant to speak anymore on that topic.

Natascha took her cue to change the subject. "Do you live in London?"

"Er, no," Richard said, regaining some of his composure, "no, I live just outside London, in a small place called Essendon in Hertfordshire. It's a decent commute to my office," he said, with a little less aggression.

"I live in North London. Winchmore Hill, actually. It's practically on the border of Hertfordshire."

"Winchmore Hill, near Enfield? I virtually pass there on my way to work."

"I see," Natascha said, but decided not to provide any further details of her address.

The conversation faded for a moment, sustaining the rather careful atmosphere.

"You're looking really well, Natascha," Richard said, with a deep, unrestrained honesty. The candour of his statement stunned Natascha into silence, struck momentarily dumb by his unexpected capability to flatter. Richard was never known for his generosity in giving compliments so these words coming from him added up to more than just a polite remark. Something changed on the turn of those few words. "You look better than I remember."

Whatever emotions had been simmering beneath the surface, they were now exposed. A deep and unique understanding filled the space between them, together with the return of a warm familiarity, an unfathomable closeness, an odd feeling of belonging. Questions surged through Natascha, wishing to know more about him although she said nothing; she felt wrapped in a strange sense of comfort.

"Thank you, Richard," she said quietly, as she looked into his eyes, intrigued by his comment and felt her heartbeat quicken from both happiness and trepidation.

It was difficult to know what he was thinking. The change in his countenance was almost imperceptible but there was a definite change and deep down, it was a surprising relief to Natascha to realise that perhaps there was another side to Richard after all, one that was possibly not so dark and reserved. It was also conceivable that based on the evidence fleetingly betrayed on his face, he was finally admitting that they did have a childhood history together, one that he had not forgotten. Could it be possible that they could at least become guarded friends again?

The atmosphere evaporated as quickly as it had descended when they both realised that a casually dressed man was standing at their table.

"Richard, good God, what are you doing here?"

With a detectable expression of discomfort, Richard introduced him.

"Bradley Sampson, this is Natascha Hamilton."

Bradley held out his hand. "Pleasure to meet you."

"Bradley is my business partner," Richard informed her while straightening up in his seat.

"Wait a minute... Natascha Hamilton. The name's familiar. Aren't you from Colonia Events?"

"Yes, I am. I'm working with Richard to plan the Client's Appreciation Party."

"Ah yes, I thought I'd heard your name before. Marissa Clarke, one of your colleagues, I presume, mentioned your name during a conversation I had with her although I can't for the devil remember why. Richard, this is unusual for you to have a business meeting outside of the boardroom."

Bradley turned to Natascha. "Don't let him get carried away. I know what he's like. It's after hours and I'm sure you have something better to do than discussing the colour of the napkins!"

Richard shed a hasty glance at Natascha and looked back at his friend. "When have you known me to get carried away?" he said, lightly but poignantly.

"That is true. Still, this should be considered a social meeting and not a business one. Carry on your business meeting tomorrow, old man, during office hours. Don't be a fool, enjoy the company of this charming and very beautiful young lady," he said, cheerfully. "Anyway, I must leave you. My wife's over there waiting for me. I had a moment of madness and promised I would take her last minute Christmas shopping!"

He shook Natascha's hand again. "It was lovely to meet you, Natascha." And patting Richard on the shoulder he said, "I'll see you in the office tomorrow."

With Bradley gone the silence returned as they both tried to hide their embarrassment. And since neither of them knew what else to say, it was a natural fissure for the dubious rendezvous to draw to an end.

Once outside, Natascha realised that in spite of the awkward moments, it had not been as bad as she had expected.

"It was kind of you to invite me for a drink. I've had a nice time," she said. Then went a step further and tentatively added, "To be honest, I wasn't sure that I would enjoy it, but I did." Natascha knew that this moment could be the resurrection of their former friendship or the irreversible breaking of it. She waited for a response from him.

He stood facing her and said nothing, his tall frame bearing down on her. Then he began to lean towards her and Natascha thought he was going to kiss her. In that very instant she wondered whether she should step aside now, and then was absolutely appalled with herself when she contemplated not moving at all.

But what he did next was unimaginably insulting. Suddenly, he stood up straight, gave what sounded like a little laugh and reverted to exhibiting the familiar domineering expression.

"I thought I should make the effort. I suppose we were neighbours once."

He was cold, arrogant and rude again and the change had happened so quickly that it was as though he had struck Natascha in the face. The shock must have been so clearly written in her eyes but he was unaffected by it. But the death of this fragile union came when he reached into his breast pocket and pulled out a business card.

"Oh, and the other reason why I wanted to meet you. I nearly forgot to give you this," he said, as he handed her the small piece of card. "I should have given you my card when I came to your office. It has my direct line telephone number."

She took it from him in total bemusement.

He then held out his hand and Natascha could do nothing but slowly extend her own. He shook it soundly, "I'll see you again in the New Year." And with that, he turned around and strode haughtily away.

There were no pleasantries, no 'thank you,' no 'I've had a nice time, too,' or 'we should do this again sometime.' He left her in the middle of the pavement staring at the back of him, mortified. As she stood there paralyzed, the cautious but nice afternoon metamorphosed into a terrible illusion. The moment of emotional honesty was only her absurd imagination and the potential of a new friendship, an ugly joke. She looked down at the card: '*Sampson & French, Software Engineering*' and below that, it had his name, '*Richard French B Eng MSc (Hons)*', printed in bold letters across the middle. Very impressive, she thought, cynically. Richard had become a pretentious and repulsive boor.

Natascha moved her fingers across her forehead, trying to erase the disbelief and confusion while she made her way home. The further she walked the more her confusion turned to anger.

Stinging tears of fury blurred her vision as she screwed up the business card until it was a scrunched up little ball and threw it into her handbag. He had insulted her once too often and for that she could see no reason why she should ever forgive him. It wouldn't ever happen again.

***

Ha! Richard took long buoyant strides as he walked along the street (other pedestrians instinctively making room for his tall and imposing figure as he passed), feeling quite pleased with himself. When he had first asked her to go out for a drink with him, he had been furious with himself for inviting her on a whim before thinking it through. He soon changed his mind, though. He decided it could be the ideal opportunity for him to find out what Natascha was really like as a woman and to somehow gain a little insight into what made her tick. Although he was curious, he wanted to sound casual when he asked what she had been doing for the last twenty years. He wanted her to see it as a neutral sort of question just so that he could gauge her reaction - test the waters, so to speak. Would she be excited to tell him all about her life or would she be retentive and secretive? The way she answered this simple enquiry would tell him exactly how she saw him after all this time; what she thought of him; whether their old friendship meant anything to her. Well, the look on her face was a picture, telling him everything he had set out to find out. He could almost see her mind go into overdrive thinking of what she should say. It was clear she sure as hell didn't want him to know anything about her! She gave as little detail as she could and even then was reluctant to let him have that loose run down of her life. It couldn't have been sketchier if she tried. She may as well have told him to mind his own business! But when she inadvertently admitted to the help he used to give her with schoolwork when they were kids - well, needless to say, the poor thing, always so cock-sure was really disappointed with herself at having made such a huge faux pas! She'd only gone and done it; mentioned the unmentionable, the one thing she didn't want to speak about - the existence of their past! It was such a superb moment he even had to look away. And then there was her mastery at making eye contact, working it so hard that she actually thought it would divert his attention away from the blatant lack of information she was willing to give him and her terrible blunder referring to their linked childhood. The 'you look good' compliment he threw in was meant to create nothing more than a little bit of mischief; to see how she handled the whole vanity thing and she had played it true to form - she revelled in it. "*Thank you, Richard,*" he mimicked, out loud. It's a good job Bradley turned up when he did. Otherwise, he wasn't sure how he was going to keep up the farce!

Having congratulated himself on how well he had tested and figured out grown-up Natascha, he was suddenly hit with a picture of the look that was written in her eyes when he more or less told her that he felt duty bound, and nothing else, to invite her for a drink and it left him feeling a little less convinced of his actions. It can't have been hurt looking back at him - could it? Was she really that good at being able to conjure up such authentic looking emotion in her eyes? That would be such a clever party trick! But then again, why would she bother to fake a look of hurt if their past didn't mean anything to her anymore? All at once, all his motives had become confused and no longer made any sense. Maybe he'd got it wrong. What if he'd got her all wrong? What if she really did care? He had asked her whether she'd like to go out for a drink and she'd said yes. It wasn't a cryptic question. She only had to say no if she didn't want to go. Richard closed his eyes as he recalled his next 'good idea'. At the end of the pseudo friendly drink, as they were saying goodbye, he gave her his business card - his business card, for crying out loud! Why the hell would any decent man hand out his business card after taking a woman out for a drink? Richard answered his rhetoric question; only a self-centred, egotistical pratt would! She must see him as some kind of ill-mannered, uneducated and socially inept ignoramus. He had actually said to her that the only reason he had asked her to join him was because they were once neighbours. Neighbours! If it was normal for plain old neighbours to spend each waking moment with each other, then what the hell would you call the closest friend you ever had? And Laugh? Did he actually laugh in her face? Why the hell did he do that?

Maybe he'd got a bit carried away trying to prove a point on the adult Natascha Hamilton, a point he hadn't even stopped to consider whether needed to be proven at all. Accept the way she is now and get over it was all he had to do and not harp on about how she used to be. It wasn't complicated. He'd been rash and deep down he knew that it was because he was spineless, pure and simple. He didn't want to be friends with her again, he didn't want to feel anything for her, he mustn't feel anything for her, especially not the way he felt about her when he was only a kid - when he was a sixteen year old coward. She had been his childhood sweetheart, only she didn't know it. He never had the guts to tell her. But it was too late. Only minutes ago he had to stop himself from kissing her and that was proof enough. It was already too late. He had behaved like a total moron and was being a total fool.

Richard was so absorbed in his thoughts that he hadn't even realised that he had reached the car park, found his car and was already sitting in it. No longer feeling self-righteous, the only thing he knew for sure was that now he was feeling like crap.

***

Chapter Ten

The satisfaction of being surrounded by her work made little difference; her office felt cold and unwelcome. No matter how hard she tried, Natascha could not eradicate the picture of her, standing outside the bar, holding his business card and watching him walk away from her. Nor could she erase the humiliation she felt when she thought he was about to kiss her and it actually went through her mind as to whether she should let him or not. And only moments later the contemptuous man stepped back away from her and laughed. He had laughed at her right in her face. How could he have been so immature and so childish? But although she was angry with him she was incredibly frustrated with herself for allowing him to get under her skin and disrupt the, up until now, smooth pace of her life. The whole experience had to be obliterated from her mind. She did not even want to pack it away in one of the boxes she kept hidden in the dark recesses of it. She wanted to be rid of it! She just had to get back to the place she had been in herself before he had so rudely gate-crashed her life.

Natascha's thoughts were interrupted by the phone and she jumped. "Er, Colonia Events."

"*Hello, is that you Natascha? It's Rachel. Have I picked a bad time to call? You sound busy.*"

"Rachel. No, not at all, you've timed it just right. I'm due a little light relief," more than Rachel would ever realise. Closing her eyes Natascha rolled her head left and right to loosen the knots that had formed at the base of her neck.

"*I was thinking,*" Rachel went on, "*maybe we should all get together for a chat about the wedding and in particular, ideas about a group wedding present. What do you think?*"

Meeting up would be the perfect diversion. "I think it's a great idea. When and where do you want to meet?"

"*How about tonight at the King's Head? Shall we say at around seven-ish? And since Sue and Matteo have already gone to Italy, there's no need for any covert operations!*"

"Yes, they left this morning. All right then, the King's Head at seven tonight. I'll see you there."

Natascha replaced the receiver, happy at the prospect of meeting up with the team later. It was definitely the best thing to do to take her out of this irritating pothole that she had fallen into.

"The usual, everyone?" Dominic asked, as he stood up to go to the bar.

"Er, not for me, thanks Dominic. I'll have a coffee instead, if that's okay," Simon said, timidly.

"And I'll have a very small red wine," Natascha said. "I've got the car."

"What's up with you, Simon?" Dominic asked, with pretend concern. "Coffee at the King's Head? That's not your usual poison?"

"Yes, well I'm feeling a little delicate at the moment. And is that '*Rockin' around the Christmas tree*' playing again? If I hear that song one more time I'm going to kill myself!"

"Ah, now I remember. It was your Christmas lunch with your old university pals today, wasn't it? Is that what's made you feel suicidal?" Dominic laughed.

"I suppose I had just a tad too much of the old 'Christmas spirit'," Simon replied, feeling a little worse for wear.

"Well, if you will translate 'Christmas spirit' into knocking back copious amounts of Jack Daniels and Coke…" Dominic laughed again but seeing the look on Simon's face, he raised his hands in surrender. "Coffee it is, then."

"Right then," Rachel began, when Dominic was back, "any ideas?" She looked round the table to see everyone shaking their heads.

Natascha had adopted her usual calm eyes and relaxed exterior but underneath she wasn't feeling her usual self. As the day went on she'd managed to diffuse the anger she had been harbouring after the so-called drink with Richard but the small hollow it had burnt inside was still quite raw and her mind was not as alert as it should have been. "No, not a single one right now Rachel, sorry."

"Well, I have one," Rachel enthused. "Matteo was raving about one of those state-of-the-art curved TVs to Dominic, telling him he was thinking about getting one once he'd moved to Italy."

Dominic put on his techy hat. "It used to be a problem trying to get a TV from the UK to work in another country but nowadays, what with everything being digital, it's not a problem anymore."

"Well, that sounds even better," Rachel continued. "Matteo's already seen the make, model and blah, blah, blah that he was thinking of buying. How about we club together and see if we can buy it for them as a wedding present? What do you think?"

"Might be a bit of a hassle trying to get it on to the plane with us," Simon piped up, trying to sound perfectly sober.

"Don't be daft," Rachel retorted. "We'd obviously give it to them before the wedding."

Planning the wedding present had given Natascha a reason to try and centre her thoughts on other things. "And since I have the spare keys, once we buy it, we could conceivably take it straight to the house and leave it under their Christmas tree as a surprise gift when they get back. I think that would be nice."

"Yes, and we can wrap a great big red satin bow around it," Simon added, with a wobbly smirk.

"Ooh, not feeling quite so wasted anymore, Simon," laughed Dominic, poking yet more fun. "The thought of big red satin bows making you feel more yourself, is it? The liquid Christmas spirit must be wearing off."

Simon humphed.

Rachel felt sorry for him. "Dominic, leave him alone."

"Yes, well he shouldn't get plastered so early in the afternoon and not expect any repercussions!"

"It's seven o'clock in the evening!" Simon cracked back in his defence. "Ow!" He put his hand up to cushion his head. "That hurt!"

"Come on, guys," Rachel interrupted. "What do you think, a TV for the new house?" There was a general nodding of heads and no objections. "Well, that's sorted, then. We can get it organised properly when we all get back after Christmas. Since Sue and Matteo are staying an extra week in Italy after the New Year, we should have plenty of time."

Simon swallowed the last of his coffee. "If you don't mind, I think I'll take myself off home, now. I need to lay myself gently upon my bed."

"Seeing as it's Christmas, Simon, I'm going to be extra nice to you and take you home," Natascha offered. "I don't feel that you should be left to make your own way home in your current condition. Consider it my Christmas gift to you."

"Oh Natascha, you're too good to me. Public transport is not endearing itself to me right now!"

"Come on then, let's go. And in case I don't see everyone beforehand, make sure you all have a lovely Christmas." Natascha moved around the table and gave each of them a warm Christmas kiss and a hug.

On the journey to Simon's flat, the conversation was mainly based around plans for the holidays.

"My brother and his wife have invited me to their Christmas Eve party and to stay over for a couple of days which I'm quite looking forward to. We've always got on, even when Mum and Dad thought we didn't. Did a lot of fighting when we were younger, you see but it was just boys' stuff. I was jealous as hell when he said he was going out with a Swedish girl, you know, more boys' stuff. But she's great. Julian and Frederika are married now and have two great kids as well. He's a lucky guy."

"That sounds nice. I wish I had a brother..." Natascha realised she was drifting into prohibited waters again and shaking the thought away, she carried on. "I think children make Christmas. It's all about Santa and their faces on Christmas morning. It's a shame there aren't any young children in my family..."

Memories tumbled into her head again. That's what it was like when she was a child, unwrapping presents from under the tree while she was still in her pyjamas. A misty picture hovered in her mind. It was Christmas morning and because they were so close, Richard and Natascha both had presents under each house's own Christmas tree. They were both waiting impatiently for the go ahead from their parents to open their gifts from under the Hamilton's Christmas tree...

"Oh, wow!" Richard said, as he pulled a very posh looking microscope from its box. He easily put it together and put a rogue pine needle from the Christmas tree under the lens. "Take a look at this," he said, excitedly. "What do you think it is?"

Natascha left her present to try and share Richard's excitement and peered into the small glass aperture. "What am I supposed to be looking at?" she asked, not quite managing to match his enthusiasm.

"It's a pine needle! Amazing isn't it? You can't even tell what it is, there's so much detail. This is fantastic!"

"Oh, yes," Natascha said, unimpressed, "amazing."

She went back to finish opening her own present. The large box housed a hard-shelled case and inside the case, lying in crushed emerald green velvet, was her very first guitar. Her eyes grew wide in awe. She took it out carefully from the soft lining and placed the instrument on her knee. "How about this, then?" she said, as she lovingly smoothed her hand over the body of the guitar. She read the tag that was attached to the neck. "It's made of real Indian rosewood, too!" And running her fingers across the shiny strings, she marvelled at the sound. "It's so beautiful, don't you think, Richard?"

Richard looked up and Natascha could see that he wasn't all that interested. "And, d'you know what?" she said, with a slight sting in her little voice, "you don't even have to stick it under a microscope to work out what it is, either!"…

"…So, what are you up to?" Simon asked.

The images in Natascha's mind dissolved. "Oh, I'm spending a few days with my parents in Oxfordshire, as usual. I'm looking forward to the peace and quiet. Getting away from here for a while will be a really special Christmas present to myself." Never was a truer word spoken, she thought.

There was nowhere to park outside Simon's flat so Natascha drove around and found a space not too far down on the high road but which required them to walk back a little way.

"Having trouble walking unaided?" Natascha asked, as Simon linked arms with her.

"Well, I would have liked to walk beside you at a gentlemanly distance. But you're right, you're helping me to stay in a straight line!"

"Well, alright then, just this once," she said, smiling. For the first time in some time she was feeling in a genuinely good mood.

As they arrived at the top of Simon's road, he stopped and turned to Natascha. "I'll be fine from here. Thanks for the lift. You make sure you have a lovely Christmas, do you hear?" Before she could say anything, he planted a great big kiss on her lips. "And that's my Christmas present to you," he said, boldly. "Oh, and by the way, I don't think I had the chance to tell you how ravishing you're looking again tonight!"

"You don't change, do you," Natascha said, in good humour. "You're lucky it's Christmas or you wouldn't have got away with the kiss. But thank you for the compliment. Happy Christmas, Simon," she said, and turned to walk back to her car.

Natascha pulled her coat closer to her. It was a raw night and she didn't want to be out for too long. With Simon beside her, she hadn't noticed quite how cold it was but now she was alone, the bitter wind penetrated her coat.

As she hurried to get out of the cold, she noticed the figure of a man loitering in the beam of a streetlight. He was looking in her direction and his eyes seemed to follow her as she walked. Natascha quickened her step and shot him a surreptitious glance as she passed. However, she hadn't walked further than a few yards when she stopped, suddenly recognising Richard as the shadowy stranger. Slowly, she retraced her steps until she was stood facing him. How long had he been there, spying on her? There was an uncomfortable silence as the already cold air between them plunged to a freeze. His dark and irascible face troubled her and even in the bad light, she could see that his usual melting eyes had become icy shards of glass, boring through her, sending a chill up and down her spine.

"What are you doing here?" Natascha asked. The tone of the question left her as brash and unsophisticated, not the composed and steady stream of words as she had wanted.

"I had to work late." The natural velvety tenor of his voice had become hard and edgy.

"Is this your usual route? I've never seen you here before," she said, sarcasm lacing the sentence.

"As I mentioned to you before, I sometimes take this route on my way home if I've been to the office in Muswell Hill. I stopped to use the cash machine across the road."

"Your business card that you so kindly presented me with says your office is in Piccadilly."

"That's the main office. We also have a smaller office in Muswell Hill."

Their eyes were competing as to who's could hold the other's glare the longest.

Natascha felt panic rising in her throat. These feelings of ambivalence she had towards him were causing too much conflict within her and she was still smarting horribly from the 'business card' incident. Her self-confidence, on which she could always rely, was fading. It was obvious that there was to be no conversation between them only the preparation of a match for tossing derisory comments back and forth.

"Well, have a good evening," Natascha said sharply, as she turned to hurry away, wanting to avoid the possibility of the stand-off getting too far out of hand.

"Do you always display such acts of intimate affection in public?" Richard said spitefully to her retreating back.

Natascha, confused for a split second, stopped in her tracks and then realised to what he was referring. It was the kiss that Simon had given her a few minutes before - Simon's friendly and innocent kiss. It was a simple peck on her lips. Richard had the flagrant effrontery to suppose he was in a position to criticise her;

had, beyond all comprehension, presumed he could pass judgement on what she could or could not do. His audacity and vicious remark downright angered her. She spun round, her hair swaying violently behind her.

"I beg your pardon?" she snapped.

"Don't you think that there is a time and a place for that sort of behaviour? I would have expected better from you, Natascha."

The sneer in his voice was the last straw. Natascha was livid. "You have a cold heart and a dirty mind, Richard," she said, with razor sharp vehemence. "I don't recall ever asking you for your permission to live my life any way I please; not back then and certainly not now! Why you have decided to make my business your own, I really don't know but I don't care for it. I suggest you spend more of your time paying better attention to what concerns you - and Lord knows, your life seems to be urgently in need of some attention - and not waste your time involving yourself in mine and making a complete fool of yourself in the process!"

Richard's steely exterior did not flinch, his glacial eyes never left hers. Natascha continued to hold firm but before he could detect her failing indignation, she turned on her heel and briskly walked away, desperately trying to control her spasmodic breathing.

Once she closed her front door behind her, she leaned heavily against it, almost as if with her weight, she could shut out the rest of the world, together with Richard forever. Every nerve in her body was trembling with fury at the bitter encounter she'd just had with him. How dare he have the temerity to even think about criticising her actions? From day one, she had known him to be cold, conceited and rude but it was a shock, even to her, to have to add malicious and spiteful to the bleak list of adjectives that were making up Mr Richard French. She had thought that after that fateful day when he had left her in the middle of the pavement holding his business card, he had insulted her once too often. And yet today, after accusing her of being some sort of street harlot, he had, incredibly, managed to surpass his already deplorably low standards. Natascha wished with all her heart that she had never set eyes on him again.

Chapter Eleven

Natascha had loaded the car with her bags and was on her way to spend Christmas with her parents. Leaving London so hastily she knew she was running away but there was so much she had to get away from. The maelstrom of bad feeling, resentment and hostility were beginning to strangle her and she was finding it hard to clear her mind of it all. Richard had made such a mess in her head, she needed the time and the fresh air to tidy it up, organise it and throw out all the recent unwanted chaos. Contrary to the impression Natascha gave, it was not always an easy endeavour, and this time it was going to take a gargantuan amount of work.

By the time she arrived, the dark December winter evening was already rolling in. The sense of release she felt when she'd reached her parents' home was overwhelming and she could hardly wait to get inside and into the warm safety of it. She was so happy to see her father that as she walked through the door she dropped her bags to the floor and threw her arms around him in a way she hadn't done since she was a little girl.

"Dad, I'm so glad to see you. I'm so glad to be here." Natascha adored her father. He never had to say or do anything in particular for her to know how much he loved her, too. And without him having to say a word, she felt he truly understood her.

"Whoa, Tascha, it's good to have you home," he said, as he hugged her in return. "Is everything all right? You seem a bit tense," he added, sensing a slight change in his daughter. He hadn't seen her looking so tired for a long time.

"I am now, Dad," she replied, almost to herself as she held on to her father. Natascha felt her stressed mind and muscles begin to uncoil until, at last, she was able to step back. She sniffed the air. Her mother had been baking, since the house was filled with the sweet and spicy aroma of mince pies. How good it was to be here. "Mum in the kitchen, I suppose," she asked casually, after having collected herself.

Being used to his wife's affinity with the kitchen her father chuckled, "Where else?"

"I'd better get these to her, then." She bent down to open one of the bags and took out the baking tins for which she had painstakingly scoured the streets of London.

"Hi Mum," she said cheerfully, as her mind continued to de-frazzle. She met her mother in the kitchen, brand new baking tins in hand.

"Hello, darling." Her mother looked up while lifting pies from the cooling rack and onto a plate. "I thought I heard the door. How are you, dear? You look awful! You need some tea!"

Natascha's mind involuntarily scanned pictures of recent events. "I certainly could do with something," she said, with a sigh.

Her mother looked at her strangely for a moment. "Well, go into the lounge and keep your father company and I'll bring through some tea and mince pies." She looked down to see that Natascha was holding the baking tins she had asked for. "Ooh, they look nice... Those for me?"

Sitting in her favourite armchair, Natascha curled her legs under her and watched the log fire as it crackled in the fireplace. The smell of pine from the Christmas tree was revitalising and the tiny speckles of colour adorning it glowed in soft waves, soothing her bruised soul. There was so much she had to do to try to sort out the issues that were stagnating within her but they could wait; for now it was enough for her to chat idly with her father and absently throw a fleeting look at the TV screen to see re-runs of well-known comedy duos performing well-worn Christmas comedy sketches. It was time to relax both mind and body.

Natascha sat up leisurely when she heard the rattling of the tea things.

"Monica called just before you arrived," her mother said, as she poured the tea. "Her electric whisk has stopped working. Damaged in the move, I would imagine. And she was right in the middle of whisking her egg whites ready to make the icing for her Christmas cake. Talk about bad timing!" Her mother handed her a cup of tea. "Anyway, I told her that if you were not too tired, you'd pop over with my spare one - only if you're not too tired, of course. I told her that I couldn't promise anything..."

"Oh, Vivienne. Why on earth did you tell her that? Of course Tascha would be too tired. She's driven a long way, as you well know," her father pointed out, vigorously.

"Well, I did say I couldn't promise anything...," her mother added, rather timidly.

"It's okay, Mum. I'll go after my tea. I feel fine."

"Well, if you're sure." Perking up, she offered Natascha a mince pie. "Monica was so pleased to see you at my birthday. It's been 'Natascha this' and 'Natascha that' ever since! She couldn't believe how much you've grown but of course I had to remind her that it *has* been twenty years since she last saw you but you know how dithery she can be..."

Natascha glanced across at her father giving him an accustomed look as he shook his head, eyes drawn towards the ceiling.

"...she sees you as a daughter, you know. All that time you spent there when you were young. She sees you as quite her own!"

"It was a very long time ago," Natascha said, a touch firmly.

Her mother appeared not to notice. "Do you know that since Richard left Scotland, he only visits once or twice a year? They've never even spent one Christmas together since he left. In fact, the day you met him at the party was the first time they'd seen him this year."

Simply hearing the name 'Richard' was enough to invite a rush of bile to Natascha's stomach. "I may as well go to see Monica now," she said decisively, as she stood up and placed her empty cup on the coffee table. "I'll go and get my coat."

When she returned her mother was holding a small carrier bag. "I've put the whisk in the bag. Our French friends live where Harriet Walters used to live, the little cottage by the church."

Natascha put on her coat, took the bag from her mother and willed herself to calm down. "Yes, I remember."

"Oh, and don't forget the torch," her father reminded her.

Natascha nodded. "I'll see you in a little while." She picked up the torch and left the house.

It was not that she minded meeting them, it was just that they were so close a connection to Richard, it left her feeling a lot less than comfortable.

Natascha knocked on the door.

"Natascha, how nice to see you. Come in out of the cold," Monica said brightly, holding the door open.

She stepped into the cosy little cottage but the first thing that caught her attention was a photograph of Richard sitting proudly on the hall table, dressed in his wine coloured school jumper, white shirt and stripy blue tie. It was a traditional school photograph, taken from the waist up when he was about thirteen.

He was just as she remembered him, light brown hair with the small section at the front that was always stubbornly sticking up. His hair was much darker now. He was smiling broadly which today, would be downright unnatural. What surprised her most were his eyes. The slightly faded picture revealed that same intensity she saw in them today. They were friends at such a young age that as they grew up together, Richard was just Richard to her and she'd never taken any notice of his eyes. The photograph unsettled her, immensely.

"Come through and I'll make us some tea."

Natascha looked up at Monica and then peered down again and saw Richard's piercing eyes still staring back at her. "Oh, no thanks, Monica, I've just had one and anyway, they're expecting me back. Another time, perhaps."

Monica seemed a little disappointed. "Yes, of course, another time. I'm sure we'll meet again in the next few days."

Natascha ran a hand through her hair to calm her as she sat in her car and started the engine. That was not the best start to her few days away. Seeing the photograph of Richard was definitely something she could have done without. But it was only a photograph, a piece of glossy white paper imprinted with various shades of colour. It was a harmless, inanimate object. It bore no resemblance to anything of any consequence. She tried to instil in herself some sort of perspective.

Driving along the empty High street, Natascha switched on the radio and turned left into the quiet road which would take her up to the *Crown of The Hills Hotel*. A choir was singing '*O Come All Ye Faithful*' and she turned up the volume and began to sing along, reaching a powerful crescendo at the end of the final chorus, '*O come let us adore him, Christ the Lord'*. Belting out the hymn released some of her frustrations and made her feel so much better.

Most of the small roads on the route between the two houses were unlit but Natascha was so used to the area that it didn't trouble her. But it surprised her to see in the distance something glinting in the dark. It appeared to be a light but she couldn't be sure where it was coming from. Was someone out walking at this time in the pitch black of this icy cold night? It seemed unlikely. As she got closer she could see that the glinting was in fact the headlight of a car parked up by the trees. She would be able to see whether the occupants needed any help with directions when she passed. As she got nearer still and saw that it was parked at an odd angle, she knew something was wrong. She slowed down and stopped when she saw the car had hit a tree.

There was no one around. The strip of road was quiet and there was no other car or animal in sight. Natascha opened the glove compartment to retrieve the torch. The only other dim light was from one broken headlight of the car. The headlights of her car were an additional source of light, lighting up the eerie scene.

She got out nervously; unsure as to what she might find but from where she was standing she could barely make out the silhouette of a body slumped against the steering wheel. 'Oh my God' Natascha said into the cold night air. Her heart pounded in her chest making her feel slightly lightheaded and her body began to slowly sway, so much so that she thought she might fall. But ordering her nerves to quieten down, she steeled herself and picked her way carefully through the bracken. The inside of the car was dark but for the light from the torch which lit up the victim like an actor under a spotlight. The size of the lifeless body suggested that it was a male but his face was turned away from her. The car had hit the tree with such force that he must have been hurled forward, striking the steering wheel. He wasn't moving. She stood quivering, unable to muster the courage to go any closer. 'Where is the strong Natascha Hamilton?' she asked herself, impatiently. 'Come on, don't just stand here, do something!' Natascha moved around the car to the driver's side and tried to open the door. It was jammed. It took several attempts before she managed to wrench it open.

She crouched down onto her haunches. "Hello, are you all right?" she asked, rather pointlessly. "Can you hear me?" There was no response. She placed her hand on the shoulder of the driver and very gently shook him. The side of his face was masked by his dishevelled hair, plastered against his skin like rough lace work by the deep crimson red of his own blood and a glistening cold, damp sweat. In her heart that had begun to hammer against her ribcage again, she begged him to wake up. Then, almost inaudibly, she heard him moan.

"It's all right. You've had an accident. I'm going to help you. You'll be fine," she said to him, as much to reassure herself. "Just try and keep still." She pulled out her phone from her pocket ready to call the emergency services when the man groaned again and tried to lift his head. "No, don't try to move. Don't worry, you'll be all right," she said soothingly, gently pushing away the hair that was covering his face. The air was black and ghostly. Natascha looked closer and stared, horrified. The battering of her heart grew fiercer and her face drained to a powdery ashen shade of grey.

Despite the coldness Natascha's sudden gasp seared the inside of her chest like a red hot poker as his face was revealed. She could not believe what she was seeing. "Oh my God, Richard! What are you doing... Richard, can you hear me... please!"

The shock was brutal and stabbed at Natascha, knocking her sideways as Richard lay semi-conscious, a steady trickle of deep red blood still running down his forehead and oozing from a deep cut to his top lip. The anger she had been feeling towards him had been pushed so far back in her mind, it was as if it had never existed at all. Tears sprang to her eyes, blurring her vision, her heart was pumping furiously and her hand began to shake as panic rose up into her mouth. Her mind had become a vacuous space and it was only when she saw that he was still trying to pull himself upright did she desperately begin to fill the blankness and consider what she could do. All his attempts to straighten himself were without success.

"Richard, please stay still while we wait for the ambulance." It was only at that point that Natascha realised that she still had her phone in her hand, fingers only poised ready to dial 999. She hadn't phoned for help yet.

His voice was thin and feeble. "No... Please... you don't need to call for an ambulance. I'll be fine. Just give me a few... minutes," he said, unaware of the severity of his injuries.

"Richard, we need to get you to hospital. You've hit your head. You need to see a doctor. I'm going to call for an ambulance. Please, please stay still." Desperation was creeping back into her voice and although she tried to keep it out, she wasn't winning. "Please do this for me, Richard." she said, in a low and soft voice.

"Yes..." He managed to squeeze out a reply through a laboured breath.

With fear almost overwhelming her, Natascha dialled the emergency services and swallowed hard to try and keep her voice steady.

"Yes, I need an ambulance. There's been a car accident." Natascha gave a description of the wounds to Richard's face, informed them of the crash location and answered a series of questions pertaining to the accident. "Please hurry. I don't think that he has been able to fully regain consciousness yet and his breathing is very shallow." She was close to tears again.

"*Just stay with him and keep talking to him to try and keep him calm and awake. The paramedics will be with you very soon. Stay on the line.*"

"Natascha... Natascha," Richard whispered. "Please... help me up. I can't... breathe." With each syllable he spoke Natascha could hear the pain he was in and it hurt her. With each breath he took his voice grew weaker. It was Richard - her Richard.

She shouldn't move him - she knew that. All the advice you're ever given is to never move an injured person; the risk of causing more damage was great. But surely his ability to breathe was more important? She dropped her phone to the ground and positioned her knee on the sill of the car door for leverage. She reached across and held his shoulders and carefully began to lift him upwards to rest against the seat. With the dead weight he was heavy and she struggled to get him up. Holding his head, she gently laid it back onto the neck rest and using the lever by the side of the seat she adjusted it to a more comfortable reclined position.

"Has that helped?"

"Yes ...it's... better." After a pause, he tried to speak again, his voice sounding raspy from the effort of speaking. "I'm... cold."

Natascha took off her coat and laid it across him, shivering as the cold snuck through her thick jumper.

"How's that. Any warmer?"

"Yes... thank you."

A light switched on inside her brain and she picked up the torch. "Richard, I'll be back in one minute." She ran to the boot of her car, this time not even noticing the twisted undergrowth beneath her feet and pulled out a small First Aid kit. Within moments she was back at Richard's side, opening the little plastic case and rummaging through its contents. She unrolled a large bandage and re-folded it together with a wad of cotton wool to form a pad and placed it on the gash just under his hairline; she rolled a linen sling into a strip and carefully wound it around his head to secure the pad as tightly as was comfortable to try and stem the bleeding. She then folded a piece of gauze and placed it over the cut above his lip using an assortment of different sized plasters to hold it down. She had to stay focused - to be practical and lifting an exposed arm, she placed it under the makeshift blanket. After tucking her coat tightly against him her terror turned into a gush of compassion, engulfing her completely. She sat back down onto the sill of the open door and clutched his cold and clammy hand. Her fear for him was causing a persistent ache in her stomach. She was scared and tightened her hold watching closely at the slight movement of his chest from beneath the coat. Then, she heard him exhale slowly and then there was nothing. Natascha held her breath then quickly raised her hand to his mouth waiting to feel some warmth. Her hand was waiting for longer than it should. Panic rumbled violently inside her like an earthquake.

"Richard! Richard!" she screamed, the high-pitched sound of her voice reverberating into the night, disturbing its stillness. "Richard, don't you dare..! Don't you dare do this to me!"

After a moment's hesitation a gulp of air fought its way into his throat and he began to breathe again, his breaths coming in quick, shallow spasms.

Natascha looked out into the darkness. Where was that ambulance? She had no idea how long he had been here before she had arrived.

With her eyes unable to leave his face and both her hands wrapped around his, an ill-timed memory crossed her mind.

She saw the two of them riding their bikes into the hills, her ponytail bouncing freely behind her. They were both so young. Richard had hit a large stone, had fallen off awkwardly and lay motionless on the ground. The brakes on her bike had screeched as she stopped, jumped off and ran to him. She had taken off the small pink back pack she was carrying and had placed it under his head and then had taken off her favourite matching pink jacket and had laid it across him to keep him warm. Through the heroism, she remembered how scared she was...

"Don't worry, Richard. I'll go and get help," Natascha said to him in a serious and grown up voice.

But Richard sat bolt upright, giving her a start. "Here, you have this. I think it might rain," he said, handing her jacket back to her.

"But what about you, aren't you hurt? I was trying to help you."

He took her hand and rubbed it across his shin so she could feel the bump that was already starting to come through. "I'll probably be black and blue tomorrow but that's all," he said, laughing…

Natascha's mind had wandered to a long, lost bygone and she was only brought out of her foolish thoughts by the sound of a siren. She picked up her phone again. "I think I can hear the ambulance coming."

She looked at him. He was lying back in the seat with his eyes closed, his face, bloody and pale. She moved her mouth close to his ear. "Richard?" she whispered, "don't you want to get up and give me back my jacket and tell me that all you'll have is a nasty bruise on your leg in the morning?"

Richard didn't make a sound but the beginnings of a weak smile definitely rose to his lips and Natascha was sure that he remembered, too.

At just that moment the ambulance arrived and Natascha let the paramedics skilfully do their work. In no time Richard was on a stretcher with a brace around his neck and a blanket keeping him warm. An oxygen mask covered his mouth.

"Is the patient known to you, miss?"

"Er, yes. Yes, he is. His name's Richard. Richard French. We used to live in the same village." At least she used to know him, she thought to herself.

"Do you mind if I ask you your name, miss?"

"No, of course. My name's Natascha Hamilton."

"Will you be coming with us to the hospital? I'm sure he'll want to see a familiar face."

Rallying herself, she realised that it was not over yet. Natascha hadn't thought that far forward. "I have my car. I'll be right behind you."

She went over to Richard just before they put him in the ambulance. "I'll see you at the hospital."

He seemed to say something to her from behind the mask. She leant in lower, lifted the mask slightly and put her ear close to him.

"Don't... leave... me," he breathed.

She sat in her car holding on to the steering wheel, trying to gather her thoughts as she looked at her trembling hands, her shock blatantly visible. The ambulance drove away, its bright red tail lights and flashing blue siren, stark against the dark of the night. She took deep breaths and when she felt she was ready she turned the key in the ignition and made her way to the Accident and Emergency department of the local hospital.

Chapter Twelve

The outside of the hospital looked exactly the same as it did when she was a girl but when she entered, Natascha could see that there had been a great many changes made to it. It was much brighter, the walls now a warm lemon rather than the faded matt salmon she remembered. The large metal pipes that used to run along the ceilings had been removed or relocated and the overall impression of the interior was clean and welcoming. She approached the girl at the reception desk.

"Hello. My name's Natascha Hamilton. I've come to find out how Mr French is."

"Was he brought in here tonight?"

"Yes, he was. He was in a car accident."

The young receptionist looked down and tapped on her computer. "Ah yes. Mr French." She looked up again. "Are you a relative?"

"No, I'm a friend. I'm the one who called the ambulance."

The girl looked down at her screen again. "Richard French is in the assessment area." She lifted her head. "If you turn left here and follow the signs to A & E, you will see a nurse at the desk. Give her your details and she will give you the information. Is that okay?" she asked, happily.

Natascha forced a smile in return. "Yes, thank you," and followed the directions she had been given.

"My name's Natascha Hamilton. I've come to see Mr French," she said, to a no-nonsense looking nurse as she reached the ward.

"Oh yes, Miss Hamilton. Please take a seat in the waiting room. The doctor will be with Mr French soon." The nurse pointed towards a room at the end of the corridor and smiled a no-nonsense sort of smile.

Natascha went and sat in the smallish room. Grey plastic chairs ran along the perimeters of the walls and two teak coffee tables with last month's magazines spread haphazardly across the tops, sat in the middle of the room as a flimsy attempt to make the place feel more homely. The décor wasn't as warm as in the foyer of the building. The room was empty but for a young woman in the far corner who sat staring at the floor, a look of worry criss-crossing her face. She probably hadn't even noticed that someone else had walked in.

The scene of the accident replayed over and over in Natascha's mind as though it was a movie she had been to see a long, long time ago. The story line, however, felt too far-fetched and at times Natascha found herself wondering what she was doing here. She wasn't thinking straight. She had to clear this fog from her head. The large old-fashioned clock hanging over the door said 8.30pm; her parents would have expected her home some time ago. She stood up and made her way outside onto the hospital grounds and phoned her father.

"Hello, Dad, it's Natascha. I'm sorry about the time but I couldn't phone you any earlier. I bet you and mum have been wondering where I am," she tried to say lightly.

"*Is everything all right? You don't sound yourself. We assumed you had stayed on at our French friends for a little while.*"

"No, I'm fine Dad. I'm at the hospital, actually. I stopped at a car accident on the strip near the copse. The driver was Richard."

"*Richard? Oh Lord, Tascha, is he all right?*"

"Well, the doctor's going in to see him soon. I thought I'd better wait with him." Natascha paused, "Did you know he was coming for Christmas?"

"*No, no I didn't. I don't think your mother knew either, Monica certainly didn't mention it. Perhaps they didn't know themselves. Maybe it was meant to be a surprise visit.*"

"Well, I think that'll be mission accomplished, then," Natascha said, noting the irony. "Listen, Dad, would you phone them and tell them what's happened. Tell them not to worry, I'll stay with him. I don't really know very much at all at the moment but I'll talk to the doctor once Richard's been seen."

"*Of course, I'll phone them now. Do you want me to come up to meet you?*"

"No, Dad, there's no need. I'm fine."

"*Well, if there's anything you need just say the word. You must be exhausted. You drove so far to get here and now this.*"

"No, I'm okay Dad. It's Richard I'm a bit worried about. Tell Mum not to panic. I'll let you know what's happening once I know more myself. I'll be home soon."

Natascha hurried back inside to the waiting room, seating herself in the same chair.

A few minutes later, a doctor walked in.

"Mrs Tilling?" the doctor asked, looking at Natascha.

Natascha shook her head. "You must want to speak to the lady over there." But just as Natascha was about to point out who she assumed to be Mrs Tilling, the woman had already left her seat and was standing beside him.

"Mrs Tilling. I'm Dr Harrison. Your husband's fine and is waiting for you. Would you like to come with me? The wound on his arm isn't as bad as it looks... "

They both left the room, the echo of their voices tapering off as they disappeared down the corridor leaving Natascha alone.

As she waited, Natascha's body suddenly felt incredibly tired and heavy yet her mind was wide awake. The large clock on the wall ticked loudly, filling the room with the reverberations of its slow rhythmic beat. Nurses shuffled past the door with files in their hands and porters pushed nervous looking patients in wheelchairs. The sound of telephones ringing and babies crying was a faraway hum in Natascha's ears and the unmistakable faint hospital odour of disinfectant clung in her nostrils. And through it all she sat in her own private world with her own private thoughts.

It was nearly an hour before the same doctor returned. He looked down at the notes he was holding. "You must be Natascha Hamilton."

Natascha stood up at the sound of her name.

"I've checked Mr French and he's also been for an x-ray. The good news is there doesn't seem to be any fractures or serious injuries. The bad news is, because he had quite a blow to the head, we're going to keep him in for the night for observations, just to make sure that he'll be in good shape to go home. With any luck he should be out in time for Christmas. He's a very lucky man."

Natascha had been sitting in the waiting room wringing her useless hands in her lap, her thoughts racing to nowhere, her worry for Richard undeniable but now with the doctor's report, her anxiety was gratefully eased. "That is good news. I'm so glad to hear that. Can I see him?" Natascha asked with a spontaneity that hadn't given her the time to think and then immediately wondered if she was doing the right thing. What if he didn't want to see her? What if he had become cold and distant again? Could she cope with that? But could she turn around and walk away now when the last picture she had of him was his face covered in blood and his body weak with pain? Reality was finally setting in and she was not sure how she was to handle it all. But this time, and for once in a very long time, she decided to go with her heart and concluded that she would have to ignore the disquiet in her head.

"Yes of course. Come this way."

Dr Harrison showed Natascha to a cubicle. "He's in here," he said, holding the curtain between his fingers. "We're in the process of organising a bed for him on the ward. Try not to stay too long; Mr French will need all the rest he can get." The doctor peeped inside. "Mr French, I have a visitor for you. I'm sure you'll be very pleased to see her. I would be!" he added, as he gave Richard a knowing wink.

Natascha stepped inside with much trepidation as the doctor left them alone and pulled the curtain across behind him. Richard lay on a couch looking tired and vulnerable. All traces of blood had been cleaned away leaving a large piece of gauze on his forehead and a series of small stitches to the corner of his upper lip. They looked at each other for a long moment before Natascha spoke.

"How are you feeling?" she asked, gingerly.

Richard seemed to hesitate. "I'm a bit sore but I think I'll survive."

There was silence. Any conversation seemed out of place and her polite small talk was simply for the sake of having something to say; hence, the stilted words and awkward pauses.

"Do you know what happened?" Natascha asked.

Richard looked away, but not before Natascha could see the distress on his face as he relived the moment. She felt sorry she had ever asked the question. "I can't really remember very much. All I know is that one minute everything was fine and the next I felt the car start to skid."

"It's possible you hit an icy patch. It feels like the Antarctic out there tonight."

Richard stared ahead then slowly turned his face towards her. "I've got a lot to thank you for."

"I did what anyone else would have done. I only wish I could have done more."

Richard said nothing.

Remembering what her mother had told her about Richard never having visited his parents at Christmas, Natascha was curious to know why he was here in the first place. "Did your parents know you were coming? I saw your mother earlier but she didn't mention it."

"No, they didn't know."

She acknowledged his answer but didn't say any more when she saw that he was becoming drowsy.

"Well, I think I should leave you to get some rest," she said, relieved that the disjointed dialogue was coming to an end.

She moved towards him and instinctively leant down as if to place a kiss on his forehead, then stopped herself in time and very gently squeezed his shoulder instead. "I'll see you soon."

The bitter cold hit her as she stepped out of the building. She had left her coat that the paramedic had handed back to her in the car. It was stained with blood. On the way to her car she met Monica and Michael on their way to visit their son.

"We just got the message. We went out and both forgot to bring mobile phones - you know what us older generation are like," Michael said, gravely. "We only found out when we got home and listened to your father's message on the answer machine."

"The doctor says he'll be fine," Natascha said, as encouragingly as she could. "He seemed to be getting tired, so I left him to rest but he'll be so pleased to see you."

"Thank you, Natascha," Michael said, the sincerity softening the serious tone in his voice. His wife, perhaps for the first time, seemed lost for words.

Natascha put together a perky expression to relieve their gloom, though it couldn't feel any emptier than she herself was feeling. "I'll see you soon."

Without being able to wipe away the worry from their faces they both turned and hurried away towards the entrance of the hospital leaving Natascha to stand alone in the desolate car park.

She dug her hands deeper into her trouser pockets and raising her face to look up into the dark sky, she felt tiny flakes of snow as they started to fall, soft and icy on her face.

Chapter Thirteen

The digits on the clock beside her bed danced erratically before her eyes. The pressure at her temples squeezed a bit more and the clenching of her stomach tightened and ached horribly. Natascha had hardly slept. Her mind had raced from one image to the other, chock-full of pictures she wanted to erase and memories she never wanted to ever recall. Her trusted mental process of organising, prioritising and compartmentalising was all but lost since the congestion of thoughts in her head made it impossible for her to know where to begin. As much as her body yearned to stay a while longer in her bed, however, her mind wanted nothing more but to get up and out into the fresh air.

It was Christmas Eve and as always, her plan was to get an early start to help her mother prepare vegetables and sauces for their Christmas lunch and help her father with cutting and peeling the fruits to make the winter mulled wine as he did every year.

But this morning she couldn't face any of it. She got up, dressed, enveloped herself in her thick, warm woollen cardigan and went downstairs.

In the kitchen her mother was rolling out pastry to make an apple pie. The par cooked apples were cooling on the side and the tang of them smelt delicious. But it wasn't enough to entice Natascha to stay.

"Morning, Mum. I think I'll go for a walk. I need the air," Natascha said, quietly. "I won't be long."

Her mother watched Natascha leave the kitchen via the back door and saw her pass the window with her head held low. Last night would have been such a disturbing experience for anyone. And yet she knew her daughter would be wrestling with herself to try and take it all in her stride and be unaffected by the evening's dreadful events. She also knew that her daughter would be concentrating on nothing else but how best to deal with the whole episode, to make it all make sense. However, she fervently hoped that, for once, Natascha would come to realise that not everything in this world, did.

Natascha stepped out and closed the door behind her. She was met by a crispness in the air that exhilarated her tired mind and for a while emptied it of the tumult. It had been raining but now the cold sun was shining. She should have liked to walk in the hills but the rain had made the paths muddy and impassable so she stuck to the lane. The wet surface of the tarmac dazzled so brightly in the winter sunshine, it almost blinded her. And the leaves and bushes glistened with the rain drops that were yet to evaporate.

Natascha had to regroup and put everything into perspective. Last night she had helped someone who was in need of her assistance; that was all. She had called the emergency services, made that person as comfortable as she could and stayed with them until the paramedics had arrived; nothing exceptional about that. She had gone to the hospital to see that the victim was in a stable condition for her own peace of mind. Anyone else with an iota of common sense would have done exactly the same. The fact that the person involved was Richard was immaterial; her actions would have been exactly the same had it been a stranger. She would not let her emotions run riot and she would keep reminding herself that she had helped Richard in the same way she would have helped anyone else.

After spending almost an hour out of doors, Natascha returned to the warmth of the kitchen.

"Better?" her mother asked, sympathetically handing her a cup of tea.

"Yes, much." She sat at the kitchen table and sipped her drink, pensively. Then again, of course she would feel some emotion. It would be far more worrying if she was to become so insensitive and so detached that she was unable to sympathise at all. She was not a cold-hearted woman. But being pragmatic was more valuable to all concerned. No amount of pondering could ever affect events of the past. And that was that. Her elbow rested on the table and her head lay in the palm of her hand, her eyes slipping closed, the familiar smell of fruit pies and freshly baked bread comforting her. Samuel Barber's haunting *Adagio for*

Strings was on the radio which played softly to itself in the corner of the room; a rather melancholic piece of music to play on Christmas Eve but it infused Natascha with some of the peace that she needed, sending her suspended somewhere between being half awake and half asleep - such a sublime state to drift in.

However, she was sharply awakened at the sound of the front door shutting and Monica's usually trill voice, sounding somewhat numb, echoing in the hallway. Monica and Michael had returned from the hospital. An involuntary tightening in Natascha's chest annoyed her and she further let herself down by eavesdropping on the conversation.

"We went to collect Richard from the hospital."

The clenching intensified as all at once, Natascha pictured Richard coming through the door at any minute.

"But he didn't have a very good night, so they want to keep him in for a bit longer."

Natascha relaxed when she realised that Richard wasn't in the house. Then she felt a pang of guilt at her self-centredness. She should be feeling concern, not relief.

"They said he's suffering from some concussion, although at the moment they can't tell how severe it is. As the day goes on they will have a better idea."

Natascha left the kitchen and joined the others in the hallway. "How's Richard?"

"Oh Natascha, I was just saying to your mother. Things are not quite as clear cut as they seemed last night. We need to wait and see."

"I'm really sorry to hear that," Natascha said, trying to ignore her unease.

Michael turned to Natascha with tired eyes. "I don't quite know how to thank you, Natascha, for all that you did for Richard. I'm sure had it been someone else, things may have turned out differently. They may not have had your presence of mind and your bravery. It was such a relief to know you were there with him. You may have saved his life, you know. He was very lucky that you turned up when you did."

"He's very lucky to have you as a friend," Monica added. "I'm so glad the two of you have met again."

At these words Natascha drew in a faltering breath. No-one knew of the true relationship between Natascha and Richard. No-one realised how incredibly different it was today to how it was when they were young.

Monica turned to Natascha's mother and, out of the blue, released some of her sadness. "If only he'd open up a bit more and let us know how he felt. He keeps so much to himself it's impossible to help him. He was always quite reserved as a child, as you know, but as the years have gone by he's become more and more withdrawn." Monica was on the verge of tears. "We didn't even know he was coming."

Natascha felt something akin to a mixture of sorrow and resentment towards Richard, sad for his obvious solitary life and resentful for being the cause of such grief to his mother.

Natascha looked at Monica, feeling obliged to offer some support despite herself. "If there's anything I can do, anything at all, please let me know."

Monica acknowledged Natascha's kind words with a cheerless smile.

"Vivienne," Monica continued, turning to Natascha's mother. "I think we may have to change our plans for coming to Christmas dinner tomorrow. Richard will need some help when he gets home and I want to be there, even if he doesn't actually want me to be."

"I understand. But if you change your minds, just turn up, Richard as well, of course."

"Thank you, that's good of you. We'll see how Richard is and let you know how things are."

Monica unenthusiastically kissed Natascha's mother's cheek. Michael stood up straight and his gesture of gratitude to them both was by of a slight nod of his head.

"Let me know if there is anything I can do," Natascha reminded them as they left.

Chapter Fourteen

There is something very special about Christmas morning; the quiet optimism and expectancy for the day ahead, the unspoken love of the familiar and traditional. And children, bright-eyed with excitement, impatiently waiting to see what Santa had left them during the night. It went hand in hand with the wonderful aroma of honeyed ham and roasting turkey that filled the air. There was something definitely very cosy about it.

As soon as Natascha was up and dressed she was in the kitchen. Nothing was going to interrupt her Christmas routine. There would be no place for thoughts that were not part of the traditions that made her Christmas the way she had always known them to be - the way she would always want them to be.

The cut glass crystal and the silver cutlery were laid out on the dinner table, together with the delicate china plates as was done every Christmas. And this year Natascha had brought with her a candle, hand-decorated with rich green holly leaves and bright red berries which she arranged carefully in the centre of the table. Six places had been set, in the event that Richard and his parents should join them.

The preparations kept her gratefully contented and distracted. Such routine to most may seem trivial but to Natascha they meant everything.

Natascha was folding the napkins while listening to her beloved Elvis Presley singing *Blue Christmas* when she heard the phone ring. The dining room door that led into the hall was only slightly ajar making it difficult for Natascha to hear what was being said, although she could distinctly discern her mother saying hello to Monica. Her determination to stay focused took a dip, however, when disappointingly, she realised that she had had to resist the temptation of turning down the volume on the CD player. Coolly, she waited for her mother to relay the latest information.

"The doctor saw Richard this morning," her mother said, as she joined Natascha in the dining room, "and discharged him saying he could convalesce at home. Richard is insisting his Mum and Dad stick to their original plans, so they'll be coming for lunch after all. He himself, doesn't feel up to it but told them that a few hours of peace and quiet would be much better for him." Natascha's mother considered this for a moment and added, "I'm not sure whether that sounds selfless or ungrateful...? In any case, you can take away one of the place settings."

Her mother left her and went back to the kitchen while Natascha was left to wonder why she had been holding her breath and why her heart had started to pump a little faster before being told that Richard would not be coming. What it did tell her for sure, however, was that she still had a long way to go before she could get a proper hold of her emotions.

Lunch was a rather subdued affair. Even with the colourful party hats from the Christmas crackers and Natascha's mother doing her best to keep the atmosphere cheerful, Richard's accident and the two nights he had spent in hospital were events that could not easily be put to one side. Monica chatted and chirruped as though all was well but her mind was obviously elsewhere.

Natascha began to clear away the table after lunch. But, regardless of her protestations, Monica was adamant.

"No, no, no," she insisted, "you've done far too much already," she fussed. "I'll help your mother. You go and relax."

Retreating, therefore, to her favourite armchair, she assumed her usual position of curling her legs under her and settled to the hum of the conversation between her father and Michael and the tinkle of voices and chinking of plates coming from the kitchen. Natascha vaguely saw the moving images on the TV but could not concentrate on what she was watching.

"I have to thank you all for a lovely afternoon," Monica said as the ladies entered the lounge. "Vivienne, lunch was wonderful. But I think we ought to be going now. Richard's on his own and I feel guilty leaving him alone like that. Don't get me wrong, I know he wanted me out of the house so that he wouldn't have me fussing over him but I still feel terrible that he's at home on his own on Christmas Day. It's the first time he's come to see us at Christmas and it doesn't feel right with us being here. We'd really love to stay but I do feel awful. It isn't very fair on him."

"Yes, Monica's right," Michael added.

"It's a shame you have to leave so early. Her Majesty hasn't even begun her speech yet," Natascha's father said.

Her mother, although disappointed, nodded compassionately. "We understand. Of course you want to get back to Richard."

Natascha's eyes were fixed on the TV screen, trying to ignore the beginnings of what was turning out to be a conflict of her conscience. She could feel it bubbling up from deep down inside and was rising to her lips, fast. Both sides of the argument taking place in her head had valid reasons. 'You have to suggest it, it's only right,' one half was saying, 'but I don't think I can put myself through it,' protested the other. But in the middle of the arguing going on within her, Natascha turned, looked at her mother and heard the words being spoken from her own mouth as the quarrelling inside overflowed.

"Mum, why don't I get some food ready and take it over to Richard. I can stay with him for a little while as well." She turned to Monica. "You and Michael can stay for a bit longer and Richard won't be on his own."

Monica was overcome at Natascha's suggestion. "Really?" she cooed. "Natascha, that is so sweet of you but I can't let you go to so much trouble."

Natascha knew what was coming next but couldn't hold it back. "It's no trouble, Monica, I don't mind at all. In fact, I'd like to see him."

"Are you absolutely sure? I feel terrible taking advantage of you like this, but in all honesty, I have a feeling Richard would much rather see you, anyway. It's a wonderful idea. Thank you. You are such a good girl."

Her look of goodwill stayed firmly in place on the outside but inside Natascha wished she could have been more resilient against her mind's not so gentle persuasion to be the Good Samaritan, a proposition she was bound to regret making. But Monica and Michael could use her parents' company knowing their son was not alone, not today of all days. It was an obvious suggestion to make but certainly not an easy one. However, she would put up with Richard's mood, no matter how bad that may turn out to be.

Natascha pulled up outside the little cottage, picked up the small basket of food that sat on the seat beside her and reached for the car door. Then she hesitated, going through again in her mind what she was going to say when Richard came to the door. This first meeting after the accident had the real potential of being an unpleasant one; it would be nothing like visiting a sick brother. In point of fact, it was unlikely that Richard wanted any visitors at all. Her presence would probably be more of an inconvenience than anything else, which he would have no problem in expressing. Natascha sighed. Two days ago, she was gently wiping his hair from his face and holding his hand, worried and scared for him. And yet today, here she was, to politely ask after his health like a vague acquaintance, to smile and sympathise and make all the appropriate noises. She had to act as though nothing had changed; that their pre-accident business relationship had not altered in any way, to disregard the verbal street fight of their last meeting and be, as always, pleasant and polite whatever the circumstance. She was ready to face Richard.

She walked confidently up the path, rang the doorbell and waited, taking a deep breath to retain her calm. But when the door opened, Richard's gaunt face, devoid of colour and etched with weariness, was what greeted her. The translucence in his eyes was gone and in its place was the dull expression of helplessness. Every thought she'd had about him minutes before vanished in an instant. The tall, handsome man had disappeared and in his stead stood a frail looking figure, tired and defenceless. Natascha was so shocked at his appearance, she was hardly able to speak.

"Richard, I-I'm so sorry. It looks like I've disturbed you. Did I wake you?" Natascha asked, trying to sound natural although a note of being slightly dazed was in her voice and was giving her away.

"No, no. I was resting but I wasn't asleep. Please come in," he said, valiantly trying to hide his obvious discomfort.

The large dressing on his forehead and the sutures on his lip made him look wounded and broken but she bit the inside of her cheek to remind herself that although she should be kind and understanding, it should be no different to the kindness and compassion she would express to anyone who had gone through what he had.

Richard showed her through into the kitchen.

As an afterthought, Natascha remembered the basket she was carrying and held it up. "I brought this for you. It's your share of Christmas dinner. I thought you might like some."

He tried to muster some gratitude. "I haven't had much of an appetite recently but that was nice of you."

Natascha knew she sounded pathetic but went on, pointing to the fridge. "Well, if I leave it in here, you can have it later if you feel like it." She began clearing some room and with her back to him, she placed glass containers inside, taking the opportunity to gather herself. "How have you been?"

"Oh, not too bad."

Natascha turned to see that he was lying. "Well, that's good to hear. Shall I make us some tea?" She was beginning to sound like an imbecile but she couldn't think of anything sensible to say.

"Of course. Tea and coffee are in the end cupboard, I think. Maybe I'll try a plain black coffee. Thanks,"

Stirring the coffee, Natascha still could not string together a sentence that was of any significance. In silence she placed two hot cups on the kitchen table and sat opposite Richard like a mute. She had been taken by complete surprise. His mild manner was totally unexpected.

"They're all waiting for the Queen's speech but not being terribly interested to hear about another 'Annus Horribilis', I said I'd come to see how you are. I'll catch the highlights later." Her attempt at a little light-hearted banter did nothing more than provoke a faint smile from Richard.

"That was good of you." Richard took a sip of his coffee and winced as he placed the cup back on the table. "How was lunch?" he asked, trying to make some more polite small talk. It was evident to Natascha that he was still in some pain.

"It was fine. It was nice to have your parents over."

Richard's face formed a faraway look of agreement.

"How have you really been?" Natascha asked honestly, at last abandoning the civilised chit-chat.

"The headaches have been a bit of a nuisance and ditto for the waves of nausea." Then he added, with a brave air of casualness, "but it seems to be easing and the bouts of nausea are not as frequent,"

Natascha watched as his face blanched further.

"I'm sorry, you're going to have to excuse me," Richard managed to say before quickly leaving the room.

She heard a door click shut and then there was an awful sound of retching coming from the bathroom, agonised and weary. Natascha felt helpless, useless and awkward as she sat in the kitchen waiting for him to come back. It was ridiculous - almost as if she was simply waiting for him to come back from answering the phone. His distress and suffering pained her and weakened her. There must be something she could do but she could not think of a single thing and instead felt troubled at her state of uncertainty. A few moments later, while she was still in the middle of her disarrayed thoughts, Richard returned.

"I'm sorry about that. I don't think coffee was the best idea." He tried to make light of it, even tried to smile but he looked fragile and exhausted and his voice had become a strained whisper.

"Perhaps you're not as well as you'd like me to believe."

The noticeable waning of the little strength Richard had left was getting to her and suddenly she felt an overwhelming desire to hold him and comfort him, wanting to make him feel better and to feel safe with her. Not knowing whether she could contain her feelings, she hurriedly finished her tea, scalding her mouth in the process. "You look very tired. I think I should leave you to rest." She stood up. "Is there anything I can do for you before I go?" she added, quickly.

"No. Thank you."

"Well, I hope you feel better soon." Natascha smiled a maladroit smile and within moments she was gone.

Once back in the refuge of her car, she took a look at herself in the mirror. Her eyelashes were moist and her cheeks were flushed from the unexpected surge of emotion. Her self-discipline had started to give way again and her resilience had begun to evaporate, simply trying to feel nothing for Richard. But he was in so much anguish she could almost feel his pain, too. She was struggling to keep an even perspective but it wasn't working. She had just abandoned him, she admitted that. But she was of use to no-one in this state. And so, fumbling with the key in the ignition, she drove back to the house via the same route she had taken on her way here, deliberately avoiding the road on which the accident had taken place. On the journey to see Richard she had convinced herself that by taking the longer route, she would gain a little more time to prepare herself and settle into the correct frame of mind before she came face to face with him. Deep down, she knew that the real reason for making the detour was because the vivid memories of finding him there alone and in so much pain were still haunting her and she was not coping very well with them.

When she arrived home she made quite a convincing show of cheerfulness and said that Richard appeared to be in good spirits and appreciated the food. But he was looking tired, so she decided to leave him early. Natascha then excused herself saying she had a few things she had to attend to and left the party, making her way to the safe haven of her bedroom. The afternoon darkness was already descending and the temperature outside had plummeted to zero but Natascha opened her window wide to let in the air and lay on her bed for some time gazing at the bright, round moon.

She awoke a few hours later to find that she had fallen asleep fully clothed with the window still open. The room was freezing and she shivered in it. She closed the window and fell straight to sleep, mentally exhausted.

Chapter Fifteen

Christmas Day was on a Friday this year, followed by the weekend and the bonus of not having that Monday morning feeling, now that Monday had become the official Boxing Day Bank Holiday, was very welcome. It worked out well for Natascha since she could spend the Saturday after Christmas with her parents, leave to go back to London on the Sunday and have the Bank Holiday all to herself.

Yesterday Natascha was to take both sets of parents out for the day. However, Monica and Michael had decided that they would prefer to spend the day with Richard. Even if he kept to his room, Monica hoped it would be of some comfort to him knowing that he was not alone in the house, she had explained.

As a result, it was only Natascha and her parents who went out. They had driven to a quaint little village across the border into Gloucestershire, wandering along narrow streets, dressed in clothing appropriate for the cold, browsing around shops and galleries, passing old buildings, mills and houses built using stone from the local quarry. They visited old churches and their beautiful grounds. And with Natascha's keen interest in architecture, they stopped and had lunch at a magnificent Tudor house which had been refurbished to become a charming hotel.

The fresh air worked wonders for Natascha. The three of them spent the whole day out of doors as they did every Christmas and that brought back with it a sense of normality. They passed places where she remembered Richard and herself used to ride and the hills they used to walk across but she made sure those thoughts were short lived. As they drove through the beautiful countryside Natascha was at last beginning to find that place in her mind where she could resume the life she knew. The power of nature was a wonderful healer.

Now it was time for her to leave and her bags were packed and ready to be loaded into the car. Although it seemed that she had only just arrived, the few intervening days had the feeling of having gone on forever, the harrowing details of the accident having happened in a far off distant past.

She carried the last bag downstairs and went into the kitchen for a light lunch before she left. There was no real need to hurry back to London but she preferred to be home early enough so that she wasn't travelling for too long in winter's early nightfall. It would give her time to unpack and relax during the rest of the evening. Natascha also had to admit that for the first time, she was looking forward to leaving. She felt happy that it was time to go home but she kept this to herself.

Her mother was sitting at the kitchen table with Monica.

"Hello darling. All set?"

"Yes, I'm afraid so, Mum," Natascha said. "Hello, Monica."

"Michael and your father have popped down the road to see Harold's new vintage car, if you know what I mean." She frowned and looked rather perplexed. "New and vintage don't sound quite right together."

Natascha laughed at her mother's strangely logical statement. "Did Dad say what it is? The make and model, that is," she asked, enthusiastically. Her predilection for cars, be it sporty and modern, or old and classic, was something she had inherited from her father.

"He did tell me the name of this supposedly magnificent piece of machinery but it's slipped my mind. You know me; all these names mean nothing to me. Anyway, they shouldn't be long."

"The time goes so quickly," Monica said sadly, ignoring the conversation and altering the light-hearted mood in the room.

Natascha's mother threw a questioning look across to her daughter before turning to Monica. "How do you mean, dear?" she asked her friend rather carefully.

"Richard. He's only just got here but already he wants to leave as well - today. Michael took him down to the train station early this morning. But apparently, there are severe delays on all train lines into London Paddington until Tuesday." Monica shook her head. "I told him he should stay until he was properly rested and able to travel but he won't have it. He just says he's fine and that he has business that can't wait." Monica looked dejected.

"I'm sure the real reason is he would rather be away from here and not have me under his feet. But what can I do? I can't stop him. He's at home now, planning a new route back to wherever it is he lives. He's never actually told us where that is apart from the fact that it's in a small village in Hertfordshire. Can you believe that?"

"You know what men are like," Natascha's mother offered, trying to placate her friend, "some love to be mothered and others want nothing more but to show off their independence..."

Natascha didn't hear anymore. She found herself in exactly the same scenario she was in just two days ago when she was forced to visit Richard on Christmas Day. Here she was again, wondering how to escape the dilemma of doing what she knew was impossible to ignore. At that moment she heard her father and Michael come through the door, the car they had just been to see being the topic of their animated discussion. Although Natascha would normally have been interested to join in, she didn't stop to chat and made a veiled excuse to go back to her room. She hastily left the kitchen taking with her this new and demoralising impasse.

She shut the door and fell onto her bed. How on earth could she go home alone in her car when she knew he would be travelling in the same direction? He'd already mentioned he didn't live too far away from her. Visiting him for a few minutes on Christmas day had been so much simpler and yet it had affected her in a way she hadn't foreseen. Offering him a lift home was a very different matter. It would mean having to spend around two hours with him in the intimate proximity of her car, trying to uphold a healthy atmosphere in which she would be comfortable to drive. How was she going to execute that? All her plans were being sabotaged and her options had been reduced to none. There was only one way in which this new development was headed and only one way for her to manage the control of it. Summon up calm, trust in her logic and maintain a clear head. Just keep it all in proportion. It was only offering someone a lift home. Her strength of character would keep her immune to any attempts at intimidation. And it would also hold her firm against falling into the trap of over-sentimentality again. Natascha looked at the clock on her table. Three o'clock. It was time she started off, so she left her room and went back to the kitchen to face the others. She was ready.

"If it will help, Richard can come with me. We live in the same general direction so it makes perfect sense that we travel together." Everyone turned to look at her as if she had said something amazing.

"Oh Natascha, that is a good idea. If he's determined to go today," Michael said, turning to his wife. "I don't think we can keep him here if he doesn't want to stay, dear. We should put Natascha's proposal to him and see what he wants to do."

Monica half-heartedly nodded in agreement.

Michael looked at Natascha's father, "If I can use your phone, Patrick, I'll give him a call now. He may have changed his mind about going home today in which case, Natascha, you can go back to your original plans."

"

Chapter Sixteen

Less than half an hour later Natascha was sitting in her car outside Monica and Michael's little cottage. She had said goodbye to her own parents and had followed Monica and Michael to their home. Natascha opted to wait outside in her car while they went in to help Richard with his things and was happy enough to let them sort themselves out without her participation. Watching as they came out of the house, she chuckled discreetly when she saw Monica fussing over her son as any mother would and watched his lack of reaction to all of it. He glanced across to see her waiting in her car and their eyes met. He held her stare and from the expression of uncertainty on his face she realised at once that the journey would indeed, not be an agreeable one. After her initial misgivings, Natascha had finally acquiesced that all things considered, she was doing the right thing, although she rather doubted that Richard was equally as philosophical about the arrangement.

"Now, Richard. Make sure you ring your father when you get home. You're still not 100% well, so don't go overdoing it. Did you remember to take a jumper with you for the journey?"

Richard rolled his eyes. "I'll be in the car, mother. I'm sure it has heating!"

"Yes, well don't forget to ring," Monica went on.

"I will," he said, impatiently.

Monica stood in front of Richard and straightened the lapels on his jacket. "I still think you should have worn a jumper." It was quite a comical sight to see the tall, cool Richard having his over-zealous mother stretching up on tip-toes to reach his shoulders and brush non-existent fluff from his jacket.

Richard put his bag in the boot of the car and went to sit in the passenger seat as Natascha smoothly got out from behind the steering wheel and went to Monica and Michael who were ready to wave their son goodbye. "Bye, Monica," she said, kissing her lightly on the cheek and then shook Michael's hand. "Don't worry, he'll be fine."

"Well, I hope his mood changes," Monica sighed, "for your sake!"

Slipping into the driver's seat, Natascha closed the door, converting the inside of her car into a capsule, isolating them both from everything and everyone. Her breath caught momentarily in her throat at the intimacy. The invisible barrier that Richard hid behind tripled in density the moment the door clunked shut. But it didn't have the effect it might have had just a few days ago. She felt all right. The self-confidence she had spent years perfecting was still there when she needed it most. She had managed to locate a piece of her armour behind which she could protect herself and at last felt strong enough to believe in her own capabilities and depend upon herself. Richard could build his barrier as high and as wide as he wanted, it would not have any effect on her - not anymore. Not long ago she had had the insane thought that he was 'her' Richard. Now she knew with every nerve in her body that she would never think that way again.

After they had been driving for a little over ten minutes, Natascha turned towards him. The large dressing he had worn had been replaced by a much smaller piece of gauze and as the wound lay so close to his hairline, it could only just be seen. The tiny stitches near the corner of his top lip were barely visible, now that the inflammation had diminished. A few days' worth of beard had grown altering his clean shaven face to appear hardy and tough although not quite unkempt. The addition of the manly stubble to his already seductive good looks would be, to most women, nothing short of irresistible and based on what Natascha had witnessed at the bar the other evening, most women was a rather conservative estimate. However, she knew, far too well, the character of the man sitting beside her. And perhaps if he wasn't so haughty and self-righteous she might agree.

She turned back to concentrate on the road. "How are you feeling?"

He was staring straight ahead and from the corner of her eye, Natascha saw him flinch. "I'm much better, no more headaches and no more nausea. I've only got the drowsiness to contend with."

"Are you still in much pain?"

"No. It's more of a case of feeling sore than actual pain," he replied, and changed the subject before Natascha had a chance to ask any more questions. "The insurance company got in touch to say that they'll be checking my car to see why the airbag didn't deploy when the car hit the tree."

The scene of the accident flashed through her head and she pictured his body lying lifeless against the steering wheel. Silence followed and when Natascha turned to glance at Richard again, she saw that he had fallen asleep, his head resting against the head rest and tilting slightly towards her. He looked harmless and childlike.

In hindsight, Natascha judged it to be a good thing that he was not able to catch a train this morning since despite his arguing to the contrary, he wasn't well enough to travel alone. She sighed as she switched on the radio and let the music play quietly in the background to keep her company while she contemplated. Everything could not have gone further from what she had planned. She had been grateful to leave London for a few days and get away from her growing problems with him and yet, the paradox was that somehow, she had managed to spend such a large and disproportionate amount of her time in his company, anyway.

It was an odd feeling having him seated so close beside her in the confines of her car. She could smell his cologne and she could hear a faint snore as he slept. The tranquillity reminded her of their youth.

He had always been calm and meditative and often kept himself to himself even though he always seemed to be glad of her company. When they were together he would laugh and joke as any normal boy but he never threw caution to the wind, never did anything on impulse - not Richard. Everything he did was cool and measured. Looking back at it now, Natascha couldn't remember a time when she had ever seen him lose his patience or become angry. Now, he seemed to be nothing but angry all the time. He was so much fun when they were youngsters even with his reserved nature but as he got older it was possible that the underlying introversion that was always part of him had caused him to become more reserved and untrusting. She was always ready to seek out the best in people but with Richard, she could only guess at what his good traits may be, so well did he keep everything about himself hidden. He had changed so much. Not only had she been unable to recognise him as she stood face to face with him on that day at her mother's, but right now, she didn't recognise any of him as being Richard at all. Natascha had once thought she knew everything about him but now realised she knew absolutely nothing. And yet, in the past few weeks, he had become the sole reason why her life was so altered. Her unstinting rationale and solid determination were central to the way she led her life. But the unpredictable blend of despair, irritation and animosity had become a stubborn obstacle. Her strength of mind had helped her to circumvent such useless emotions for years; these feelings had not been part of her life for a long time, not since - well, not since Laurent. Abruptly she put on the mental brakes. Laurent was a part of her life she did not wish to revisit - ever.

The traffic on the motorway started to slow and become heavier before it came to a complete stop displaying a line of lorries and cars neatly lined up. She engaged the handbrake, slipped the gear into neutral and took her foot off the brake. The scene in front of her presaged a long wait. She reached for the volume button on the radio and turned it up a little as she tried to find a traffic news station and tuned in as the announcer advised motorists to avoid that section of the M40 as an incident involving two lorries was causing a six mile traffic queue.

"Oh, great!" Natascha moaned, louder than she had intended and saw Richard straighten in his seat. "Sorry. I didn't mean to wake you." She raised her arm and introduced him to the stationary vehicles. "It looks like we're going to be here for quite some time."

Richard stared out of the window and turned to look back at her, eyes glazed with confusion and looking a little lost. "Have I been asleep long?"

"You were awake for the first fifteen minutes or so and since then you've been drifting in and out. You could not have travelled by train alone."

Richard appeared to be a little self-conscious but any embarrassment was undetectable in his voice. "Sorry. I was hoping I would be able to stay awake. Falling asleep in front of strangers is not always a good look."

His words caused her to take a quick and sharp breath. "Don't be sorry," Natascha said, "it's fine. And I'm not a stranger - not really," she added with more sincerity than perhaps he would have wanted to hear. Richard had nothing to say. The word 'stranger' hung in the air and a nerve deep inside Natascha was touched by a kind of sadness; Richard saw them as strangers. His silence seemed to confirm how little value he put on the years they spent together. Natascha did not see them as strangers. She saw them as two individuals, once close but who now no longer shared any common ground. She had become a strong and confident woman and he had become moody and cold thus resulting in the absence of any further interaction between them. His lack of any discussion on the point was confirmation that it was finally settled between them. And she was glad, glad to know that she didn't need to question the relationship anymore. It was time to move on.

Leaving behind the poignancy of those few words, Natascha switched the course of the conversation. "You'll need to be a little more specific as to whereabouts in Hertfordshire you live." Broaching the subject of where he lived immediately reminded her of the night she had taken Simon home and how they had met on the High Road outside the cash machine. He had told her that he was on his way home. He never knew that they stood arguing not twenty minutes away from where she lived. The grim memory of how coarse and aggressive he had been towards her still left a bitter aftertaste she could not fully swallow. But it really didn't matter anymore, so she let it wash over her.

"I live in a small village called Essendon. It's about forty-five minutes from Winchmore Hill. I sometimes pass Winchmore Hill on my way home, depending on which direction I'm travelling from. I'm surprised we've never bumped into each other..." A marked pause followed. He knew that it wasn't true. They had, indeed, bumped into each and he too, remembered the vicious exchange of words that had taken place. He closed his eyes when he realised what he had said.

"We did bump into each other, one night, on the High Road," Natascha said, keeping her tone light, as if nothing remarkable had happened. "If you had not met me at my mother's birthday, you would never have recognised me, anyway," Natascha added, preferring to ignore the details of the verbal battle that night.

He opened his eyes and turned to her, looking steadily into her face. "I would have. You've changed, but not that much," he countered smoothly, his voice quiet but effective.

Natascha, taken aback by his reply, stared at him and thought back to his reaction to seeing her when they met outside her parents' house. "You didn't look as though you recognised me."

"I recognised you straightaway." He paused. "It was you who didn't recognise me."

There was no way she could dispute that, recalling how she had scrutinised his face for too long without knowing who he was until he was introduced to her by her mother and even then it hadn't at once been apparent.

Natascha was confused. Moments ago he had referred to her as being a stranger and now, by admitting he would have recognised her he had contradicted himself. He was making no sense.

The traffic started to crawl forward. Natascha turned to face the road and tried to decide whether she should ask him to clarify once and for all exactly where they stood; it was so frustrating. Brake lights lit up like the Las Vegas strip in front of her as the traffic halted for the second time. She was tired of skipping around the issue. She was not used to tip-toeing around a difficult subject and so seized the moment. "Are you glad we met again?"

He hesitated. "I am."

"We're not strangers then, are we? Strangers don't meet 'again'," Natascha stated without confrontation. It was a straightforward statement.

When Richard did not answer, she felt she had taken the upper hand and began to feel even more in control. She was getting used to him continuously dumbfounding her from all angles. They both turned to face the road ahead as silence fell once more and when she glanced back at him, she found him to be asleep again.

Chapter Seventeen

Natascha had been on the grey and vapid motorway for what seemed like hours and hours and had been sitting in the driver's seat for even longer. What with the traffic jam, it had taken an age to reach the junction for the M25. She needed a break. So, before getting onto the M25, she took the preceding exit that would take them to a local town where she could find somewhere to stop for a rest. She also wanted to check the map to have a visual sense of the route to Essendon before putting the details into her Sat Nav. She parked outside a small coffee shop and reached behind her for the map that was sitting on the back seat. The action brought her face close to Richard's sleeping face and suddenly her heart skipped the next beat. She quickly picked up the map, breathed deeply and continued to study the roads before inputting Essendon into the useful extra of her car. When Richard next woke up she would ask him for more specific details of his address. All the while, he still slept. He looked so peaceful. It was easier when he was asleep, no uncomfortable vibes to put up with; no awkwardness as they sat in silence in the ungenerous amount of space. It afforded her time to think clearly and sensibly.

As she turned to pick up her handbag, he opened his eyes.

"Ah, you're awake. I was about to ask you if you needed anything," she white-lied. She would have bought him a bottle of water, anyway, but she didn't actually want to wake him. "I'm going to get some coffee."

He stared at her blankly. "Um, yes... some water, er please." He looked around him, "Where are we?"

"I took a slight detour. I need to stretch my legs a little."

"Oh..., oh..., okay," he said, while still trying to find his bearings. "God, I should be sharing the driving," Natascha heard him mumble to himself, "What a useless idiot."

Natascha did feel a bit sorry for him. This situation of having to be chauffeured home by someone he didn't particular want to be in the company of must be like a living nightmare to him, she thought, trying not to feel too pleased at his discomfort. She opened her door. "We could sit inside if you're up to it? I should think you're in need of a change of scenery, too."

They sat at a small round table in the bright little café.

"I've checked the map and it looks as though I should leave the motorway at the Potters Bar junction, is that right?" Natascha asked.

"Yes, that's right."

"But from there, you'll have to give me directions."

Richard hesitated slightly. "I don't expect you to take me to my front door."

"Well, unless you have any strong objections, I really don't mind. And it is getting quite late," Natascha said. If Richard wanted to keep the exact details of his address private, it was too late.

"I don't want to take you too far out of your way."

"Well, to be honest, Richard, we've been driving now for hours and it's still another hour to Potters Bar. I've estimated that from there Essendon can't be more than ten or fifteen minutes away. In the scheme of things…"

Richard looked rather sheepish. "Yes, I'm sorry. It sounds a bit stupid you now dropping me off at a bus stop." He stopped and added with a whisper of reluctance, "I'd appreciate you taking me home. Thank you."

Natascha ignored the pause. "You're welcome."

They were back on the motorway in twenty minutes and during this second leg of the journey there was an unexpected but gradual ease in the atmosphere and a near comfortable calm.

"It's a very small part of the world," Richard pointed out suddenly, for no apparent reason.

Natascha, for once, was oddly glad to hear Richard's voice which was a distraction from the monotony of motorway driving. "Essendon?"

"Yes. It's all right there but I'm thinking of moving to somewhere a little further out. I still feel too close to London."

Natascha was very surprised at how forthcoming he was without being cajoled in any way. "I understand. I love living where I do but I miss the vastness of the Oxfordshire countryside."

"It was great growing up there. It felt so free," he continued. It was probably just a throwaway comment but it sounded very odd and very profound coming from Richard.

"That's the beauty of youth. You don't need to know anything about anywhere as long as you're happy with where you are," Natascha said. She fleetingly wondered whether his thoughts of moving were a recent concern when he learnt of the relatively short distance between their two lives. In spite of the whole world being at their disposal, they had managed to live not much more than ten miles from each other without ever knowing it.

"How long have you lived there?" she enquired further.

"About four years. Before that I didn't stay anywhere for any longer than eighteen months. As long as my business was secure, it didn't matter to me where I lived. If I could get to work and back, I didn't really care."

It was a strange attitude to have about your home. However, Richard's way of thinking seemed to suit his personality. Natascha kept these thoughts to herself. "That sounds interesting, in a nomadic sort of way."

"It's not interesting at all. It was just the way it'd become," he said, short and sweetly.

"I see," Natascha said, getting the impression that Richard was not going to elaborate.

Then, and without any inducement, he began to explain random facts about the history of the large county of Hertfordshire, from the Roman Conquest to the industrial revolution and Natascha watched him as very slowly he began to transform into the Richard with whom she used to spend so much of her time. He could relay all the details, dates, names and origins. He knew it all. She had once considered him to be some kind of human encyclopaedia, committing to memory all kinds of obscure pieces of information and in that respect, he hadn't changed. When children needed answers to questions, they would ask their parents. In Natascha's case, anything she needed to know, she would ask Richard. She now could see why she used to hang on to his every word when he spoke, with that quiet authority. Another scene from the past entered her head. She remembered one afternoon on their way home from school, she had yet another question…

"Richard, why do the stars twinkle?"

"They don't really twinkle. It's only because the light from them has to get through the air in the atmosphere. The air is quite thick in some places and when the light hits a thick area, it bounces to an area where the air is thinner and because it keeps doing that over and over, it looks like the star is twinkling."

"Oh."

"That's how the stars in the sky twinkle. That doesn't explain why your eyes do, though!"…

She remembered laughing at his comment at the time but thinking about it now, it struck her as being an odd thing for someone like Richard to have said and for some reason, she did not want to recall any more of that afternoon.

Chapter Eighteen

They had left the motorway and were on the way to his house. "You need to take the next left and then left again."

The left turn took them into a narrow lane and the next led them along a long gravel driveway at the end of which stood a large Georgian style house. What appeared to be old-fashioned gas-lamps, illuminated the drive. There were no other houses around so Natascha could only assume that this was his home. It looked so grand.

She knew his company had done well, he had told her so himself, but he hadn't indicated exactly how well it had done. "Is this your house?"

"Yes...yes, it is." Where most people would parade their pride at being owners of such a property, Richard's modest reply showed no sign of it.

Natascha got out of the car and gazed at the fine-looking house with its careful symmetry and elegant façade. She appreciated the uncluttered appearance of a Georgian house and had always been especially enamoured with the tall sash windows and large panelled doors.

"You did tell me your company had done well, but I didn't realise it had done quite so well."

"The house was in a bad state when I saw it and was able to buy it at a reasonable price. The inside had to be completely gutted and restored."

There was no such thing as a 'reasonable price' when it came to this type of property, no matter what the condition of it, Natascha knew. However, the architectural epoch of the house piqued her interest and she spoke freely, in awe of the building. "Well, it's stunning. Georgian architects found a way of building such simple yet subtly grand houses. Houses built today have absolutely no character." She continued to gaze at the house. "I personally find Georgian styled houses the most beautiful."

All around her and against the now night sky, dark Hertfordshire hills framed Richard's home and in the dusky surroundings, acres of barren fields swept about it. She closed her eyes and inhaled the perfume of the cold, damp earth and the smell of nature.

"Come in," he said blandly as he turned and walked ahead in front of her.

So enraptured was Natascha she did not think twice about going inside. Nor did she pay any special attention when he appeared to be distancing himself from her again. She followed him into the house.

Inside, the hall was large with a grand sweeping staircase that ran along one side of the vast area. There were mirrors, paintings and plants and the original waxed parquet flooring. However, Richard's rather eclectic taste in art caught Natascha's attention the most. An abstract painting of bold lines and deep coloured squares, the artist of which was unknown to Natascha, was hung beside a print of Renoir's rich impressionistic *Bal du moulin de la Galette*. Below that was a charcoal sketch of a nude woman and beside her was an Edward Hopper watercolour. They were all very beautiful in their own right. However, housed in such close proximity to each other, the rather unbalanced look unearthed a hidden vulnerability in Richard's character that was slightly mystifying to her.

Richard placed his bags on the floor and showed Natascha into the spacious lounge with its high ceiling and large windows. The usual wood panelling for this type of house had been replaced by pale Wedgewood blue walls but the cornices had been restored and still retained their intricate carvings. The flooring was again polished floorboards with delicate inlaid wood tile detailing around the edge. A beautiful white marble fireplace was the focal point together with a magnificent ivory black grand piano in one corner. Natascha was very impressed. There was something missing however, and it didn't take her long to realise that not a single trace of Christmas cheer decorated the house; not a single bauble or Christmas card. At this time of the year where everywhere was warm with colour the room seemed stark and sad.

"Make yourself comfortable and I'll get you something to drink. I can't offer you much by way of something to eat. I didn't bother to get much in since I wasn't going to be here, but you're welcome to anything that's edible," Richard explained, matter-of-factly.

"Thank you, just tea would be nice. I'll have that and then be on my way. I can't be very far from home and I should get there well within the hour."

Richard left her, leaving behind him a roomful of gelid air, cooled by the change in his mood. For reasons unknown, the small degree of zest he had shown in the car had died away and again, was inexplicably replaced with a detachment from her which he obviously felt needed no disguise. But Natascha was tired and just needed some time to relax her muscles which had become stiff from sitting in one position for so long, and to work up the energy to go home. It had been a gruelling journey so far. After having had part of the motorway closed off by the police and the surrounding roads gridlocked by the sheer volume of cars and lorries trying to find alternative routes, it had taken over four and a half hours to get here. She settled back into the sumptuous armchair, taking in her luxurious surroundings and closed her eyes for a moment.

"Natascha? Natascha." She heard her name being whispered from somewhere far away and opening her eyes she realised she must have dozed off. She took the cup Richard held in front of her.

"I was only meant to rest my eyes for a moment."

"I think you've done enough driving for the day. You might be less than an hour from your home but you're not in any fit state to drive. You're exhausted. Stay here for the night. I have plenty of room. Leave in the morning when you've had a decent rest."

Asking her to stay was sensible and logical and Natascha was genuinely grateful. But the delivery of the invitation was far less than inviting. It was made so coldly that it was on the tip of her tongue to decline. But Richard was right. The thought of now getting back behind the driver's wheel filled her with dread. Driving while being this tired would be unwise and not to accept his offer would be churlish.

"Maybe if I could just stay for a couple of hours, I'll be fine. Thank you. I'll go and get my things."

Once outside she needed to hone her thoughts. Richard's transformation was as severe as *Jekyll and Hyde*. His words were short and sharp again; the near uninhibited state he had shown only an hour ago had gone and she had no idea what had changed so abruptly. Feeling obliged to ask her to stay the night under his roof may be the reason for it, perhaps? It must have proved tormenting for the man who liked to keep his private life so well concealed. Whatever it was, he had grown very prickly very quickly and Natascha was too tired to even attempt to decipher what had gone wrong. She had little option but to stay for a while, but had no desire to spend a moment longer here than was necessary. As soon as she was rested enough she would leave this place and allow the owner to wallow in his own bad temper. However, she had to take more care, she warned herself. Towards the end of the journey she had gradually begun to feel dangerously at ease with him. She had thoughtlessly been mixing the past with the present in her mind, finding herself grateful to hear him chat as he used to when they were young. She had, for a brief period, recognised Richard, the friend that she had loved back then, relaying interesting facts and figures just as he had always done. This had caused the carefully constructed invisible fence she had built around her to keep Richard away at a safe distance, to begin to slip. She would rectify that now. Her mental defences had to be put firmly back in place and her cool, strong-will restored. Recovering her bags, she inhaled a lungful of cold air and headed back towards the house.

As she stepped into the hallway, Richard was standing at the foot of the stairs. "I'll show you to your room," he said, austerely.

Standing tall, she brushed off the absurd show of disdain towards her and followed him up the stairs.

The first floor led onto a sizeable galleried landing from which a narrow hallway led away to the back of the house. It was plainer than the hall downstairs, sparsely furnished with a Queen Anne style chair nestled in one corner and a long side table set between two of the five or six doors that lined the walls. The whole floor was covered in thick cream carpeting. The open space felt rich and warm, in direct contrast to the master of the house. Natascha followed Richard as he escorted her down the hallway to the furthermost room and gallantly opened the door before her. She assumed his room was behind the last door at the opposite end of the landing.

"I think you'll be all right in here. There's a private bathroom where you should find everything you need but let me know if there's something missing. Goodnight," he said, quickly.

Natascha thanked him as he walked away and closed the door behind her. Inside, the room was spacious and plush. There was even enough room for a decent-sized coffee table and a small leather sofa over by the window. The large ensuite bathroom was clean-lined, bright and modern with large white tiles, white suite and natural coloured stone. The shower that stood in the corner was large enough to allow three people to shower simultaneously and an abundance of green leafy Boston ferns draped from glass shelving. In fact, of what she had seen of the house so far, it was very well-kept and stylish, not always usual for a man living on his own - unless of course, he did not live alone. He was aware of her marital status since she still went by her maiden name and this was generally a good indicator... 'Stop it!' she thought and reproached herself for even contemplating his personal circumstances. All she needed was to make herself as comfortable as she could, rest her weary body and escape this place for her own, comparably tiny home. She would then be out of his personal and oppressively secretive life for good.

She took a warm shower to alleviate the exhaustion and leave her sleepy. And after having carefully folded her clothes and hanging them on the back of a chair, she slipped on a robe and lay on the roomy bed.

Although her eyelids were heavy, she had spent the best part of two hours restlessly tossing and turning, unable to sleep. There were so many unwanted thoughts in her mind which she could not control. They whirled around and around keeping her awake and after trying to clear her head without success she sat up. She would go and get herself something to drink. Tying the belt of her robe around her, she left her room and cautiously made her way down the stairs in the dark, tiptoeing around and quietly opening doors until she found the kitchen. Soundlessly, she prepared herself a hot drink and stood by the window sipping the satisfying warmth of it.

The moonlight illuminated the kitchen. And peering out into the darkness her eyes gradually grew accustomed to the surrounding fields and trees that were silhouetted against the cloudless night sky, displaying a bleak and wintry beauty. In the midst of winter, it seemed nature was waiting for spring when it could awake from its months of slumber and boast new life...

The sound of a 'click' startled Natascha out of her poetic reverie. A light was switched on. It was a single diffused beam of light that subtly lit up the area in which she was standing. Richard stood in the doorway.

"I heard a noise."

"Oh, I'm sorry if I woke you but I was thirsty. I was admiring the view of your garden in the moonlight," she added, a little tongue in cheek, as he came over and filled a glass with water. He glared at her but said nothing and quickly finished his drink in one gulp just as Natascha finished her tea. They placed the empty glass and the empty cup on the side, but as they did so, his hand unintentionally touched hers. Instantly, he drew it away as if he had just made contact with a boiling kettle. Richard's reaction was no surprise. To have her under his roof must be vexing enough for him. But to have any kind of physical contact? Well, that would be more than he could bear, surely! He had behaved exactly how she had expected. Inwardly, Natascha was pleased to see him so uneasy with the arrangement.

"I'll say goodnight, then," he said, as he turned away and strode decisively out of the kitchen keeping his eyes on anything but Natascha, obviously troubled.

So that she would avoid having to fumble her way in the darkness again, Natascha quickly left the room and stayed close behind him as he led the way up the stairs. Never had she experienced a tension in the air so acute that it could quite easily be sliced with a blunt knife. The screaming silence was stifling and the growing pressure between them felt as though it could rupture at any moment. The need to be safely within her four walls was rapidly increasing. She reached the top of the stairs but accidentally, tripped on the last step and lurched forward, falling into the back of him. As fast as lightning he spun around, reached out and grabbed her to prevent her from falling. She regained her balance as he took her hand and pulled her away from the top of the stairs.

"Are you all right?"

"Yes... yes, I'm fine."

He stared at her and she could see his eyes become hard with an unrecognisable look. Suddenly there was quietness and the air was loaded with a heavy sense of unease as time seemed to grind to a halt. Natascha steeled herself against the impending ice-cold remark or sarcastic comment that only Richard could unleash on her. But then something strange began to happen. This should have been the moment when he released her from his grasp - but he did not. 'This is outrageous!' her head screamed. Then again, it should have been her obvious reaction to pull her hand from his - but she did not. Natascha, not knowing what was happening, quickly looked away and did not dare lift her eyes again to see his face, too embarrassed by the inexplicable naturalness to leave her hand in the daring, yet safety of his. Richard said nothing. Instead, he slowly raised a hand and hesitantly placed it under her chin, tilting her face towards him, forcing her to look at him. The expression in his eyes had changed but Natascha still did not understand what they were saying. Eyes locked, confusion was written on their faces. The strong magnetism was overpowering, imprisoning her in his presence. It was so strong she was unable to move away. He made no attempt to flee as he had done minutes before but began to caress the skin of her hand beneath his fingers until an invisible thread intertwined them with hers. Gently, he began to trace the lines of her face, brushing across the fullness of her lips with unsure fingers. Natascha began to shiver, even as the icy tension that had played such an imposing role moments ago gradually started to melt away. It was replaced by a soft, cloudy and terrifying warmth. 'Leave now!' she shouted to herself in her head. No response.

The moonlight that radiated through a window shone on him and the intense emotion reflected in his eyes was becoming too much for her. She had to look away but it was impossible. His eyes did not leave her - couldn't leave her, as if absorbing every detail of her face. The strong magnetising force was pulling them closer and closer together and Natascha didn't know how to stop it. He was feeling it, too - she knew it; frightened and reluctant, wanting the moment to end but powerless to do anything about it. Natascha was still shivering as he gently buried his fingers into her hair. She began to feel a persistent ache for him, yet she found herself unable to react. The wall she had erected stood firm, her mind was clear and she wanted to stay in control. But it was a battle she was going to lose. Her body continued to tremble and the reasoning between right and wrong started to blur. She was paralysed. Against all the mental obstacles she had put before her, the clarity in her mind steadily began to soften and the wall around her started to crumble as she moved in closer still. The moment was incredibly surreal. Richard lowered his head until his mouth was close to hers.

"I have wanted to hold you from the very first moment I saw you," he said, quietly. The words tumbled out like a dam that had buckled under pressure.

What was happening? Night had turned to day, black to white. She closed her eyes and almost gasped in astonishment when she recognised that it was what she had wanted, too. All the anguish she had suffered in the weeks leading up to this moment was her way of denying how much he really meant to her. She was still so confused. What was she doing? Why was she letting this happen? The didactic voice in her head was trying to make one last attempt at keeping her from making a decision, the consequences of which, she could never take back. She was Natascha Hamilton who did not allow any man to make her feel as defenceless as the way she felt right now. But she couldn't stop it; it felt good to, at last, have this person whom she had been missing so much without realising it, back in her life. She felt safe and warm with him, the same sense of security she used to feel with him when she was just a girl. This was what she had been craving all this time. This was where she wanted to be. It was a strange feeling, as though after walking for an eternity, she had finally come home. When she was young all she had wanted was his friendship. Now, standing so close, all she wanted was him. She pressed her body into his. His lips hovered temptingly close to hers; the feel of his breath was warming her face. For so long now, she had been pushing him away when all the time she only really wanted to be with him. Their mouths were now too close not to touch and as his mouth covered hers she shuddered at the sensation. He gently grazed her lips with his. But the moment his tongue pushed through and entered her mouth, something clasped the bottom of her stomach like a vice. A groan of pleasure and fear bubbled in her throat as her tongue tasted the warm silkiness of his. This feeling of an intimacy they had never before shared shocked them both and the unchartered waters they were now stepping into was so daunting. Yet it felt so right.

They pulled away from each other, their mouths still teasingly close. The same look of confusion was still written in their eyes. There were questions that had unclear answers and there was that line; the line which neither could decide could or should ever be crossed. Richard's sultry and smouldering eyes looked deep into hers.

"I love you. I think I've always loved you," he whispered.

Natascha was stunned by his declaration. "Why are you saying that? Do you know what you're saying?" she asked breathlessly, her heart beating wildly in her chest.

"Yes, I do. I know exactly what I'm saying."

She took a moment to try and digest his reply, dazed by what he'd said. "Maybe you're confusing it with what we had. We did love each other, Richard, the way close friends do and we were so very, very close."

"No, that's not true. You always meant more than just a friend to me. I wanted to be with you every minute of the day. I hated the times when we weren't together. I know we were young and my feelings were inexperienced; maybe I didn't even know it at the time but I think I was always in love with you."

"We were too young to know about love, Richard."

Natascha said this although she, herself, couldn't be sure that she too, hadn't felt the same. In her girlish ways, maybe she had loved him more than a friend, too. She tried to unravel the unsettling thoughts in her head but they would not untangle. He rested the side of his face against her hair and his fingers massaged the nape of her neck. She closed her eyes and a picture in her mind saw a young Richard walking a little ahead of her as the two of them went for a stroll in the hills one afternoon after it had been raining, their shoes wet and covered in mud...

He jumped over a large puddle.

"I don't think I can get across this one, Richard."

He turned back, "Here, give me your hand."

She placed her hand in his and jumped using his strength to help her but once she was across, his hand never left hers and she didn't feel the need to let it go. They continued to walk across the hills hand in hand...

Natascha couldn't remember ever feeling that there was anything unusual or improper about it. It had felt so natural, just as it was beginning to feel right now.

Natascha opened her eyes and gazed up at him. "What we had was very green, very innocent and very tender."

He searched her eyes. "Maybe what was once green, innocent and tender has changed, is different now, it's something more special," he said, with a sincerity that melted her inside. "We shared such an incredible connection. Didn't you ever feel it, too?"

"I... I don't know. Yes... maybe... I don't know..."

He slowly began to step back and held her hand to draw her towards him and as she diffidently followed, he turned around and still clasping her hand, led her to his bedroom, both finally deciding that the line between friends and lovers had to be crossed.

They stood facing each other in a shaft of moonlight and in his eyes she saw an indescribable richness and tenderness. He untied the loose knot of her robe and gently pulled it from her shoulders where it fell to the floor. He slid his fingers under the thin straps of her nightdress and skimming them over the skin of her shoulders, let it too, slip easily and silently down her body. He picked her up in his arms and laid her on his bed, stretching himself beside her, tenderly smoothing away a tendril of her hair that had strayed across her face.

His fingers began to follow every contour of her body from the nape of her neck and down her throat, between her breasts to the flatness of her stomach and the curve of her tiny waist. And where his fingers trailed his lips followed. His warm tongue delicately caressed the silkiness of her skin. His hand massaged the roundness of her breast and he moved his lips to where he could draw the soft flesh into his mouth and sweep his tongue over the aroused nipple. Natascha felt a searing heat emanating from her centre, flowing through her like lava. He kissed her face and she saw in his eyes an intense passion, scorching her like fire. She began to tremble as he tasted every inch of her. It ignited something deep inside that was uncontrollable, a feeling that had lain dormant in her for so long. Natascha pulled his t-shirt up over his head to reveal his strong upper body and raised her head to kiss the smooth skin of his chest. Her hands slid over his wide, strong shoulders and down his firm muscular arms. Every inch of him was lean, taut and powerful. She held his face between her hands. She wanted to know every feature.

"Your injuries must still be sore. I don't want to hurt you," Natascha said, quietly.

Richard's eyes held hers and he spoke with calm conviction. "Natascha, I have never felt so alive in my life. You seem to flow through me and inside me. And I know you're going to heal me. You're everything I need. I don't feel any pain when I'm with you... none. " His voice was deep, sincere and reassuring.

She drew her fingertips across his forehead before pulling him towards her. She put her lips to his wounds and carefully and lovingly kissed them. Her fingers stroked the lines of his jaw. Her thumbs slowly moved over his closed eyelids and strayed across the striking outline of his high cheekbones that were softened only by his beautiful eyes. His lips were so very sensual. His hair slipped through her fingers as she ran her hand through the sleekness of it. They stared into each other's eyes and both could see the burning flames in the other.

His mouth came down on hers, no longer gentle and tender, but with impatience. He was lost in a lustful delirium. She wrapped her tongue around the probing excitement of his; her need to be part of him was consuming her. He kissed her long and hard. Their skin glided against one another, hot and silky and it felt good. His hands moved freely over her body with a desperate need to touch her, to feel her and to have her. And as he pressed hard against her the fire that raged within every cell of her body flared with a breath-taking intensity and she knew she could no longer hold back. The initial doubts that had played so harrowingly on her mind were now gone - far, far away. He reached inside her, dismissing every spare inch of space between them and as she raised herself to meet him they both began to drown in an unrelenting tide of blistering passion, an insatiable hunger, melting away any last traces of fear. The wave was too strong. It carried them together towards the centre of that turbulent ocean and when they reached it, they clung to each other, bodies shaking, as though it was the only thing they could do to stay alive. Richard buried his face in her hair and breathlessly inhaled the light, citrusy scent of her perfume.

"You are so beautiful. I love you. I always have," he murmured, simply.

And with Natascha cradled in Richard's arms and the moonlight shining peacefully upon them, they both fell asleep, reconciled and happy.

Chapter Nineteen

Natascha awoke to the daylight that squeezed through the drawn curtains where the moonlight had streamed in the night before. She was lying on her side, staring at the sliver of sunlight. For a moment she was disorientated but as the tiles in her mind quickly fell into place, so did the memories of last night. Had she not felt the weight of Richard's body behind her, she would have described the pictures in her head as the most extreme dream she had ever dreamt. But it was not a dream. What they had shared last night seemed to be the ripening of what they had shared when they were young, a rare closeness that had always been there and despite all outward appearances and senseless interaction between them, it had survived, all these years later. Still dozing in the outer reaches of sleep she felt him shimmy towards her and tuck himself behind her, moulding his body against hers, nuzzling his face in her hair. She could feel the gentle rise and fall of his chest on her back which told her that he was still not yet fully awake. Here lay a man, complex and distant but inside, Natascha had finally witnessed a simplicity that tempered his stormy character. She closed her eyes and an involuntary smile crept onto her lips. A feeling of calm, relief and satisfaction enveloped her and she too, began to slip into semi-consciousness.

Suddenly, she felt him spring back from her. Her eyes shot open. She quickly turned to face him.

"What's wrong? Is something wrong?"

At first, he seemed to be a little bewildered but what Natascha then saw in his eyes shook her to her soul. She had expected to see a warmth, a tenderness even, perhaps a small hint of the love he had professed to her last night, for until right now, she felt a happiness in her heart that only stemmed from the inklings of love. Instead, his face reflected a sort of fear and maybe a look of horror. But by far, the cruellest and loudest word expressed in his eyes was pure and undiluted regret. Oh God, he regretted last night. Natascha suddenly felt foolish and embarrassed. She pulled the sheet around her, pushed back her dishevelled hair from her face and stood up, picking up her robe which lay exactly where it was left the night before.

"I'm going to shower and then I'll gather my things," she said hastily and fled from his room.

She stood under the hot shower and desperately tried to unscramble the crazed thoughts that were clashing against each other. Nothing was making any sense. Last night had been so wonderful and unimaginably special. The fervent emotions, the passion and his words were beyond description. This morning he looked sickened at the very sight of her and wanted nothing more but to have her out of his bed. Had she suddenly become that repulsive to him? Was she so insignificant that he was able to play with her feelings in such a cold-hearted way? And could he have been as callous as to have used her for his own self-gratification and be so brutal as to toss her away once she had served her purpose? Who was this man? What was this man? A few hours ago Natascha thought she had found in Richard everything she had been searching such a long time for. And now she realised that she had been nothing but a cheap pawn in that same man's evil game. She felt stupid and ashamed and she couldn't get out of his house fast enough.

Minutes later, Natascha was downstairs with her bags ready to leave when Richard appeared. "I'm going now," she said coldly, as she headed for the door without so much as a glance in his direction. He couldn't see the conflicting fusion of anger and embarrassment on her face.

"Don't you want some breakfast before you leave?" Richard said, quickly.

Natascha turned around slowly and faced him. "I beg your pardon?" she said, as coolly as she could. "Do you mean to say that after opening your eyes and staring at me with such loathing this morning, you are actually now offering me a cup of tea?" Her external calm was already beginning to feel a lot less stable as she tried hard to rein in her emotions. "What's the matter with you? Do you consider that normal behaviour?"

"I'm sorry. I didn't mean to make you feel uncomfortable. I'm sorry if I did." At first Richard sounded hesitant and a little unsure but then he straightened up, lifted his chin and added more height to his already tall figure. "Perhaps there has been some sort of misunderstanding."

The volume of Natascha's voice rose as the patience in her tone diminished. "What is there to misunderstand? Last night you were telling me that you loved me and this morning you were so appalled by the sight of me you couldn't even speak. What is there to misunderstand, Richard? Which part of it have I got wrong?"

Unexpectedly, Richard's tone softened. "Please don't, Natascha. I'm sorry if I gave you the wrong impression. I've got so much to be thankful to you for. You've done so much for me, I couldn't possibly..."

"Now I've heard it all," she interrupted abruptly, with a sarcastic smile. "You're telling me that you thought that by letting me have the privilege of sharing your bed, you would be adequately recompensing me for all my trouble? What kind of a depraved monster are you?" Natascha shouted, now unable to hold back her anger.

"No... no, Natascha, that's not what I was going to say..." Richard said, with an uncharacteristic suggestion of desperation.

"I can't believe I let you seduce me, let you whisper those ridiculous words 'I love you' to me and actually start to let myself think that perhaps things were going to be back to the way they were all those years ago - to be better than they were. I can't believe that I actually fell for your puerile pick-up line." Natascha's voice had now risen to the point where she was virtually screaming at him. She was so full of shame and anger. "You practically ignored me from day one and left me with the absolute conclusion of you being a very cold, unapproachable and conceited man. You were rude to me on so many occasions I knew then that I didn't want to have anything to do with you. You're not even a shadow of that warm human being you once were and I wasted all those years worshipping the ground you walked on. God, how stupid do I feel now? What happened to you? What have I done to you to deserve this? I never imagined that I could ever say this about anyone but," Natascha's voice quietened to a low, abrasive whisper, "I hate you Richard French. You disgust me. You're a vile and sick man and I'm going to do everything in my power to make sure that I never need suffer the misery of having to meet you ever again. Do you understand? Never!" As she was speaking, she started to shake and the tears that were threatening to fall sounded thick in her voice. But before she could give him the satisfaction of seeing even one tear roll down her face, she turned and ran out of the house. She flung her luggage into the back of her car, threw herself in the driver's seat and slamming the door shut, moved off at an incredible speed, her tyres screeching on the gravel on her way out. She could see Richard run out of the house behind her but she was not going to wait for him to utter a single word.

As she got to the end of the long driveway, she stopped the car and thrust her face in her hands. Tears were streaming down her face in torrents. She felt stupid, dirty and fallible and everything was so much worse because it was her own fault. She had let it happen, had allowed herself to fall prey to his maliciousness and wanton lack of any common decency. She had let her heart believe, even when her head had told her otherwise, that she should give him a second chance. She had also indulged herself into believing that perhaps his words of love were true. How could they ever possibly have been true when he had always gone out of his way to be bad-mannered and insulting towards her? She only had herself to blame. She had given in so easily. When had she become so trusting and naïve? His behaviour had been atrocious towards her at nearly every encounter and yet she had decided to forget all about that in the blink of an eye. Natascha was appalled with herself and miserable to the core. She brushed away the tears from her face and inhaled deeply to try and allay the sobs. And with her confidence in pieces, her dignity in tatters and her heart shattered, she gripped the steering wheel and made her way home, the hurt inside crushing her.

***

What an idiot! What a bloody idiot! Richard said to himself as he stared after the car roaring down his driveway in a cloud of dust. What the hell had possessed him to do what he did? At the beginning of the evening, he wished he hadn't had to invite her to stay but by the end of it they were making such wondrous love that he felt he had been floating in paradise. When Natascha had looked at him last night with her dark blue eyes that had become like pools of crystal in the moonlight, he had been instantly hypnotised; an emotion in him had been awakened after a very long time. It would have taken nothing less than a crowbar to prise her out of his arms last night. But he should never have let it happen.

But it wasn't all his fault, was it? No-one could accuse him of forcing her into doing anything she didn't want to; she was a consenting adult. She could have happily slapped his face if she was at all repulsed by his actions. All that unnecessary bravado she put on made him mad. She riled him and intrigued him at the same time and there was something about her that made him become some other person, some another man he didn't recognise... Admittedly, he wasn't much good with women but to have one racing out of his house on the verge of tears? Well, that was something of a massive blow to his male ego.

When the car had disappeared into the distance Richard marched back into the house still trying hard to justify his behaviour by that of hers; her expert cunning, the attempted look of innocence. She had provoked him and he was only a man after all. He went and sat in the armchair in which she had fallen asleep last night and pictured her deliciously silky skin, her exquisite figure and that unbelievably sexy mouth. It had been too much for him to ignore. She'd grown into such a gorgeous woman. He'd never seen a more gorgeous woman - ever.

But then he gave an angry little laugh. Who the hell was he kidding? Stop it! Stop playing these fucking games with yourself! Suddenly he was overwhelmingly furious and disgusted with himself. What's the matter with you? It wasn't the sex. It was never about the sex. He wasn't that type of man nor could he ever be. He should have stopped it but he just didn't want to. He felt sick with self-contempt and knew that he would rather have spent the rest of his life alone than to have done what he had done. He'd given in to feelings he promised he would never give in to again. Beautiful or not, she was Natascha and she was the last woman he would ever want to be intimately involved with. She was now a business acquaintance and that's how he should have kept it but even that looked like it was soon to be a thing of the past, anyway, which, on reflection, Richard decided to be something of a blessing. He didn't deserve her.

After a moment he tried again to feel unaffected by it all. Hey, why was he letting it bother him? She said she no longer wanted anything to do with him and if that's how she felt, so be it! Why should it matter to him? She would get over their one night of passion soon enough. She was a grown-up!

But then the pendulum of his actions and their reasons swung back the other way again. He was still lying to himself. She was right. His face this morning must have shown his disappointment. But how could she have known that it was reflecting the disappointment in himself?

'I'm a fucking idiot!' he said aloud, the harsh, angry words reverberating around the room before fiercely raining down hard on him like sharp pieces of glass. But there was nothing he could do to undo what he had done. As difficult as it would be, he had to somehow, move on. He could never face her again.

But did he really want her to live the rest of her life believing him to be the most insensate bastard who ever walked upon this earth?

His feelings were all over the place.

***

Natascha arrived home. She took in her luggage, closed the door and locked it. This was where she felt unshakably safe. No-one could touch her here, here in the sanctum of her own home. It enveloped her like a warming blanket. No-one could hurt her here.

Lowering herself into her armchair, she tried to steady her breathing and closed her eyes when she could feel the tears prickling again. Her mind was a mass of nothingness. She couldn't think, couldn't plan, couldn't decide. She just felt empty. She sat staring into space, then thought of her parents. She hadn't phoned them yet. Picking up the phone, she dialled the number, cleared her throat and fixed a smile on her face. It would help to keep her side of the conversation casual.

"Hello Dad, how are you? How's Mum? Both recovered after Christmas?"

"*Yes, love. We're both fine. It was nice to have you here. Can't say it wasn't an eventful one this year though, can we?*" Natascha squeezed her eyes tightly shut. Her father would never know quite how eventful it had been. "*Monica and Michael can't stop talking about you and what an angel you are. They can't thank you enough for all you did for them and for Richard. You're certainly on their Christmas card list for next year!*"

Natascha held her head in her hand and cringed. She didn't deserve the accolade, not after what she had just done. She couldn't bear to hear any more about Monica and Michael French or Christmas and certainly not Richard. She frowned slightly to keep the smile on her face and the cheerfulness in her tone. "Mmm... Oh, well, I'm glad everything turned out fine in the end."

"*Are you all right, Tascha? You don't sound yourself.*"

"Oh no, Dad, I'm fine," she said, sitting up in the chair and widening the smile, "just a bit tired that's all. There was an incident on the motorway and it took hours to get home. By the time I dropped Richard off, I was so tired I went straight to bed when I got home. That's why I didn't call yesterday."

"*Oh, that is bad luck, love. I'll tell our French friends that you both got home all right, shall I? Just in case it slips Richard's mind to phone them himself and from the impression I got, he may well not even bother. I have a feeling that all is not too well in that family.*"

"Yes, I got that idea, too. But let them know that Richard's okay, would you, Dad?" Natascha wasn't a bit keen on discussing the French family any longer and quickly added, "Anyway, I just wanted to let you know that I'm home safe and sound. Give Mum my love and I'll see you both sometime in the New Year."

She replaced the receiver with care, glad the conversation had come to a speedy end. She didn't like telling her father these little white lies but certain situations asked for nothing else. This Christmas had been one as no other and all Natascha wanted to do was wrap it all up in thick black paper and lose it from her mind. Failing that, she would have to keep it locked in the secure box in a corner she'd labelled as 'forgettable history'. This practise of extinguishing incidents and experiences from the cognitive areas of her mind was recently becoming much too frequent.

She was exhausted. The whole experience at Richard's house had been a hideous, hideous nightmare. She had already accepted that she was equally as guilty; at no point could she lay the blame exclusively at Richard's door. The balance had shifted even further in his favour. She had totally lost any self-control. She had allowed herself to become so wholly exposed and vulnerable. Over the years she had kept her emotions firmly in check and had been able to remain calm and cool under all circumstances. She was known for her unflustered and unflappable personality and breezed through her life with only herself to look after, never letting any man come close enough to change that. She was very happy with the life she had. But in the space of one night, she had compromised herself and everything she believed in.

Natascha also discovered, to her horror, that for the very first time in years, images of Laurent had begun to figure in her mind. As well as teaching her much about music, Laurent was the man who had taught her a very hard life lesson and she thought she had learnt it perfectly. But when Richard reappeared, she had ignored it all and had yielded to his temptations so easily, convincing herself that all his sickly sweet words would somehow defy logic. From the very first moment they met he had treated her as though she was an enemy. But in one night he had uttered three stupid little words to her and she had believed them to be true. How did she ever consider that to be possible?

Richard had undone it all, years of her blood, sweat and tears after Laurent had left her and she had allowed him to. Natascha could not stop the hurt from falling as tears. She brought her hands up and covered her eyes to try and stem the stream. And as they gradually abated, she promised herself that this would be the last time she ever shed a single tear over the whole affair. He had invaded her life and she let him wreak untold destruction. It was never to happen again. And more importantly, she would do her damnedest to make sure that neither of these nefarious men ever entered her head again.

Chapter Twenty

As was usual, Natascha was the first person to arrive at the office on the first day back after Christmas to work the few days before the New Year's Day Bank Holiday. She wanted to get an early start on whatever work was waiting for her. The day's calendar was already open on her screen: *Gavin - meeting; 1.00pm, Stevenage - to see Alex Charles, CEO of Charles Logistics.* She opened her top drawer and took out the train ticket she had printed off when she had booked his seat on the train in advance. Natascha didn't want to read what was next on the list. It wasn't necessary for her to check the next job on the calendar. The site visit to Brooke Park Hall had to be confirmed. It was one of the potential venues she had approached before Christmas to host Richard's client event and to which Richard had already said he wanted to visit with her. But someone else would have to deal with that now. She would have to tell Gavin that she wasn't able to look after the Sampson and French project after all. With all the terrible problems she was having with another client, the extra work she had agreed to take on would suffer as a result. She shook her head in resignation. How far she had fallen; now forced to make excuses for imaginary shortcomings.

She phoned Gavin as soon as he got in later that morning.

"Good morning, Gavin. Do you have a free moment? I've got your train ticket to Stevenage for your meeting with Alex Charles this afternoon," and trying not to stall she continued, "and I also need to speak with you about something else."

"*You know I've always got time for you. Why don't you come over now? I've got something I want to talk to you about, too.*"

Natascha knocked lightly on Gavin's door.

"Come in." Gavin sat behind his desk and looked up from the mess of paperwork in front of him. "How was your Christmas? Parents okay?"

"Er, yes, they're both really well. Oh, here's the ticket. The train leaves Euston at 12.06pm and should arrive in Stevenage at a quarter to one. Alex Charles' office is five minutes from the station." She handed the ticket over and waited a few seconds. "Gavin, about the Sampson and French project..."

"Ah yes, Sampson and French. That's exactly what I want to talk to you about.

Gavin had caught her by surprise. "Oh?"

"I've had an email from Richard French. He says he wants to cancel. He didn't go into any detail, only asked us to invoice him for the work already done. Do you know anything about this? I'm puzzled. Did something happen between the two of you, some sort of disagreement? It's not like you not to be able to work your magic on your clients, Natascha."

"Um, no, I really don't know why he's changed his mind," Natascha lied. It didn't take much to work out what was going on. Richard had had his fill of her. "I was about to confirm site visit details with him. It was the last thing we spoke about."

"Well, I'm going to phone him to try and find out what's gone wrong and try to convince him not to bail. What did you want to talk about?"

Natascha was ready with her excuse. "I was about to say that I'm going to find it difficult to deal with the extra work with Sampson and French. I'm having real problems with the Salter conference next week. Castle Green Business Centre have double-booked their large conference room and don't have anything else available that can cater for the amount of attendees. I have to find somewhere else and soon." It wasn't a story, it was the truth. The untruth was Natascha telling Gavin that it would be too much for her to deal with both projects simultaneously. But this case was different. She just couldn't see how she could ever face Richard again. Obviously, step one of getting her life back on track was to never see him again. She'd told him she'd have nothing more to do with him and that was exactly what she intended to do.

"Oh, I see," Gavin mumbled, "that is a problem. Salter's are big clients."

"So, I was hoping to hand the project back and have it allocated to someone else... although, of course, it seems that that might all be irrelevant, now that they've pulled out."

Gavin thought for a moment. "Let me ring Richard French now, find out what's going on and let you know the outcome as soon as I've spoken to him."

Back in her office Natascha thought it highly unlikely for Gavin to be able to talk Richard around once he'd made a decision. She sat back and breathed a huge sigh of relief. It had all been very conveniently sorted out with very little input from herself.

A little later that morning, after she'd settled her mind into some semblance of normality, she picked up the phone to call Brooke Park Hall and explain that she wouldn't be looking to the hire the venue after all. As she was about to dial, Gavin knocked and popped his head round the door.

"I've just spoken to Richard French. It seems there was some sort of internal misunderstanding in his office and he doesn't want to leave us after all. He'd be grateful if we could ignore his email and carry on where we left off. Good news, eh?"

Natascha had to hide the look of horror that was about to flood her blanched face. "Yes.., very good news," she stammered.

"Oh, and I've heard Marissa's coming back to work at the end of the month. So if you could try and hold on until she gets back I'd be eternally indebted. It's only for another couple of weeks or so. Anyway, got to dash if I want to make that train. I'll see you tomorrow."

"Are you sure you can see me tomorrow?" Natascha queried. "That would be perfect for me. In fact, you'll probably be doing me a huge favour."

"Yes, I'll be very happy to meet you tomorrow. The thing is, we're having part of the building remodelled and the work is due to start next week," Mr Byers, the manager of Brooke Park Hall explained. *"Unfortunately, the hall I was going to suggest for your event is now to be one of the first to be to be tackled. However, I have detailed drawings, plans and virtual graphics for the new hall that I can show you and I think you will be very pleased with what we have in mind. We expect the work to take approximately six weeks - plenty of time until your party. If you're not able to come before the work begins we can arrange a date for when it should be finished."*

Natascha didn't need to think too hard about it. "No, I think leaving it until the middle of next month may be cutting it a bit fine. I'll look forward to seeing you tomorrow morning at 11 o'clock."

If only she could persuade Larkswood Manor to see her tomorrow, too. She could kill two birds with one stone and get that out of the way as well.

"... well, I'm visiting another venue within an hour's drive from yourselves and I wondered if it would be at all possible to visit you tomorrow afternoon... Yes, I know it's very short notice and I feel very cheeky in asking," Natascha said, in her most friendly and attractive tone. "I really won't take up much of your time, ten to fifteen minutes at most, just to take a quick look around and have a short chat." She smiled warmly into the receiver knowing that somehow, the person at the end of the line would sense it. "Well, thank you very much. You're very kind and at such short notice. Yes, I look forward to meeting you tomorrow afternoon."

Natascha hung up feeling very relieved. Although her wish to pass Richard's project over to Marissa had not been possible, at least by having both meetings tomorrow, it would be far too short notice for anyone to visit with her as was originally planned. And there was no way that Richard would ever show his face again after what had happened between them. It was very tidily wrapped up.

She would pay them the courtesy of an invitation, anyway but there was nothing for her to worry about - she'd be going alone. She turned to her computer and typed up an email:

'*Mr French,*
I have confirmed details to visit both venues we spoke about previously for tomorrow am and pm. I can fully appreciate the inconvenience the very short notice may cause, but Brooke Park Hall will not be in a position to accommodate us for at least another month if we are unable to make the appointment tomorrow. Please do not feel obliged to change your plans. I will make all the necessary arrangements on your behalf.

Natascha Hamilton.'

She clicked on the send button before she had a chance to lose her nerve. But no sooner had she sent it when a reply was received:

'*Miss Hamilton,*
Thank you for your email. I have no meetings scheduled for tomorrow and will therefore be available to make the visits with you as promised. I currently have a rental car so please let me have the details and I shall meet you there.
Richard.'

You've got to be joking!

'*Mr French,*
Please find the times, addresses and directions to Brooke Park Hall and Larkswood Manor attached to this email. Again, there is no need for you to attend.
Natascha Hamilton.'

"Damn!" Natascha said out loud. She couldn't believe that this was happening. He still intended to make the visits with her, even after his shameful behaviour! Was there no end to his audacity? Wasn't there even an ounce of remorse? He was probably incapable of feeling anything at all. Natascha swiftly moved the cursor across the screen and closed the email - she couldn't even bring herself to look at his name. She was furious at his brazen cheek to feel he could come along and join her as though nothing had happened, as though the other night was all in a day's work for him. She had made a reprehensible mistake, she had to admit that much. It was a mistake that she could not fix. But she did have some control over the future and she would start by detracting the focus away from the impending meeting with Richard.

Sue had given her a list of instructions regarding her bridesmaid's dress and armed with this information, Natascha googled all the bridal shops near Bond Street and made a list of each one she could visit. Tomorrow would be a good time, after the, no doubt, grim site visits with Richard. It was the obvious evening to tackle the list and the perfect way to forget all about her 'day out'. Browsing the shops in Bond Street would lessen the trauma of having had to endure spending even one more minute with him. Organising her dress for Sue's wedding carried far more importance than any meeting she had to sit through with that man!

Natascha parked her car in the visitor's car park of Brooke Park Hall and made her way to the front of the building where Richard stood waiting for her.

"Good morning," she said, holding out her hand for the briefest of handshakes before pulling it away.

"Hello, Nata..."

"We need to ask for a Mr Byers," Natascha interrupted and led the way towards the sign to reception.

"Mr Byers? Hello, I'm Natascha Hamilton and this is Richard French."

The talkative Mr Byers took them on a guided tour of Brooke Park Hall. "This is the main room that is large enough to hold 200 guests. At the moment, the bar is situated across the hall in a little snug area. However, we're hoping to have it incorporated into the main room for the comfort and convenience of the guests and also to avoid unnecessary traffic in the hall."

"Well, it all sounds very well thought out," Natascha remarked pleasantly, once they were back in Mr Byers' office. "But I must admit that personally, I find having separate areas for the bar and cloakroom makes for a more interesting venue. It can be quite nice to have the freedom to roam around, as long as the facilities are not too far away, of course. Don't you agree?" Natascha asked and turned towards Richard who was staring out of a window. "Don't you agree, Richard?"

"Yes... I agree," he finally replied, without any real interest.

Mr Byers looked a little put out by Richard's blatant lack of enthusiasm so Natascha smoothly carried on. "You say your cloakroom facilities are located on the first floor. Could you tell me whether there are lifts available? I'm thinking of elderly guests or those with disabilities."

Glancing quickly across at Richard, Mr Byers decided that he would not bother to address him but would only speak to Natascha. "At the moment, there are no lifts. However there are separate toilet and washing facilities for the disabled on the ground floor." He tried once more to include Richard into the conversation, "I hope that will not be a problem. I have had no complaints so far...," but to no avail. Richard was not listening.

At the end of the visit, Natascha held out her hand. "Thank you again, Mr Byers. I'll be in touch."

"I'll look forward to hearing from you, Miss Hamilton," he replied, as he shook Natascha's hand. He turned towards Richard and without offering his hand he addressed him civilly by a quick nod of his head, "Mr French."

Once Natascha and Richard were back outside, she was pleased that she had been able to conduct the meeting professionally without having the insolence of Richard affect her. "What did you think?" she asked him. "The house itself is very nice but I'm not certain that the impending makeover will be an improvement."

"Yes, you're right," Richard muttered.

The visit to Larkswood Manor was much more pleasing. The floor space and decor of the suite were very comfortable and the facilities were excellent. It was a grand yet welcoming house and in Natascha's opinion it was the perfect venue. But Richard's attention was still lacking. She again ignored his attitude.

"What are your thoughts on Larkswood Manor?" Natascha asked when they were back in the car park. She looked about her. "The woodlands at the end of the gardens make for a very nice setting and with all the car parking space available, I feel it's worth serious consideration," she said in her business-only style. Again, Richard said nothing. "Richard," she said raising her voice slightly, trying hard to keep her irritation in check, "what do you think?"

"I think we should talk."

Natascha's patience was beginning to wane. "I hope you're not referring to anything that is unrelated to the issue at hand because if you are, then I have no interest in talking to you," she replied, her heart somewhat in her mouth yet still holding her composure.

"I really need to explain..."

"I don't need you to explain anything to me. I am only too well aware of your barbaric ways and what you think of me. There is nothing more to explain. But whatever it is you have against me, I don't think our hosts deserved your disrespect and bad-manners,"

He carried on regardless. "Please Natascha, let's talk..."

"No, Richard. Me handling your project is a very temporary arrangement, thank God. The thought of having to see you again made me feel sick. So, unless you have any questions about your 'grand' event, I don't want to hear from you." Natascha turned her back and walked away towards her car and gracefully slid into the driver's seat. And as she glanced in the rear view mirror she saw him watch the back of her car as she drove away.

***

For God's sake, what's the matter with me? Richard questioned. I should never have come to this blasted place, meeting those blasted people I never had the slightest interest in meeting. Why didn't I just do what I said I would and move on from the whole, goddamn business with Natascha? Haven't I caused enough of a mess? I shouldn't have said yes when that Gavin 'whatshisname' guy rang to ask me to reconsider my decision to cancel. I shouldn't have said that I would meet her here. But no, instead I had to go and make a bad situation worse! I seem to be hell bent on complicating everything, as if everything isn't complicated enough already! Every single decision I've made has been the wrong one - me, Mr 'I-Can-Handle-It-All', he sneered to himself. I was supposed to have walked away and leave her alone. Play it cool, I promised myself. Play it cool? I've done nothing but shown myself to be a sad, filthy sleaze ball! Annoyed with himself, Richard got into his car and slammed the door shut. "And to top it all I hate this bloody car!" he said in frustration, as he shoved the car into gear, released the handbrake and sped away.

***

Natascha returned to the office and sat behind her desk, recovering. What a dreadful day she had spent in Richard's infuriating company! He had made it unbelievably difficult for her but she thought she had managed to maintain her dignity throughout the meetings quite well. It was he who looked uncomfortable although she couldn't, for the life of her, fathom why. Had he suddenly had an epiphany and discovered the error of his ways? She very much doubted it. Anyway, she should never have to meet with him again and it would not be long before she can hand over the file to Marissa. Her complication-free life would soon be restored. She sighed with relief. But it didn't last long. She switched on her computer to see a new email in her inbox from Richard staring at her. Natascha groaned with disappointment. He was beginning to feel like a perverted stalker who wouldn't leave her alone. But, not knowing whether the email was work orientated or not, reluctantly Natascha had to open it:

'*Natascha,*

I have not been able to put the weekend out of my mind. I have to talk to you. Could we meet? Is there any way you would give me a second chance? I hate to contact you by email but I doubt very much that you would have spoken to me on the phone.

Richard.'

Natascha didn't have to think twice. She clicked on 'reply':

'As I politely asked you earlier, please do not contact me again unless work related. And I'm sick of giving you second chances.'

A second email came straight back:

'Please, Natascha. I really need to see you. It's very important. I really need to talk to you.
I'm sorry.
Richard'

This man did not know how to take 'no' for an answer; his nerve showed no bounds. She felt as though she was being bullied and so the answer was simple - a plain and straightforward 'NO'. So why, then, was she hesitating? Could she honestly be considering meeting with this pitiful man she wanted nothing more to do with?

'I'll be in the West End tonight. Meet me in the Royal Café in Davies Street at 6.30pm.'

Chapter Twenty-One

Her mind had been unable to concentrate on a bridesmaid's dress and although she had chosen one, she wasn't at all sure she had made the right choice. And the moment Natascha entered the coffee shop she began to question whether she had made the right decision to come here, too. She never used to question her judgement - she never needed to. But recently, belief in herself kept rocking backwards and forwards. Everything inside her said turn around and walk away. However, beyond all reason, she found herself giving him yet another undeserved opening to acquit himself. He was a poor excuse for a man and she should not be entertaining his demands. Yet absurdly, here she was, something inside of her urging her not to leave. If he had nothing of any worth listening to, then she would simply get up and walk out. Right now, however, she found herself compelled to hear what he had to say, needing to know what it was he wanted to talk about.

Scanning the room, she saw Richard at a table in the far corner away from everyone, portraying a lonely figure, sitting on his own staring into a coffee cup, deep in thought. She moved towards him.

It took him several seconds to realise she was standing beside the table. He stood up and faced her squarely.

Natascha summoned up some resilience to use as her improvised shield. "I don't have to be here. In fact, I don't know why I am and I don't know whether I want to be." She looked him steadfastly in the eye. "But I'm here now. I'll only ask that you do not insult my intelligence by telling me that I've got it all wrong."

"I know that and I'm not going to try to convince you of anything. I just wanted to talk to you about some things I should have talked to you about a long time ago."

Natascha had never seen him look as humble as he did now, not even after the car accident. Just by looking into his eyes she felt the shield she had built around her begin to slide.

"Please," he said, inviting her to take a seat. "Can I get you anything?"

"No. No, thank you." Natascha removed her coat, placed it on the chair beside her and sat perched on the edge of her chair, waiting.

Richard took his seat opposite her and cast his eyes downwards as if he was trying to find somewhere to begin. He looked up. "I just wanted to tell you a bit about myself."

"And what makes you think I'm interested in knowing anything about you?" Natascha asked, a cool inflection in her tone. "And why now?"

"Because once upon a time you were my best friend and you knew everything there was to know about me. And talking to you is long overdue."

"Yes, and you were my best friend, too but, as you say, that was a very long time ago. Things have obviously changed a lot since."

Richard didn't rush his words. "I know I'm not the same person you knew. Things happen that changes a man. Life and its twists makes a whole lot of difference to who you become."

Natascha said nothing and waited for him to continue.

"Certain experiences I've been through forced me to reassess and I finally came to the conclusion that I had to get used to a life in which I was going to be my own boss, completely self-reliant and have no need for, and no room for anyone to complicate it."

Something struck a chord with Natascha but she ignored it. "So, have I complicated your life?"

Richard lowered his eyes and stared into his coffee cup again and picked a spot from where he would go on. He looked up, giving Natascha a half-smile; losing the matter-of-fact air he was trying so hard to hold onto. "I haven't forgotten how much of a friend you were to me, you know. How we used to ride in the hills and how you would carry your backpack filled with drinks and chocolate in case I got thirsty or wanted something nice to eat. I liked you because you were different to all the other girls. You didn't giggle all the time, or dye your hair some God-awful colour or wear bright pink lipstick. You were sweet and mature and really nice to me. You made up stories to tell me in case I got bored with talking to you. You even used to sing your new songs to me and ask whether I thought they were any good or not, as if I was some sort of music impresario. Do you remember any of this?"

Natascha didn't have to say anything. The wistful look in her eyes was enough to convey that she remembered all of it and seeing the recognition on her face he went on.

"You were so good to me. You listened to me go on about the universe, about safari animals, frogs, Einstein's theory, anything and everything that took my fancy even though it probably must have bored you stupid." An amused expression lit up in her eyes, as if all her well-meant 'try to look interested' intentions she had back then while she used to listen to him ramble on and on, had just been discovered. "I thought so," Richard said, as he laughed lightly. I remember you trying to teach me the guitar and how patient you were even when I proved myself to be totally tone-deaf. I didn't really have many friends but I didn't need any - not when I had you. You were the perfect friend and all I ever wanted."

All of this was a surprise to Natascha. She had no idea that Richard had ever seen her in that way. All she ever believed was that he was the one with the most to contribute to their friendship; she didn't actually have all that much to offer except an ear to listen to all the complex explanations of subjects she never really understood. "I didn't know you felt that way."

Richard looked into her eyes. "I was a bit shy and too embarrassed to ever say. I was supposed to be the older one looking out for you when, in fact, it would be fair to say that you were actually looking after me. And plus, I thought you were quite pretty. I was definitely not going to tell you that, not when I was trying to be a cool sixteen year-old, was I?"

A smile touched the corners of his lips but Natascha couldn't detect any trace of it reflected in his eyes.

He repeatedly lowered his gaze throughout as if he was trying to hide some of his feelings behind his dark lashes, still unsure whether he was doing the right thing by speaking so candidly. Natascha, stunned by these revelations and feeling less belligerent, slipped back into her chair.

"When my parents told me that we were moving away I was heartbroken and so angry with them for not bothering to ask me how *I* felt about it. They were taking me away from the place where I had grown up, where I was happy, where I had everything I could ever wish for and they were taking me away from the best person I ever knew. I couldn't bear the thought of not seeing you every day." He paused for a moment. "I must have had a pretty bad crush on you, don't you think?" he said, with a half-hearted chuckle.

"Are you sure you want to be telling me all of this, Richard? It was such a long time ago. We were just kids."

He very gently nodded his head. "Yes, I do. I think I owe you an explanation." He lowered his eyes again and stared at a coffee ring left on the table. "I had a lousy time at school when we got to Scotland. Because I joined in the middle of the school year, all the other kids had already made their own gangs so I spent most of my time on my own."

"I wrote you letters, Richard, and I kept phoning you but we talked less than half a dozen times. Every time I rang you, your mum said you were out and that you'd ring me later but you never did. I thought you had made new friends. I thought you had outgrown me."

"No, you couldn't be more wrong. I loved our phone conversations. I loved your letters even more because I knew that I could re-read them over and over whenever I wanted to or needed to. I knew that something you'd written would make me laugh. I needed a lot of cheering up at that time. But I deliberately stopped writing and I told my parents to tell you that I was out every time you rang." Richard ran a hand nervously through his hair. Dredging up the past was becoming much more difficult than he thought it would be. He looked up at Natascha and drew her into his eyes. "You used to tell me that you missed me and I told you that I missed you, too. But I couldn't tell you just how bad it was. I was so lonely and so depressed. I was worried in case my real feelings would seep into a phone call or a letter. That's why I stopped contacting you. I didn't want you thinking that I was some kind of pathetic idiot with 'wimpish' feelings - so 'not cool'." Richard paused. "I suppose this all sounds crazy to you. I was only sixteen." He shook his head. "I can't believe I'm saying all of this to you."

Natascha was so astounded by what she had just heard that she could not react.

"My relationship with my parents deteriorated. I was so angry with them for making me live somewhere I didn't want to be. If I wasn't arguing with them, then I never spoke to them. I suppose I went out of my way to disagree with them on every single thing. I never wanted to go to Scotland and I hated every minute that I was there. They knew I was having a hard time and they kept trying to make up for it. They even bought me my first car, even though I hadn't even passed my driving test yet. But all their attempts to make things better just made me more frustrated with them. I blamed them for making my life such a misery and decided that my only way out was to get into a university somewhere as far away from Scotland as I could go. So that's what I did and I've never had any interest in staying in touch with them since." Richard looked away. "I was young and I suppose I let it all get so out of proportion. The trouble was I didn't know how to make things right after that."

"You could have come down for the holidays. Why didn't you? We could have at least spent the summers together."

"What was the point if I had to leave you all over again? I knew I wouldn't be able to do it." The resignation on his face was sad and empty. "I know. You don't need to look so confused. I was an idiot." He again looked into his coffee cup, which by now, had grown cold. After a brief pause Richard let out a long sigh before going on. "I left Scotland and went to Cambridge and was there for about a year on my own when I met a girl, Carrie. She was so different to you, wild and carefree, a real live wire. But there was something about her that reminded me of you. I still can't put my finger on what it was. We started going out and had grown quite close when we found out that she was ill. She had leukaemia. The doctors did what they could but it was too late, it was an aggressive form and she died five months later." He paused to regroup. "I was a mess after that. I felt abandoned and angry that she had been taken away from me so suddenly. I didn't get a chance to get my head around what was happening before she was gone and once again I was left on my own. But I found that every time I thought of Carrie I thought of you. Maybe the loss of her reminded me of how we were separated so quickly. My feelings for you and for Carrie had strangely become intermingled and I felt so guilty about it."

"You should have called me, Richard," Natascha said, in an unsteady voice

"Don't ask me why I didn't. Pride? Stupidity? Shame? I have no idea."

"I don't understand. What could you possibly have been ashamed of?"

Richard shook his head slowly, wearily, "I don't know..." After a moment, he cleared his throat as though he hadn't quite finished. "Anyway, I stayed on at Cambridge to study for a

Masters. I think I decided to stay on mainly because I felt sorry for myself and didn't feel ready to join the real world. Then, after a few months, I made friends with Grace. I was quite happy studying and messing about with my motorbike on my own but when we met and I found out that she was into motorbikes and long bike journeys a friendship sort of clicked. And as a bonus for me she seemed to quite enjoy my company as well," he said, with a small laugh. "We shared a lot of common interests and spent a lot of our spare time together. We promised ourselves that as a reward for completing our finals, we would spend three months biking across Europe. It was going to be a holiday of a lifetime for me and I scrimped and saved every penny. And for once, in a very long time, I was actually excited at the prospect of spending the summer with someone who enjoyed the same things I did, just like you and I used to." A moment passed before Richard again cleared his throat, calling upon some courage to carry on. "We were going to ride to the south of France and down into Spain and on our way back we would travel through Switzerland and Germany… Anyway, it was going to be quite a trip. We knew that Grace's brother was getting married so we factored it into our schedule and made plans to get back to London for the wedding. We would carry on our holiday afterwards. Maybe it was a crazy idea. Maybe we should have waited until after the wedding to go. God, so many maybes…" A distant expression clouded his eyes. "We were meant to go back together but when the time came Grace insisted I stay on in

France and find us another place to stay while she returned to London on her own. She was only going for a couple of days. At first I said no and that we should stick to our original plan but she persuaded me that it was a waste for us both to go back. She said she'd bring me back some wedding cake." A deep hollow laugh bubbled in his throat for just a moment before it disappeared and that distant look that took him a million miles away returned. His gaze passed right through Natascha. "She didn't even get ten miles away before she was hit by a lorry. She was killed instantly. The driver said he hadn't seen her ..." He broke off.

Natascha closed her eyes and gasped at the horror of it. How did he ever manage to live through all of that alone? A pang of guilt found its way inside her. And how did she never come to realise that something might have been wrong when he severed all ties without having given her any indication of his reasons? If only he'd come to her, had got in touch with her, she would have been with him in a heartbeat.

The painful memories were etched on his face and it took him a while to return to real time. He straightened in his seat and took a deep breath. "The whole purpose of telling you all of this was to try and explain my actions. I'd come to the conclusion a long time ago that somewhere along the line I had done something so wicked in this life that I was punished with the loneliness of never having the privilege of a real friend. It wasn't enough that I was separated from you against my will and went to a new school where no-one actually realised I existed, two very good friends had to die before I understood that friendships were not going to be part of my life's agenda. Don't get me wrong, I know I wasn't always the life and soul of the party but I didn't exactly plan to spend the rest of my days having no-one but myself to have in-depth conversations with. It seemed that I was doomed to lose anyone I ever really cared for. But when I saw you again at your mother's I couldn't take it in, that after all these years you were standing there, right in front of me. It was the one moment I had been waiting for all my life. All the conclusions I'd made about friendship went straight out of the window."

"It didn't seem as though you were happy to see me at all," Natascha said, as she pictured the scene outside her parents' house, his expressionless face and his haughty attitude.

"I was shocked at first. I've always wondered what it would be like if we ever met again, how I would be, how you would be. I thought it was going to be incredible. But it didn't turn out as I had imagined. Suddenly I saw images of Carrie and Grace and a picture of you standing outside your house with tears in your eyes waving goodbye to me twenty years ago. I asked myself why I should believe that meeting you, my once closest friend, after so long, why it would be any different, why something terrible wouldn't happen to you, too, the same as it did to the others. When I realised that, I could hardly speak to you." His eyes rested on Natascha's face and she could feel her stomach tighten when she saw them glistening; his long black lashes damp with sadness. "That night at my house was a mistake because I had let you down. I was putting you in danger just because I selfishly, couldn't stay away from you anymore. I'd tried so hard to ignore you that I didn't even realise just how much I wanted to be with you. And that night, I ignored a promise I had made to myself - that I would never get involved with another woman..." He looked into Natascha's eyes, as though he was speaking deep into them. "But I could never regret that night with you, not as long as I live... I'm so sorry I hurt you."

At that moment, Natascha could not hold back any more. She got up to go to him, wrapping her arms around him to comfort him - to do something, something that would also help her to try and manage her own pain. They leant against each other, supporting one another, helping one another, the way they used to.

Natascha pulled away and dragged her seat nearer to him to sit close beside him, to take his hand in hers.

"My troubles have left me a difficult man for people to get close to, I know that. I deliberately don't need people to like me and if something hasn't got anything to do with my work then I'm not interested. I'm better off on my own. I tried to make that theory apply to you, too. But it didn't work. I still care about you too much." He stared into Natascha's eyes, as if he was trying to see inside her. "I promise that I'll never ever make you feel bad again." After a moment, Richard said calmly, "We've both changed so much and things won't ever be the way they used to be but I'd like us to stay in touch. It won't be the same, I know, but I wouldn't like to think that it would be another twenty years before we heard from each other again."

Natascha was helplessly drawn to the eyes that had held her prisoner from the very first moment they met. "No, we'll never let that happen again."

They left the café and stood facing each other in the darkness of the cool night.

"Look, I'm sorry to have to bow out now but I've got a flight first thing in the morning. I'm going on a business trip for a couple of days and I really should throw a clean change of clothes into a bag," Richard said, as casually as he could, wanting to finally engrave a line under those sad chapters in his life.

"You're going abroad to work on New Year's Eve? You won't be working on New Year's Day itself, will you? It's a Bank Holiday."

"I'm going to Israel and it isn't a Bank Holiday there. It's business as usual. Anyway, it doesn't really make any difference to me."

"Well, before you go, let me give you my number." Natascha pulled out a small notepad and a pen from her bag. "Here, this is my house phone number and my mobile number. Let me know as soon as you get back and perhaps we can toast in the New Year, albeit belatedly."

Richard took the piece of paper and placed it inside his breast pocket, tapping it lightly to indicate it was being kept in a secure place.

He gazed at her with a melancholic look in his eyes and a solemn note in his voice, "I just need to tell you again, Natascha, I'm so sorry for hurting you. I promise I'll never do that to you again."

Natascha looked at him tenderly. "You've said that already and I believed you the first time."

He leant forward until his mouth was close to hers. "Take care of yourself," he whispered, as he very softly kissed her cheek.

Then each went their separate ways. They had finally parted as friends.

The short walk to the train station gave Natascha a few minutes to digest all that she had heard. This account of Richard's life was very different to the vague one he had recounted to her the evening they met for a drink after work. With so much tragedy for one person to have to live with alone, it was no wonder he had changed so drastically. Scepticism and indifference was his life now and everything else paled into insignificance. With no real friends and an estranged family, he had become a lonely man leading a rather sad and hermitic life. The words 'I love you' rang in her head. Richard's feelings that night must have been so confused and she should have realised that before now. She had been so distracted in the moment that she, herself, had been unable to separate the platonic relationship from an intimate one and for that she was so very disappointed with herself. While he was speaking to her, however, she could not fail to see certain similarities she did not want to think about; all the hurt and disillusionment that had shaded different areas in their lives. Laurent was the darkest part of her history and she still wanted it left well alone. Turning her thoughts back to Richard, Natascha didn't know how to help him or, indeed, whether she could and Richard certainly had not asked for any. He had told her, in so many words, that he was happy they had met after so long but he had no intention of trying to re-ignite what they once had and he was right. So much water had passed under that legendary bridge that it would be a mistake to try and make up for lost years. They had both grown up to be two very different adults to what they had been as children. Both of them were now so very independent and exceptionally self-reliant, that somewhere along the line their personalities were bound to clash. An occasional phone call, the odd email was sufficient for them to keep in contact and Natascha was happy with that. Natascha could now file the whole thing away neatly in her head.

***

Richard sat in his car. If he hadn't lost control of his need for her that night, all of this would never have taken place. He would have avoided the humiliation of disclosing the story of his whole sorry life. All those memories he had finally managed to come to terms with were all stirred up again and he hated it.

The one person he wanted, the only person he knew could have helped him was Natascha and he had needed her. But bizarrely, he couldn't face her. It would have been easy to find her but the more he thought about the prospect of seeing her again, the more he had convinced himself that it wasn't the right thing to do. She could have been married, with children she loved, a husband she adored and living a very happy life. Would he have been able to cope with that? And what if she really didn't care whether she saw him again or not? Or much worse, what if she didn't even remember him, anyway?

Jeez, it was so long ago and he was making such a meal of it. So, he had told her everything - big deal. It's not as if she could change anything. No, he had made certain decisions about his life and knew how he was going to live it. As far as he was concerned, those decisions still stood. It's true he hadn't made any provisions for meeting her again - how could he have predicted that? But hey, he was strong enough and single-minded enough to deal with it. There was no reason to change the order of his plans. He'd just send her a birthday email every year on 22nd January. That was the only date that ever meant anything to him. He'd have one hell of a tough time trying not to get in touch with her more often, he knew it. But that's just how it had to be. Oh God, what if she was feeling pity for him right now? He didn't want her pity but she must be feeling it, how could she not? He had just admitted to her that his life was nothing but one long lamentable tale. Blast it! He should never have told her any of it. He'd done it again; let the sentimental drivel overrule his head. It would have been better if she still hated him; it would make it a lot easier.

Richard felt his head start to throb and unexpectedly, he had to brush a tear from his cheek.

***

Chapter Twenty-Two

Making herself comfortable in front of the television, Natascha sat with a glass of wine watching the New Year festivities being televised from London's South Bank. New Year's Eve this year was to be a very quiet one for her. Sue and Matteo were still in Italy, Simon had stayed on with his brother's family after a last minute New Year's Eve party had been arranged and both Rachel and Dominic were nursing dreadful colds. She glanced up at the clock. It was 11.55pm so must be 1.55am in Tel Aviv, she calculated. And if Richard's flight left this morning, the duration of which was approximately four and a half hours, he would have arrived hours ago. She had given him her number but he hadn't phoned. Natascha stalled these absurd thoughts before they developed into full blown paranoia. Why was she expecting him to ring? He didn't say he would and she hadn't asked him to. In one breath she planned on having very little contact with Richard and in the next she was wondering why he hadn't called. It was not going to be as easy as she once thought. But that was okay. It would not take long to come to terms with their new relationship and keep it in order. As long as he'd reached Israel safely, that's all she needed to know.

She turned to the TV in time to see the last remaining seconds of the year being counted down by the thousands of New Year revellers and listened to the deep authoritative chimes of Big Ben welcoming in the New Year. The crowd roared Happy New Year and began singing Auld Lang Syne while an impressive firework display lit up the London skyline with a shower of dazzling diamonds and shimmering colour. Any minute now the phone would ring and her father would wish her a Happy New Year. It was supposed to be a silly little race to see who would telephone first but admittedly, every year Natascha let her parents win. Her phone rang.

"Hello, Dad, you win again..."

"Natascha, it's Richard. I just wanted to wish you a Happy New Year!"

The unexpected sound of Richard's voice left her feeling slightly dazed. The line was not very clear and a buzzing made it difficult to hear. "Oh Richard, this is a really nice surprise. How are you?"

"I'm fine. I arrived here at around lunchtime and I had a meeting as soon as I left the airport."

"It must be the early hours of the morning in Israel."

"Yes, it's two o'clock."

"Well in that case, Happy New Year to you, too!"

"You shouldn't be at home, you should be out having a good time!" Richard said, cheerfully.

"No, not this year. It's a rather muted affair this year, unfortunately. I'm watching it all happen on TV."

He didn't seem to hear her. "Well, enjoy whatever you're doing. Take care."

And before Natascha could reply, the line went dead. Suddenly, she felt very strange. Her body was tingling and she could feel her heart racing. Tears of happiness distorted her vision and her face was bright enough to light up any room. Despite her earlier convictions, she astonished herself at how incredibly happy she was to have heard Richard's voice - and how terribly saddened she was that he had gone so quickly.

***

He had to do it. There was no way he could watch 31st December roll into 1st January and not think of her, not now. He was about twelve years old when they started their own little tradition of exchanging gifts themed around the animal which would represent the New Year in the Chinese calendar. Every year she would ask whether it was the year of a particular rodent (she couldn't actually bring herself to say the name of it) because if it was, she wouldn't be giving him a present and she didn't want one either - she was terrified of them. And every year until he left, he would tell her that the year of that rodent she didn't like (he wasn't allowed to mention the name either) had passed and it wouldn't come round again for years. Richard laughed to himself when he thought of it. Slowly he placed the phone back onto its cradle, folded the piece of paper on which she had written her telephone number and held it in his hand just for a moment before laying it down on the table by the bed. He switched off the lamp, turned over and closed his eyes and the very last thought on his mind before he fell asleep was Natascha.

***

Natascha sat in the kitchen watching the dawn of another wet and miserable day. Yesterday had been a very quiet New Year's Day and Natascha was pleased to have heard from Sue who was still in Italy but had made sure she was able to spend a few minutes on the phone to her friend. She said was having a good time with Matteo's family and their friends. To spend both Christmas and New Year in Italy away from her friends for the first time had been a little daunting to her at first. However, there were so many parties and so much entertainment that she surprised herself at how much she had enjoyed it all.

"I'm having a great time, but I still miss having our usual little New Year's Eve party, just the six of us," Sue had added. *"But never mind. How was your Christmas?"*

Natascha had had to think carefully about what she was going to say. "Oh, you know, the usual, Mum and Dad, Christmas dinner and *Miracle on 34th Street*. It was quiet, just the way I like it."

"*Sounds as though it was a bit too quiet, if you ask me.*" The phone line had gone silent for a moment. "*You sure nothing else happened?*"

"No, nothing, why do you ask?" Natascha had been slightly nervous and had tried to keep her voice even but she obviously hadn't done enough. How did Sue do it? Natascha couldn't get a thing past her, not even over the phone.

"*Oh, I don't know. Something in your voice doesn't sound altogether convincing.*"

"You're imagining things, Sue. There was nothing of much excitement."

"*Really? Oh well, if you say so.*"

Natascha had had to change the subject. "So, a good time is being had by all, you say."

"*Yep, it's been fun, but I'm looking forward to seeing you. We're coming back for a few days next week and I want to meet up as soon as we can. I'll give you a ring when we're home. See you soon.*"…

She added a drop of milk to her tea. Everything was changing already, she thought sadly. It would have been the time when Natascha would tell Sue all that had happened and would ask for her opinion and advice. It would have been enough just to talk to her about it. It wasn't appropriate anymore. Sue had her wedding affairs and a brand new life to get to grips with. She certainly did not need to have Natascha's problems added to what she already had piled high on her plate. They would meet next week but

Natascha would say nothing more about her sagas involving Richard. From now on, she would look after herself.

Less than a minute after Natascha had sat down to her breakfast the phone rang. Who would be calling her at seven o'clock on a Saturday morning?

"It's me. I'm at the retail park. How soon can you get down here?"

Natascha was really pleased to hear his voice. "Simon, you're back. Firstly, Happy New Year, secondly, how was your Christmas and thirdly, why are you ringing me at seven o'clock in the morning from the retail park?"

"Happy New Year, my beautiful Natascha, Christmas was great and I'm at the sales. You'll never believe how many people are already here and have been queuing all night. It's not even daylight and it's like Piccadilly Circus on a bad day."

"It sounds irresistible, Simon but I think I'll take a rain check."

"Sadly, I'm not asking you on a date. Besides, you could credit me with a little more imagination than to arrange a romantic rendezvous outside PC World!" Simon said, with some drama. *"Anyway, you're distracting me. Listen, I've seen that TV for Sue and Matteo, the one we're supposed to be buying as a wedding present. It's on sale so I doubt whether they'll keep very many in stock. We need a car to take it away but no way is it going to get into my Mini. I've spoken to Dominic but he can't*

help. He's still wrapped around a hot water bottle. Can you do anything?"

"I'll be there in half an hour. I'll bring Sue's keys so we can take it straight round to the house. Wait there for me, I won't be long."

Natascha was soon in her car. Before locking her front door she checked her handbag to make sure she had Sue's keys with her, they only lived ten minutes away from each other. She then left to meet Simon.

Although there was a constant flow of cars going in and out of the car park, Natascha found what seemed to be the only empty parking bay and as she slid the car into the space she saw Simon waiting for her outside the electrical store. The telephone banter earlier was just habit. In reality, she was really happy to see him. The whole of Natascha's Christmas and New Year holidays had been a whirlwind of traumatic and surreal events all of which she had kept to herself. However, just seeing Simon seemed to put everything back to where it should be. This was the life she knew, her music, her work and her friends.

Natascha kissed Simon on the cheek and he seemed to sense the extra warmth in the gesture.

"Wow! What was that for? You've never, no matter how hard I've tried to get you to, ever done that before! Did I miss my birthday or something?"

"Oh, don't be silly, Simon, I'm happy to see you, that's all. Nothing wrong in that is there?"

"No, no, nothing at all. I'm not complaining. It's just that it was rather unexpected. Very nice though! I just wish you were always this pleased to see me!"

"I'm always pleased to see you but normally, I'm able to restrain myself from making it too obvious," Natascha said, playfully.

"Well, in future please don't feel the need for any restraint. Feel free and furnish me with as many kisses as you feel will make you happy. I'll be happy to help. Don't be shy!"

Natascha feigned a theatrical expression of gratitude. "Oh thank you so much, Simon. I'm very grateful!" She rolled her eyes upwards towards the still dark morning sky. "Anyway, enough of all that nonsense, let's get on with our mission," Natascha went on, pushing Simon towards the entrance.

Simon and Natascha survived the crush of determined sales shoppers who filled the store to capacity and emerged relatively unscathed. Between them they carried the boxed TV to Natascha's car.

"Let's head straight to Sue and Matteo's and leave the TV there. No problem in letting ourselves in," Natascha said, jingling a set of keys, "and I've brought the ribbon with me." She manoeuvred out of the car park. "How did Christmas at your brother's go?"

"Actually, it was pretty good." Simon said, bashfully. "I'm going to have to confess. I met someone who almost matches your magnificence and beauty. She's a friend of my sister-in-law, Frederika and we got on *really* well, if you know what I mean!"

"That sounds interesting. Tell me more."

"Her name's Dana and she's Canadian. She was Frederika's flatmate and good friend for a couple of years before Frederika and Julian got married. She left five years ago to go back to Prince Edward Island, where she lives. Now she's back on a three month holiday in Europe and it's the first time she's been back since she left. She's staying with them and was meant to be there for only a couple of weeks but now she may try and find somewhere to stay in London for the duration of her holiday."

"What happens after three months?"

"She goes back home. I know. Therein lies the small problem." Simon shrugged his shoulders. "Oh well, maybe it's just a holiday romance thing but I really do like her. She's a really lovely girl. I just don't quite know how it's going to pan out with her going back in a few months."

"Well, I think you should enjoy her company while she's here. You can sort out the details later. It's great that you've met someone, though. I'm happy for you."

"How was your Christmas?"

"How was mine?" Natascha hesitated. "It was okay."

***

This is absurd, Richard said to himself, irritated as he waited behind a queue of traffic streaming out of the retail park. After a rough flight back from Tel Aviv, this was all he needed. I bet eight out of ten of these people have wasted their hard earned cash on gadgets they don't need and don't actually want, he thought as his gaze wandered into the car park. Richard thought he was seeing things as a woman resembling Natascha was loading a box into the back of a car. He looked again and recognised at once, the sleek black Audi A4 in which he had spent hours alone with her locked inside the intimate space as they drove back from Oxfordshire; the journey that had paved the way for that night... Richard cut short his recollections and concentrated on what he was seeing. Natascha was with the same man with whom she had linked arms with on the High Road on that fateful evening and who had blatantly kissed her in the middle of the street. Seeing them together that night had annoyed him to the point of unwarranted anger. That was another meeting he would rather forget. He watched as they left the car park and squeeze into the line of traffic ahead of him. He could not ignore his awakened curiosity and with a degree of self-loathing, he followed them.

He parked at a safe distance behind them and watched as they got on with unloading the car and carrying the large box through the gate of one of the houses. He then saw Natascha reach into her bag and pull out what must have been her front door keys. They both entered the house looking relaxed and happy and shut the door behind them leaving Richard with the sad feeling of having been shut out of Natascha's life.

Richard's heart sank and he sat at the wheel of his car trying hard to comprehend what was going on inside of him. All his emotions were so mixed up that, together with the difficult meeting he'd had in Israel, he felt so weary he couldn't even begin to sort out a way to toughen up and forget that woman. He needed to go away.

***

Natascha came out of the house to retrieve the large bow and ribbon to decorate the TV from her car. She glimpsed the back of a car turning around in the road but paid no attention to it, she didn't recognise it. The road was a cul-de-sac and it was probably someone who had lost his way.

Chapter Twenty-Three

With all the Christmas and New Year's holidays out of the way until next December, Natascha arrived at the office early as usual. But her normal drive and enthusiasm for work was seriously lacking and so she busied herself with taking down the office decorations that had looked so festive in the run up to Christmas but today looked rather insipid and out of place, now that the holidays had come and gone. However, now stripped of all additional adornments that had been hanging from the walls for the best part of a month, her office now looked bare and gloomy, mirroring her own lethargic spirit.

She closed the cupboard door after packing away the last box of tinsel and went to her desk to answer her phone.

"Natascha, it's Sue."

Natascha looked at the digital calendar on her desk. She still had not heard from Richard. She was definitely finding it a little difficult practising the 'every now and again' arrangement they had agreed on. "Oh Sue, wonderful, you're back! How was the flight?"

"It was fine. How are you coping with being back at work post-holiday?"

"Work's the same as any other normal working day. Nothing's changed," Natascha replied. The palms of her hands grew damp with the dishonesty.

"*That's a relief then. There isn't anything worse than going back and nothing seems the same as it was before Christmas and you have to re-adjust all over again just to get back into the usual routine.*" Sue had no idea of just how right she was. "*Anyway, as you've already gathered we've just arrived back from Italy and planning to have you all come over to us after work tonight. Are you up for it?*"

"Tonight is good. I look forward to it."

Everyone was already at Sue's by the time Natascha arrived. The Salter conference was still without a venue and she had had to work later than she had intended. A meeting had finally been arranged with the manager of a recently completed, multi-function sports stadium, who promised her an excellent suite for holding large conferences.

"You'll never guess what Santa left under the tree when we got home? A brand new, state of the art TV! Can you imagine our surprise when we realised that it was exactly what we had been looking for!" Sue exclaimed.

"What a good idea it was to post your Christmas wish list off before going to Italy," Simon teased. "And seeing as you've both been good little children, Santa was definitely going to come through on the pressie at the top of your list!"

"It is very generous of you all and is very much appreciated. Thank you all so much," Matteo said, his little laugh hardly masking his heartfelt gratitude. "It was also a good idea to leave it in the house. Now it can be packed away together with the rest of the furniture we are having shipped to Italy tomorrow."

A thin mist of both sadness and happiness descended while individually, they all tried to come to terms with the fact that Sue and Matteo were soon to leave for good and that this was, more than likely, to be one of the last occasions when they would all be together as a group.

Simon deliberately tried to dispel the somewhat awkward morosity in the air. "So, Sue," he asked, "what was it like abroad at Christmas? Would you recommend it?"

"I genuinely had a fantastic time," Sue enthused. "Matteo's family knows how to have a good time and you would have felt right at home seeing as there was more wine flowing at the dinner table than there was water in the kitchen taps!" Sue explained, realising that everyone needed something to smile at, including herself.

"Looks like I'll be inviting myself to your next Christmas dinner, then!"

Matteo laughed with the others but was serious after a moment. "Changing the subject to something just a little more important," he continued, "I know Sue has already spoken to Rachel and Natascha about being her bridesmaids but that leaves me with the question of a best man. I have very close friends here and I also have a cousin in Italy who I am very close to. We more or less grew up together. And so the decision of who to ask was a very difficult one. But I have solved it. I have decided to have two best men. My cousin has agreed to be one of them and I would be so happy, Simon, if you would be my other best man. Believe me, there will be plenty to do to keep both of you extremely occupied."

"I can't think of anything I would rather do. Thank you, Matteo, I would be honoured," Simon answered, pride lighting up his face.

"And the reason why you are not invited to be part of that boys club, Dominic," Sue continued, "is that I need a man I love like my own family to walk me down the aisle. Without having a father or anyone I trust more, I was hoping you would step in."

Dominic looked shocked and his face expressed a real slushiness that no-one had ever witnessed in him. "I-I really don't know what to say," he said, eyes brimming. "I'll be so, so proud to walk you down the aisle."

"Don't worry, Dominic. I'm sure it has nothing to do with the fact that you look old enough to be Sue's father, of course," Simon bantered, recovering from the heavy emotion that had settled over the proceedings.

"Oh be quiet, Simon. I only hope Matteo has the good sense not to let you have the responsibility of bringing the rings to the church," Dominic returned, once he had got over the shock of being asked to be proxy father of the bride, "because if he does lose his matrimonial head and asks you to be the ring holder, a plan B will need to be put in place for a backup set of rings to be on standby. I can just picture you standing up by the altar searching all your pockets in a cold sweat wondering whether you were wearing the right suit jacket!" Dominic started to laugh.

Simon opened his mouth ready to come back with something equally facetious.

"Now, now, children," Sue cut in, "I think we should take this opportunity to make a toast to our friendship and say a prayer for this wedding which may otherwise turn out to be quite a spectacle, and for all the wrong reasons," she giggled.

Sue, Matteo and Natascha stood by the front door waving off the others.

Natascha reached for her coat. "I really should make a move myself."

"Can I, er, just have a quick word before you go?" Sue asked.

Sue's hesitancy had Natascha eying her cautiously. "You can but you're making me nervous. You don't usually ask for permission to speak."

"Yes, well this one is a bit unusual."

"How unusual?"

"I want to ask if you would do something for me."

"I'd do anything for you, Sue, there's very little I wouldn't - except decline a proposal of marriage from Bradley Cooper if you asked me to. But something tells me that I'm not going to like this. Am I allowed to refuse?"

Sue shut the front door. "Why don't you come and sit down. Another glass of wine?"

Natascha went in and sat down and accepted the drink which she felt was offered as a way to cushion whatever it was Sue was about to say.

Sue came and sat beside her and raised her glass. "Cheers! Oh, I was meaning to ask," she said, after a mouthful of wine, trying her utmost not to appear to be skirting around the reason why she had asked Natascha to stay behind, "whatever happened to your long lost friend? The last I heard was he'd asked you out for a drink. Wow, that seems such a long time ago, way before Christmas! I can't believe it's been so long since we last had a decent catch up," Sue remarked. "Did he eventually call you?"

At that moment, it dawned on Natascha on how much had happened since the last time she had spoken to Sue about Richard. Sue didn't know that they did, in fact, meet for that strange drink and since then, there was so much to tell. A list of events rolled out in Natascha's mind like a seamless ball of string: the persistent hostile vibes that led to the ugly words in the street. There was the car crash at Christmas, the torrid night of unmatched passion and the shocking argument that ensued. All followed by the revelation of the tragedies he had endured and the near recluse he had become as a result. There was just too much of it. "Yes, as a matter of fact, he did phone. We went for a drink after work one evening. There was a lot of small talk; you know, the sort of conversation you have with someone you barely know. It was all very polite," Natascha explained loosely, doing as best she could to sound blasé about it all.

"Oh, that's a shame. And you haven't got together since?"

Natascha hung on to her carefree manner and then lied. "Good Lord, no! That was the last time. It was nice meeting up again after so long but I don't think we'll be seeing each other again. I'm handing his client's party project over to Marissa when she's back in the office. No, we're very different people now and don't seem to have much in common anymore," she said, offhandedly. From Sue's expression, Natascha could see that her friend was considering asking more questions. The conversation needed a very swift change in direction. "Anyway, we're getting away from why I'm here. You had something you wanted to ask me."

"Ah yes, there is," Sue said, uneasily.

"Come on, out with it. I've never, ever seen you stuck for words, Sue Robinson."

With a deep breath, Sue said quickly, "I'd like you to sing at the wedding."

Natascha's eyes shot wide open. "Sorry?"

"I'd like you to sing at the wedding. Please. It would be the best wedding present I could ever wish to have. Please," Sue pleaded, when she saw the horror on Natascha's face.

"Oh Sue, I can't believe you're asking me to do this, I really can't," Natascha mumbled in a small voice.

"I can't think of anything I'd want more." Sue softened her tone. "You've got such a beautiful voice which you keep hidden under years of convincing yourself that you're not interested in singing anymore."

"But I'm not. I-I just don't do that anymore. You know I don't," Natascha stammered. Not known for ever being tongue-tied, she suddenly found herself floundering in a plethora of words to make up an explanation for why she couldn't do it but none of them could express her feelings adequately. "I just can't do that, Sue."

"You can do it, I know you can and deep down, I think you know that you can, too." Sue could see the fright in her friend's eyes. "It only has to be one song; a short one will do." She paused. "Natascha, you can't let your talent die; not because of someone else. Don't forget that credo, the one you painstakingly created for yourself; you call all the shots when it comes to making decisions in your life. Don't let that one person continue to have a hold over you. It's only you letting that happen."

"Laurent hurt me so much," Natascha murmured, trying to hold back tears.

"I know he did but that was then," Sue said, understandingly, "but you're not that person anymore. You're stronger, wiser and in the driver's seat."

Sue was right, it was up to her what she did and when she did it. Natascha held her head up and collected herself. "I can give it a try, but I doubt..."

"You'll give it everything you've got, I'm sure of it. I've never known you to back away from a challenge. And doubt? You don't even know the meaning of it!"

With her spirit resigned and her thoughts defeated, Natascha looked at Sue. "Any particular requests?"

"Just surprise me."

Of all the things Sue could have asked her to do, she decided on the one thing that terrified Natascha the most. She would have walked on hot coals if her friend had asked her to. But to sing again in public? That was something entirely different. Her guitar stared at her from the corner of the room, innocently evoking long buried memories. Once upon a time singing used to mean everything to Natascha. Now her voice was relegated to being heard within her own four walls only. When she was young, she was known to be a little shy, not unlike other children. However, singing in front of a crowd never frightened her. It was something she enjoyed which needed no coaxing. Her singing voice was mature and strong for someone so young and she would stand up in front of family and friends to sing and play her guitar out of pure pleasure. Singing in the front room of her home soon moved on to singing solo parts in school concerts and then on to village fêtes and local community festivals. She enjoyed every minute of it.

When she arrived in London, it had developed into a more serious pastime when Sue introduced her to Laurent, a session musician from the outskirts of Paris who was lodging with Sue and Matteo. He had persuaded her to sing with him at a small nightclub where he was working part time as the resident guitar man. Their stints on stage became longer and more frequent and it wasn't long before their names were beginning to be recognised across a wider audience and they began to perform at larger venues, supporting some well-known names in the entertainment business at that time. Laurent had been the biggest inspiration in her life. However, that was a long time ago and things had changed dramatically, leaving Natascha no longer interested in performing.

She didn't think she would ever sing in public again. The thought of faces looking to her, waiting for her to sound beautiful filled her with excruciating panic. It was a world away from the excitement she used to feel back then. But she finally accepted that she would do this. It was time. She didn't know where the courage was going to come from but resolved that after so many years, she would once again sing to an audience at Sue and Matteo's wedding, no matter what.

Chapter Twenty-Four

Wedding plans had begun in earnest. The church, reception venue and catering were in the process of being organised in Italy. However, dress, shoes and all accessories were to be bought in London. Hunting for the perfect wedding dress was not an easy one and given the little time they had in which to find one, it had become something of an after work ritual which had Sue and Natascha traipsing around a multitude of bridal shops all over London.

The dress Sue finally settled on was a delicate ivory satin creation that left her shoulders bare and fell gracefully to the floor. A sprinkling of tiny sparkly stones added a splash of drama and a short tailored jacket in the same satin was the finishing touch.

"I am so glad I didn't settle for that third one. It was really beautiful but there was something not quite right," Sue said, as she made herself comfortable at a table in the 'Salon de Thé', where they had decided to rest after a shopping marathon.

Natascha put her bags down. "Your dress is perfect."

They watched as worn out waiters hurried back and forth between tables, negotiating the 'shopping bag obstacle course' while carrying trays of tea, coffee and cakes from the patisserie.

Sue and Natascha waited patiently for their order to arrive. Late night shopping meant they'd shopped 'til they nearly dropped! Anything that could vaguely be justified as being necessary had been purchased. However, from the amount of glossy bags, colourful bags, big bags and small bags they had amassed, it was evident that perhaps a few unnecessary items had made their way in, too. Sue slipped her purse back into her bag.

"How's the song coming along?"

Natascha had rummaged through an old file that held completed songs, half scribbled lyrics, fragments of melodies and portions of chord sequences. Amongst all the bits of paper that had potential, her heart kept coming back to the song she had written when she was a teenager and which was currently undergoing a makeover. However, the original version of the song she had composed all those years ago was more suitable, no matter how romantic and syrupy it was. It was the perfect choice to be sung to a bride and bridegroom on their wedding day. Natascha had gone back and discarded all the alterations she had made and left the song in its original form - sweet and simple. "Well, I have been working on one and I think it's nearly there."

"Oh, that's good. I'm so glad you agreed to do this for me. It's going to make my day perfect. I can't wait to hear you sing again. I know it won't be easy for you but I'm confident that you're going to be great!"

A pale look of 'you're welcome' crossed Natascha's face, wishing she could be as confident as Sue was.

"Matteo's cousin, Cristiano, the other best man, is a musician and he and his group will be providing the music at the reception. I was speaking to him on the phone last night and I mentioned that you'll be singing a song and he asked me to tell you that if there is anything you need, to let him know and he'll try to organise something for you. He also asked me to tell you that if you wanted some accompaniment, he would be happy to help out. Just send him a CD of the song and any information that might be useful and he could arrange for his band to put something together as backing. He'll talk to you about it when you get out there. That sounds great doesn't it? I'm not sure what kind of information he means but I suppose you musician people understand!"

Oh. Natascha's heart sank. This was not what she had planned. Her intention was to do the song with her guitar, get it over and done with and disappear back into the crowd of guests. She was sure this Cristiano fellow was only trying to be helpful, but having others involved just complicated matters. Her song was simple and amateurish and to another musician, would undoubtedly sound juvenile. It was definitely not worthy of having a band accompanying it. But if she refused his offer, she might give the impression of being arrogant and egotistical. "That's really kind of him. Any help he can offer will be very much appreciated. Please thank him for me," she fibbed. "I'll get something prepared for you to take with you when you go."

Sue eyed her friend. "You can smile until those beautiful cheekbones ache, Natascha but I can see that you're worried. You don't have to be. Cristiano is a really lovely man. You'll get on with him, I'm positive you will. I don't know anyone who doesn't."

Natascha was still very much unconvinced.

The waitress brought their drinks to the table.

"By the way," Sue said as she stirred her coffee, the spoon clinking merrily against the side of the cup, "any news from your long, lost amigo?"

The reference to Richard startled Natascha. She had heard nothing from him since his phone call on New Year's Day and she had done well cordoning off any thoughts of him to the back of her mind, making wedding preparations her strict priority. It had been the perfect diversion which left her with very little time for reflection and having already handed the Sampson and French file over to Marissa Clarke she had had no further communication from his company, either.

"Er, no, not really. I heard Marissa say he went to Israel on a business trip but that must have been a few weeks ago... Anyway, Marissa's dealing with him now and I haven't heard from him." Natascha still had no inclination to tell Sue the entire story. "It all seems to have fizzled out quietly into oblivion..."

Without having had any word from him, it said everything Natascha needed to know. Richard had absolutely no plans to get in touch, if only to say hello.

Chapter Twenty-Five

'You are my rock whenever I stumble
You are my pillow whenever I cry
I give you my heart and I give you my soul
Such a pure love like mine will never grow old.

Days are covered in sunshine
And in the night sky the moon turns to gold
I give you my heart and I give you my soul
Such a pure love like mine will never grow old...'

Bridge:
Do you know what this means?
Don't you dream what I dream?
I'm in love, I'm so in love
Time won't change the way I feel

Deep in my mind, deep inside my body
Deep in the middle of my simple heart
I give you my life and I give you my soul
A pure love like mine will never grow old

No, a pure love like mine will never grow old'

With her guitar balanced on her knee, Natascha strummed the last chord at the end of the song and let the sound of the notes echo in the air for a few moments before bringing it to a final close. This was exactly how she had written it when she was a shy teenager and these were the words and the melody she would sing at Sue and Matteo's wedding. It was a relief to have finally found a song, but it worried her that someone she'd never met and knew nothing about was to hear her sing. What would he think of her? Natascha ran a weary hand through her hair and shrugged her shoulders. She'd just have to go through it again... The phone rang and she was forced to put down her guitar.

"Natascha? It's your best friend."

For a second, air got caught in Natascha's throat before she recognised the voice on the other end of the line. "Hello, Simon. Where are you now? Don't tell me... Standing outside B&Q! Or is it Toys 'R' Us? Maybe Argos' jewellery section, perhaps?"

"Very funny. It's a shame, you know. You're such a beautiful woman and yet your witty repartee lets you down every time! Ah. Er, forget what I just said. I was only joking, obviously," he added meekly, remembering the reason why he had called. *"Actually, I'm in dire need of your assistance. I'm in Arnold & Co. on the High Road, standing in my stockinged feet, hopelessly staring at three suits and facing a massive dilemma. Natascha, you've got to help me. I have to choose one but all I know is that*

it should be navy. I can't make up my mind which one I should go for and you're the only person I know who has any flair for style and knows what would look sharp! Is there any chance at all that you could just drop everything to come and help... Please?" The tone of Simon's voice rose to a high pitched plea.

The shop wasn't far and Natascha could be there in a matter of minutes.

"Well, as long as you're not standing in your underwear I'll be there in ten minutes."

"Oh, thank you, Natascha. You're an absolute saint!"

Through the large window of the shop front, Natascha saw Simon speaking to the assistant while buttoning up a jacket and scrutinising the cut, his back to the full length mirror and head looking over his shoulder at his reflection. The old fashioned bell on the door tinkled as she pushed it open.

"Oh, am I glad to see you! Thank goodness you were home."

Natascha suppressed a look of amusement when she saw the panic on Simon's face. "Right then, what have we got? Three contestants, I see."

Simon tried on the first suit and had to agree with Natascha that it wasn't quite right. It was then a difficult decision between the remaining two. Simon went back into the fitting room to try on the second finalist again, hoping it would be the decider.

While she waited, Natascha went and stood by the window and gazed out. It was large enough to have a clear view of the

High street and she watched shoppers bustle in and out of the shops, scurrying around one another trying to get to the next store. Many were carrying large bags filled with sale items from the last of the 'Well-Into-The-New-Year' sales, that had been eagerly purchased but were probably never to be utilised, she thought, mildly entertained. Others strolled casually along window shopping, much to the annoyance of the experienced bargain hunter. A mother with three little children, pushing a child's buggy and carrying two large bags caught Natascha's eye. She watched as the woman tried to juggle the children, the buggy and the bags along the pavement to the pedestrian crossing.

"What do you think?" Simon asked behind her, as he stepped out, adjusting the hemline of the jacket. "I definitely think it's going to be this one! ... But I'm not sure. Oh, help!"

The sound of Simon's voice brought Natascha out of her daydream and she turned around to see stress lines criss-crossing his face. "I honestly think that it is the best one," she said, taking a good look at the suit. "They're all very smart but I think that this one just has the edge on the others."

"Yes, you're right," Simon agreed enthusiastically, as he went back to the mirror to take one last look, examining the suit from every angle. "It definitely has a better fit than the others. I'll take this one," he said to the shop assistant. He was so excited and grateful for Natascha's help that he rushed over and wrapped his arms around her. "Thank you, my angel," he said, as he hugged her, relieved that with any luck, he wouldn't need to try on another suit for a long time.

***

The lights turned red and Richard slowed the car to a stop. 'Great!' he mumbled to himself and tried to calm his vexations at having been caught at this particular set of traffic lights, knowing that he was in for a long wait. Getting stuck here meant you weren't going anywhere soon!

He looked down and fiddled with the radio and tried to find something worth listening to. There seemed to be more inane chatter than music on every station these days. Since picking up the new BMW he'd picked out quickly and haphazardly from the showroom, he hadn't had the chance to play with any of the extra 'on board' toys, and took the opportunity to press a few buttons at random to see if any of the fancy gadgets could keep him amused while he waited. But he soon grew bored. He just didn't have the patience right now. Optimistically, he looked up to see whether the lights had changed yet but was distracted by a woman struggling to cross the road pushing a buggy, carrying shopping bags and dragging along the kids in tow without much success. Another glutton for shopping punishment, he thought, cynically. He looked to his left and absently redirected his attention to the row of shops. His eyes rested on a woman staring out into the street from the huge window of the menswear store, presumably waiting for her husband or partner. Richard looked closer and frowned inquisitively at the woman; he was stunned to see it was Natascha.

He wondered if he should park up somewhere and go to say hello - or maybe not... but it would be rude not to. Then again... The internal debate was resolved within moments. Richard watched as she was joined by the same man he had seen her kissing in the street and with whom she had gone into one of those nice houses in Branscombe Gardens, carrying a box between them. He looked on with profound disappointment as the man threw his arms around her, locking her in a tight embrace and Natascha, looking to be nothing but relaxed and comfortable in his arms, hugged him back.

Richard was tooted from behind when the lights turned green. Trying to wipe out what he had just witnessed from his mind, he turned up the volume of the radio to nearly full blast, thrust his foot down on the accelerator and moved off at almost breakneck speed.

***

Chapter Twenty-Six

Suitcases had been packed and re-packed several times to try and squeeze in everything Sue wanted to take with her. She was leaving tomorrow with Matteo to give themselves plenty of time in Italy before the wedding, making sure that all plans were progressing smoothly and to be on hand to iron out any potential problems. There had already been numerous telephone calls between the two countries, finalising and confirming plans. But actually being there would be less stressful for both of them. Natascha was on hand to help with the cases.

"Right then Natascha, it looks like we're all done at last," Sue said, surveying the three large suitcases. "I think we deserve a break. Time to sit and have a drink."

"I feel I should be going with you to help out. There's so much you need to take care of. I'm not entirely sure how much help I can offer seeing as I speak zero Italian, but I'm sure I could do something." Natascha felt somewhat guilty for having decided not to travel with her friend.

"Don't worry. You have your dress to sort out and the rest of the paraphernalia that goes with it and time is running out."

"It's all under control. I have all my wedding day accessories, shoes, handbag underwear, just waiting to be packed. I just have my bridesmaid's dress to pick up which I'm going to do on the Monday before I leave. It's only clothes for the rest of the time while I'm out there that I don't have room for!"

"Of course you're ready. I should have known you'd be organised well ahead of time," Sue said, with a sigh. "What made me think that you would be running around like a headless chicken like I've been doing?"

"Well, I haven't got it completely wrapped up. I'm trying to work on plan B just in case something unexpected goes wrong with the dress. I mean, I won't have long to sort anything out if they've altered it three inches too short."

"Oh yeah, that's bound to happen - I don't think! Don't be so negative and drink up," Sue said, as she handed Natascha a glass.

Natascha opened her bag and pulled out the CD of her song that she had prepared. "Don't forget this. It's the CD Matteo's cousin asked for. And don't look so excited, soon-to-be Mrs Sant' Angelo, it's for his ears only. I'm sure I can trust you not to give in to the temptation of a sneak preview. It's meant to be a surprise, remember?"

"I promise I will not listen. I promise I will do my best to hand it to Cristiano personally." Sue lifted three fingers in the air, "Scouts honour!"

Both Natascha and Sue were trying to keep up some semblance of normality, determined to spend these last few hours together cheerfully.

Sue took the CD and shoved it into her handbag that was sitting on the table beside her.

"So, what progress have you made in your search for your step-sibling?" Natascha asked, keeping the conversation bright.

"It wasn't as difficult as I first thought. Aunt Jessie actually had more information then she let on the first time. She thinks it was a boy. But she did have a name and the area in which she thought the adoptive parents used to live so I could check it out if I wanted. She warned me it was years ago, though. Anyway, I did some investigating, made a few phone calls and managed to get the most recent address. I'll try and make contact when I get to Italy." Sue had a distinct look of excitement in her eyes. "What a turn up. My family, previously consisting of one old aunt and her audio impaired husband, is now complete. From nowhere, I have a brother - a brother! It may well turn out that he wants nothing to do with me, of course, but I can still say I have a real live BROTHER!" Sue wrinkled her nose. "Okay, okay a step-brother, then!"

She looked truly contented. To any other person, the addition of a new member to the family may perhaps give rise to nothing more than a certain level of curiosity but to Sue it was everything. Without any parents to make up a proper family, a sibling, even though there was no blood tie, was absolutely the next best thing. Natascha was still concerned that perhaps she was being a little too optimistic. She could so easily be let down. But Sue was Sue. She didn't mind finding out the hard way. She was used to it.

"Well, best of luck." Natascha put down her glass and stood up. "I'd better be off. You'll need an early night before tomorrow," she said, hugging Sue. The joviality of the evening had somehow dissipated and the sobering mood brought with it reality.

"I know I'll see you soon but I'll be desperate for you to arrive. I'm going to need you there for the run-up so much." Sue paused to try and control her emotions. "And don't forget your dress. I can't wait to see what you've chosen."

They looked at one other with the fondness of close sisters, and again pulled each other in for a tight hug.

"I really do wish you were coming with me tomorrow," Sue whispered, her voice breaking down. "I'm really going to miss you."

"Sue, you'll be so busy that the time will rush by. I'll be with you in no time, I promise."

And for the last time they said their goodbyes. Natascha turned and walked out of the door and the tear that had been teetering in the corner of her eye could no longer be held back and finally slipped over the edge to roll down her cheek.

Chapter Twenty-Seven

Sitting in the staff restaurant and nibbling at the sandwich which she held in one hand, Natascha studied the notepad that lay in her lap. Her other hand held a pen which she twisted between her fingers as she concentrated. The dining hall was fairly busy with lots of chatter and lots of movement but she didn't notice any of it. She went over her 'to do' list, making notes where necessary:

- Apply for leave and book flights √
- Shoes and handbag √
- Arrange taxi pick-up to airport √
- Buy new Italian phrase book   (Waterstones this weekend)
- Purchase Euros (this weekend)
- Record song for Matteo's cousin √ (CD already sent via Sue)
- Pick up dress (Monday)
- Mum's shopping list √
- Rehearse song again and again and again...

Natascha was so engrossed in the bullet points and their suffixes that she hadn't noticed Marissa until she was already sitting beside her.

"A penny for them?"

Natascha looked up. "Oh Marissa, I didn't see you. I'm just going through my list of what I need to sort out before I go away."

"Well, you look like you're trying hard to work out how to make a square peg fit into a round hole!"

"A friend of mine is getting married in Italy and I'm going over there in a couple of weeks."

"Oh yes, I heard. A wedding in Italy, how romantic!" Marissa bubbled, impressed. "It's a bit of a shame that the wedding isn't in the summer, though."

"Oh, I don't know, a winter wedding sounds rather charming to me."

"Of course it is, but what are the chances of meeting a nice young Italian guy in a tight t-shirt and matching shorts in the snow; a sight to be appreciated purely as a work of art, obviously!" Marissa tried to sound serious but was having a lot of trouble hiding a naughty grin.

"Marissa, you are incorrigible. And you, a mum to be! You should be ashamed of yourself," Natascha laughed.

She then mmm'd and ahh'd whether she should ask or not but in the end decided that it could do no real harm. "How are you getting on with Mr French, you know, from Sampson and

French? Is he any friendlier with you than he was with me?" Natascha asked, casually.

Marissa swallowed her mouthful of coffee eager to convey some news. "Didn't he tell you? Richard French isn't dealing with Colonia anymore. He handed the clients' event over to his partner, Bradley Sampson, to look after. Not quite as nice looking as Mr French but definitely more normal!"

Natascha was taken aback. "Oh," she said, indifferently, "no, I didn't know." But she was even less prepared for the next missile that Marissa was about to launch.

"Yeah, apparently, he's moving to Mauritius to take over the company's newly set up offices there. New offices? Huh, what an excuse! That's not work, that's just one long, all expenses paid, holiday! Maybe, taking your laptop to the beach counts as work! What do you think?" Marissa giggled. But when she realised that Natascha hadn't uttered a single comment, she cleared her throat and quickly carried on. "He's going next week, I think. It's not been confirmed exactly how long he's going for, but it's for a year at least, if not indefinitely, Bradley told me. I thought Mr French would have mentioned it to you."

"Really? Moving to Mauritius? No, no he never mentioned it," Natascha finally replied, as evenly as she could without betraying her shock. She made the gesture of checking her watch. "Oh, is it that time? I'd better get back. I'll see you later, Marissa." She sprang to her feet and took her leave, doing her best to regulate her breathing which was now coming in short bursts.

Back in the privacy of her own office, she shut the door and lowered herself into her chair, numbed by what she had just found out. It felt as if she had physically suffered a blow to the chest, leaving her breathless.

Closing her eyes, Natascha thought back over the sequence of events leading her here, to this moment. After the evening when Richard had poured out his life story to her, she had agreed with him that it was right that they should not try to pick up their friendship from where it had been left to wither away so long ago. An occasional phone call or an email would have been enough for them to stay in touch. However, since his phone call at New Year, she had been subconsciously counting the time that had elapsed between then and now, every day unknowingly disheartened that she had had no word from him. Sue's wedding had been a useful distraction but Richard's silence had been tapping away at her like a soundless woodpecker - she didn't hear it but she could definitely feel the vibrations of its actions.

Maybe, it was time to be honest. There was no point in deceiving herself anymore. A rare phone call or rogue email would never have been enough for her. Her real expectation of a friendship with Richard was very simple. What her heart truly desired, perhaps over-optimistically, was the chance of meeting with him regularly, it didn't even have to be often. She wanted to share any news and tell him about recent events in her life and he would do the same. A mere fraction of what they used to have would have been perfectly enough for her, as long as she could still call him her friend. Richard, on the other hand, had kept true to his word. He did not feel as she did and so his idea of keeping in contact did not match hers. A yearly Christmas card was maybe all she should expect from him.

But Natascha was not prepared to be so far down his list of priorities and so insignificant, that he didn't even feel it necessary to let her know of, what she considered to be, a monumental development. He was leaving the country, perhaps for good but didn't think it was important whether he told her about it or not. That thought was painful. Richard had let her down and the disappointment was upsetting. But again, it was her own fault for making such baseless assumptions on what she now saw as a very brittle attachment. Twenty years ago there had been no real finish to their friendship and perhaps this was the reason for her misjudged hopes of a new relationship. It was time to resolve that and end it as should have been done all those years ago. The finale to this story would at last enable her to pick up her life where she had left off months ago. She reached for the phone and calmly dialled his number.

"*Hello. Richard French.*"

"Hello Richard, it's Natascha."

"*Oh, er, Natascha... I've been meaning to get in touch with you.*"

Natascha squeezed a little light-heartedness into her voice. "It's just that I haven't heard from you in a while and thought that perhaps you'd decided to stay in Israel, so I thought I'd give you a call."

"Yes... I'm sorry. Work has been frenzied."

"I understand." Natascha waited for him to speak, waited for him to tell her his news. He did not. Staying painfully pleasant, she continued. "I'm told you're moving to Mauritius."

"Er, yes... Their developing I.T sector is growing well and is business I don't want to miss out on. It's only for... well actually, I'm not sure how long it's going to be for...," he said, trailing away his reply.

"Wow! What a location to expand your business! How exotic. Mauritius is a beautiful island. Extraordinarily beautiful beaches, I'm told. Yes, I suppose it can be difficult to estimate how long these things will take."

There was a pause and Natascha could hear Richard take a deep breath. *"I was about to let you know, but..."*

"You're, no doubt, going to be extremely busy over the next few months, I suspect," she cut in, before he had a chance to finish his sentence. "Settling in will probably take up all of your time." It was the moment for Natascha to deliver her message. "I suppose then, that this might be the right time to be honest with ourselves and end this well-meaning but hopeless new friendship. Maybe we both wanted it to work but I don't think either of us really believed it could. We had a wonderful childhood together but so many things have happened to us in our lives that we're very different people now. We've both changed so much that I'm not sure we have very much in common anymore. Why don't we keep hold of those precious memories, say goodbye properly this time and both get on with our own lives the best way we know how? I really think we were meant to meet again to do just that."

Richard made no comment. He did not even try to disagree with her.

"It's about time everything started to work out for you, Richard. You deserve it. And who knows, this could be the new beginning you've been looking for." There was a long and very heavy pause. "Goodbye Richard," she said, tears catching in her throat, failing now to disguise how she really felt. She waited for a moment, but hearing nothing, she ended the call.

A sudden sense of release came over Natascha but this was almost instantaneously drowned by incredible sadness and regret; sadness that she had to do what she had just accomplished and regret because deep down, she had really wanted their once beautiful friendship to go on. But it was not meant to be that way and now she could put the whole affair in order and lose it in her mind's repository.

However, Richard had changed something inside her. He had set alight in her the need for a deeper relationship with someone with whom she could share at least some part of her life. It had become an alien feeling for a long time but it was coming back. Not since Laurent had she felt such deep emotions. It was impossible to know how she would deal with this unveiling of her heart but she would no longer set up barricades against a more meaningful connection in her life, should this person ever appear.

***

The phone lay limply in Richard's hand. He could hear the faint uninterrupted beep of the disconnected line but was finding it hard to replace the phone in its cradle. Natascha was right, of course. This was how it should be. He had wanted to call it quits a long time ago but putting the phone down now would really mean the end - like he was irreparably severing all ties. Richard suddenly felt angry with himself. Why the hell was he feeling like this? Get over it. Wasn't this exactly what he wanted, not having to see her or even talk to her again? But the anger was short-lived. Oh, for the love of Pete! Why do you keep trying to fool yourself? Just be straight with yourself for once and admit it. You're going to miss her. You're going to miss her so very, very badly. He stared at the rows of numbers on the phone, 'but it's finished now', he said aloud putting it back in its proper place, 'it's over'. And packing the last of his belongings into the small crate, he shrugged into his coat, picked up the box and closed his office door for the last time.

***

Chapter Twenty-Eight

'Tickets? Check. Passport? Check'. Natascha zipped up her handbag for the last time and placed it by the door with the rest of her luggage.

Her suitcase, although large, had been taken up by dresses and flower baskets for the flower girls, two vases of sentimental value from Sue's mother's house (wrapped in copious amounts of bubblewrap for a safe journey) and a small satin bag, in a larger than necessary box, that matched Sue's wedding dress that she would carry on the day. They were perhaps the larger items in amongst additional wedding trappings. Natascha's own shoes, handbag and other accessories had to be squeezed in and any clothes she had managed to bring with her were only for the purpose of packing in between all the other items so they wouldn't be thrown about during the flight. Her bridesmaid's dress had been expertly packed by the bridal shop in a strong, specially designed box and would be taken on board the plane as hand luggage. Her guitar took pride of place among the luggage.

Sue had pointed out that the severe lack of clothing she was bringing with her was the perfect excuse to acquire some of the latest Italian designs. Shopping in Italy was an absolute necessity. Natascha laughed as she always did when presented with Sue's sometimes dubious sense of logic. In the middle of this thought there was a knock at the door. The taxi had arrived.

After watching her luggage being carried away on the conveyor belt, she checked her watch and searched for somewhere to sit while she waited to board her flight.

She spotted a vacant seat and made her way over to the end of a row of chairs, positioning her guitar and bridesmaid's dress beside her. A few moments of inexplicable panic earlier had subsided when she realised that she was simply experiencing a side-effect of recent events that would soon pass. It was all part of the process of regaining her inner calm.

Broodingly, she ran a finger over the guitar case and allowed her mind to slip back in time. It slowed to that time in her life when performing was nothing but an absolute joy.

The mixture of nerves and excitement before she went on stage was exhilarating. Laurent's encouragement to turn a pastime into something more significant was the push she had needed. He had persuaded her to join him at the nightclub where he was the resident entertainer.

They sang together and, to look aesthetically more pleasing on stage, he also played the guitar. Their compatible singing styles produced well-received performances. And it was their growing popularity with the audiences and their mutual love of music that threw them closer and closer together until their professional relationship evolved into a romantic one. The natural step of moving in together was inevitable and for two years they shared a life together. Laurent taught her how to improve her guitar playing technique and gave sound advice on song-writing. He was a true musical talent and she had learnt a great deal from him. But a sick mother in France meant that he often had to stay away for short periods. His sweet, caring nature only made Natascha love him more.

It was a time when she was truly happy, with a man she increasingly loved with every day they were together. And she was on a career path that would have taken her across the country and maybe beyond. Life was fun back then, travelling to so many different places and meeting so many new people. The money wasn't great at first but it was enough for them to live a fairly decent life and it was getting more financially rewarding all the time. It was an amazing time for her but, like all good things, it had come to an end...

A sigh escaped her as she opened her eyes and floated back down into her seat and into the present. She was looking forward to her holiday in Italy. Christmas had not exactly been the relaxing break she had envisaged. In fact, it had all been a harrowing nightmare and it was long overdue that she got away to enjoy a proper break - an extremely hard earned break. Sue had begged Natascha to come out to Italy well before the wedding so that she could enjoy more of a holiday rather than just simply being roped in to help with wedding preparations. At the time she had, a little reluctantly, allowed Sue to persuade her to change her mind and leave for Italy a week earlier than originally planned. Now she was thankful she did. Meeting her friend again and, no doubt, being absorbed by wedding fever, was just what she needed. In her present state of mind, exploring a different place in the world, listening to the melodies of a different language and wandering amongst new people far removed from those she knew, could not be better therapy.

Pulling out the book she had not opened in far too long from her handbag, she bent down to pick up a battered piece of paper which had fallen out with it and dropped to the floor. As she began to unravel it, it didn't take her long to recognise what it was. She straightened out the business card Richard had given to her outside the café, an episode in their recent reunion she would really rather forget.

The words on the card became a blur of letters as irrational tears filled her eyes. But she had to smile at the irony of trying to get away from all that reminded her of Richard, only to find that she had been carrying a little bit of him with her wherever she went, hidden underneath a paperback in her handbag. Natascha smoothed her fingers over his name '*Richard French BEng MSc (Hons)*'. When he had given her the card she had taken a look at his name and the handful of abbreviations that followed it and cynically thought how arrogantly impressive it looked. Now it looked perfect - just how it should be. Her eyes travelled over the office address and the now familiar telephone number and email address. However, the details were redundant, now that he was moving to Mauritius and it was silly to keep hold of the card. She clasped her fingers around it to crumple it up and discard it but something held her back and without making a conscious decision, she straightened it out as best as she could and slipped it back into an inside pocket of her bag.

The monitor indicated that her flight was boarding. She stood up from her seat, confidently slung her handbag over her shoulder and, picking up her belongings, she made her way to the departure gate with her bridesmaid's dress in one hand and her guitar case in the other.

Part Two

Chapter Twenty-Nine

Italy

Pushing her trolley through into the arrivals hall, Natascha peered into an ocean of faces waiting for friends and relatives who had disembarked from flights that had recently landed. Names of passengers were randomly being called out from the lively chatter of excited voices, although the smartly dressed chauffeurs, holding up pieces of card with the names of the strangers they were to meet, did not appear to share the same enthusiasm. The description of the person who was to meet Natascha was rather vague; the only information Sue had given her was that he was a young man with messy light brown hair and bluey-grey eyes. The piece of paper Natascha held in her hand only had details of his name and telephone number.

Then, from amid the bodies, she could hear her name repeatedly being called and as she scanned the area she saw an arm waving up above the heads of the crowd. The sound of her name was coming from the same direction.

"Nata-scha." A fresh-faced young lad was smiling and waving at her. He pointed to a spot at the end of the line of people where the crowd thinned and Natascha weaved her luggage through the other passengers to make her way there. The young man who had been waving appeared beside her.

"*Ciao*, Nata-scha," he said, with a lilting Italian accent. "You are Nata-scha, no?"

"I am." She glanced down at the piece of paper she was holding. "You must be Alessio." He ignored her outstretched hand, grabbed her by the shoulders and kissed her gaily on both cheeks instead.

"I saw you with your guitar. Sue said you would have a guitar. That's how I knew you, you see!" He paused, stepped back and took an admiring look at her. "*Molto bella!*" he said, with a roguish twinkle in his eye. "Sue told me also that I would know you because you are very beautiful."

Natascha smiled and laughed lightly. "*Grazie.*"

Alessio was a friend of the family who had offered to meet her at the airport and take her to Sue and Matteo's home where they would be waiting. A prior engagement with the local parish priest prevented them from meeting her themselves.

"It's nice to meet you," she said, still amused from his unabashed earlier comment.

"It is nice to meet you, too. You can come with me? My car is outside."

He was much younger than Natascha had expected, somewhere in his early twenties, she guessed. He was friendly with boyish good-looks and a bubbly personality, and taking charge of the luggage, he pushed the trolley towards the car park.

As she stepped out into the afternoon air, Natascha breathed in the delicious perfume of the Mediterranean that greeted her. It all felt fresh and new and the pace of life seemed to have slowed to a leisurely stroll. It was as if she had landed on another planet. Home could have been a million miles away. Natascha also had the curious feeling that an adventure was awaiting her and she wondered at the vibes of excitement and expectancy that teasingly stirred inside her.

Alessio guided her to a sturdy, yet very elegant looking Land Rover, carefully arranged her luggage and guitar inside with plenty of room to spare, then moved to the front of the car and held open the passenger door. "Please, come in. You are tired from the journey, I think?" he asked.

Natascha thought about it. "No, as a matter of fact I'm not," she said, realising that she wasn't in the least bit tired. "I'm very happy to be here and I'm looking forward to my holiday."

"I am afraid we have quite a long journey to Siena. We will be perhaps one and a half hours. It is a long way."

"Yes, I realised that when I was booking my flight but it seems that Perugia airport is the closest to Siena. It's really very kind of you to take the time to come and meet me."

"Oh, it is my pleasure. It will not be nice for you to take the train with all the bags."

"Well then, perhaps it will give us a chance to talk and get to know one another."

Natascha appreciated the passing scenery. Going through the towns and villages before getting onto the main highway gave her an opportunity to admire the architecture and with some of the trees leafless in the winter, she could pick out some of the finer features on the buildings and houses. Not since her short visit to Richard's house had she come across such historical beauty. The drama of that night suddenly made a threat to drive forward to the forefront of Natascha's mind but she quickly blotted out the memory and its details.

The day was bright and in the more rural areas, the sunshine reflected off the acres of bare vineyards transforming the vista into a watercolour.

"You are working in England?"Alessio asked, after a few minutes.

"Yes, I do. I'm an Events Organiser, helping people and companies arrange their parties and festivals, that type of thing. Sometimes I organise large events such as pop concerts and exhibitions but day to day I mainly deal with business conferences and social events. It's an interesting job but it can also be quite demanding. What do you do? Are you still studying?"

"Oh no, I finished at the college last year and I have been helping my father on his farm until I can have enough money to have my own one. At college I learnt about business in farming."

"That sounds very practical. And what do you do in your spare time?"

"I like to go to clubs and listen to music. I like music very much." Alessio nodded towards the back of the car. "You have brought a guitar. Do you play?"

"Well, yes, I'd like to think that I do, just a little."

"Are you in a band or do you play, er, *chitarra classica*, you know? Me, I am in a band. I play the drums."

Natascha was comfortable when it came to the topic of music. "No, I don't play classical guitar although I would like to and I'm not in a band. A very long time ago I used to sing with a friend but I don't do that anymore."

"Okay." Something seemed to be going through Alessio's mind. "Oh, wait a minute! You are Sue's friend who will be singing at the wedding?"

"Oh." Nervously, Natascha cleared her throat as the reality of why she was carrying her guitar around with her hit home. She was so enraptured with being in Italy and enjoying the scenery, that she had been able forget for a while the dread that niggled at her incessantly as the time for her to sing at the wedding gathered momentum. She turned and looked at her guitar lying on the back seat, seeing it for the first time as being something of a sinister object. "Er, yes. I'm doing it as a special favour."

"Me and the group have been practising your song."

In that very moment, Natascha lifted her eyes towards the heavens as the connection dawned on her. "Are you in Cristiano's band?"

"Yes, I am the drummer." Alessio looked excited. "This means we will be playing together at the wedding." His face lit up at the prospect. "This is very good, no?"

Natascha winced inside. When Sue had told her that Cristiano and his band would be playing at the wedding, at no point did she suspect that the group members were a bunch of teenagers. "Are you all very young?" she asked him, anxiously having visions of looking like an old 'has been' trying to resurrect her career by singing with a trendy new boy band!

"Oh no, I am the youngest," he said, casually.

"Right..." Natascha was trying to get to grips with Alessio's announcement. "...so, obviously you've heard the song. I'm sure it isn't the type of music you are used to playing." She felt a cringing within. To Alessio, Natascha's song probably sounded as though it had been written back in the dark ages.

"I like all music. In Cristiano's band we have to play all music because we play for all kinds of people. Sometimes it is for the party for the *bambinos* or sometimes it is maybe for the *nonne e i nonni*, er, how do you say it, grandmothers and grandfathers." Alessio looked proudly at Natascha. "But my mother likes your kind of music very much!"

'Hmm...,' Natascha thought. That sounded about right.

Changing the subject, Natascha decided to move the conversation away from music. "Your English is excellent. They must teach it very well in school."

Alessio laughed. "Oh no, perhaps they teach it well in school but I did not listen very much while I was there. It is my girlfriend. She is from England. Usually, she studies tourism at university in England. But at the moment, she is here, in Italy, working for one year in a hotel, not far from Siena to make her Italian better. I help her to speak Italian and she teaches me a little bit of English. I do not think that it is so good. I went to England when I was younger for a little while but I did not learn so much."

"No, believe me. Your English is very good." Alessio was so bright and vivacious that Natascha couldn't fail but be cheered by his enthusiasm, providing her with some much needed respite from her vexing and preoccupied mind.

Chapter Thirty

"We are here," Alessio announced, as he pulled up outside a charming Mediterranean farmhouse.

Natascha stepped out of the car and was very impressed by what she saw. The house, built using traditional pale-coloured stonework and a warm terracotta roof, sat in the middle of approximately half an acre of beautifully maintained lawn, edged with rich, green Cypress trees. She looked up to see light grey smoke swirling out daintily from the chimney. I'm going to like it here, she thought, with a smile lifting the corners of her lips. It was as pretty as any picture you would find in a holiday brochure.

Natascha scarcely had time to shut the car door when she heard Sue calling her name, running towards her with her arms wide open before flinging them around her friend.

"Oh Natascha, I couldn't wait for you to get here. Boy, am I glad to see you!" she said, as she squeezed Natascha in a tight hold. "Your timing's perfect. I've just got back myself. Oh, this is great! How was the flight? Did Alessio behave himself? He can be quite a cheeky chappy...," she babbled, unable to contain her excitement.

"He was the perfect gentleman," Natascha replied, after having been released from Sue's embrace.

"Well, that's a relief! I had visions of this young whippersnapper trying to chat you up!"

After the luggage was brought into the house, Natascha accompanied Alessio back to his car. "It was very kind of you to meet me. Thank you very much."

"It is my pleasure to have such a beautiful passenger," he said, with a wink. "I will see you again at rehearsals, yes?" he said, eagerly.

An irregular heartbeat upset her blissful contentment for just a moment. She took a small deep breath. "Yes, of course. I'm looking forward to it."

Alessio grinned, kissed her on both cheeks and drove away.

"Come on, let's put your things in your room and then I can take you on a grand tour of the house," Sue said excitedly, as she shut the door behind Natascha. She picked up the suitcase and led the way to the spare room.

"Ooh! Am I going to be sleeping in that gorgeous, huge bed?" Natascha gasped, when greeted with the enormous super king-sized bed, dressed in crisp white sheets, stark against navy blue cushions. "And just look at the beautifully carved wardrobe and drawers! I'm going to love it here." The brightness of the room was enhanced by the blast of vivid colour coming from an abstract painting and a beautiful arrangement of winter flowers. "I feel like a real pop diva! This, my friend, is yet more irrefutable evidence of your very expensive taste!" Natascha added, with a knowing smile.

Sue shrugged her shoulders. "I don't know what you mean," she retorted, "I got this lot from a car boot sale!" An innocent expression played in her eyes but it didn't last long and she ended it by pulling a face.

The fresh, bright room and Sue's excitement did much to lift Natascha's spirits yet a little higher.

After taking Natascha around the house the tour ended in the kitchen. Sue put on some coffee and assembled a small spread of traditional miniature ricotta cheese and spinach Panini's and some local sweet biscuits on the large rustic table and they sat down.

"It's really beautiful. I think you and Matteo will be very happy here," Natascha said, gazing around as true peace of mind settled comfortably within, now she knew that her friend's decision to make such a huge change in her life was the perfect one. "It's much bigger than I thought. And so much space!" she continued cheerfully, putting aside her deeper thoughts to share in Sue's excitement. She nibbled her sandwich. "Do Matteo's parents live far from here?"

"It's about a ten minute walk. You can see the Sant' Angelo's house from here."

Natascha got up from the table and ambled across to the window.

"It's towards the right, up on the hill."

A very grand sandy coloured building, what could only be described as a stately farmhouse, sat proudly on the plateau of a gentle hill, surveying its acres and acres of vineyards. The rows of vine, stripped of any foliage, were sectioned off into neat squares and sewn together like a patchwork by the tall, rich forest green of the Cypress trees. Orderly squares of olive groves and their silvery leaves added contrasting texture to this quilt that covered the land and the scenery rolled way off into the distance until it became an undistinguishable mass of grey, blurred against a hazy blue sky and diluted yellow winter sun.

"When you told me the family ran a vineyard, I certainly did not expect this. The estate is huge. Does it really all belong to them?"

"It does. It might look a bit desolate at the moment but as soon as spring arrives and the leaves begin to appear on the vine it takes on a totally different feel. And in the summer, when the grapes are abundant, it really is a fantastic sight. At harvest time, everywhere you look great vats of grapes are moving all over the grounds and up the country roads; although all I can picture when I see so much fruit are hundreds and hundreds of bottles of wine. And that, I can tell you, is quite an image!"

Natascha came back to the table.

"Come back in September when harvesting starts. We can go to all the festivals, drink wine to our hearts content and have a great laugh! What do you say?"

"Stop now, Sue. You're making me very envious of your new life," Natascha said, trying to sound light-hearted when in fact, she was beginning to feel that a change in her own life as major as the change in Sue's was perhaps something that needed serious consideration.

Earnestness replaced the fun on Sue's face. "There's plenty of room for you here, you know. All you need to do is say the word and we can get something sorted out."

A wistful smile shaped Natascha's lips. "You're a lot braver than I'll ever be."

The mood had changed to become quietly sober which Sue broke before it had a chance to take root.

"Why don't you go and freshen up and then we can have a glass of wine. The coffee was just to line the stomach!" she suggested, with a cheeky smirk.

"Good idea. I won't be long."

After having showered and changed, Natascha took out the bridesmaid's dress from her luggage, ready to hang in the wardrobe and as she straightened out the few inevitable wrinkles, her mind wandered. The thoughts she had had while speaking to Sue about making a drastic change in her life, were not as remote as they once may have been. The straight path to her future had grown bends and turns that were making her dizzy, leaving her road in desperate need of remodelling. And since the idea of a new life in a brand new environment had somehow now topped her list of important issues for evaluation, perhaps it should be seriously considered as part of her major life rebuild.

The movement of her hand smoothing the material of the dress slowed until she was hardly touching it at all, when an audible moan full of logic escaped her as unexpectedly it all became clear. It was obvious. It had all become mixed-up in her head. It wasn't really Richard's friendship she wanted to hold onto, she was trying to cling onto Sue's. She was losing her soul mate and it was hard for her. Sue's permanent move to Italy was a massive loss which, deep down, Natascha had not been fully able to accept. She had tried to compensate for it by searching for a substitute. Richard's arrival had simply capitalised on her, then unperceived, insecurities of Sue's future plans and had played tricks on her. The Richard she once knew would have been the perfect substitute. He would have helped to alleviate the deprivation of Sue's company. The old Richard would have understood, would have been her confidante just as Sue had always been. He was the only other person who had ever really known her, the only other person she would have trusted with her life. But the old Richard was gone and in his place was a whole new other person. The old Richard no longer existed. How could she have become so confused? This was the explanation she had been looking for, to make sense of it all. It explained why she felt so strongly about her misguided feelings for him - it had to be.

Her glass of wine was waiting for her when she returned to the kitchen. She had left her troubles back in her room and would leave them there for now.

"Mmm, this is very nice," Natascha commented, impressed by the quality of the wine. "I assume this is a bottle produced from the very grapes of this very vineyard?"

"You assume right. It's a couple of years old and I'm proud to say that I helped at the grape harvest that year." Sue held her glass into the light and swirled the liquid around. "Look at the colour," she said, with the lofty manner of a connoisseur and holding the glass to her nose, she carried on, "smell the fruity underlying tones of raspberries and blackcurrants, strawberries and cream and just the hint of my mother's hearty sausage and mash!" she said, almost choking with laughter.

"You may well laugh now but I'm willing to bet that it won't be long before you're dissecting the qualities of every sip you drink, swishing it around your mouth and letting it glide down your throat, studying its merits as it passes over your well-versed and discerning tongue." Natascha tried to stay serious but could not and she also started to laugh.

They were acting like a couple of schoolgirls.

When the laughter died down, Sue looked seriously at Natascha. "You'll have to tell me all about it now."

Natascha looked puzzled. "What do you mean? Tell you about what?"

"You can let down that fancy smokescreen now. I know you too well. You've been hiding something from me for a very long time and I think that maybe you'd feel a lot better if you came clean. It's the body language; it can be saying one thing - always the calm, confident Natascha. But your eyes? Your eyes tell me a totally different story."

Sue couldn't be more right, but Natascha had been adamant that she would not breathe a word of her anxieties and the current state of her problematic life to anyone, especially Sue. However, she knew she wasn't going to be able to pass it off this time by wearing an innocent smile and a baffled expression. "All right, all right, you win," she said, at last. It took her a couple of seconds to decide how she was to tackle it. "It's this friend of mine or more to the point, this so-called friend. Things got a little more complicated between us, that's all."

Sue narrowed her eyes. "Complicated?"

"Yes, just a bit… confused." Natascha hesitated. "We met up for that drink, as you know and one thing led to another..."

"Led to another what?"

"It ended with us sleeping together. There, that's it. That's all it is."

"What?" Sue shrieked."

"I know, I know. It was a moment of weakness, I suppose," Natascha said, nonchalantly.

"You went to bed with him and you call it a moment of weakness! Natascha, I've known you for a very long time and there's no way you would ever suffer a moment's weakness that resulted in you jumping into a man's bed!"

"I didn't jump into his bed."

"Sorry, that was a bit harsh but you know what I mean."

Natascha slowed her breathing to compose herself. "Perhaps it had something to do with a feeling of 'for old time's sake'. Maybe it was the familiarity, I don't know..."

"'For old time's sake'? Hey, you didn't say it was *that* kind of a relationship!"

"No, it wasn't, we were just friends. I don't know why I said that..."

"You told me it had all 'fizzled out'."

"I know. I'm sorry."

Sue shrugged her shoulders and took a gulp of wine. "So?" she then asked, with a mischievous grin.

"So...?"

"So, what was it like?" she asked again, expectantly, eyes wide open in anticipation.

"What?" Natascha saw the look on her friend's face. "Oh no you don't! You surely don't expect me to..."

"Okay, okay." Sue raised her hands in surrender. "Anyway, what's the latest? When's the next date?"

Calmly, Natascha continued. "Next date? No, I don't think there's going to be a next date. I haven't heard from him since." This wasn't strictly true, but Natascha did not want to go into it.

"Wow! A 'wam bam thank you ma'am' kind of guy, is he? He sounds like a bit of a creep to me - no disrespect." Sue's tone of voice had returned to normal. "So, it was a one-off."

"Oh yes, definitely a one-off - a big one-off mistake! It wasn't right. *He* wasn't right. He's such a different person now. I thought that I recognised something of the old in him but I was wrong." Natascha tried to speak evenly and casually and hoped that her explanation was enough to satisfy Sue's curiosity.

"Well, I can't quite believe it. No man even reaches first base without you being absolutely sure that it's what you want and even then, it's only on your terms."

Natascha raised her eyebrows and nodded slowly in agreement. "I know. I admit I slipped and I can't deny it. I do regret it but there's nothing I can do about it now. I just hope I never have to see him again..." She paused. "But anyway," Natascha continued at last, needing to change the conversation, "turning to more important things, aren't you in the least bit curious to see what your Maid of Honour will be wearing at your wedding?"

Sue was still pondering over Natascha's story. She still wasn't sure that her account of it was as simple as the tale that had been related to her. Natascha didn't dance to any man's tune. Something wasn't quite right but it was obvious that her friend didn't want to say any more about it.

Sue brightened her mood. "Yes, of course I am, let's take a look at it," she said, as she got up and moved towards the bedroom with Natascha following her.

Chapter Thirty-One

"There, what do you think?" Natascha removed the dress from the wardrobe and held it up for Sue's inspection."

"That is gorgeous! The colour is even nicer than I remember. I'm glad you went for a long straight skirt. I knew that I could count on your good taste. You're going to look sensational in it."

"Not that sensational, I hope. My job is to enhance the bride. I don't want to be accused of trying to upstage her!"

"Natascha, I want you to have as special a day as I'm going to have and for that to happen you've got to look and feel amazing."

Sue's sincere words moved Natascha. "I know for sure that you are going to look spectacular on your wedding day. I just want to complement you." She paused for a moment, "And I want to be there for you. I'd like you to know that you can always rely on me."

Before emotions had a chance to bubble over, Sue grinned mischievously, "And perhaps you can be there to keep one of Matteo's single male friends company too, eh! There'll be quite a few to choose from. You'll be spoilt for choice!"

Natascha shook her head. "I don't think so, somehow. I've had my fill of all that recently. Come, let's go. We have half-drunk glasses of wine waiting for us in the kitchen."

Back in the kitchen Sue munched on a biscuit. "So, how are you feeling? Revitalised? Ready for action?" she asked, with her mouth full.

"I feel great," Natascha enthused, still not quite telling the truth but doing her best. The subject of Richard was still crazily emotional and it also dawned on her that moments like these with Sue were soon be a thing of the past. But she was determined not to let any negative thoughts colour her mood

"Good. Then you'll be okay about meeting Cristiano later. He asked me to take you over to see him as soon as you were ready and I guess there's no time like the present! He's looking forward to meeting you."

Ah. Now this was different and Natascha had been caught out. She wasn't ready to meet him yet, this person who had listened to her song and had heard her sing although she'd never set eyes on him. He made her feel, in a way, exposed and she didn't like it. But making up an excuse to get out of it would, no doubt, fall on deaf ears. Natascha didn't say yes or no, but constructed a look of interest.

"Well, Matteo will be home soon and I can get him to take us there. I need to get a few bits and pieces from the shop, anyway. We'll be able to do that while you and Cristiano get acquainted. How does that sound?"

Natascha replied as convincingly as she could. "That sounds fine."

"And don't forget, *la mia casa è la tua casa* or something along those lines. Well, whatever the Italian is, do whatever you have to do to make yourself at home."

"Thanks Sue. I'll go and unpack my case." She tried not to but Natascha was feeling just a little bit nervous about meeting this man; to make public to him what she had long kept very personal.

Her guitar was sitting beside her in the car on the short journey to where they were to meet Cristiano. Natascha wasn't sure what the plan was so she had brought it along just in case.

"Here we are," Matteo announced. "Cristiano said that he will be in the hall."

Leaving her guitar in the car, she followed Sue and Matteo into the community hall.

"Hey, Cristiano," Matteo shouted. At the other end of the hall a man wearing worn jeans and a loose fitting pullover was squatted on the floor, rummaging around for something, ankle deep in cables.

"*Ciao, Matteo.*" At the sound of Matteo's voice, he got up, waved and made his way towards them.

Cristiano De Luca's tall, slim figure showed off his golden olive complexion and a healthy, sun-kissed Mediterranean glow.

"*Cristiano, come stai, amico mio?*" The two men hugged each other, slapping each other on the back, revealing an undoubted closeness. "Let me introduce you to Natascha. Natascha, this is Cristiano, my cousin and also my very, very good friend."

Blond highlights, bleached by the summer's sun, had tinged his chestnut brown hair which hung in soft curls and bounced playfully as he came forward to kiss her on both cheeks. "It is very nice to meet you at last. I have been listening to you before I ever saw you. Strange, huh?" His bright, sea-green eyes twinkled and the slight upturned corners of his lips gave the impression that he was always smiling.

He must have been somewhere in his early thirties, much the same as Natascha but his overall appearance had a fresh and youthful radiance. Natascha didn't quite know why she had expected an older, slightly balding and hippy-ish musician-type look, so in Cristiano, she had a pleasant surprise.

Turning to Sue, his manner took on an air of familiarity, "And you, *bella*, it is always lovely to see you," he said, as he kissed her, too.

"Cristiano, I don't really know what you intend to do but can we leave Natascha in your capable hands and you can talk about whatever it is you need to talk about? Matteo and I have some shopping that we can take care of in the meantime. We should be about an hour or so. Is that all right?"

"Yes, of course."

"Will I need my guitar?" Natascha asked Cristiano. "It's in the car."

"Yes, why not. It will be a good idea to have a practice."

Natascha walked out of the hall with Sue and Matteo and for the first time, admitted to Sue just how nervous she was. "He's going to expect me to sing, obviously, but I don't think I'm going to be able to do it. I haven't sung to anyone in five years. Only my four walls at home have been subjected to my singing and they've been very forgiving. This is going to kill me."

"You've met Cristiano and you can see that he's a lovely guy. If it was anyone else perhaps I might understand but he's so sweet and patient that he'll probably do more for your confidence than you realise." Sue handed Natascha her guitar. "Now, go knock him dead!"

When Natascha got back to the hall, Cristiano had returned to the cables which he seemed to be sorting out and rolling up. She walked towards him, trying not to let the nerves slow her pace. He turned around when he heard her footsteps.

"Ah, hello again," he said, while holding a handful of wires. He tiptoed his way around the cables to meet her. "You do not need to look so nervous. After all, it is only me," he said, as if they had known each other forever. He stood in front of her. "If you sound half as good as you do on the recording you sent me, it will be fantastic. Do not to be scared. Sue told me that it has been a long time since you last sang in public so I understand your fear. But it is like riding a bike, as they say in your country. After the first few notes, it will seem as though you never stopped singing. The only nerves you are allowed to have are from excitement, okay?" he said, smiling warmly.

He was calm and laid back and had an attractively placid personality. Natascha liked him. She did wonder at how much Sue had told him about her, though.

"So, have you had a chance to visit any of Italy yet?" he asked, as Natascha was taking her guitar from its case.

"No, not yet. I only arrived today. I think one of my first visits will need to be clothes shopping; I didn't bring very much with me. And I also have some very important Italian kitchen shopping to do for my mother." Natascha kept smiling through her qualms.

Cristiano laughed. "Well, you are in the right place for clothes. There are many boutiques in Siena."

He went over and sat at the keyboard. "Okay. Just start whenever you feel like it and I will join you."

Natascha took a deep breath. 'Like riding a bike'. Cristiano's words repeated in her head as she finally began to sing:

'*You are my rock whenever I stumble*
You are my pillow whenever I cry
I give you my heart and I give you my soul
Such a pure love like mine will never grow old

Days are covered in sunshine
And in the night sky the moon turns to gold
I give you my heart and I give you my soul
Such a pure love like mine will never grow old...'

Natascha ran through the song in its entirety and after having sung the last note she stood and waited, holding her breath. She didn't quite know what she was waiting for - approval perhaps? But when Cristiano started to applaud, it surprised her.

"That was great. It is a lovely song and you sound beautiful. Your voice, it is rich and yet very sweet. The boys will love to hear it."

It didn't appear as though Cristiano was humouring her. He didn't look as though he was just being kind. It seemed to Natascha that he genuinely liked it. "Are you sure? Sometimes I think that the song is just a little too simple. A bit immature, perhaps?"

"It is perfect the way it is. A wedding is romantic and your song is romantic. It is perfect," Cristiano said, his eyes twinkling. "I am looking forward to hearing you with the others at a rehearsal."

The rest of the time turned into quite a musical interlude. Natascha found singing in front of Cristiano less and less intimidating and amazed herself at how comfortable she felt doing so. She sang some more, he played and sang Italian songs and they sang songs they both knew together.

They were both singing the last line of a song when they heard applause. Sue and Matteo had been standing at the door listening to the little impromptu jamming session.

"You seem to work together really well." Sue commented, as she walked towards them. "That was so nice."

"I think that she is very good. She is too modest," Cristiano said, reassuringly. "I don't think that we will need many rehearsals. We will have one with the boys and maybe another one a bit nearer to the day but it is already perfect."

He then turned to Natascha, "In fact, I don't think that you need any accompaniment behind you. It is very nice just with the guitar. Would you like to sing with just your guitar?"

Natascha hesitated. Her mind drifted back to thoughts of long ago when she couldn't have been happier to be up there on her own. But although she had been quite sceptical when Sue told her about the band, she had now changed her mind. "I'd be happier if I wasn't on my own, if that's all right." No, she would rather be part of the performance than the centre of it.

"That is no problem." Cristiano turned to Sue. "Natascha tells me that she would like to go shopping. Perhaps I can take you both tomorrow, Sue? I have to go into the city in the morning. I can maybe, give you a lift?"

"Oh, I would love to go but Matteo and I have an appointment with the photographer and videographer tomorrow morning so I won't be able to make it." Sue looked towards Natascha, "So, that'll mean shopping on your own unless you want to wait until the afternoon?"

"You go and do what you have to do. I'm sure I'll be fine. Don't worry about me. I'll be armed with my phrase book. What could possibly go wrong?"

There was a small chuckle of laughter. "Well, that seems to be sorted, then. You'll be taking Natascha into town tomorrow morning, Cristiano, and we'll meet up again in the evening. Oh, and by the way, don't forget to bring her back, will you!"

Later that evening, Natascha thought of Cristiano and how his obvious affinity with music reminded her of Laurent. She had really enjoyed playing and singing with him earlier; it was something she used to do all the time when she and Laurent were together. She had loved it then and she loved it now. Soon, her memories of her time with Laurent began to crowd her and she didn't want to think of him anymore so she dismissed him from her mind.

Chapter Thirty-Two

Natascha and Sue breakfasted together the next morning. Matteo had left the house sometime earlier.

"I've got the guest list and need to transfer those names to a seating plan. I'll do that later," Sue explained. "Do you fancy helping out?"

"Of course. That's what I'm here for. I'm going with Cristiano into the city this morning and I assume we'll be back by the afternoon. There'll be plenty of time to sort it out together."

"That sounds great! I'd be grateful for any help you can give. I would ask Matteo but he's been so busy with the business recently that I'd rather not bother him. The poor thing, there's so much to do before he takes over. If he's not out with me for the wedding, he's at the solicitors with his father signing papers. Sometimes I think that the last thing he needs right now is the thought of getting married!"

"Oh Sue, don't be silly. I'm sure that having you as his wife is the only thing he really wants right now and that's the most important thing. I've told you before, just let me know what I can do to help. That's why I'm here." It was the first time Natascha had noticed that perhaps Sue was feeling just a little more anxious about her impending marriage than she let on.

Just before leaving to meet Matteo, Sue handed Natascha a key. "If you get back before me, use this spare key to let yourself in. I'll be back as soon as I can."

The house was quiet and looking out of the window Natascha couldn't imagine scenery more picturesque than the sight of vineyards and Cypress trees living side by side. Smiling to herself, she dried her hands and after putting away the breakfast things she heard a car tooting in the drive. She peeped out of the window to see Cristiano in a small white van waiting for her. And picking up her coat and bag, she left the house to meet him.

Even though the sky was a solid mass of blue and the sun was dazzlingly bright, it was a very cold day.

"Good morning, Natascha," Cristiano said, as she slid into the passenger seat. He leant over and gave her a kiss on both cheeks. "*Buon giorno.*"

"*Buon giorno,* Natascha replied, noticing how his eyes gleamed even more in the daylight.

"Did you have a good night?"

"Yes, thank you. It gives me such a thrill waking up on the first morning of a holiday. Everything feels so fresh and exciting and this is such a wonderful place. The view from my room is amazing!"

Cristiano started up the van and moved off. "Maybe you should think about moving to Italy, too, like Sue."

Perhaps he thought that he'd made a rather casual remark, but Natascha didn't want to mention that the idea had already entered her head, that maybe a complete change in her life and environment was the remedy she was looking for. She returned his comment with a smile. Cristiano glanced across as Natascha looked out of the window and seeing the expression on her face, his eyes squinted, inquisitively.

"I am sorry, but I hoped that Sue would be able to come, too because unfortunately, I will not be able to stay to accompany you to the shops as I have an important package to collect and some business to do. I feel very bad that I will have to leave you on your own."

"Please, Cristiano, don't worry. I'm quite happy to go shopping on my own. In fact, it has been my experience that to go looking for clothes with a man is not always such a good idea."

The corners of his eyes crinkled as he smiled. "Ah, well in that case, I shall leave you to shop in peace. It is true, I am not very helpful when it comes to clothes. I know what looks nice when I see a girl wearing it, but I am not able to say if it looks nice when they are trying it, if that makes sense."

Natascha laughed. "Yes, that makes perfect sense." There was a lull in the conversation which Natascha curtailed. "So, apart from your group, what do you do for work?"

"I work for myself as a sound engineer. I also run my own business, hiring and selling electronic tools. I also spend a lot of time setting up PA systems, music systems and other audio equipment."

"Wow, you're a busy man! And setting up PA systems sounds very interesting. I've always been intrigued at how sound systems are put together. I work in Events Management and a lot of the time I have to organise for PA systems to be installed. I try to be around while it's being done but I don't always have the time."

"Well, I would be happy to take you with me when I go to do a job if you would like. In fact, I will be setting up the sound system for the wedding. You can help me."

This prospect of at last having any kind of involvement in installing a sound system was really exciting to Natascha. It had been something she had always wanted to try ever since she used to watch the soundmen coordinate the set-up of the audio equipment during the time when she used to perform on stage with Laurent.

"I would love that. Thank you."

The car park was almost full but Cristiano managed to find a space to park the van. "It will be easier to walk into the city from here. It is only about ten minutes. Driving within the city walls is strictly prohibited so you have to find somewhere outside to park."

When they arrived, the city of Siena became a maze of small roads and pretty alleys lined with buildings and houses, all an architectural pleasure for Natascha. The wider roads appeared to be reserved for all the main shops and boutiques.

"Here, you can see all the shops. I think this is what you want. I am so sorry that I cannot be with you but I hope you will be all right on your own for about two hours?"

"That sounds perfect, I'll be fine."

They swapped mobile numbers in case of any emergencies.

"Okay. So I will see you here in say, two hours? If you have any problems, please phone me straightaway. I will not be very far," he said, as he walked away in a different direction.

This was how Natascha liked it best. She was on her own, in control and could please herself. She wandered in an out of the shops and browsed through rails of well-known designer wear. Most of her time, however, was spent in small independent boutiques that sold one-off designs and hand crafted accessories. It wasn't long before she was carrying far too many bags, evidence of her one major flaw - clothes shopping. It showed the only shortcoming she could ever really be accused of when it came to perfectly tailored linen trousers, fine knitwear and excellent quality tops and silk blouses. In addition, she had also yielded to her fancy of a pair of leather boots and an unusual yen for a very stylish pair of jeans.

A little further away from the boutiques and fashion stores were traditional Italian food shops selling fresh fruits and seasonal vegetables, cakes, pastas, cheeses and cured meats. The air was filled with the aroma of freshly baked Italian rolls and good food. The kaleidoscope of colours from the fruits and vegetables tempted Natascha to fill a basket with foods she did not necessarily recognise and try her hand at some authentic Italian cooking. When she returned to the house she would look for recipes to prepare the evening meal.

There were so many Tuscan wines that Natascha didn't know where to begin to choose. She appreciated good wine but faced with such a large selection it was difficult to know what to buy. And how fitting was the saying 'bringing sand to the Arabs' when she had finally made a choice of the three bottles that she would set on the dining table of one of Tuscany's finest wine producers?

Picking her way through the other shoppers, all attempting to pass each other in the small spaces that were available along the tiny roads and alleys, Natascha made her way back to the meeting point to wait for Cristiano. Here, she thought to herself, was one of life's good guys; a rare and seemingly dying breed of men, keen to be friendly and witty yet remaining courteous and respectful at all times; no risqué innuendos or cheap double entendres. Last night he had been so considerate and thoughtful towards her, a relative stranger to him, that she felt slightly overwhelmed by his kindness. Within minutes of being introduced to him, Natascha had sensed his unaffected and open honesty. It seemed nothing in the world could ruffle his sweet-tempered feathers and she knew straightaway that he was a genuine and dependable person. He had treated her with such sensitivity as she practised her song with him, and even though he appeared to know that she used to sing semi-professionally, he was still patient and understanding of her apprehensions. He was easy-going and uncomplicated and that was just the sort of company Natascha needed right now.

Cristiano was already at the bottom of the road.

"I'm not late, am I? I nearly lost track of time for a while," Natascha said, as she reached him, a little short of breath from having walked up and down the narrow, steep streets at a lively pace, "but there is just so much to see." He raised an eyebrow. "At least I don't think I'm late," she said again. Perhaps she really did lose track of time? She checked her watch again and looked up only to see him trying to smother a smile.

"Ladies are all the same," he went on, in an attempt to be diplomatic, "they all love shopping. And when they are in the shops time does not exist!" Cristiano glanced down at Natascha's hands and this time began to laugh openly. "And I can see by all of the bags you are carrying that you are not so different! Let me help you with some of those." Cristiano bent down and unburdened her hands of some of her purchases. "Don't worry, I have only arrived just now," he said. "You are not late. Come, let us walk back to the van."

Leading the way back to the car park, Cristiano held up the bags he was holding. "I think that perhaps you have found everything that you were looking for?" he teased, again. "There cannot be very much left in the shop if you have not!"

Seeing as her hands were full, Natascha gave him a good-natured nudge on the arm with her elbow. "I have a feeling that you're still making fun of me."

"Who me? Never!"

They were both laughing as they arrived at the van. Natascha was feeling very relaxed.

Moments after leaving the city, the landscape suddenly opened out to reveal a backdrop of undulating hills all in colourful shades of winter greens, acres of bare vineyards, olive groves, their delicate foliage rustling in the breeze and the red and white dots of houses nestled in amongst the hills. The scenery was so beautiful that Natascha drew in a deep breath.

"This is really beautiful and so close to the city."

"It is nice. I prefer to drive home this way when I am coming back from the city. There are many other places of beauty. Perhaps we can go and visit some of them?"

"I would like that very much," Natascha said, still in awe of the panorama before her.

"But first you must visit the attractions of Siena. It is not only the boutiques that are nice, there are also some beautiful buildings and piazzas. If Sue is not able to take you, I will be very happy to show you some of the places to see."

"If you can spare the time, that sounds lovely. Thank you. I'm very interested in old buildings."

The scenery passing by her was so breath-taking that Natascha spent the rest of the journey staring out of the window and was slightly disappointed when in no time they were back outside Sue and Matteo's house. "I'm not sure if they're back yet but perhaps you'd like to come in for a cup of coffee and maybe give me a few ideas for an authentic Italian dish I can cook with the food I bought."

Once inside the kitchen, Natascha found everything she needed to make coffee and jokingly, looked warily at the traditional percolator. "Don't worry, I have one of these at home which I use when I can but I'm afraid that's not very often. I'll do my best, though." Cristiano laughed when she pretended to be mystified by the shape of the sturdy aluminium jug.

Just as Natascha set the percolator on the stove, Sue and Matteo came through the door. Sue fell into a chair, worn out. "How do the simplest of tasks become so complicated? The photographer had us scheduled in his diary to take our photographs a week after the actual date of the nuptials and the videographer had my name spelt as 'S' double 'O' 'Soo'! Can you believe that? I don't need all this stress!" she groaned. "Can I smell coffee cooking? I really need a good strong cup!"

After some light chat over coffee, Natascha offered to make dinner and it felt totally natural to expect Cristiano to stay.

"That sounds very good," he said, "but unfortunately I cannot stay. I still have a few things I need to do but thank you, maybe another time." Cristiano stood up to go. "Natascha, I will speak to you again about a rehearsal with the rest of the group and also about the guided tour of the city."

"Okay, I'll wait for your call. Thanks again for taking me to the shops." She gave Cristiano a warm look of gratitude.

Sue noticed this and raised a curious eyebrow.

Chapter Thirty-Three

In bed that night, Natascha felt pleasantly sleepy. The day had been long but extremely satisfying. She had very much enjoyed her trip to the city visiting the eclectic mix of shops. She'd spent a wonderful evening with Sue and Matteo, sorting out the guest list and trying to work out who should sit where, making sure that any feuding relatives were not seated together. And she couldn't forget the generosity of Cristiano, offering to take her sightseeing and very importantly, for making her laugh more in the little time she had spent with him than she had done in a very long time. Everything was such a long way away from the complexities and the disarray of her life back in London. She closed her eyes. They were such a long, long way away..."

The winter sunshine was flooding into Natascha's room. Unable to resist another look at the view outside she left her warm bed and went across to the window. It was another sparkling day with a cloudless blue sky. But from the lingering frost on the grass and the mist her breath left on the cold glass, it seemed that once again she would be donning her new thick winter coat. She had already been in Italy for almost a week and so far, the weather had been the same every day, Siberian-like temperatures but with brilliant blue skies and a champagne-coloured sun. There had been only one day when it started rather cloudy. However, by mid-morning, the clouds had dissipated to reveal yet another chilly but sunshiny day, the sun dazzling high in the winter sky.

Shivering, Natascha ran into the bathroom for a hot shower, before her toes turned blue.

By the time she arrived in the kitchen, Sue was wrapping a scarf around her neck. "Oh, you're up. I didn't want to wake you; I know you were up late working on those stupid little things but Matteo and I still have some legal paperwork that have to be completed. No paperwork - no wedding, apparently! Our appointment's at half past nine but we want to get there as soon as the office opens in case of any changes to the timetable, you know, latecomers, appointment mix-ups or 'the wedding's off!' cancellations, that sort of thing." Sue looked at the kitchen clock on the wall. "Oh sh-sugar! Matteo's waiting for me in the car. I've left you a note of what's where. I know you'll keep yourself amused. I don't think we'll be too long. See you later." And with that she was gone.

The percolator was still hot and Natascha poured herself a cup of coffee before turning on the radio, leisurely wondering how she had managed to stay in bed for so long. In her defence, however, she had undertaken the task of making up the hundreds of wedding favours, which Sue had so eloquently referred to as 'stupid little things'. Because of the sheer number of them,

Natascha had set herself a daily goal of the numbers that had to be completed. Last night, carefully folding glossy pieces of pre-scored card into boxes the size of a matchbox, and filling them with shredded tissue paper and sugared almonds, had taken Natascha into the early hours of the morning before she had finished her quota.

She sipped her first coffee of the day and lost herself in the sounds coming from the radio. The DJ was speaking with great excitement and introduced a slow ballad with such enthusiasm that it had Natascha trying to guess what amusing titbit of trivia could possibly accompany such a mournful melody. Without understanding a word, Natascha was fascinated by songs sung in a different language. The basic theme of a love song was normally the same the world over - most about love lost and found. But somehow, the same song sung in two different languages, usually had a totally unconnected feel; it was as if the pain of a broken heart in one part of the continent differed to that of a heart that had been broken in another part of the world. The tone of one language and technique of a voice could make the same song sound so much more intense and full of drama. Natascha was grateful for Laurent's intuition into the choice of songs to build their varying repertoire. It included a range of French songs that she could sing so fluently, that she was able to deceive her audience into believing that French was her first language - another of his little gifts to her… Natascha abruptly cut short her recollections. Memories of Laurent were continuing to infiltrate her thoughts more and more frequently and that, she knew, was deeply disturbing.

Then, the sound of crackling gravel coming from the front of the house and a soft knock at the door brought Natascha back to the present. She went to the window to see who was there. It was Cristiano.

"*Buon giorno*, Natascha. I think it is a fine day for sight-seeing. Would you like to have a walk in the city of Siena today?"

"Now? Are you sure?" It sounded perfect. Natascha threw him an excited smile. "I'll just get my coat and leave a note for Sue," she answered, as she rushed back inside.

Chapter Thirty-Four

The *Piazza Del Campo* was an ancient square and even in the winter it did not suffer from a lack of visitors. It throbbed with people wandering across the redbrick herringbone paving, surrounded by gothic architecture that showed-off the intricacies of medieval design. Natascha cast a studious eye over the building's design while behind her Cristiano pointed out some of the main features.

"As you know, *piazza* means square in Italian but in fact, as you can see, this *piazza* was actually built as a semi-circle. Over that side, in the white marble, is the *Fonte Gaia* which means 'Fountain of Joy' and on this side is the *Palazzo Pubblico*, the town hall." Natascha strained her neck to look up at the town hall's tower that rose like a sky-scraper into the sky. "And the tower you are looking at," Cristiano continued, "is called *Torre del Mangia*. It is the second tallest tower in Italy."

"It's beautiful," Natascha said dreamily, as she watched tourists file in an out of the busy shops and restaurants below the *Torre del Mangia*. There was a real bustling vibe about the place.

"Every year on two days in the summer there is an event here called '*Il Palio*'. It is a special horse race in honour of the Madonna. They put dirt and sand around the piazza to make it like a horse track and the jockeys ride the horses without saddles. It is a very, very old tradition and at these festivities there are also parades and pageants with soldiers dressed in medieval costumes. Many people like to visit during this festival and it can be very busy, but it is a lot of fun. Perhaps you will come back in the summer?"

"Try and keep me away!" Certainly, regular visits to this fine-looking city was something that Natascha was definitely going to do - and frequently.

They strolled on.

"And this is the *Piazza del Duomo*."

Natascha gasped in awe at the building in front of her.

"And I think that you will agree that the *Cattedrale dell'Assunta* is the most majestic cathedral you have ever seen."

"Oh yes, definitely! I've read about the horizontal dark green and white marble striped tower but it's even more beautiful than I expected! It seems to be nothing but walls and columns of incredibly intricate carvings!"

"Let us go in. There are more sculptures and paintings inside and I am sure you will not be disappointed with them!"

The bold shock of thick green/black and white striped marble columns inside looked almost primitive compared to the elaborate walls outside. Exquisite golden stars looking down from the high dome did their best to outshine the breathtakingly detailed marble flooring that was spread like a carpet of tapestries covering the entire floor space which, in Natascha's eyes, was the most splendid thing she ever saw.

"This is a masterpiece," Natascha breathed, almost to herself. "Can you imagine the affluence and wealth of this city when this was built?"

"This is the *Ospidale di Santa Maria della Scala*," Cristiano continued, as they left the cathedral and walked across to a building with a façade of old brickwork. "It used to be a hospital until the 1990s. Now it is full of exhibitions and so on."

At every turn there was yet more elegant architecture for Natascha to admire and different monuments to enjoy. She was in her architectural design heaven, soaking up the atmosphere of this great city. And Cristiano played the role as the expert and well-informed tour guide perfectly. He stood behind her leaving her to gaze in wonderment, providing running commentary on the landmarks and tourist attractions and giving detailed information on the more notable pieces of art.

"I'm impressed by your excellent knowledge of this city...," Natascha said as she turned around to face him, "You know so much..." She stopped mid-sentence. "Is that what I think it is?"

He didn't need to say another word. Cristiano's horrified expression, which swiftly switched to mortification, answered her question.

She snatched the book out of his hand and read the cover "*A Tourist's guide to Siena – in glorious detail...*" Natascha stared at him for a short while and watched him squirm.

"It is not that I don't know about the attractions, perhaps I don't know them in as much detail as you might wish to hear...?"

She continued to stare saying nothing. Then she began to laugh and laugh until she nearly cried. "At least tell me that you're the author...," she went on, through her fits of laughter.

As they roamed around, it wasn't long before an old memory slipped back into her mind. She and Richard were on school holidays and he had promised to take her on a day trip to London. They had taken the train in the morning and had spent the day visiting London as tourists.

Richard had been as informative and as knowledgeable as he ever was. Every road, every building, every park - Richard could recount its history...

"... no, Richard, I don't think that he'll be too pleased with us having our picture taken with him."

They had stopped at Horse Guards Parade.

"Of course he won't mind. Why wouldn't he want to have his picture taken with us?" Richard teased.

"But look at him... he looks so... angry. If he was okay with it, shouldn't he at least smile a bit?"

Richard looked at her seriously, "If he really doesn't want to have his picture taken with us, he'll slice us up into tiny pieces with his sword!" he said. Then he began to laugh.

Natascha nudged him in the ribs, "You think that's funny do you? Well, come on then, let's do it. I'm going to stand really close to him and smile like a mad person and if he chops my head off it'll be your fault! You'll have my blood on your hands!" Natascha said, dramatically. Finally, she plucked up the courage to stand beside the statue-like guard who was armed with a long shiny, silver sword and Richard joined her. He handed his camera to a passer-by and asked if he would take their picture.

"Ready? Smile..."

Although Natascha had now wandered back to the present, part of her was still floating along with the past. She had vivid memories of the day as though it had only been a few months – not years ago. They had walked up and down the city of London. They had burgers and chips for lunch which they ate in Green Park and Richard had helped her to climb up onto the lions in Trafalgar Square. It was the first time she had seen the famous sights of Buckingham Palace, Big Ben and the Houses of Parliament. Richard had taught her everything she knew about the London landmarks and she had always listened attentively when he was explaining anything to her since she wanted to know as much as he knew. It was the first time she had travelled on the underground. It was his first time too, but they never got lost - Richard was too careful for that to happen. He had studied the Tube map before leaving home. Natascha recalled it as having been one of the most fantastic days out that she and Richard had ever spent together.

She wondered what had ever happened to the photograph.

Cristiano pressed pause on the movie that was playing in her mind. "You are very quiet, Natascha. Are you getting tired?"

Natascha realised that she must have spent more than just a moment lost in the past and in that time had said very little to Cristiano. "Tired? No, not at all. I love it! I've been struck dumb with so much to see, that's all." She took a moment to redirect her thoughts. "Mmm. I'm feeling a little hungry, though. Shall we stop for some lunch?"

"That is a good idea!"

"Where would you recommend we eat? I can see there are only a few dozen restaurants and cafés to choose from!"

Cristiano spoke with an air of mystery. "Ah. Come with me."

They walked along the tiny and sometimes quite dark meandering streets and alleyways before reaching a small, friendly looking restaurant.

"Here is the best restaurant in all of Italy, I think," Cristiano said, proudly. "It is owned by my brother. Let us go and eat!"

From the moment they stepped inside, Cristiano began chatting to the other patrons. He seemed to know them all personally and they were all very happy to see him. It was also the first time Natascha had heard him speak fluently and easily in his mother tongue, switching seamlessly from English to Italian, which absurdly, Natascha had taken for granted. The soft poetic melody of the Italian language poured from him like honey and the mellow, harmonious sound suited him perfectly.

A man stepped out from behind the bar. There was a slight resemblance to Cristiano but perhaps he was a little older and Natascha guessed that he was his brother. They kissed each other in the customary greeting.

"*Ciao, Romano. Questa è la mia amica, Natascha.*"

"Natascha, this is my brother, Romano."

"*Ciao, Natascha*," he said smiling, as he kissed her cold cheeks. "*C'é un tavolo libero, qui. Venite.*"

Before Natascha had the chance to reply, he was leading the way to a table in the corner of the restaurant.

Looking through the menu, Natascha was grateful for the English translation but could not decide on what to try.

"I'll leave it to the experts and have whatever you're having. I have great faith in your taste," she said to Cristiano, "if you pardon the pun!"

For the first time, Cristiano seemed as though he didn't quite understand and just looked at her, frowned and shrugged his shoulders. "I suggest we have the fettuccine pasta in a very nice tomato sauce, wild boar meat and a green salad. Does that sound good?"

"It sounds very Italian. I'll give it a try."

"It is very good; it is my favourite. My brother is a genius when it comes to pasta."

Romano came over with a bottle of red wine and a carafe of iced water.

"*Questo va bene?*"

"Is red wine all right for you, Natascha? You can have white wine if you prefer. My brother brings the red because he knows which dish I will order!"

For a fleeting moment Natascha debated in her mind whether she should indulge in a glass of wine seeing as she did not usually drink at this time of the day. Today, she had a very rare 'devil-may-care' attitude and so broke her own rules. She was on holiday and had the right to be a little less inflexible and more relaxed. "Red's my favourite colour," she announced.

"*Sì, va bene, grazie*," Cristiano replied to his brother.

Romano began to fill Natascha's glass but as he turned the bottle towards her companion's, Cristiano held out his hand to motion that he did not want too much. "*Non troppo. Purtroppo, io sono alla guida*," he said, gesturing that he was driving. And so pouring just a little wine, Romano placed the rest of the bottle on the table. Cristiano grinned. "I will be in big trouble with Sue if I do not take you home safe and sound!"

As they waited for their food, Natascha picked up her glass. "Hmm, this is really good."

"Take a look at the label."

She held the bottle and read the details. "Ah, I see. It's from the vineyards of *Sant' Angelo's.* That explains it."

After a very good meal, Natascha took out her purse ready to cover the bill as a small token of her thanks and appreciation of Cristiano's kindness, but Romano refused to take payment.

"He says that any friend of mine is a guest in his restaurant and not a customer. He would never charge me and would never charge my companion."

Natascha turned to Romano, "That is very generous of you, thank you very much. The food was delicious. I hope to return the compliment one day."

Her words of gratitude were translated by Cristiano and Romano turned to her, "*Prego. Una bella donna non deve pagare il pranzo.*"

Natascha shot a questioning glance in Cristiano's direction.

Cristiano smiled, his eyes sparkling as a ray of sunlight gleamed through the window as he translated. "A beautiful lady must not pay for her lunch."

Chapter Thirty-Five

"So, you used to sing more often, Sue tells me," Cristiano said casually, as they left the restaurant.

Although she had been in Cristiano's company all morning, somehow she had managed to bury the song somewhere, deep in the back of her mind - until now. The mention of singing brought her back down to earth with a bump. "Er, yes I did," she answered, unsteadily, "with a very good friend of mine but that was many years ago. He was an excellent guitarist and could teach very well and in fact, most of what I learnt, I learnt from him."

"You sound like you enjoyed it. Where did you play?"

"Well, we started by playing in small clubs and bars. Then it became more serious and as we began to get more work we played in bigger venues. My friend, Laurent Olivier, was the one who..." a confused expression replaced Cristiano's usual uncomplicated look as he pondered on what she had said. "I know, I know, but apparently his parents were great fans of the old English thespian," Natascha explained, with a giggle. "Anyway, it was Laurent who encouraged me to do it. We sang as a duet and as the better guitarist he would also play. So, by day I sat behind a desk and worked in an ordinary office and by night

I would get dressed up in nice dresses and stand in front of an audience." Natascha wondered why she had felt it necessary to impart such detailed information, even referring to Laurent by name, but then Cristiano was so easy to talk to that it flowed from her very easily and naturally. And at that moment she realised that it was the first time she had ever spoken to anyone but Sue about Laurent, and to her surprise, it felt okay. It was testament to how she felt in Cristiano's company. "From the name, you can probably tell that Laurent was French. He was a session musician so as well as improving my guitar skills, he did a lot to improve my high school French. By the end, I was quite fluent. Perhaps it was a shame he wasn't Italian. That would have been more useful!"

Cristiano laughed then paused for a moment. "You say 'by the end'. Are you no longer friends?"

This was where the story wasn't quite so easy for Natascha to narrate. "No, we didn't stay friends." She took a deep breath and gave a nervous little laugh. "Well, actually… Laurent was my fiancé and we were together for two years but it didn't work out." Could she say any more? Could she tell him the whole story? "He, er, fell out of love with me and fell in love with someone else, another girl in his hometown. So one day he left in a taxi, taking his belongings with him and moved back to France to be with her. He also went back when he decided he wanted to be more involved in bringing up his one year old little boy." Natascha raised her eyebrows at him, inviting him to work it out.

"I'm sure you can do the maths. It was all rather a shock to me at the time." It was all she could do not to choke on her words but she hoped she had convinced Cristiano that she was completely over the whole affair with her matter-of-fact manner. In no way did she want to give him the impression that she was a damaged woman with a pathetic history, forever plagued by a broken heart. She wanted him to know her only as she was today.

Cristiano fell quiet for a little while. "I am sorry to hear that."

Natascha sighed. "It was a long time ago." Then added more cheerfully, "But, I'm over it now," she said, wanting to end on a lighter note.

They continued their leisurely walk up the steep streets of Siena for a little while after they'd had lunch, stopping every now and again to browse in the shop windows and hunt for small souvenirs that Natascha could take back to England. They also made time to stop for coffee and pastries at a small espresso bar before making their way back to the van.

On the journey home, a little bell of disappointment tinkled in Natascha's mind. Though she had spoken easily about Laurent, it had not escaped her notice how difficult it had been trying to avoid memories of Richard and their trip to London. He was still playing far too much of an important role in her head. She would have to try harder still to forget.

It was coming close to getting dark and by the time they arrived, Sue and Matteo were already home.

"I have had a fabulous day," Natascha declared, as she came through the door. "Siena is a gorgeous city and I've completely fallen in love with it."

"It seems that Natascha likes history very much," Cristiano said, as he walked in behind her, happy at seeing Natascha's excitement.

"I can see that you've had a good day," Sue commented. "I haven't seen you so hyped up for such a long time, Natascha." She turned to Cristiano. "What have you done to my friend?"

Cristiano shrugged his shoulders and shook his head innocently. "Nothing."

"Why don't you stay and have something to eat, Cristiano? You missed out on a fantastic meal Natascha cooked the other night."

"I wish I could but unfortunately, my legs will not allow me to stand up again if I sit down. I think Natascha could have continued to walk up and down the streets of Siena all night without any trouble."

"Oh, I didn't realise that I was tiring you out that much," Natascha said, a little guiltily.

"Not tiring me, just my knees," Cristiano teased. "No, I am joking, I too, had a very nice day. It was fun."

Cristiano changed the subject. "I am sorry to have to talk about more serious matters but it seems to me we will have to rehearse soon. There is not very much time left and I would like to practice at least once before having a final rehearsal at the reception hall. I will phone the rest of the group later and see if we can make a date. Is that okay?"

Although she had enjoyed the musical evening with Cristiano when she arrived in Italy, she was a little unsure of doing the same with the rest of the band, especially since it was very possible the group was Italy's take on the *Backstreet Boys'* younger siblings. However, she wanted to keep these feelings to herself. "Yes, that sounds like a good idea."

"I will let you know what has been arranged. I will phone you soon." Cristiano winked at Natascha.

"I'll wait to hear from you then," she said, as she fashioned a pleasant and affectionate smile on her lips.

Before making his way towards the door, Cristiano turned to Natascha once more, "Thank you again for a lovely day, I had a very nice time."

"No, I should thank you. It wouldn't have been the same without you. You were the perfect tour guide, even if I could have easily read the book myself!"

Cristiano laughed somewhat ashamedly before leaning forward to kiss her on both cheeks. "*Ciao.*" Then, looking across to Sue and Matteo, he gave a little wave. "*Ciao*, I will see you all again soon."

Closing the door behind him, Natascha felt a tiny relaxed glow, warm and contented somewhere deep inside of her.

"I see you and Cristiano have 'hit it off'," Sue said at breakfast, as she peered at Natascha over the rim of her coffee cup.

"If you mean do we get on? Then yes, we get on very well. He's a lovely person."

"Is that all he is, 'a lovely person'?"

"What do you mean is that all? Cristiano is a very nice man, really friendly and I like him very much. I feel we've actually made good friends in the short space of time since I've been here."

Sue stared into Natascha's eyes and waited for more and when nothing was forthcoming she forced Natascha to be more specific. "So you're just good friends are you? Nothing more? I mean, I saw the way you looked at each other when you came in after your sightseeing trip."

"I think you're letting your imagination run away with you. It was nice of him to spare the time and show me around the city and he has been very kind to me. So, the answer to your question is yes, we're just good friends and no, we're nothing more." Natascha realised what Sue was trying to do and knew that she was disappointing her.

Sue stopped with the roundabout small talk and came clean. "Well, if you want me to be up front with you, I was hoping that you were going to tell me that you'd become more than just friends, that you'd become *very* good friends - in the intimate sense!"

"Sue, come on. You know I'm not interested in the whole 'boyfriend' thing - not now," she finished, with more care than she expected. Natascha had had this topic of conversation with Sue many times before. Normally, it didn't bother her, she just went along with it but with Richard still haunting her, an undercurrent of confusion ever so slightly coloured the usually docile subject.

"Yes, I know, but I was hoping that this time it would be different. Cristiano is such a lovely guy. I mean, he's fun and easy-going and so calm and unassuming. And I think he's rather gorgeous to look at as well, wouldn't you agree?"

The expectation in Sue's eyes was making Natascha faintly nervous but she injected casual laughter into her reply. "Yes, I agree, he is fun and easy-going and extremely good-looking," she added for good measure, "but that's it."

"But you both make such a great couple. I haven't seen you so happy in years." Sue noticed the unease in her friend's eyes. "I know you, Natascha," she said, more quietly, "I do know how things are with you, but I think they're changing."

"What do you mean?"

"You let your long-lost friend get very close to you, didn't you? Although, for whatever reason, something obviously went wrong there." Sue gauged Natascha's reaction and took her time. "It's been years since you last let a man get that close to you."

Natascha said nothing. She just looked at her friend and knew that there was a certain ring of truth in what she was saying. But she wasn't prepared to be that honest just yet, mainly because she wasn't ready to be that honest with herself.

"I think you're ready to move on. You're looking for something else now."

Natascha moved her eyes away from Sue's face.

"Cristiano is one of the nicest men I know and you two seem to have a real connection. Maybe you could really have something together."

After a few moments, Natascha looked up at Sue. "I know that you're only looking out for me and that you're worried for me but honestly, I'm fine. I'm happy with the way things are. You're reading too much into it, Sue. I'm afraid you're wrong. I'm very lucky to have met Cristiano and I agree, he is a wonderful man, but really, we are only friends and that's how I would like it to stay. With no complications there is little chance of unwanted dramas," she added, with a watery and apologetic smile.

Getting up from the table, Natascha sought to change the tack of the conversation. "I'd better go and carry on with making up the favours."

Watching Natascha leave the room, Sue felt that familiar weight of disappointment and worry. Since those dark times after Laurent left, her friend had shied away from any potential relationship with any man. After the awful depression she had gone through she had courageously picked herself up and had assumed the new character of a confident and self-assured woman always in total control of her life, never letting anyone disrupt her ordered existence. But as far as Sue was concerned, that's all it was - an existence. Natascha had repressed any feelings of passion and verve so robustly that she had lost herself somewhere between caution and liberty. She had created for herself her own little world where she was safe and comfortable but she made sure that there was no room left for anyone else to move in. Sue had known the old Natascha when she was a spirited, warm, and ambitious young woman and had a real thirst for life. And now, she prayed for the day when something of the real Natascha would find its way back, where she would finally be able to find a happy balance of self-reliance and the freedom to share her life with someone special.

Chapter Thirty-Six

It was all arranged for Cristiano to come and collect Natascha to meet the rest of the group for their first practice. Her initial anxieties were still very much alive but a small amount of excitement was now beginning to emerge and she found that she was quite looking forward to it for the first time.

Cristiano had arrived at exactly the time that had been decided and came into the house just long enough to say hello to the others before they were in his van and on their way.

"Nervous?"

Natascha nodded her head, "Just a little."

He reached across and gently squeezed her hand. "You do not need to be, you have a wonderful voice. You should be proud of it. The guys are a great bunch and they have put in quite a lot of work with your song. It sounds very good. I think you will be happy with it. And… I will be there for you. I will be there to help if you need it."

Natascha noticed a wistful look in his eyes and smoothly slipped her hand out from beneath his. Just as quickly, the look disappeared and once again his eyes were twinkling as they always did. "I have every confidence in your judgement," Natascha continued, completely disregarding the split second of an intense moment as if it had never happened, "so I'm going to try and enjoy this. It's been such a long time. I just need to get over some unpleasant memories and I'll be fine, I know it."

Natascha closed her eyes and fell away inside herself; she had to absorb her own advice. She used to enjoy what she did and her audience seemed to enjoy what they heard. There was nothing that could stimulate her senses more than performing on stage and yet she had turned away from it all because of the inadequacies of just one man. But for the first time, like a flickering light in a dark room, a shadowy feeling in her core started to make whispery noises. It was telling her, without unbearable pain, that the corner in her mind where that deep, dark chasm of fear had stubbornly refused to leave; that area in her mind where she had kept locked shut the story of Laurent for so many years and vowed never to return to, had at last been gently confronted. She had gingerly taken that prodigious first step and had uttered Laurent's name to someone else who wasn't Sue. Although she had re-invented herself, her character now virtually unrecognisable to what it used to be, after all these years she still had not dared to face the very reason why she so desperately had to make that transition - until now. Without realising it, she was finally staring her demons in the eye - she had spoken to Cristiano about Laurent and what he had done. Gradually she would start to deal with the whole affair in the same way that she would approach any problem today; coolly, rationally and logically. For the very first time in five years, Natascha just might at last be ready.

Glancing across and seeing Natascha's face turned towards the world outside, eyes closed, body pensive and still, Cristiano realised that perhaps she had things on her mind that she needed to think through. He hadn't known her for very long but it was already clear to him that she was the type of woman who needed space to be left to mull over and contemplate whatever problems needed her attention. For her to do that, she needed no distraction or intervention from anyone. No amount of advice or meaningful words could influence her decision. It was more than just the prospect of performing in public that had so occupied Natascha's thoughts, the real source of her anxieties lay somewhere within the story of her broken engagement. Cristiano said nothing. The rest of the journey, therefore, continued in silence.

"Are you ready?" Cristiano asked, as he handed Natascha her guitar case. He'd parked the van and now they were standing in front of the small building where they were to have their first rehearsal.

"I'm ready." With the help of that dim light within her she had made up her mind that she would master this. She was always ready for a challenge, and in some ways, she thrived on them and singing in front of strangers for the first time in years would be just another one of those challenges. "Let's go," she said, clutching her guitar case to her.

He led her down a warren of softly lit corridors before they reached a low-ceilinged, darkish but cosy room illuminated by brightly lit floor lamps. There were electric guitars resting on stands, ready to be wired to amplifiers, several different styles of keyboards all placed side by side, half a dozen microphones held in stands and a drum kit that was set up on a low platform behind the other instruments. Through a large glass window that acted as the wall to an adjoining room, a long table was loaded with mixing desks and their rows and rows of controls, switches, sockets and gauges for audio metering. There were cables running everywhere.

"This is a proper recording studio," Natascha whispered, impressed by the sight. "I've never been in a recording studio before; we nearly did but it never happened. It all looks so professional - and a bit intimidating, as if it only wants to hear good music."

"I am glad you like it. It is not very grand, but it is ours. It was used as an office filing room but the company left, taking their files with them and I took over the lease and converted it into a recording studio."

"I thought that we'd be rehearsing in someone's garage or at best a small church hall."

The door swung open and four young men came bursting through, laughing and chatting.

Cristiano turned to his friends as they came in. *"Ciao, amici miei. Come va?"*

"*Tutto bene*," they answered, in a babble of high spirits and high-fives.

"Natascha, please meet my friends. This is Elvio, he is our bass player, this is Andrea, he plays keyboard and this is Pascal, he is our guitarist although sometimes he plays the saxophone. The lead guitar is played by either Pascal or myself. Ah, and you have already met Alessio, I think."

"The drummer," Natascha added, "yes, we've met."

One by one they came over to Natascha and gave her rather long drawn out kisses.

"It is very nice to meet you," Elvio said. "*Alessio ce l'aveva detto che eri bella da mozzare il fiato, e aveva ragione!*"

Natascha looked across to Cristiano for help.

He laughed an amused laugh. "They were told that you were an incredibly beautiful woman. Their source of information was correct!"

Natascha blushed uncharacteristically, "Thank you very much. That's very nice of you to say."

"We Italian men are never shy to tell a woman how beautiful she is," Pascal said, winking at her saucily.

"Hey," one of the others said. The room fell silent. "Natascha is not just a beautiful woman... she is a very beautiful lady."

'*Ah, si, si. Naturalmente*', they concurred, in a din of voices that was once again back in the room.

"Guys, guys, you are giving us Italian men a very bad name," Cristiano joked. "And stop staring. You are scaring her!"

They all seemed very comfortable with each other. They had been playing together for years and the relationship between the band members was more like one of brothers than of friends. They were a fun lot, all in their late twenties or early thirties apart from Alessio, although it was sometimes difficult to estimate their ages since their playful behaviour and rakish manner could lead anyone to believe they were much younger.

After a few minutes, Cristiano held up his hands as a gesture to end the bantering.

"Okay, okay, let us get to work."

Cristiano introduced Natascha to a few simple ideas he had devised.

"Okay Natascha? The first eight bars of the song you will sing *a cappella* and then the band will join in with you. Elvio and I will sing some backing in places. I also had the idea of a short lead guitar solo. We will go through it once to see how it works and if you like it. I will motion to you where the instrumental comes in. I think it should be just before the last verse but we will see. Does that sound all right?"

Natascha could only nod.

They all got into their respective positions and immediately the atmosphere changed from one of rapid and witty chatter to a calm and professional one.

Cristiano counted them in and Natascha started to sing. At first it was rather tentative but as soon as the others started to play it inspired her to project her voice with more confidence.

They reached the end of the song and Natascha sang the last line of the lyrics solo again with the band joining in and ending on a very pleasing discord. Natascha was surprised at the difference the addition of the other instruments and voices made, enhancing the quality of the song to a whole new level. No longer was it a simple, sweet melody. It had become a real song with substance and a professionalism she never expected. The group played together like a well-oiled machine, supporting her. And it was clear that they all had put in a lot of work to bring her song up to such a high standard. Natascha was pleased and excited at what she heard and privately, she felt proud of herself, that she had composed a song that not only had worth but could, in her opinion, match the composition of any experienced and well-seasoned songwriter. Cristiano was a maestro.

"That was excellent. You see Natascha, how good it is?" Cristiano said. "You have nothing to worry about. When we play together, we are one, like one heart beating together and we help each other. You do not have to feel alone." His last sentence was delivered differently, more seriously as his eyes penetrated hers, as if trying to convey a secret message. The others didn't appear to notice. She gave him a quizzical look but the moment quickly vanished when Cristiano's face brightened. "Right, I think that there are a few things that need more work."

They ran through the song a few more times adding agreed alterations and tweaking any sounds until it was just right.

"That sounds perfect." Natascha was delighted and overwhelmed at the finished product. "I think you all deserve a huge round of applause." She put her hands together and started to clap. Everyone relaxed again and each of them took a bow.

"I have been told by the manager of the reception hall that it will be free two days before the wedding and he has given us permission to set-up our instruments at any time. This means we can have a last rehearsal there and do not need to wait until the morning of the wedding to set up and have a full sound check. I have been assured of the security of the equipment. Is that okay with everyone?"

With no objections the session came to an end and they all went their separate ways.

"You're rather quiet this evening," Natascha said, as Cristiano was giving her a lift back to the house after the rehearsal. Ever since she had met him, although he wasn't always very talkative, it was never because he was inattentive or preoccupied; he was a very good listener. This evening, however, he seemed different. "Is everything all right?"

"Er, oh yes, I am all right. I was just thinking about a job I have to do tomorrow evening and I expect some problems, that is all. I am sorry, I did not mean to ignore you."

"No, no, you didn't. It's just that I've never seen you look so serious before."

He hesitated for a moment before his eyes regained their sparkle. "Would you like to come with me? It is for an 18th birthday party. They have invited another band, a rock band, to play at the party. We do not normally play that type of rock. I very much like the group *Deep Purple.* They play some interesting music. But I do not think that heavy rock suits our band." Cristiano gave a little chuckle. "Do you?"

"Deep Purple? Hmm, maybe not," Natascha smiled.

Cristiano went on, "The person who normally does the sound check has broken his arm and it will be difficult for him. I have therefore offered my services."

"Tomorrow evening, you say? Yes, I think that I might be able to. I'm going with Sue in the morning to pick up her dress which has had last minute alterations then we're going to confirm the order for her flowers. But I think the evening is free. If Sue doesn't need me, I would love to go with you." Natascha looked at him again, not entirely convinced that the birthday party was the only thing on his mind. "Are you sure everything's all right?"

"Oh yes, everything is fine. I will phone you and pick you up if you can make it."

Chapter Thirty-Seven

Stepping out of the shower the next morning, Natascha grabbed the warm towel and wrapped it around her. She dressed herself in one of the new cashmere sweaters she had bought on her shopping trip and teamed it with the pair of well-fitted jeans and knee-length boots. It was a style of dressing she was unused to, but for the first time, she felt quite comfortable to try it. She sat in front of the mirror and pulled the brush through the thick waves of her hair, the sound of her song resounding in her head over and over. It had been transformed into more than she had ever hoped. Inevitably, and what seemed to be the natural way nowadays, memories of when she was young filtered into her thoughts…

"...well, do you like it?" she asked Richard, when she had strummed the final chord.

"Yes, it's nice."

"Hmmm. 'It's nice'. That's all you ever say, 'it's nice'! Go on then, tell me, what's *nice* about it?"

"The words are nice and the tune is nice."

"That's not very helpful, is it? You should have said that it was a beautiful love song, full of emotion, but instead, all you can say is 'it's nice'." Natascha shook her head, disappointed. "You boys, you're all the same. I bet you don't even know when something is beautiful, even if it came up behind you and bit you on the bum! I don't think I've ever even heard you say the word!"

Richard shrugged his shoulders.

"I hope you don't plan to be one of those film people who go to the pictures to watch films and then write about them in the paper," Natascha said, defiantly, "I'm sure the readers are going to want to know more about a film instead of it being just 'nice'!"…

She hadn't been angry with him, just a bit annoyed. His comments were so 'Richard'. If it didn't involve facts and figures, he wasn't that interested, though he did try sometimes - she'd give him that.

"Breakfast, Natascha," Sue called from the kitchen.

"Wow! That's a new look. Very sexy!" Sue commented, as Natascha entered the room. "I just love those jeans!"

"I haven't overdone it, have I? It's been such a long time since I wore such clingy jeans. Back in the bedroom I thought they looked okay but now I'm not so sure."

"Natascha, Natascha, Natascha, calm down. You look fantastic! You're never usually paranoid about what you're wearing," Sue said, as she wondered what or who had made such a change in her friend. But for the moment, she decided not to ask and changed the subject. "A local seamstress is altering the dress," she said, as she buttered a piece of toast. She's a friend of Eva's, Matteo's mum, and came highly recommended. I've lost a couple of pounds since I last had the fitting and it's made quite a difference. I just needed it to be taken in a little - I want everything to be perfect."

"With all the work you're both putting into it, why shouldn't it be?"

Sue was quiet as they ate their breakfast but suddenly perked up. "Oh, by the way, how did rehearsals go last night?"

"It went well. In fact, it went better than I expected. It wasn't quite as bad as I thought it might be. It's actually given me quite a boost and it's made me feel so much better about it all. Cristiano's very good at what he does."

The minute Natascha mentioned his name she knew it was a mistake.

It gave Sue the bone she had been digging for. "Didn't I say so? And he's so modest with it, don't you think? Do you know, I've known him for some time now, he's such an important part of the family, but in all that time, I have never seen him upset or even heard him whinge about anything? He takes everything in his stride. If you're feeling stressed it takes just a few minutes in his company to make you feel better. He's quite a guy. He's going to make someone a wonderful husband one day," Sue went on, as she waggled her eyebrows at Natascha.

"Oh no. You're not going to start that again, are you?"

"Well, you should know me by now, I don't give up that easily."

The portrayal of some of Cristiano's attributes were features that up until recently, she recognised as once being her own. Not long ago, she had enjoyed that uncluttered feeling and a deep, personal serenity. But of late she felt she was losing this, having bouts of demoralising uncertainty. At home, she had been having a difficult time of it, battling to keep hold of these merits that had kept her going for so long. But since she'd been in Italy, it was all coming together again - she had been able to find some of what she had lost. Whether it was simply down to having had the chance to leave it all behind or whether it had, indeed, been because she had been in Cristiano's company, was somewhat unclear.

"He was married once, you know," Sue informed her, "but his wife ran off with a local footballer. It caused quite a scandal at the time."

"Oh?" Although she had never paid it much thought, Cristiano had never spoken about a wife or partner.

"I've known him to have had a couple of girlfriends since, but they were nothing serious. I think after his wife ran off, it left him a bit sceptical about the whole 'marriage' thing."

A darkness clouded Natascha's eyes, "I can understand that."

It was to be a very busy day as preparations for the wedding were in their final stages. Natascha went with Sue for the final dress fitting. The alterations were perfect and so they were able to take the finished gown with them. They then went to the florist to check that the order of fresh flowers that were to make up Sue's bouquet was still on course to be delivered. With a quick lunch in between, it was on to the venue to confirm the final guest numbers for the reception and finally on to the hairdresser who was to come to the house on the morning of the wedding. And at the end of it all, Natascha was afforded a few minutes to freshen up before Cristiano came to pick her up in the evening to go and set-up the system for the 18th birthday party.

She watched him as he plugged cables into the amplifiers, a mixing desk and microphones for which he had set up stands. The speakers had to be positioned in exactly the right location for optimum sound quality and all the cables from the instruments were bundled up and secured with tape to avoid potential accidents caused by tripping over them. When he was finished the band members came in and all the sound levels were tested and set. The whole process took nearly an hour. Natascha was impressed by the obvious skill needed in order to achieve a balanced sound but of course, Cristiano worked smoothly and efficiently making it all look like child's play.

"Have you always worked as a sound engineer?" Natascha asked as they left the hall.

"When I left school, I got an apprenticeship working with a sound engineer but I knew that if I wanted to start my own business, I would need to study. It took four years before I qualified. I have had my own company for three years now. I did my studies in London and supported myself mostly by working as a guitarist wherever one was needed. Sometimes a guitarist is needed at very short notice. I enjoyed my time in London." He paused. "I did at the time, anyway," he added, as a quiet afterthought.

"Oh, so that's why your English is so good. It's a shame we didn't know each other when you were in London."

"Yes, a very great shame," he repeated, looking straight into her eyes.

At that moment, Natascha's phone rang.

"Natascha, it's Sue. Whereabouts are you?" Sue sounded mildly panicked.

"I'm with Cristiano and we're on our way back. Why? What's the matter? Is everything okay?"

Natascha could hear a deep breath being taken. "The shop printing the place names has had a flood on the premises. All their stock and paperwork have been ruined. Everything is now just a soaking wet mess on the shop floor! They don't have any useable stationery or equipment that's in working order and I haven't been able to find anyone else who can do more printing for us in time for the wedding. 'Houston, we have a serious problem'!" She finally let out the breath.

"Are there stationery shops around here? Maybe we can get some blank ones and we'll just have to do them manually."

"But that will take hours, if not days!"

"I don't see we have much of a choice at the moment," Natascha said, calmly.

"Well, in that case, maybe Cristiano can help to find a stationer. If anyone knows, it'll be him. I don't want to call Matteo yet, he's got a lot on today."

"Consider it already done," Natascha said, reassuringly. "Don't worry, I'll sort it out. Everything will be fine."

Finding a stationer that stocked what they needed was not an easy task and they had to travel quite a distance to find what they were looking for. When Natascha finally bought the pile of blank place cards, calligraphy pens and ink, she realised that she was in for at least a couple of very busy days. She persuaded Sue and Matteo to go out for the quiet, pre-wedding meal that they had originally planned for that evening while she and Cristiano sat for hours working on the place cards. He read the names of the guests as per the table plans and she wrote out the cards, putting the skills learnt from a calligraphy course into good use.

"Okay, the next one is Tony Androsciani."

Natascha narrowed her eyes and raised her eyebrows. "I think I can manage Tony but 'Andro...' what?"

Cristiano gave a little laugh. "Perhaps I should spell that for you, then," and went on to spell out the rather complicated surname to an Italian non-speaker. "And the next one; 'Mario Lanza'. That is M,A,R,I..."

"Oh, very clever!" Natascha said, laying her hand on his shoulder and light-heartedly pushing him away. "As far as I was aware that renowned tenor died over fifty years ago!"

A moment passed between them when their eyes held the others' for just a second longer than should have been natural. But the moment was very brief and in the next second they both began to laugh - although Natascha had to consciously stop herself from lifting her hand to ruffle his curls.

Chapter Thirty-Eight

Simon, Dominic and Rachel were due to arrive for the wedding and Alessio had happily volunteered to take Natascha to meet them at the airport. As they drove through the villages, Natascha recognised the route they had taken a couple of weeks ago when Alessio had come to meet her. But it felt like only yesterday when she was travelling along the same road with her luggage in the back of his large car.

"So, what about getting married? Do you have any plans to marry, if you don't mind me asking?" Natascha enquired.

"Oh no. Maybe one day but now we are still very young. She is still studying and I have to save some money. Anyway, I want to be very sure that we are making the good decision. I do not want to be married and then to think if I have made a mistake. I want to be very sure that it is what I want to do and, of course, that she is the right girl."

Natascha knew all too well of having plans and aspirations only to realise that you had made a gross mistake. "I think you're very wise. There's no need to rush to get married, especially nowadays, when both men and women can have a career and be settled first before making such a huge commitment."

"Yes, that is true. I heard one day, the story that someone had made a very big mistake. When I was still at college, Cristiano took me with him to London in the school holidays when he was working there."

"Oh yes, he mentioned that to me." Natascha recalled Cristiano telling her that he had studied and worked in London a few years ago.

"I used to go with him to a recording studio sometimes where he was a guitarist. He was working on an album with other musicians. In one break time, I went to the coffee room where I had left my bag and Cristiano came into the same room with another one of the guitarists. They did not see me at one corner picking up my bag from behind a big *armadio, armadio*..."

"A wardrobe? A cupboard?" Natascha tried to guess, based on her knowledge of French.

"Yes, yes, a cupboard! I know that it was not a good thing that I stayed but they were talking very seriously before I could leave. The man told Cristiano that he felt so bad because he had a fiancée in London but was in love with another woman who lived in France, I think, where he visited many times."

What a coincidence, Natascha thought at first. Then she froze. Her mind began to race in overdrive, thoughts flitting backwards and forwards, not knowing where to go. If this was a coincidence, then the odds had to be several million to one - a French session guitarist engaged to a woman living in London who travelled to

France regularly and who fell in love with another woman? This really was in a league of its own.

"He told Cristiano that he did not know how he would do it but now he had to tell his fiancée that he did not love her anymore and wanted to leave her and go back to France to live with the other woman and their child. But he also had another problem. He would not tell her that he was already married to the woman in France because it would hurt her too much."

"Married?" Natascha somehow managed to restrain herself from screaming. "He was already married?"

"Yes. He said to Cristiano that his fiancée was such a sweet girl that it would be more cruel for him to tell her the real truth. That is a very sad story, no? That is why I want to be very sure when I decide to get married."

Alessio had casually been relating a little bit of innocent gossip. But since his eyes were on the road, he didn't notice the pallor on Natascha's horrified face. Icy-cold blood ran through her veins as she tried to assimilate the details of the story that she had just heard. Could it be possible Alessio had been speaking about Laurent? The chances of it being the same person were simply too incredible to comprehend.

Natascha hesitated to ask the next question, frightened to hear the answer. "What was his name?"

"Oh, I do not remember properly, it was a very long time ago but it was something like Lorenz or Lorenzo, the same as my father; my father is called Lorenzo. But it was a French name. Why, do you know him?"

"Er, no... No, I was just curious, that's all."

How she managed to utter a single word, she did not know. Her breathing had quickened as she fought for air. This was ludicrous, she tried to reason. This type of script was only meant for the big screen, not real life. She could have misheard or misunderstood Alessio, couldn't she? Maybe he was wrong about the name. Maybe he'd misunderstood the conversation between the two men. This was far too surreal. It was too much for her to even begin to deal with. Her head began to swim and her body began to tremble silently. She struggled to find her logic, her sensibleness, her rationale. This was all too crazy to be true. Cristiano could not possibly have known Laurent - it was just not possible.

She would soon be meeting the others. Her mind was in shambles and her body felt like lead but she had to recover at least a fraction of her now, perilously unstable calm. This was, by far, the hardest challenge she had ever faced. Having gone through the aftermath of Laurent leaving her under the most brutal of circumstances imaginable, watching her whole life die and disappear into the back of a taxi all those years ago, she never expected that after all this time the drama would rear its ugly head once more to add such a punishing epilogue.

Her mind had disintegrated but she needed to dig out something from deep inside to present an exterior that resembled something close to her usual composed demeanour.

The arrivals hall seemed to be more crowded than the day she arrived but amongst the sea of bodies trundling by, she sighted the three of them and ran to meet them, hugging them all tightly as she reached them.

"Hey, I've got to go away more often," Simon said, with usual mischief. "What a welcome!" Natascha never thought that she would be so happy to hear his annoying repartee. "Natascha, please meet my guest and friend, Dana. I think I mentioned her to you when we met after Christmas."

"Yes, of course," Natascha said, holding out her hand. "I'm very happy to meet you at last."

Dana seemed to be the contrast of Simon. She was shy and quiet and smiled timidly.

Natascha forced herself to return it with her own welcoming smile.

"How's it all going?" Rachel asked, looking excited and raring to go.

"The last few days have been all go but I think it's all going more or less to plan."

"Are you sure, Natascha? Because, if you don't mind me saying so, for the first time since I've known you, you actually look a tiny bit stressed."

Natascha grabbed Rachel in another tight hug. "I'm just glad you're here."

Back at the house, they met with Sue and Matteo and the reunion was a moment of genuine happiness amongst the close friends, each expressing their excitement at meeting up again in a mêlée of babbled words and gestures. After some minor objections, mainly from Simon, it was decided that the girls would stay with Sue in the cottage and the boys would stay in the guest apartment close to the Sant' Angelo's house.

With the team back together, hugs, kisses and wild chatter galore filled Sue's kitchen. However, despite Natascha's outward appearance of the same elation and her participation in the animated conversation with the others, somehow, she felt she was hovering just outside the circle of her friends, looking in. The disturbing revelation she had learnt from Alessio continued to simmer within her.

Chapter Thirty-Nine

Later that afternoon, Alessio gave her a lift to the reception hall on his way home so she could help set up for the wedding. Cristiano's van was parked outside.

"I'll be fine getting back, Alessio. I'm sure Cristiano will take me home," she said to him, after he had offered to pick her up when she had finished. "But thank you very much for the offer."

She waved him goodbye as he drove away and then turned to make her way towards the real purpose of her visit.

The beautiful grounds were deserted but for the breeze that gently brushed in between the leaves providing the only movement in the quiet air. But Natascha didn't see much of her surroundings - her mind was focused. She calmly entered the building, and through the glass of the doors leading into the main hall, she could see Cristiano on his knees busy joining electrical cables and wires into a range of equipment that he had obviously spent the best part of the afternoon carefully arranging. She pulled open the door and moved towards him, her expression cool but her steps deliberate. She crossed the hall. Her intention was to stay composed and in control when she confronted him, but these hopes were shown to be rather optimistic as the ire churned and the throbbing in her head banged with increasing intensity.

Cristiano turned in her direction when he heard her heels clicking on the shiny wooden floor. "Natascha," he started cheerfully, as he stood up, "how are you? Are you ready? It is good we have the hall early. The rest of the band will be here soon to begin..." but his words trailed away when he noticed that her usual friendly and tranquil aura had transformed into a severity and indignation he had not seen in her before.

Now that she was standing face to face with him, Natascha tried to contain her anger but to no avail. She looked at him with hard dark blue eyes. "Did you know Laurent?" she asked. Her question was simple and needed a simple 'yes' or 'no' answer.

It was as though Cristiano had been expecting this moment. "Natascha, I..."

"Did you know Laurent?" she asked again, her words spoken crisply and directly.

"I... I was so shocked when I realised that you were talking about the same person I knew and... I wanted to tell you... I nearly told you but... "

She interrupted him again. His reply had begun lamely and she had no patience to listen to any excuses. "But you didn't," she said, angrily, "you didn't tell me. You say you were shocked? Believe me, you cannot have been more shocked than I was when I found out that you had both worked together." She paused. "Why didn't you tell me that you knew him?" she asked, coldly.

Cristiano stared at Natascha, not knowing what to say. The moment he realised that the man Natascha had spoken of during their day out in Siena was the same man he had worked with in London, his mind had been in a state of disarray, wondering whether he should admit to having known him or just to leave it all alone so she could enjoy her holiday and get on with her life. He had let her go on talking about this man who had obviously caused her so much pain but he didn't have the heart to tell her what he knew. He hadn't known what to say to her then and right now his predicament hadn't changed. Cristiano did not even attempt to offer an explanation and his lack of argument infuriated Natascha more.

"You let me tell you something that was so private and so personal, a part of my life that even some of my closest friends know nothing about and you chose to say nothing when all along you knew everything. You knew more than I did!" she shouted at him, no longer concerned about controlling her rage.

Cristiano still said nothing as he looked at her with sorrow in his eyes. Their twinkle had long died away.

"But I know it all now, too. You needn't bother about trying to hide it from me anymore," she continued to shout. "I know the whole story. He was already married when he left me, wasn't he?" Cristiano stayed silent. "Wasn't he?" Natascha shouted again. "He told you that he wasn't going to tell me - he wasn't going to tell me the part where he was already married, didn't he?" Deep down, she knew what she was really feeling was extreme hurt and embarrassment and an overpowering sense of loneliness; alone in the middle of this huge lie when strangers all around her, people she did not know even existed, had known the whole truth all the time. Her words did not betray any sign of her grief. When the words left her mouth they were full of hostility and there was nothing she could do to lessen the venom in her tone. "You knew that I was completely unaware of that small but vital piece of information and you decided that you'd keep it to yourself." Her frustrated emotions tasted like acid in her mouth.

Cristiano could see the strange melange of sadness and resentment in her eyes. "No, Natasch…"

"Did you honestly think that I didn't need to know? You knew that I only had half the story but you let me go on believing something that wasn't true. Out of everyone you know, Cristiano, don't you think that I had the right to be told the truth? Don't you think you should have said something to me? Why didn't you tell me? That story belongs to me! It's my life!" she screamed. At this point, Natascha didn't know whether she wanted to laugh or cry. She felt so ashamed of the fact that a complete stranger had known for all these years how stupid and naïve she had been.

"Natascha, I really did not know whether you knew. Did Laurent decide to tell you everything? I did not know. Maybe, you did not want to tell me. I was not sure what to say to you. If you did not know, I would be the one to cause you more hurt and I did not want to do that to you. Also, I could not know for sure that he was the same person. What if I was wrong?" Cristiano said quietly, trying to calm her, "I only knew his first name".

"Hurt me? Who gave you the right to make decisions about my hurt? You telling me nothing is what really hurts," she hissed. "I don't know why I ever thought I could trust you, seeing as I hardly know you! I thought I had found a friend that I could talk to." Natascha paused to breathe. "But by keeping the truth from me, you may as well have lied to my face. You let me down, Cristiano. I don't know why I ever thought that you were different." The fury inside her was reaching boiling point.

His face was lined with distress; the perpetual smile that shaped his lips was gone. "How could I risk telling you something that would have brought you so much pain without being totally sure? I had to be sure, Natascha," he tried to reason.

But Natascha was not prepared to listen to any more of his pathetic excuses. With the ferocious storm tearing her apart inside she finally lost control of her own actions as instinctively, she felt her hand fly up ready to slap his face. With a strength that conflicted with his gentle personality, he caught it and gripped her wrist in a vice-like hold before her hand had a chance to make contact with his cheek. Her automatic reaction was to reach for the other side of his face with her free hand but just as she lifted her arm she stopped abruptly. Cristiano's penetrating gaze held Natascha's eyes with an intense energy. His hand was still wrapped around her wrist in a tight clasp when suddenly and without warning the emotional tension between them detonated and he pulled her into him, capturing her body tightly against his, thrusting his tongue into her mouth and kissing her deep and hard, his mouth, hot and sensuous. She kissed him back without hesitation. The anger that had taken hold of her had, in an instant, developed into a violent desire for him that she had no power to resist. Cristiano was strong, attractive and simmered with a quiet passion. He had a calm openness which Natascha found refreshing and the understanding they shared from the moment they met was so special. Natascha needed security, stability and reassurance. She needed to be held and to be told that everything was going to be all right, that her life would be all right. The sudden intensity of that second and the uncontrollable spontaneity of their actions had taken her by complete surprise but she was enjoying it, begging that his mouth wouldn't leave hers. Then, from nowhere, she was seized by a crazy sense of betrayal - of disloyalty as she was beset by a barrage of vivid pictures of Richard coming to life in her head. Her mind just as quickly cleared and she came to realise that this was not where she would find what she so hungered after. Being in Cristiano's arms would not give her what she wanted. She swiftly pulled away.

"I'm sorry," she uttered, breathlessly. "This isn't right. I'm so sorry." She could see the rapid rise and fall of Cristiano's chest as he breathed heavily, trying to control the passion now that the moment had shattered. He closed his eyes to regain his equilibrium and carefully released her from his hold. The electricity was still raw in the air and when he opened his eyes he looked deep into hers. She badly needed to say something, to explain herself but no words came to her. She didn't know what to say.

"Cristiano…, I…" It was at that precise moment a movement caught her attention from the corner of her eye. She looked towards the stage and saw an orangey-yellow light flickering at the bottom of the curtain backdrop. It was on fire.

"Cristiano!" she screamed, "The stage. It's on fire!" Without waiting another second, Natascha rushed towards the beginnings of the small blaze, tearing off her jacket and grabbing a large broom that was propped up against the wall on her way. "Where's the extinguisher? Get the fire extinguisher!" she shouted, as she ran up the few steps that led onto the stage. The broom was heavier than she expected so she had to haul it up behind her, nearly tripping over in the process. Her first thought as she reached the top was to protect herself, so she hastily removed her scarf and wrapped it tightly around her nose and mouth. She picked up the cumbersome broom and using its extra wide-head, she tried to beat the fire into submission, to keep it under some kind of command while she waited for Cristiano to arrive with the extinguisher. But the broom was too heavy and awkward for her to lift easily and the growing flames that continued to climb, had now reached above her head.

The fire was quickly taking a firm hold and Natascha's eyes were beginning to sting from the thickening mass of grey-black smoke that started to swirl around the stage. She scoured the immediate area around her through blurred vision, hoping to find something that would be easier for her to hold but she could see nothing to hand. She had to do something, the fire was getting out of control at a terrifying rate and she was forced make a rushed assessment and decide her next action. Time was not a commodity she had on her side therefore she had to think fast. 'Think, think, think, Natascha,' she pleaded with herself. She had to pull the curtain to the ground. Bringing the fire back down to floor level was the only way Natascha would stand any chance of tackling it. 'Please don't let it be too securely fixed' she prayed. She violently yanked at the weighty material several times with all that she had before eventually, metres and metres of thick, coarse fabric came crashing down at her feet, together with the strong metal curtain rail. It caused a colossal smash as it hit the stage. Grasping the handle of the heavy broom, she heaved it up over the burning cloth and gripping the end tightly, she let it drop with a thunderous bang. Natascha repeated this over and over, her eyes streaming and her hands red raw from holding onto the rough wooden handle. She pounded at the growing flames, each time summoning up a brute strength she didn't know she possessed.

The heat was rapidly intensifying and she felt her face begin to prickle from it. Large beads of sweat were running down from her forehead and her arms were weakening from the constant motion of lifting the broom. The weight of it just seemed to grow heavier and heavier after each hoist as she tried to smother the flames. Her whole body was wet with perspiration and the tears that covered her face were hot from the sweltering heat. She would not be able to keep this up for much longer but she had to keep trying. She kept on, beating the inexorable flames as best she could until she could see the savage colours of the fire begin to die on the destroyed piece of material.

Her determination to put out the fire began to shift to an immobilising sense of panic when she looked above her head. The fire was blazing across the fabric of the pelmet that ran the length of the stage. Pieces of burning material began to fall around her. Where was Cristiano? He'd been gone too long!

The angry flames were now too high for her to reach and she was physically exhausted. Natascha stepped back from the red, glowing fragments dropping from above and agonised in silence as she waited for help to arrive. She knew that there was little more she could do other than stamp out the flames that had fallen at her feet. She stood trying to take in deeper breaths but the scarf that was safely in place, restricted her breathing. Although she knew that to remove it and expose herself to the smoke would have much more serious repercussions, the mask, rather than keeping out the acrid smell that was filling her nose, seemed to be holding it in, capturing the pungent taste of smoke in her mouth as it grew ever thicker. Where was Cristiano? She began to feel light-headed but just as she knew she had no more to fight with, she heard a pressurised whooshing sound as Cristiano now stood beside her, holding the large cylinder and aiming the foam which was being spewed out from the hose up onto the heavy fabric burning above her head, dousing the flames as they continued to lick their way across. On its own, the one extinguisher was having little effect but at long last, after what seemed like an eternity, more men appeared on the stage each carrying their own piece of equipment to help fight the fire that had given up any initial leniency and raged on.

There was a frenzy of activity as more staff and workers of the building started to fill the hall, together with a thickening cloud of smoke that had begun to drift from the stage area. People were running in all directions shouting instructions in Italian, all of which Natascha could not understand. She ran down the steps and found her way to the edge of the commotion and pulled the scarf down from her face. It was only at that point was she able to properly take in what was happening. The loud and high pitched ringing of the fire alarm had imbedded itself in her head and only seemed to add to the mayhem that was unfolding around her. She heard the sound of sirens in the distance and the noise was getting louder and louder in her ears. She felt like a lone spectator as she watched the onslaught of chaos being played out before her eyes.

"Natascha!" She nearly wept with relief on hearing the familiar voice. "Natascha!" The very sound of her name alone gave her the feeling of having been rescued. Cristiano came rushing to her, seized her by her shoulders, and held her tightly to him.

"Oh Natascha I did not know where you were. There are so many people everywhere that I could not see you. I was so worried when I could not find you."

Natascha felt overpowering relief within the confines of Cristiano's arms that were folded around her. The adrenaline that had heightened her acute awareness suddenly drained from her body leaving her to feel dazed and depleted of comprehension. She was so weary and was grateful at being able to rest in the arms of her friend. He continued to hold her, then gently he pushed her away from him so that he could look at her. Her face was streaked with the black smoke.

"Are you all right?"

She weakly looked up to see his worried face. "I-I just need to get out of here," she answered, in a thin voice, "I need some air."

Chapter Forty

Natascha sat on a wooden bench in the grounds of the hall waiting for Cristiano to return with some water. He had helped her outside from the hysteria inside and she had asked him to take her as far away from the hall as possible so that she could sit on her own and see the comings and goings of the fire from afar but hear only the relative quiet of the gardens.

It can't have been much more than half an hour since the time she had walked into the hall to now sitting outside in the chilly air. However, it felt as though she had been here for hours, everything unfurling in slow motion in her head. It was the most frightening few minutes of her life when she realised just how close she had come to serious injury. The high drama of the fire then began to merge with recollections of the bizarre swing of passion from one extreme to the other between Cristiano and herself moments before. It left Natascha's mind dangling in mid-air for some sort of explanation as to what she had experienced. It was all a jumble of sensations; the details of the afternoon had fused together making a fine, hazy veil draped across her thoughts. Occasional watery pictures filtered through the mist, as if Natascha was watching random images from an all action silent movie. She closed her eyes to try and block them out - she was so worn-out, she hadn't the energy to process it all. So much had happened in such a short space of time it would take a lot more than sitting in a park for a few minutes to try and understand it all.

Her eyes opened and drifted skywards. The brightness of the day had gone and clouds had rolled off the hills to cover the sky with a blanket of grey. The earlier quietness of the day had now turned bleak under the caliginous sky and the breeze had changed to a gentle wind that tugged at her smoke-ridden hair. Natascha pulled her inadequate woollen cardigan closer to her. Her body was limp, spent of energy and emotion. And as much as she didn't want to think of it now, her words with Cristiano resonated in her head, together with images of maddened flames. Both started to hound her sooner than she was ready for.

She had lost her temper, something Natascha considered unforgivable. He hadn't deserved her reproach and accusations. On reflection, she knew that he hadn't done anything wrong. He had wanted to shield her from further hurt and for that, she had berated him. She was totally ashamed of herself for losing her self-control and spitefully treating him like a criminal. Where was all this hostility and hatred coming from? It wasn't that long ago that she had had that dreadful argument with Richard after the night they spent together. Towards Cristiano, she had behaved deplorably. Little by little she was assuming the personality of someone she didn't want to know. The fire seemed to symbolise the shambles of her life: the unbearable heat, the rage of the flames, the gradual and painful destruction.

Movement ahead of her halted her train of thought. Cristiano was coming towards her.

"Here, drink this."

She took a glass from him and sipped the water to lubricate her throat which had become dry and sore.

The silence between them became an unseen barrier, separating them, holding them apart. Natascha was hardly able to look at him; such was the embarrassment she was suffering, sourced by the cruel words that were issued from her own mouth not so very long ago.

"How are you feeling?" he asked at last, in his quiet way. "You were so brave. I don't know what would have happened if you had not acted so quickly."

A feeble smile and a tired shrug of her shoulders acknowledged his comments but her predominant thoughts were no longer focused on the fire.

"Cristiano, I don't know how to tell you how sorry I am for the way I spoke to you. It was inexcusable."

Cristiano put his finger to her lips, "Ssh," he said, gently, "we do not need to speak of this now. You are all that is important right now. We can talk about everything else another time."

Natascha looked at him and feeling too tired to argue, she nodded weakly.

"Natascha." She turned to see Sue running towards her. "Natascha! Oh my God, I just heard about the fire. Thank God you're all right." She looked across at Cristiano. "How are you? You both look exhausted. Can I give you a ride home, Cristiano?"

"Thank you but I have my van. I will be fine."

"Well, let's get you home," she said, helping Natascha to her feet. "Matteo's waiting in the car."

"Look after her," Cristiano said, softly.

"I will. Come by later and I'll look after you both."

A knowing look was exchanged between Natascha and Cristiano which did not go unnoticed. Something had happened between them but Sue let it go.

"I'll phone you later then, Cristiano, to make sure you're okay," Sue called, as she put her arm around Natascha guiding her across the grounds to the waiting car.

On their way to the house Natascha only had the energy to garble a thank you to Matteo for coming to meet her. But no sooner had she spoken those few words, she fell asleep in the car, hoping she would feel better soon - physically and mentally.

A bad dream woke Natascha that night and she opened her eyes to the moonlight that had formed a dim shadowy mist, lighting up the room with a muted glow. Her body felt heavy with exhaustion, but her mind raced between dramatic clips of a movie that was replaying over and over in her head. Flames danced in front of her, alive and restless, falling around her like great drops of rain. The fire had been frightening but it was not what was so confusing her. She was wide awake now and could feel panic tightening in her chest. The afternoon's experience with Cristiano had blown apart the murky recesses of her mind in which she had locked away the horrors of her past life. She had wanted to open it up herself, slowly, in her own time one day, but it was too late. The re-emergence of those bad memories were now beginning to suffocate her.

Never, since her break-up with Laurent, had he been the subject of any discussion with anyone. When his name came up in conversation with Sue it was usually just a passing comment and never spoken about in any real depth. When she had allowed Cristiano the rare insight into her past, it had been vague, brief and handled matter-of-factly. However, in truth, the recent and increasing reference being drawn to him, and with every mention of his name, Natascha gradually felt as though her life was slipping undone. The hard shell that had encased her heart from him was disintegrating. She thought she was ready but the truth was too much, too soon.

Laurent's trips to France were not because he was the devoted son or because he had been cheating on her or even because he didn't want to shirk his responsibilities as a father. It was far more than that. She'd been blissfully unaware of the double life he was leading. Natascha had been too busy planning her own life, to spend the rest of it with a man who had captured her heart so completely and to whom she had given of herself so wholeheartedly, that she hadn't seen what was happening before her own eyes. She had never seen a reason to question him and so saw nothing of the messy entanglement her love for him was to cause. She had believed their love was unbreakable when all along she was in a contest she was always fated to lose. The day he told her that she shouldn't blame herself, that it wasn't her fault; that she would always be very special to him, Natascha's world had crumbled into pieces. He told her that she was a wonderful woman but she could never give him what he wanted. He loved another woman more, a woman who was bringing up his child. Those words had ripped a hole in her that proved nearly impossible to heal. Laurent loved another woman more than he had ever loved her.

The bottomless pit of depression had hit her hard after he left and would have engulfed her completely had Sue not been in her life to help her climb out of it. She had been Natascha's lifeline, offering unending support when she needed it most, giving her the strength to turn her life around. That was the last time sweet-natured Natascha was ever seen. She had come out of her depression to become the strong, confident and self-assured woman she was today and she never looked back.

Natascha shook her head dejectedly. Even after everything she had gone through, she still hadn't known the whole truth. All these years later, she now knew that while Laurent had been living with her, pretending to love her, masquerading as her future, all along, the woman she thought was his mistress, with whom he had fathered a child was, in fact, already his wife. Laurent had been going back to France to go home to his wife and child, living his other life as a husband and family man.

Natascha filled her lungs and very slowly let the air escape into the grey shadows and with that breath she finally let go of that entire part of her life - no longer hidden inside her like a secret beast. She would find a way of ridding herself of every trace of it forever, of leaving it way back in her past, out of her head, beyond the boundaries of her personal galaxy and look for real happiness in her future. She knew the whole story now; it could be put to rest. It couldn't hurt her anymore and she would never again let it.

Closing her eyes, other issues still lay heavy inside. The unfinished business between herself and Cristiano began swishing around, turning her stomach. But it was a camouflage for a truth more profound. When her mind stopped swirling, it stopped at the point when although she was in Cristiano's arms, Richard was the man she was thinking of. This was the moment she had been dreading, the moment when she had to face what she had known for some time. No matter how hard she tried, she had failed to destroy her suspicions. Ever since he had come back into her life after so many years away, Richard had been consuming her thoughts. He had ensnared her; he was part of her, unobtrusively trickling through her veins. Somewhere along the roller coaster ride since their first meeting, in between the acid arguments, his terrible mood swings and her initial despise of him, she had fallen in love with him.

All the life-changing training she had put herself through to make certain her head always made the decisions in her life had come to nothing. All the self-instruction she had adhered to like a set of commandments to harden herself against the complications of love had been a waste of time; he had slipped into her heart unnoticed. The firm attachment she had to him when she was fourteen years old was as strong today as it had always been except now, at the age of thirty-four, it had become deeper, it had matured and he had become intrinsic to her life. How was it possible that he did not feel the same? He had become a stranger she once knew so well. He did not need her anymore, was not interested in her anymore.

The night he told her he loved her was evidence enough of how he could be a cruel and hard-hearted man, cold and calculating. How could he have said that? Since he never spoke those words to her again, it proved that he hadn't meant a word of it. And such was his indifference, it easily allowed him to exit her life for a second time and move thousands of miles away without feeling the slightest obligation to say goodbye. It was a mystery to Natascha as to why he had decided to open up and tell her of his deep-seated troubles so truthfully. He seemed to care; he must have cared, surely? She could see it in the warmth of his charismatic eyes. Natascha exhaled deeply. She would never know. But whether they were real or not, she could not run away from the undeniable truth anymore; she loved Richard and her agony now was to forget him all over again.

Her whole life's truths, half-truths and full-blown lies were now all laid bare in front of her.

Natascha closed her eyes and begged for sleep to come.

Chapter Forty-One

The day of the wedding had finally arrived. And as dawn broke, Natascha had left her room, thrown her warm coat around her shoulders and sat on a bench outside the house with her hands wrapped around a mug of hot coffee, her face turned towards the frosty early morning sun. Since the fire, the boys had been chasing all over Siena for an alternative venue to hold the reception and in the midst of the panic a small miracle had taken place. The hall of a large hotel had become vacant due to the last minute cancellation of a fashion show that was to be held there. Sue was ecstatic with the silver that had lined her cloud, considering it to be an even nicer venue than the one they had originally booked. The doctor had given Natascha the all clear although she was advised to rest her voice for a day or two. Yesterday, the caterers who were on standby were informed of the new location, the flowers and bouquets collected and the boutonnières put together. And in the evening, everyone had gathered at the Sant' Angelo's house for a pre-wedding meal. To Natascha's quiet relief, Cristiano, who had been had been invited, could not be there, saying that a problematic PA set-up needed his attention.

Natascha had not seen him nor spoken to him since the day of the fire.

She sipped her coffee and lowered her head in shame, heavyhearted in the silence of the new day. She had made a terrible mistake yielding to that moment of uncontrollable desire for Cristiano. She knew from the moment she met him, there was something about him that made her feel safe and comfortable. She was so used to that look on people's faces when first making her acquaintance; finding it difficult to approach her easily, so strong was the independence and the self-confidence she effused. Cristiano never let any such impression influence him. At the very start, he made her feel as though he had known her for years. He was a breath of fresh air in her life, rejuvenating her spirits with his sense of fun and his easy-going nature. The unwavering calm that seemed to be the cornerstone of his personality had easily broken down those ramparts in Natascha's life that she herself had built. A strong bond had quickly formed between them and their mutual love of music had only served to make that bond even stronger. Since the tragic end of her engagement to Laurent, Natascha had never again felt inclined to share her passion for music and had kept it to herself for years - until now. It was Cristiano alone who had been her inspiration to revive her fervour for it. She saw traits in him that mirrored her own and she found comfort in the familiarity. And for all that he had given her, she owed him everything. But even with all the priceless qualities that Natascha found so appealing in him he could never be more than a very good friend. A good friend that she had been blessed to make at a time when so much disquiet had intruded her world.

The sound of tiny stones crunching underfoot cut short her deep contemplations and Natascha turned to see Cristiano walking towards her.

"*Buon giorno*, Natascha," he said, as his warm smile tried to disguise the apprehension in his voice.

"Cristiano, *buon giorno*." The object of Natascha's thoughts materialising in front of her was slightly unnerving and from the sound of her own voice she knew that any words she spoke would betray her unease. "It's er, good to see you. What are you doing here so early?

"I was about to ask you the same thing, sitting outside in the cold."

"I was awake, saw the start of a beautiful sunrise and couldn't resist being in the open air to watch it come up over the hills."

Cristiano came and sat beside her on the bench and squinted to look into the rising sun. "You are right, it is very beautiful."

The quiet of the morning was stark as they sat side by side in silence, both staring out into the distance watching the golden rays light up a pink-tinged sky.

"A faulty electrical socket was the cause of the fire," Cristiano said at last, without altering his gaze.

"Oh, I see..." Natascha waited for her nerves to settle a little then turned towards him. "Cristiano, simple words are not enough to tell you how sorry I am. I said some terrible, terrible things. It was so wrong and I'm so sorry. There is no excuse for my unacceptable behaviour." She felt so humiliated she could no longer look at him and turned away to face the sun again. "I can't even think of how I screamed such awful words at you without feeling so dreadfully ashamed." She paused and closed her eyes as she remembered the words with which she had lambasted him. "I know that you were not lying to me or that you had any intention of ever deceiving me. I know that the only reason why you said nothing was to protect me and I should have thanked you for your compassion, not accuse you for my misery, for something that happened a long, long time ago, something that you could not have known about or done anything about." Guilt-ridden tears filled her eyes. "You didn't deserve my cruel words. You were being kind to me; you've always been so kind to me and I treated you as though you were the villain. I should have understood your dilemma. Of course, I understand it now…" A tear escaped her eye and travelled down her face. "Please Cristiano, can you ever forgive me?"

He turned towards her and touched her shoulder so that she would look at him. Delicately, he brushed away the tear from her cheek. "You do not need to apologise. You were upset and I understand why. Perhaps it was bad judgement not to tell you what I knew. But I know that you are not the kind of person to be so angry so easily. Let us forget about it."

"I don't think I could ever forget but I do want to stay friends with you."

Cristiano's eyes twinkled. "Yes, I do, too."

There was another painful silence which Natascha knew was up to her to assuage. "We also need to talk about something else."

"The kiss?"

"Yes... the kiss." Natascha tried to arrange the right words to say. "I don't think it was right. You are such a wonderful man and it would be so easy for me to fall in love with you but ..."

"... But your heart is with someone else."

Natascha was stunned by his words. "No... I... I mean yes... yes I think so," she garbled.

"Natascha, there was so much tension between us, so much hurt that it became too much for both of us and in that moment we comforted each other. You are a beautiful woman inside and outside." Cristiano paused. "I want you to be happy. I wish I could be the man to do that for you but if I am not, then I want you to go and find the person who can."

Natascha was lost for something to say. His sensitivity surpassed anything she could have hoped for.

"But I will always be your friend," Cristiano said, as he searched for her hand, brought it to his lips and gently kissed her fingers.

A great feeling of relief enveloped her. "Thank you."

Whether she deserved the luxury of this feeling was a separate issue.

Later that morning, wedding day preparations were at full tilt. With hair and make-up already ticked off the list Natascha helped Sue into her wedding dress. Her blonde hair had been swept into a classic French pleat and gypsophila had been intertwined to create a mist of tiny white flowers.

"You look beautiful, Sue," Natascha whispered, as she stood back to check for any final minor adjustments. "You look absolutely perfect."

"Thanks. I feel great!" Unexpectedly, Sue lowered her voice. "I couldn't have done this without you, you know," she said, sounding more profound than she had hoped. Brushing it off, she quickly brought the fun back into the moment. "But that could easily change if you don't go and get that dress on!"

"And there I was thinking you were on the verge of being all bride-esquely emotional," Natascha laughed. "I'm going. It won't take me long. I'll see you in a minute."

Natascha went to her room to get herself ready. She slipped into her dress and took a look at herself in the mirror. The criss-cross pleating of the pretty bodice clung to her, shaping perfectly over her bust line and down to her tiny waist. The long, A-line skirt accentuated her long legs for an elegant silhouette and the sheen from the dark burgundy satin dramatically clashed with the cool fire of her midnight blue eyes. Sue wanted all the bridesmaids' hairstyle to match her own and so Natascha's hair had also been gathered into a French pleat into which the same spray of the tiny white flowers had been entwined. The colour of the flowers contrasted vividly with her burnished black hair and tendrils of the natural waves that refused to stay in the pleat fell softly around her face and down the nape of her neck.

Through all her frustrations, however, Natascha continued to present her trademark personality, of quiet calm, able to assist Sue in all that she needed. But within, she was having insurmountable trouble in trying to bury her thoughts of Richard. As she stood in front of the mirror, another snippet of a memory surfaced.

Richard had come to the house to accompany Natascha to the end of term school dance, the last school dance before he left for Scotland, as it turned out. He wasn't one for dancing but she had begged him to come with her...

She walked into the kitchen in her new amethyst-coloured satin dress where Richard stood waiting for her:

"Wow, you look nice," he said, sounding a little embarrassed.

"There it is again, 'nice'. But never mind. Why, thank you kind sir!"

Richard straightened up and summoned up some renewed confidence. "In fact you look more than nice. You're beautiful." It was the first time she had ever heard him use the word...

Natascha took a deep breath as she folded her shawl over her arm, left her room and produced an easy smile to illuminate her face. And in spite of the complicated secrets she was concealing, unsurprisingly, Natascha looked stunning.

Sue, flanked by her two bridesmaids, made for a memorable portrait.

"You really do look amazing, Sue, I'm so happy for you," Natascha said, as the car took them the short distance to the church.

"I hope I look as good as you on my wedding day," Rachel added.

"I feel wonderful. I have my best friends around me, I'm marrying the man of my dreams and to make it complete my new step-brother phoned a few days ago."

"Oh?" Natascha exclaimed, surprised.

"Yes, I know, I'm sorry but it's been so hectic that I didn't even have a chance to tell you."

Natascha nodded her head gently in agreement. "I know - a little too much drama, in my opinion."

"He was sorry he hadn't got in touch with me sooner but he'd been away," Sue went on. "He said he knew he'd been adopted; his parents had sat him down on his eighteenth birthday and had told him but they obviously never knew I existed. He can't wait to meet me. He's going to try and make it in time for the reception. I'm just so excited!" She moved her hands in a downward motion to help her slow down. "Everything's at last coming together and today is going to be the most fantastic day of my life, just fantastic!" Tears of happiness shone in Sue's eyes.

"Just don't make me cry!" she sniffed, as she dabbed a tissue under her eye makeup.

As they reached the small village church, Dominic was outside waiting to escort her in. Everyone had already taken their place inside while the girls fussed around Sue, making sure her dress was hanging perfectly and her hair was still neatly in place.

"Ready?" Dominic asked, as he offered her the crook of his arm.

"Ready." She placed her hand on his arm and gracefully walked into the church. It was, alive with pink roses, lilac orchids and cream lilies. Dominic walked tall and proudly beside her, taking her towards the front of the church where Matteo stood at the altar waiting for his beautiful bride.

To hold with tradition, Matteo's father released a pair of white doves as Sue and Matteo emerged from the church after the ceremony.

"Rachel, take this," Natascha called loudly over the 'ooohs' and 'ahhs' from the guests milling about as they watched the birds fly away into the sky. She handed Rachel a basket full of small boxes of confetti to distribute and also lucky rice, believed by the Italians to encourage a prosperous marriage. "See if you can hand them out to everyone!"

"Okay, will do! Hey, Natascha! At least the rice isn't cooked!" Rachel shouted back

At the reception, a small room had been set aside for close family and friends to enjoy a quiet drink together before joining the other guests who were having drinks and appetisers in the main banqueting suite.

Sue crossed the room and came over to Natascha, a smile on her face as wide as the River Po.

"I think it's all going well so far, don't you?" she said, looking eagerly around the room. "There are so many people here and I hardly know any of them," she giggled. "But it's great, it all adds to the fun!"

"Wait until you get out there," Natascha said, nodding in the direction of the main hall. "I can't believe we sent out so many invitations."

Sue was unperturbed by the amount of people, appearing to be more excited than anxious. Natascha had rarely seen Sue let nerves hinder her and today she openly basked in the effervescent atmosphere and the attention that was centred on her and her new husband.

"I'm going to introduce myself to the aunts, uncles and cousins I haven't met yet. Hopefully I can find Matteo to help me out!"

Sue took a closer look at Natascha. "Is everything all right with you? You seem to be a bit 'vague'. Aren't you having a good time?"

"Are you joking? This is a great wedding. I can't wait until it really gets going," Natascha said, in an air of rapture. "It's all running wonderfully smoothly and there's a great atmosphere!"

"Is it the song? Is that what it is? If you're really feeling uncomfortable we can leave it out. It's no big deal. I'll totally understand. All I want is for you to kick back and let your hair down - for once."

"No no, I'm actually looking forward to my fifteen minutes of fame!"

"Good. I know you'll be fine."

She squeezed Natascha's hand and winked. "Why don't you go and do some mingling, too. You never know who you might meet, 'Mr Right', perhaps? Cristiano's around here somewhere," she added, raising her eyebrows to give Natascha a cheeky look.

Natascha bent her head closer to Sue. "Cristiano and I had a chat. We're really good friends but we both think that anything more wouldn't be right." Sue looked disappointed. "...not right now, anyway. But you never know...," Natascha added, as a positive note to soften the evident blow to Sue's wily plans.

"Aha! I thought there was something going on," she said, feeling pleased with herself as she turned to make her way towards a small gathering of older looking guests. "Keep me informed of any developments!"

Natascha rallied herself and wandered amongst the people. She kept her smile in place, pleasantly saying *buon giorno* as she passed. Images of Richard flashed constantly in her head; images of when he was young, a bit shy but always funny, pictures of him now, sombre and introverted and pictures of that night when he ran his fingers through her hair and gazed at her with an intense tenderness, smouldering in the rich colouring of his compelling eyes. A deep sigh left her. She just couldn't let go of that dream that would never be. As always, her smile was still intact as she went on grappling with her confused mess of feelings and tiring thoughts. Why was her strength of character letting her down now when she needed it most? How did she allow herself to fall in love again with a man who didn't love her - a man she knew nothing about but wanted more than anything? She was a fool. What she felt for Richard was incomparable to anything she had ever felt in her life. Please God, she pleaded, let me hang on to the hope that all these memories and these wasted feelings will soon fade and be forgotten.

Dominic, Rachel, Simon and girlfriend Dana were on the other side of the room and Natascha, with her bright smile expertly still in place, meandered through the crowd and went to meet them.

Chapter Forty-Two

The reception was an extravagant affair - the amount of food served to the guests could easily have fed a whole regiment of soldiers. Natascha had often heard of the emphasis placed on an Italian wedding reception; however she would never have been prepared for the seven courses that left the kitchen in a steady stream, juxtaposed with periods of respite while guests rested, ready for the next plate. The waiters and waitresses delivered dish after dish to appetites that heartily ate their way through the finest food and drink Italy had to offer. And as the wine flowed, the spirited and diverse topics of conversation became louder, the laughing bordered on the rowdy and a buzz full of energy filled the hall.

Countless speeches were made following the three-hour long meal. '*Eviva gli sposi*' was cheered at the end of every speech as though everyone was singing 'Amen' at the end of a Pentecostal prayer.

Natascha looked down the table and caught Matteo's attention. "What does it mean?" she mouthed. "They must have said it a hundred times."

"It's a sort of hip, hip hooray to the newlyweds! That's us!" he called back, as he waved his finger between Sue and himself proudly, laughing ecstatically.

Cristiano and the rest of the band made their way towards the stage to set themselves up and started to play.

At first the upbeat tunes were intended as background music while the staff moved the tables to the sides of the hall to create a large dance area. Then it slowed down to a gentle waltz.

"Please, can we have the Bride and Bridegroom on the dance floor?" Cristiano invited Sue and Matteo to open the dancing as he sang a beautiful rendition of *Pledging My Love*.

"And can we have new partners, please?" Cristiano then called, partway through the song. Sue and Matteo separated and she turned to her father-in-law, Fabio, Matteo pulled Sue's Aunt Jessie to her feet and Dominic asked Eva, Matteo's mother, if she would like to dance. It was a strong symbolic union of the families to which everyone applauded.

The music swiftly moved on to the traditional Italian tarantella and every guest, young and old joined hands to form a circle. The tempo of the music was even paced as the circle danced in a round. The speed gently increased and the direction of the circle changed as the dancing became a little faster to keep up with the music.

"Come and have a go at this, Natascha!" Simon shouted, from within the circle he had joined. "It looks like fun!"

Natascha smiled but didn't dance. She was more content to sit and watch as the tempo grew ever faster until it had become so furious that the circle fell apart, leaving everyone crying with laughter. The mere pleasure on the faces of everyone in the hall was enough for her. It gave her some welcome relief.

Her gaze wandered towards the stage to see Cristiano nodding at her, his eyes asking whether she was ready to sing. She stared at him, unconvinced that she ever really would be but she nodded discreetly - yes, she would do it now.

Cristiano tapped on his microphone to call the crowd to order.

"Ladies and Gentlemen. Sue's good friend Natascha, who has travelled all the way from London to join us in celebrating this special day, has agreed to sing for us a beautiful song she has written especially for Sue and Matteo. Please, let's make her feel very welcome to Italy."

People briskly made their way to the front of the hall and applauded as Natascha climbed the few steps up onto the stage. Her legs were trembling and her heart rate was racing, pounding in her ears until she could barely hear anything at all. She stood in front of the microphone, looking blindly into the crowd and waited - waited for her courage to come. It took a few moments before she was ready. At last, she turned to look behind her and was heartened to see Cristiano's twinkling eyes smiling back at her, the way they always did. The familiar expression conveyed to her all the encouragement she needed to begin her song.

Her audience was now silent, ready for her in quiet anticipation and then she heard Richard whispering in her ear as she prepared for her last attempt in the school high-jump finals... 'Go on, you can do it!'... And with the palms of her hands damp with nerves, she eased the most frightening first note she had ever sung from her throat:

'You are my rock whenever I stumble
You are my pillow whenever I cry
I give you my heart and I give you my soul
A pure love like mine will never grow old.'

Natascha looked down at the guests gathered below, determined not to let the sheer number of faces staring back intimidate her. Then she peered closer. She began to stammer her words and lose her place in the verse when she thought she saw Richard amongst the sea of bodies.

D-days are covered with sun...sh-shine
And in the... night sky the moon turns to... gold...'

How could she let herself become so nervous she would actually begin to hallucinate? Richard had got to her in a serious way, she knew, but surely not like this? Suddenly a deep and creamy smooth voice took over:

...I give you my heart and I give you my soul
Such a pure love like mine will never grow old.'

Her hallucination was moving towards the stage. Every muscle in Natascha's body was frozen keeping her solidly bound to where she stood. Her voice was lodged firmly in her throat and as the band continued to play she told herself over and over, *'forget about him, you have got to forget about him'*. And yet, the image of Richard grew closer and closer. It was still singing; the warm and rich tones resonating around the hall, filling in the words when Natascha could hardly sing a note.

'Do you know what this means?
Don't you dream what I dream?
I am in love; yes I am in love,
Time will never change the way that I feel.'

But she was not dreaming. Richard was standing beside her and had slipped his arm around her waist. Natascha opened her mouth and her voice streamed out desperate to be heard. And for the first time in twenty years they were singing together.

'Deep in my mind, deep inside my body
Deep in the middle of my simple heart
I give you my life and I give you my soul
Such a pure love like mine will never grow old.

386

No, a pure love like mine will never grow old.'

There was a hush and then the crowd started to clap wildly, assuming it was all part of the act. In Natascha's ears a distant echo of *'Bravo! Bravo!'* filled the hall. She turned to see Richard applauding her, smiling; she hadn't seen him smile in a long, long time. And taking a bow as graciously as she could, she left the stage in a daze.

Sue met her at the bottom of the steps and grabbed her, clutching her tightly.

"Natascha, I just don't know what to say. That was so beautiful. Thank you so much. You were just brilliant!" When she finally released Natascha, her gaze strayed beyond her and a questioning frown replaced her beaming face. "And it seems you've already met my step-brother, Richard French." Sue's mind seemed to be working overtime trying to figure it out. "But how do you know each..."

Natascha turned around and still in a state of shock, she moved towards him. "I didn't know I'd met your step-brother but I met Richard a long, long time ago. Hello again."

Sue gaped in astonishment, the proverbial penny finally dropping with a thud.

"You're never going to tell me that *he* is your childhood friend, your long-lost friend, the one you haven't seen for years?" Natascha nodded slowly, her eyes still fixed on Richard, staring at him as though she was witnessing a celestial apparition. "And your long-lost friend is my long-lost step-brother?" Sue's mind was still ticking frantically. "You never told me his name and I never told you what I'd found out. I don't think either of us ever mentioned any names, did we?"

"No, I don't believe we did."

Richard stepped in. "I hope you don't mind, Sue, if I just borrow Natascha for a moment,"

Speechless, Sue slowly nodded her head.

Richard took Natascha's hand and led her to the small empty room adjacent to the hall.

"I can't believe this is happening," Natascha said, in a tiny voice. "Are you real?"

Richard said nothing but smiled a smile that was calm, collected and soothing.

"But... but... how can it be possible that out of the whole of the human race, *you* are Sue's step-brother?"

He gave a slight shrug of his shoulders. "It's too crazy to try and work that one out. Sue wrote to me in London although it took a few days for the letter to reach me in Port Louis where the offices are, in Mauritius. Sue explained to me that a few years after my biological father had given me up for adoption he met and married her mother but he died before he'd said anything about my existence. I phoned Sue and we spoke for the very first time a few days ago. She told me she was getting married and invited me to the wedding. Of course, I booked myself on the next available flight - I was really impatient to meet her. I had no idea *she* existed."

Natascha took another moment to try and get her breath back. "How did you know I was going to be here?"

"I didn't. Sue met me outside and brought me into the hall. And then your voice started ringing in my head. I thought I was going mad but when I walked in and saw you up on that stage... I couldn't believe what I was seeing. I thought I was delirious, jet-lagged from the flight."

Natascha still could not register what was going on.

"I thought you were settled in a relationship," Richard announced, the pertinence of which was somewhat obscure.

"What? A relationship? With who?"

"I saw you with the same guy a few times."

Natascha was confused, "What do you mean? Which guy?"

"I saw him kiss you. I saw you both in each other's arms through a shop window." Richard started to look a little embarrassed. "And I saw you both carrying a box into a house which I assumed was where you lived - where you both lived. You had a key... I thought you were together." He looked really embarrassed now. "Honestly, I wasn't stalking you."

"Oh, you mean Simon! He's here - with his girlfriend."

"Yes, I know. I saw him as I came in with his arm wrapped around another girl's waist."

"He's a friend of mine, a really good friend."

"I know. I'm sorry. I should have realised that. That night would never have happened if you were..." Richard deliberately changed the course of his thoughts when his calm seemed to falter. "I don't really know why I'm talking about Simon." He breathed deeply and regained his composure. "Natascha, I need to explain. I've told you some of it but you don't know all of it." He took a moment, as if trying to make sure he was starting at the very beginning. "When we met again after all those years, I thought it was fate, as if after the mess my life was in, everything, at last, would be all right; the beginning of my life's recovery. The minute I saw you I had to stop myself from running to you and scooping you up into my arms. I was so happy and I felt strangely relieved, like that moment was always going to happen, the moment I'd been waiting for. I wanted to tell you everything, all my feelings, all my regrets, things I've wanted to say for a long time. But then you didn't remember me. I'd kidded myself for years that if we ever met again it would be great but when it happened, it didn't quite work out that way."

"That's not true. It's just that you'd changed so much..."

"I don't know why I thought it would be so amazing; there was no real reason why it should have been - we weren't best friends anymore. I tried to convince myself that it was a good thing you didn't remember. Given my history, sooner or later it would have all gone wrong, anyway. And that's when I got back into my car. I had to get away from you, in case I said something stupid. I had to leave and forget all about you, pretend that I hadn't seen you at all; pretend it didn't happen."

Natascha thought back to that first day and recalled how confused she was when he had left in such a hurry having spoken not much more than a dozen words.

"But I didn't realise that that was only the beginning. Out of all the companies in the UK I could have used to sort out the clients' evening, I went with the one you work for. And on top of that, you were the person who was going to be dealing with it. I tell you, something or someone definitely had it in for me."

In her mind Natascha saw him standing in reception, so cool, suave and handsome.

"What with my curse when it came to friends," Richard continued, "I'd told myself there and then that I should walk away, find another company..." His gaze wandered past Natascha. "But from then on, it went from bad to worse. Everything was going horribly wrong." He turned his eyes towards her again. "I admit, I wanted you to think that I'd become some kind of low-life that you would never want to see again but all I managed to do was to show myself to be some sort of disturbed pervert!" he said, with a tiny hint of humour. He then grew sober again. "But I went too far. Every time I met you, it turned out to be one disaster after another. It was such a mess. And then there was Christmas. God, what a nightmare! Just when I thought it couldn't get any worse..."

Natascha tried to stop him from having to say any more. "You don't need to go on. I think I understand now."

"I'm glad you do because I didn't know what the hell I was doing." Richard laughed lightly but then spoke seriously. "All I knew was that I had to put things right. I couldn't bear to have you thinking so badly of me for the rest of your life and that's why I was so desperate to tell you my depressing story; about my pathetic life. It was important that I explained."

So, the sad stories he had related to her were all true. Natascha had begun to believe that maybe he had fabricated the whole thing.

"But after I'd told you it all, I was determined that I'd never try to see you again, I'd done what I set out to do. I know I called you for New Year; I had to laugh when I remembered that stupid game we used to play when we gave each other little model animals." Natascha was taken aback by the trivial details he obviously, still remembered. "But that was going to be it. I'd decided never to contact you again; my past was still haunting me, telling me what I should do. And when the job in Mauritius came up, it was perfect timing. I could get away for good. That was the biggest mistake I ever made. I thought I could handle the whole thing - like I always do."

"Oh Richard, I wish you'd told me..."

"I know I was wrong. I was wrong about everything. I got to Port Louis but couldn't concentrate on anything. I thought about you all the time. I'd left you for a second time, feeling just as bad as I did the first time only this time, it was so much worse - because this time, it was my decision to leave. I finally had to admit to myself that I wasn't made of steel and I certainly couldn't control everything, not even my own feelings." He stopped, wondering whether he would be able to say everything he had ever wanted to say to her.

"What I'm trying to say Natascha, is I love you. What I said to you that night - the most beautiful night of my life, was not a lie. I really do love you."

Natascha's head was spinning. She was fantasising - she had to be fantasising. Any moment now she would tumble back to earth on a cloud of heart-breaking disappointment. But when Richard gently touched her face it felt too real. His fingertips were warm and trembling. The distant sound of music and voices faded away into another world.

"Natascha..." The sultry warmth of his eyes was melting her very soul the way they always did. "I don't ever want to be away from you. I can't leave you again and hope that this time it would all be all right. It never was and it never will be. I can't believe I almost threw away my one chance to tell you that I love you. I've always loved you and it's taken me twenty years to say it."

"Oh, Richard, I've got so much I have to tell you, too but that can wait... What is important is that from the moment we met again something happened to me," she said, at last, "and I didn't understand it. I learnt a long time ago how much pain love can cause and I vowed that it would never happen to me again. I learnt to have faith in no-one; I learnt to distrust everyone. But when you came back something started to change and I didn't even know it; I couldn't understand my own feelings. I expected them to be the same as they were when I was young, but they're so different. All grown up I didn't realise how much I loved you, until you left me all over again." Natascha reached up and slipped her fingers through his dark hair. "I love you so much, Richard, and I've been missing you for so long. I've loved you in so many different ways... but I've loved you all my life."

After a moment, Natascha stepped back from him and gave him a curious sideways glance. "Just one thing... How did you know the song?"

"You sang it to me a very long time ago and I've never forgotten it."

Memories of the past and dreams of the future at long last drew them together.

"We never really forgot each other did we, Richard?"

Richard pulled her in close to him. No, we never did," he said quietly, as his lips touched hers in a destined kiss.

The End